M000169638

INVESTIGATION,
MEDIATION, VINDICATION

ALSO BY CHRIS TULLBANE

The Murder of Crows

See These Bones
Red Right Hand *
One Tin Soldier *

Stories from a Post-Break World

The Stars That Sing
The Storm in Her Smile
Fire of Unknown Origin *

The Many Travails of John Smith

Investigation, Mediation, Vindication
Blood is Thicker Than Lots of Stuff *
Ghost of a Chance *
The Italian Screwjob *
A Dead Man's Favor *
Godswar *
John Smith Doesn't Work Here Anymore *

*Forthcoming

Investigation, Mediation, Vindication

CHRIS TULLBANE

GHOST FALLS PRESS

NEVADA

First published by Ghost Falls Press 2020
Investigation, Mediation, Vindication. Copyright © 2020 by Chris Tullbane.

GHOST FALLS PRESS

All rights reserved. No part of this publication may be reproduced, stored or transmitted in any form or by any means, electronic, mechanical, photocopying, recording, scanning, or otherwise without written permission from the publisher. It is illegal to copy this book, post it to a website, or distribute it by any other means without permission.

Publisher's Cataloging-in-Publication Data
provided by Five Rainbows Cataloging Services

Names: Tullbane, Chris, author.
Title: Investigation, mediation, vindication / Chris Tullbane.
Description: Henderson, NV : Ghost Falls Press, 2020. | Series: The many travails of John Smith, bk. 1.
Identifiers: ISBN 978-1-7334824-5-5 (paperback) | ISBN 978-1-7334824-4-8 (ebook)
Subjects: LCSH: Vampires--Fiction. | Mediators (Persons)--Fiction. | San Diego (Calif.)--Fiction. | Humorous stories. | Paranormal fiction. | Fantasy fiction. | BISAC: FICTION / Fantasy / Urban. | FICTION / Fantasy / Humorous. | FICTION / Occult & Supernatural. | GSAFD: Fantasy fiction. | Humorous fiction.
Classification: LCC PS3620.U45 I58 2020 (print) | LCC PS3620.U45 (ebook) | DDC 813/.6--dc23.

Book cover design by ebooklaunch.com

This novel is entirely a work of fiction. The names, characters, places, and incidents portrayed in it are either the product of the author's imagination or are used fictitiously, and any resemblance to actual persons, living or dead, events or locales is entirely coincidental.

FIRST EDITION

For Nami,
the reason for everything

ACKNOWLEDGMENTS

Publishing order notwithstanding, this was the first book I ever wrote. It's taken a number of years and even more rewrites and revisions for it to finally see the light of day. Along the way, the usual heroes played their parts:

Nami, my wife, editor, agent, best friend, and narrative compass. Just knowing her makes me a better person.

Johanna, the first friend I ever shared my fiction with, who spent many, many months referring to Lucia as 'Queenie.'

Jamie, my model for all of John's good qualities and none of his bad, who remains both the best and the only brother I've ever had.

Shawn and Keith, my former partners-in-crime and current Slack channel buddies. One day, Shawn will learn how to spell my name.

And last but never least, my mother and father.

Thank you all.

CHAPTER 1

IN WHICH COSPLAY IS A CONTACT SPORT

I was having a pretty good day until the crab men tried to kill me.

May Gray and the all-too-aptly-named June Gloom had finally given way to summer in San Diego, and it was a warm and sunny day with nothing but blue skies and seagulls overhead. My ten o'clock appointment had been a no-show, which was a huge bummer, but I'd used my suddenly free morning to go check out the costumed crazies that flooded the city every year for Comic Con.

And that didn't suck at all.

People-watching was a favorite pastime of mine. I often told clients it was the reason I'd become a private investigator in the first place. It wasn't true, but it sounded way better than *I dropped out of community college and didn't want to intern at my dad's accounting firm.*

These days, my job-related people-watching was frequently of the skeevy variety, which made the hundred-thousand-plus comic book, anime, and video game fans a breath of fresh air. And getting to spend Friday morning out on the sunny streets of my hometown?

Like I said, I was having a pretty good day.

Unfortunately, I had to cut the people-watching short once my stomach started growling. I didn't have the cash to pay even regular downtown prices for lunch, let alone what the street vendors charged during Comic Con, and the peanut butter and jelly sandwich on my desk in Logan Heights was calling my name. Thankfully, the length of the trek back almost justified the half-box of cookies I'd packed with my sandwich.

As I left downtown, the number of costumed would-be crusaders swiftly petered out, replaced by the debris and urban decay of one of the few neighborhoods in San Diego in which I'd been able to afford office space. Still, cosplayers remained very much on my mind. Maybe that's why I didn't pay the crab men much attention. Whatever part of my brain actually noticed the pair dismissed them as con-goers who had mistakenly wandered into a very bad part of town.

I didn't know what show featured crab men, let alone crab men in trench coats, but it seemed like the sort of thing that could have been a failed Teenage Mutant Ninja Turtles spinoff.

Nodding amiably to them both, I went to unlock the front door of the three-story building that housed my two-hundred-square-foot office. I was still a few feet away when one of them spoke.

"John Smith?"

In most places and for most people, that would have been the setup to some sort of lame joke, even before you considered the cosplayer's oddly slurred speech. After all, it was 2013, and nobody with the last name of Smith would be so cruel or oblivious as to give their son the name John.

Unfortunately, nobody had told my parents that. Or my dad's parents, for that matter. Or anyone in our overly long and narrow family tree. I was the seventh in a long line of John Smiths, and well on my way to being the least remarkable.

"Yes?" I gave the crab man a confused look. Up close, his costume was even more impressive. The red shell and pincers looked like they'd been sculpted out of something more solid than the usual foam. In the sunlight, they gleamed with an oily sheen, and matching antennae poked through the holes in his floppy fisherman hat.

If I'd had any constructive criticism to give at all, it would have been that neither crab man had thought to cut similar holes in their oversized trench coats. As result, their extra limbs were visible only as weird lumps beneath the fabric. Anyone who put that much effort into a costume really deserved to show it *all* off.

The crab man's face, at least, was a creative marvel… and also the stuff of nightmares. Two wide, slightly glowing eyes had been set in the center of a disquietingly lumpy and otherwise featureless face.

"Hey, how do you even see through—?"

I never got to finish my question, because he was already attacking.

ooo

Fist of Legend came out when I was six, but I didn't get to see it until almost six years later. That was my *true* introduction to Jet Li—a thousand times better than his part in the Lethal Weapon movie or that one film with Aaliyah. As the end credits rolled on the DVD, I knew—as only a twelve-year-old can truly know—that my destiny was to become the greatest martial artist the world had ever known. I swore to move to China, find a sifu, shave my head, and dedicate myself to the ancient arts of ass-kicking.

Instead, my parents signed me up for taekwondo, taught in a strip mall just a few miles from our house in Chula Vista.

I muddled through classes for a while, waiting for my promised destiny to materialize, but it turned out training was really hard work. Or maybe I just wasn't all that talented. Either way, whatever dedication I had to my craft went right out the window when I turned thirteen and finally discovered girls.

It would be another few years before girls discovered me back, and even then, it was more of a bemused awareness that I existed than any sort of tangible interest, but that's not the point. The point is that my dream of becoming a martial artist had amounted to little more than six months of learning to bow and one failed test for yellow belt.

So when I dodged the incoming pincer, it was pure luck, not skill. In truth, I stumbled backwards, tripped over my own feet, and very nearly ate concrete as I fell to the ground.

This wasn't the first time someone had tried to jump me on the streets of Logan Heights, but the crab costume was a new touch. The only good news was that he didn't seem to be carrying a gun. If I could make it back to Comic Con, security there would protect me. Two miles was a long way to travel—especially for the third time in one day—but given the bulk of the crab man's costume, I should have an edge in speed.

A slight edge; I hadn't done much running in the seven years since high school.

Or *during* high school, for that matter.

Or really any time since I was six.

As these thoughts raced through my mind, far faster than my purely corporeal body could ever hope to manage, I rolled to one side and scrambled back to my feet. The crab man lunged for me again, but I was already running full-steam back in the direction I'd come from.

Unfortunately, I'd forgotten that there were *two* crab men.

I bounced off the second enraged cosplayer and went down hard. Whatever that shell was made of, it was solid, and the man in the costume was built like a linebacker. That too-wide mouth opened under his lump of a face and he screeched, showering me in spittle.

I crab-walked backwards, too scared to even appreciate the inadvertent pun, only to bump into the lower feet of my original attacker. My position gave me a spectacular view right up the now-open trench coat of my attacker, and I could see those extra limbs wriggling in a manner that defied modern cosplay technology. He raised one of his hind legs, preparing to bring it down upon me like a ketchup-colored spear. In that brief but endless moment, I was forced to accept the truth that was, quite literally, staring me in the face.

There's just no way these guys are human.

I'd spent my entire life avoiding the Pacific Ocean, but that was because I got seasick even standing on a pier. Nobody had ever warned me about homicidal humanoid crabs.

It seemed like the sort of thing someone should've mentioned.

Then time caught back up with itself, and that leg came crashing down.

ooo

I may or may not have squealed like a seven-year-old. Nobody caught the moment on camera, so the world will never know for sure. Even a witness would've been hard-pressed to hear any noise I may or may not have made over the far louder shriek my attacker gave when a tall shape interposed itself between us, shunted the killing strike aside, and spun the crab man into the wall of my office building so hard I thought the whole structure was going to come down.

I was still flat on my back, like a baby in his crib, when that same tall shape hurdled me to attack the crab man who had been bringing up the rear. I couldn't see what happened next, but from the sound of things, it wasn't good for the crab.

Whoever or whatever had just saved me had clearly taken more than six months of martial arts classes.

The first crab man finally staggered away from the building it had collided with, its shell now cracked and split. One of its many legs was hanging limply, and any last doubts as to its inhumanity was dispelled by the greenish blood oozing out from lacerations in its flesh. Even from ten feet away, the fluid smelled like raw sewage. Glowing eyes blinked twice as the crab man shrugged free of its trench coat, exposing its full ugliness to the world. Then that lumpish face focused back on me.

That lasted for all of a second, because my protector—who had slowed down just enough for me to see that she was both human and female—had taken out my other attacker and was coming back to finish the job on its buddy. She met it a few feet in front of me, bobbing and weaving through the storm of pincers and extra limbs the other creature was unleashing.

After my late introduction to Jet Li, I'd watched every martial arts movie I could get my hands on. Jackie Chan, Bruce Lee, Tony Jaa, Donnie Yen… even homegrown heroes like Chuck Norris and Cynthia Rothrock. To the best of my rather expansive knowledge, none of them had ever fought mutant crab men on the streets of San Diego, but it was hard to imagine them doing any better than the woman defending me.

In the blink of an eye, three of the crab man's eight legs were just *gone*, torn away in another shower of green goo. One of its pincers waggled drunkenly to the side, and she slipped past the second to grab hold of the lumpy head, right beneath its antennae. She jumped up, braced her booted feet on either side of its thorax, and pulled.

The crab man's lumpy head flew over her shoulders like the world's foulest missile, and my defender rode the now-decapitated body down to the street. The creature's shell became a makeshift island in the rapidly spreading pool of noxious blood.

It was simultaneously the most disgusting and awesome thing I'd seen in twenty-five years of life.

I really should have kept going to taekwondo.

CHAPTER 2

IN WHICH THE WORLD GETS WEIRDER

Start with the shoes.

It's something my old boss and mentor taught me while I was accruing the hours necessary to apply for my private investigator's license: always look at a person's shoes. He claimed they were one detail people forgot to change when traveling incognito.

In my experience, very few people bothered with disguises in the first place, but the lesson had stuck.

The woman who'd just killed two monsters with her bare hands wore leather boots with almost no heel at all. Given the amount of crustacean ass she'd kicked, I'd have expected combat boots, but these looked like something you'd get from a high-end designer instead. If someone had walked into my office wearing boots like that, I'd have gleefully tripled my usual rates.

Above the boots, long black pants and a blue silk blouse had been transformed into fashionable biohazards by gratuitous quantities of crab blood and goo, but my crab-killing savior almost made the whole thing work. She was tall and slender, with shoulders slightly broader than her frame suggested, and posture so perfect that the buildings around us seemed even more decrepit by comparison.

"John Smith?"

That was the point where I should have said something back—preferably something suave that she'd recount to our children twenty years down the line—but my heart was hammering a million miles a second, and oxygen was in short supply. Still flat on my back, the best I could do was nod.

Thankfully, the blood-soaked woman standing above me didn't seem to mind. She returned my nod with one of her own, somehow elevating the simple gesture to a thing of elegance.

"Mr. Smith, my name is Anastasia Dumenyova." Her voice was smooth and deep, like warm chocolate. Even her name was lovely; an exotic blend of rounded consonants and vowels. I'd never regretted my own utterly bland name quite so much as in that moment. "As you can see, your life is in danger. I need you to come with me."

Anastasia pulled me to my feet with astonishing ease. Now that I was finally upright, I realized she was a good four inches shorter than I was. She'd seemed taller when I was flat on my back.

It was my turn to speak again, but face-to-face with my future wife, the world's softest hand still firmly gripping mine, the words stuck in my throat. It was eerily reminiscent of the time I'd tried asking Marie, our school's Canadian exchange student, to Homecoming.

Except that Anastasia hadn't laughed in my face.

Yet.

As we stood there, two black Escalades pulled up to the curb. In a movie, there'd have been an accompanying squeal of brakes and some sort of ominous music, but this was real life, and there was nothing but the throaty purr of oversized engines. Judging by the shine of their glossy paint jobs, both SUVs had been washed, detailed, and waxed that morning.

I was glad my gently-used Corolla was parked around the corner. It had enough self-esteem issues already without being directly compared to vehicles like these.

I looked from the Escalades back to the woman who had just saved my life, and somewhere along the way, I found my voice. "Shouldn't we call the cops?"

"And tell them what, exactly?" She arched one delicate eyebrow, slightly darker than the auburn hair she'd pulled back into a neat bun. "That you were assaulted by a pair of *karkinos*?"

"Maybe?" I had no idea what a karkino was, or how I could actually hear the italics she was giving the name, but my well-honed investigative instincts and the two bodies lying in multiple pieces around us made me think she was talking about the crab men.

"The rest of the consortium is no doubt on its way, Mr. Smith, and the police have better things to do than get killed."

I blinked. I wasn't sure what a consortium was either, but… the rest of what she'd said sounded an awful lot like a quote from Big Trouble in Little China.

It might have been the near-death experience talking, but I decided then and there that I was going to marry this woman if it was the last thing I did.

I was busy planning our elaborate Coronado wedding—I'd wear a tux with a red cummerbund… she'd wear whatever she damn well pleased—when a man emerged from the driver seat of the first Escalade. He cut an imposing figure in aviators and a suit that had been purchased at whatever store stocked XXXXXXL, but there was something deferential in his manner as he came around to open the rear passenger door.

Clearly, he'd seen Anastasia's fight.

The second Escalade disgorged a handful of additional men in similarly black suits. Unlike the driver, most were average-sized, but they were all fit and far too attractive for Logan Heights. Or even downtown San Diego, in general. It was like someone had hired an entire modeling agency to play bit roles in a government conspiracy thriller. Wordlessly, they unrolled plastic tarps along the sidewalk, and began to mop up the carnage. The cracked concrete had been stained that disturbing shade known as puke green… which was appropriate because I was about ten seconds from losing my breakfast.

"After you, Mr. Smith," said Anastasia, disengaging from my increasingly sweaty hand and gesturing to the empty rear seat.

I turned back to her and felt my nausea transform right back into butterflies. That Homecoming disaster hadn't been the end of my crush on Marie—nor had her eventual return to Canada, where she'd gotten married and was now somehow already the mother of two—but at that particular moment on the blood-soaked streets of San Diego, I couldn't remember what the former love-of-my-life even looked like.

There was no space in my world for anything but the woman in front of me. From a few feet away, her eyes were pools of liquid jade.

"Two girls with green eyes," I recited. "What can it mean?"

"I beg your pardon?"

Maybe she hadn't been quoting Big Trouble in Little China after all. That was actually kind of disappointing.

"Never mind." I cleared my throat, and voiced the questions I should've asked at the start. "What's going on? Who are you people? Why would anyone try to kill me, let alone whatever these things are?"

"We do not have time for explanations, Mr. Smith. I promise they will come when you are safe." She had a small ring of gold around her pupils, almost lost amidst the green. As she spoke, it seemed to catch light and sparkle. "Get in the car."

The private investigator side of me wanted answers before I went anywhere, while the side of me that could never have survived a regular nine-to-five bristled at the idea of anyone giving me orders. But Anastasia had literally just saved my life. If she thought we'd be safer elsewhere, I was willing to trust her.

Besides, God loves a strong woman, and so do I.

I got in the car.

○○○

The interior of the Escalade was closer to a small apartment than a car. It was one hell of an upgrade from my Corolla, whose interior had already been trashed *before* I bought it, and now most closely resembled the dumpster I parked it behind every morning. I let myself sink into buttery soft leather and luxuriated in the ability to extend my legs without encountering day-old fast food wrappers or any of the other stakeout trash that had made my car's back seat a wasteland. As we pulled away from the curb, the SUV's shocks effortlessly handled the pothole-ridden streets outside my office.

It was like riding on a cloud. Only less damp.

I was alone in the back with Anastasia. The oversized driver had passed her a fluffy white towel, but crab guts were proving to be the sort of stain that never comes out. With a sigh, she folded the now-ruined towel and placed it on the floor by her booted feet.

"I'm sorry about the mess," I said. My 'Stay Classy, San Diego' t-shirt was a lost cause too, but I had an extra back at my house. Besides, I was pretty sure her one outfit had cost more than my entire wardrobe. And maybe my monthly rent.

She shrugged. "It is a small thing, Mr. Smith, when measured against your life. What matters is that we arrived in time to save you."

In the confines of the Escalade, the impact of her voice was only magnified. It was unfair that anyone so good looking could also have a voice like that. *Barry White* would have been jealous if he were still alive. Part of me wanted to just sit and listen to her speak for the rest of my life. Especially when she made it sound like I was someone important.

But I'd been promised answers.

"How did you know I was in danger? And for that matter, *why* am I in danger? I don't even eat crab. Anymore." As a small business owner, my food budget mostly went to beer. "Why would they want me dead?"

"The karkino are not concerned with your dietary habits. Nor do they bear any direct relation to actual crabs. They are a species of assassins. I believe their consortium was hired to kill you because of what you are."

"And what's that?" I'd read fantasy books that started out this way. A hidden bloodline. Secret powers. Women way more attractive than the protagonist warranted. The hitman crabs were admittedly a new wrinkle, but everything else was going precisely according to script.

Instead of answering, Anastasia retrieved a black folder from the pocket of the seat in front of her. She flipped through several sheets of varying color and size and handed me a torn yellow scrap of paper.

It was a Yellow Pages ad. That was weird enough as it was. Even weirder? It was mine.

ooo

The ad had been one of my many attempts to drum up business for the agency. My best friend Mike and I had been on our third pitcher of beer when I purchased it, and the ad copy, printed just above the address and phone number for my office, reflected that fact:

Investigation. Mediation. Vindication.

No case too small, no fee too large.

(Tips gratefully accepted, but not required.)

Needless to say, it hadn't been very successful. I'd written the whole thing off as a lesson on never drinking again… and then, when that lesson proved impossible to follow, as a lesson on never buying Yellow Pages ads when drunk. Or at all.

As bad as the ad was, however, it didn't seem to justify someone hiring hitmen… or hit crabs… or whatever… to kill me. And why now, all this time later?

Wait. Anastasia had said they wanted to kill me because of *what* I was. So it wasn't the ad itself that had put my life in danger. It was my job. That made slightly more sense.

"Did I see something I wasn't supposed to on a case?"

I'd had two jobs in as many months. One had been a father trying to reconnect with his wayward daughter. I'd scoured social media, interviewed old friends, run a credit report, and basically struck out on all fronts. At the end, Mr. Oglestein had seemed more sad than murderous.

The second job had been a housewife looking for proof that her husband was having an affair with his personal trainer. As was too often the case, he had been. And with his secretary. And their next-door neighbor. It had taken me less than three days to fill four USB drives with the photographic evidence. Which sucked, both for the poor wife and for my billable hours.

I wouldn't have been shocked to get a visit from that dude— irate spouses were an occupational hazard—but nothing I'd seen in my brief stakeout had suggested criminal connections… let alone some sort of pipeline to syndicates under the sea.

Anastasia shook her head, sending a few wayward strands of auburn hair whispering across the silk of her blouse. "It is not your role as an investigator that is the issue here, Mr. Smith." She extended one slender finger and tapped the second word in my ad's headline. "This is why they want you dead."

I'd literally just read the ad, but I found myself doing so a second time, just to be sure. "Say what now?"

"They want you dead because you are a mediator."

"That's impossible."

"For your sake, I wish that were the case. But all evidence points to the contrary."

I frowned. Small streams of crab guts had pooled in the leather stitching of the car's seats. I wasn't sure how much it cost to have an Escalade detailed, but this one would also need an exorcism.

"Mr. Smith, I recognize that this is difficult to accept, especially for someone who was unaware of the true nature of the world they lived in. But as you have seen, the threat is real. You are, in fact, the last mediator alive in San Diego."

It wasn't the sort of thing I'd ever expected to hear, let alone on a Friday in July, after a morning outside Comic Con. Assuming I ever recovered from my own near-death experience, I was pretty sure I'd have nightmares about all the many murders that had apparently been carried out before mine. But in that singular moment, my mind was fixated on only one thing.

"But I'm not really a mediator!"

CHAPTER 3
IN WHICH MISCONCEPTIONS ARE MURDER

"I beg your pardon?" Anastasia's poker face was spectacular. The only evidence that I'd taken her by surprise was a slight sharpening of her gaze.

"I'm not a vindicator either. Assuming that's a thing? I was drunk when I bought the ad and…" I trailed off, and smiled weakly. "Rhymes are funnier after a lot of beer."

"I suppose that explains why you were listed as a Private Investigator instead of under Mediation Services. I *had* wondered. That may be why you survived long enough for us to find you."

"Lucky me, I guess." I waited, but that appeared to be all she was going to say on the matter. "So how do we inform the bad guys of their mistake? This has been nuts, but I'd like to get back to my real job."

And lunch. And especially those cookies.

"I wish it were that simple." She plucked the ad from my hands and carefully re-folded it. "The state of California does not require licenses for mediators. For our specific scenario, this document is all that is necessary to identify you as such."

Either I had hit my head harder on the sidewalk than I'd thought, or Anastasia wasn't making any sense. And given that I'd just barely survived a murder attempt by mutant crab assassins, that was saying something.

"You're saying that an old Yellow Pages ad is enough to make me a mediator, and because of that, I'm a target? That's insane!" She opened her mouth to say something, but I kept going. "And even if I *were* a mediator—and I'm really, really not—why would someone want to kill me for that? And for that matter, how do you, the human wall, and the men-in-black factor into the equation?"

There was a brief moment of silence as our car smoothly took the exit for the 8, carrying us eastward away from downtown San Diego. When Anastasia finally replied, her voice had softened. "I recognize that this is confusing, and more than a little alarming, Mr. Smith. We rarely expose mundane humans to the realities of the world around them, and for obvious reasons, I am not the usual intermediary for such discussions."

Six months of community college and one possible concussion left me completely unprepared to unpack that sentence. Thankfully, *my* poker face was infamous for being the worst in San Diego, and she had no difficulty reading my continued confusion.

"The karkino are not the only paranormal species living around and among your kind. The world is both darker and deeper than you or anyone else might suspect."

"And I'm the secret, half-blood prince of one of those empires?" I wasn't sure why she'd decided to take this tangent, but somehow, we were back in urban fantasy territory.

Anastasia tilted her head to one side and studied me. I wish I could say it was the first time a woman had given me that look. "Did you take a blow to the head before I arrived?"

"I *did* fall. Twice." I shook my head. "I'm just trying to process. So the world is full of things that go bump in the night, and somehow humanity hasn't noticed? Figures. Where does my being a mediator factor in? Not that I am one."

I was going to keep hammering that point until it stuck.

"Many of the races on this planet are prone to conflict. Wars were waged long before humanity achieved any semblance of civilization. However, in the last millennium, humankind's numbers reached a critical mass. It became increasingly difficult for those other species to keep their battles hidden and the risks inherent in failing to do so became significant."

I still didn't have a clue what she was talking about, but it was fascinating, in a low-budget, alt-history sort of way.

"And so," she continued, "several centuries ago, there was a convocation in the town of Toulon."

"Mexico?"

"Southern France."

I'd been close.

"All manner of species were represented, from the ancient to the insignificant. Out of that assembly, the Concordat was born."

Concordat. Convocation. Consortium. Anastasia was like a smoking-hot, crab-murdering, word-of-the-day calendar.

"It specifies that open warfare between species must be a last resort, lest humanity awaken to the world they truly live in. Should conflict arise, it is incumbent upon the involved parties to exhaust all manner of resolution before engaging in battle. And that delicate dance of diplomacy is overseen by one specific individual."

I swallowed. "A mediator."

"Exactly."

ooo

I chewed on that little info-bomb for a bit, barely noticing as we took another exit and headed north on the 163. "So there are two species in San Diego—not counting the karkino, I guess?—who are pissed off at each other... and only a mediator can stop things from escalating, but someone has killed all the mediators in San Diego?"

"All but one."

"Still not a mediator," I muttered. "Why not just go up to Los Angeles? It's the lawyer capitol of the world... surely, they have their share of mediators? Or if that's too far to travel—" I wouldn't want to wish the 405 on even my worst enemy. "—why not pick a random person and make *them* a mediator?" She started to reply, so I hurriedly added. "Someone other than me, I mean. If there's no license requirement, why not grab someone more qualified? I think the UN has people trained in this sort of thing."

"When the Concordat was drafted," said Anastasia, her voice still soft, "there were concerns that parties would endeavor to cheat the system through their choice of mediator. Consequently, three provisions were included."

I didn't like the sound of that. If I'd learned anything from television and superstition, it was that bad things came in threes.

"First, the mediator must be a resident in the town in which the dispute occurs. This would preclude hiring a mediator from Los Angeles."

Some people claimed San Diego was basically just a suburb of Los Angeles anyway, but those people were idiots. And they generally lived in LA.

I nodded, conceding the point.

"Second, the mediator must already be one at the time of the dispute, which means we cannot make someone a mediator after the fact."

"But…"

"Your advertisement qualifies as the modern analogue to a shop sign, and is sufficient to designate you as a mediator."

My mom had always said beer would be the death of me. I just hadn't expected it to happen so quickly. Or at the pointy end of a crab pincer.

"And third?"

"The accused party is responsible for hiring the mediator, but the accuser is given the right of rejection."

"Meaning?"

"Meaning you will have to convince them of your suitability for the role."

I'd never done well in interviews. Or tests, for that matter. This sounded like a potentially fatal combination of the two. "What happens if they say no?"

"As there are no other mediators, any hopes of peaceful resolution would be over."

"So… war?"

"Yes."

"Between secret species. In San Diego." I really, really didn't want to know the answer, but still felt compelled to ask. "How bad are we talking?"

"By the end of it, Los Angeles might well be the southernmost city in California."

Well, shit.

ooo

I stared out the window, not really seeing the blur of strip malls and scrub grass as we continued north. San Diego was the only home I'd ever known. Literally; my parents had owned the same house for as long as I'd been alive, and all three of us were still living there. San Diego wasn't just America's finest city, it was *my* city. There was no way I was willing to let it slide into the ocean.

Or a hell mouth.

Or whatever was potentially going to destroy it.

"So everyone I know is doomed unless I take this mediation."

"And are able to forge an accord between the two parties."

"Right." Just taking the job wasn't sufficient. I'd actually have to succeed at it too. Because that was totally something I was qualified for. "And I'm the only option left because all of the actual mediators have already been killed."

"Indeed. The first casualty was the individual who usually serves in such matters. By the time his body was discovered, further assassinations were already underway." She shook her head, eyes distant. "I have had a very bloody morning."

"I'm sorry."

"It is hardly your fault, Mr. Smith."

For the first time in a long while, I met her eyes. The thin ring of gold around her pupil had disappeared, swallowed up by deep green waters.

"Call me John. You just saved my life from criminal crustaceans, and now we're both doing our part to ruin this car's leather interior. I think we can be on a first-name basis."

"If you insist." What almost passed for a smile flashed across her face.

"So where do you and the men-in-black fit into this?" I asked again. "Some sort of secret organization dedicated to observing the paranormal and arranging mediations when necessary?"

All those reruns of Highlander my dad had forced me to watch were finally coming in handy.

"Not exactly. As I said, there are two parties to every mediation. The accused and the accuser."

"Right. And…?"

"And I represent the former."

"Legally?" The idea of a ninja lawyer was giving my suspension of disbelief a run for its money.

"Not exactly." Her voice shifted yet again, steel emerging from behind those chocolate notes. "I am Lady Anastasia Dumenyova, Secundus of House Borghesi. We stand accused of a crime that we did not commit, and I have come to secure your services on behalf of my queen."

"Cool." I nodded confidently. "Wait. What?"

CHAPTER 4

IN WHICH AMERICA HAS A MONARCHY

Oddly, the first thing my mind decided to trip over was Anastasia's mention of a queen. I hadn't been the best of History students—and I definitely preferred the Cartoon Network to CNN—but I was pretty sure our country was still a democracy. Had England re-assimilated us when I wasn't paying attention?

It wasn't impossible, but it seemed unlikely.

Before I could press that issue, or ask what the hell a Secundus or a Borghesi was, the rest of what she'd said finally sank in.

"*You* want to hire me? I thought this was a thing for the creepy-crawlies?"

"I beg your pardon?"

"You know... the non-humans... the crabs, the fish heads, the greys, and—" I was only guessing on this last one. "—the chupacabras."

"Mr. Smith, I don't know what *greys* are—"

"Aliens," I supplied. "Big heads, bug eyes, and anal probes."

"—but the karkino and yes, the chupacabra, are merely two of the very many species in the world. I and my kind are another. Some of us pass better among humans than others."

"Please tell me you're not a lizard in a people-suit."

"A *what?*"

I waved off the question. If Anastasia didn't know about V, I was going to let her enjoy her ignorance. "So you're not human?"

"I am not."

"What about him?" I nodded to the driver. "Is he half man, half grizzly bear?"

"Mr. Jefferson is entirely human."

That was almost as hard to believe as the whole queen thing, but I let it go. "So other humans *do* know about your kind?"

"A few. In the case of our supplementary security personnel, we take steps to insure that the information does not travel far."

"Steps?"

"Steps."

I was starting to think my interrogation technique was lacking. Which was weird, since I'd taken an online course and everything. I spared another glance out the window as the Escalade finally left the highway. Apparently, this so-called queen lived in Scripps Ranch.

I'd have gone with Del Mar, but nobody was asking me.

"So you're not human, but you're not crabs or goat people either. Are you... angels?"

"No."

"Demons?"

"No, although some would—"

"Simulacrum?"

"What?"

"Like Chucky, from Child's Play? Not that you look like a toy doll or anything. But I didn't know murdering crabs were a thing until like half an hour ago. I'm open to the possibilities."

"Mr. Smith—"

"John," I insisted.

"Mr. Smith, we are not aliens. Nor are we characters from your horror movie franchises." She shook her head. "In English, we call ourselves the People, but humanity has its own names for my kind. Moroi. Nightstalkers. Nosferatu."

"*Vampires?*"

"And yes, vampires."

I sighed, and settled back into my still-comfortable chair. The Escalade turned down a long, private driveway, and came to a halt at a gatehouse. "If you didn't want to tell me, you could have just said so."

"Am I to understand that, despite accepting the reality of the karkino and being open to, as you said, *lizards in people suits*, you reject the very possibility of vampires?" By her tone, Anastasia couldn't quite decide whether to be irritated or amused.

"Aliens are real. Probably. It's a big universe. And crabs just tried to kill me, so they get a pass too. But vampires?" I shook my head. "They're so played out. Twilight. True Blood. It's 2013; zombies are the new 'it' thing. Besides…"

"Yes?"

"The sun's out. And so are you. And nobody's burst into flame." I shrugged and spread my hands as if resting my case. "Not a vampire."

"You will find that human literature gets a great deal wrong with my kind, Mr. Smith. We walk in the sun, just as you do."

"Right." The guards waved us on and we drove through and up the winding road through lush greenery. The occupants clearly hadn't heard about the ongoing drought. At the end of the driveway, on top of its own hill, was what could only be described as a mansion or— God help me—a palace; four stories high, as wide as a football field, and with enough windows for a hundred rooms. "Can you turn into a bat?"

"No."

"A wolf?"

"We are not the Infected."

I filed away the question of who or what the Infected might be for another time. "So, no sun allergy and no magical powers. Exactly what is it that makes you vampires then?"

Our Escalade parked right in front, at the base of a long flight of stairs leading up to the imposing set of double-doors.

"Come with me," said Anastasia, "and find out."

ooo

"Seriously, dude… that's not a gun."

The guard didn't reply, but his hands—each the size of a bowling ball—moved on, patting my legs down to the ankle. My sneakers received only a cursory examination. Apparently, seven-year-old, badly scuffed Nikes weren't considered a threat in Vampire-Central.

Even on one knee, the man's head came up to my chest, intimidating in its bald sheen. He was every bit as large as our driver had been, and his tent-like blazer was open to reveal both a shoulder holster and the weapon stowed within. I didn't know a damn thing about guns, but this one was proportionally sized for the giant carrying it.

Not that I spent a lot of time thinking about the size of other men's weapons. That way lay madness. And despair.

Anastasia stood off to one side, patient and serene. We'd barely made it through the mansion's ornate, intricately carved double doors before the security team had descended upon me to make sure I wasn't sneaking in some sort of thermonuclear device in my boxers.

If nothing else, it gave me a chance to take in the mansion's interior. The floor was marble tile, gleaming like it had never seen foot traffic. Ceilings were at least twenty feet high, and a second row of windows in the exterior wall flooded the area with natural light. Directly ahead of us, an enormous staircase led up to the second floor, with an honest-to-God velvet runner partially obscuring the polished wooden steps.

Just looking at all those stairs made me tired.

To my left, another set of double doors opened onto a banquet hall, full of tables and chairs. To my right, a much less impressive single door was firmly closed, but I could hear the buzz of unintelligible chatter from within. More importantly, I could also smell something utterly fantastic.

Once again calling on my professional powers of inductive reasoning, I decided that was probably the kitchen.

If this frisking went on much longer, I was going to risk a beating and ask for a sandwich. I might as well get something out of the ordeal, right?

Finally, the enormous man ran out of body parts to grope. Rising to his feet, where he loomed over both of us like the world's most terrifying TSA agent, he gave Anastasia a nod.

"He's clean, ma'am."

"I already told you that," I muttered.

"Your pardon, Mr. Smith," said Anastasia. "Our security team takes their job quite seriously."

"No kidding." Between the gatehouse, the estate grounds, and the front-door welcoming crew, I'd counted over a dozen guards, all of them armed. Anastasia didn't sound American, but her people sure seemed to love their guns. "Is it because of the current crisis or are things always so…?"

I trailed off. Calling the woman who had recently saved my life *insanely paranoid* seemed like a low-percentage play.

"There are extenuating circumstances, yes," she said, escorting me deeper into the house. Happily, the guards stayed behind. Even better, we bypassed the staircase entirely. Nestled in the shadows, behind and to the right, was a bay of elevators. "It has been a difficult decade."

"I hear that." Prom. Graduation. My one semester of community college. Three years interning as a private investigator's assistant, and two more trying to run my own agency. I'd always assumed that I'd be rich and married by twenty-five—with the former a result of the latter—but my birthday had come and gone and I was still living with my parents.

Thankfully, things were looking up on both fronts. Judging by the mansion, this so-called queen had plenty of cash, and if I really was the only mediator left in town, my as-of-yet undisclosed rates could afford to be exorbitant. As for marriage… Anastasia had been nothing but professional so far, but a solid working relationship seemed like a great foundation to build on.

A chime sounded, and the doors to the nearest elevator whisked open. If the foyer had screamed old-world opulence—and it really, really had—the elevator was modern and efficient, like something you'd find in one of the high-tech towers downtown. As we filed inside, I took a peek at the array of buttons on the interior panel. In addition to the four floors I'd already noted on our drive up, there were two sub-floors and something called G.

"Ground?" I guessed, pointing at the button.

"Garage. Much of House Borghesi resides here full-time, but we all have our own lives, and come and go as those lives demand." Anastasia tapped the button for the fourth floor, and it lit up with a soft glow.

"I thought *this* was the House." I waved at the mansion outside the elevator doors, even as they started to whisper shut.

"A House is its people, Mr. Smith." I'd thought the interior of the Escalade did wonderful things for her voice, but the confines of the elevator amped things up even more. "Think of it in feudal terms. Every noble has a house. Everyone here is a member of that house and a sworn vassal of the queen."

"Queen Boregazy."

"Borghesi. Yes."

I couldn't hear any difference between our pronunciations, beyond the fact that her slight accent made everything sound better, but I shrugged.

"Okay. And we're heading to meet her now?"

"And the rest of the council, yes. Time is of the essence. Once you have been briefed, we can arrange for the initial meeting with Lord Beel-Kasan."

"Who?"

"The accuser."

"Is he a vampire too?"

"Most definitely not."

I wanted to ask more, but a chime announced that we had arrived on the fourth floor. The doors slid open, and I braced myself for my first view of the hidden depths of House Borghesi's... well... *house.*

ooo

"Huh."

Anastasia turned, one eyebrow arching delicately upwards. "Yes?"

"I thought it would be a little bit more... vampirey." Much like the elevator itself, the hall would have fit nicely into any of the more expensive office towers in San Diego. Wide enough for five normal people—or two of the human guards—to walk shoulder-to-shoulder, it stretched for a hundred or more feet in either direction, flanked on both sides by the glass walls of what appeared to be conference rooms.

"Our kind must do business like anyone else, Mr. Smith." So far, she didn't seem keen on calling me John. That was admittedly a bit of a setback. "The House owns an office tower in Sorrento Valley, but meetings of a more sensitive nature occur here, in the heart of the queen's domain."

The carpet was lush and deeply padded, cushioning my feet with every step. If my bedroom had carpet like that, I'd be able to forego a bed entirely. Sleeping on the floor probably wouldn't impress any dates I brought home … but the fact that I lived in my parents' basement kind of already had that covered.

Most of the conference rooms we passed were dark and empty. In the few instances where lights were on, the glass had gone opaque, hiding the room's interior. I wasn't sure how that worked, but it was pretty cool.

Our destination was two thirds of the way down the hall, one of only two rooms in that wing featuring double doors. Between this, the banquet hall, and the main entryway, it seemed like vampires used the number of doors to signify importance. I wasn't sure how that knowledge would be of use, but I filed it away anyway, just in case.

Assuming these people really *were* vampires. Anastasia didn't seem like the kind of woman to joke about that sort of thing, but you never knew.

We paused outside the illuminated conference room, and Anastasia's voice dropped to a soft murmur. "When you speak to Queen Borghesi, it is customary to refer to her as Your Majesty. As you are not her vassal, you need not kneel, but a bow would be appropriate. Above all, be respectful."

"No worries," I assured her. "I can totally do respectful."

CHAPTER 5

IN WHICH RESPECT IS NEITHER GIVEN NOR EARNED

The first thing I saw was the table. Long enough to accommodate a dozen people, its top appeared to have been made from a single piece of wood. *Mahogany*, declared a voice in my mind, blithely ignoring that I had only the faintest awareness of different wood species.

Like the house's enormous front doors, the table's surface had been carved within an inch of its life, over a dozen different scenes forming a tapestry that I couldn't even begin to decipher. The table was pristine but something told me that it and the matching doors were far older than the house itself.

The people around the table, on the other hand, looked my age or even younger.

Ahead of me, two men wore the sort of suits only CEOs and movie stars could afford, one in navy and the other in charcoal gray. The conference table kept me from peeking at their shoes, but I'd have bet my last dollar—which was unfortunately *not* just a saying, given the state of my bank account—that they were designer and from Italy. Both men could have stepped off the cover of GQ; dark and handsome, with strong jaws, piercing eyes, and carefully trimmed stubble. The one to the left kept his hair fashionably short, while the other's was long and slightly curly, pulled back into a ponytail that somehow didn't make him look any less overwhelmingly masculine.

I sucked in my beer gut and did my best to emulate Anastasia's flawless posture. I'm not sure I succeeded on either front.

Next to the two men was a woman in her late teens, lean and sharp as a knife, with cheekbones to match, and short, dark hair that she'd styled into spikes. Like the men, she wore a dark suit, but I was betting that her shoes were stilettos, heels high and sharp enough to stab a man in the heart. She looked me over, head-to-toe, and smirked, only then revealing an impressive set of fangs.

I suppressed a shiver. I'd been out of high school for seven years, but teenagers were still terrifying.

Anastasia dropped to a knee in front of the room's final occupant, a woman seated at the head of the long table. I hadn't seen an ugly vampire yet—which was honestly kind of irritating—but this woman took things to an extreme, a voluptuous vision in white with her platinum blonde hair cut into an A-line bob. The only spots of color in her entire ensemble were her golden tan and two eyes as blue and cold as an Alaskan glacier. Even discounting her obvious beauty, she had a presence that filled the room. I was still coming to grips with the whole vampire thing, but I had no trouble believing she was royalty.

Those chilly blue eyes pinned me to the wall, dismissed me with casual swiftness, and returned to Anastasia. She motioned to my companion with a ring-laden hand.

"Secundus." Her voice rang like crystal; clear, vaguely musical, and utterly cold. "Who is this that you have brought before us?"

She'd actually used the royal we. Or at least the royal us. That was kind of off-putting, actually. Nobody likes a snob.

"Your Majesty, this is John Smith, San Diego's last mediator." Anastasia rose and turned to me. "Mr. Smith, you stand in the presence of Queen Lucia Borghesi, Lady of Winter, first-born daughter of Aurelius the First, and true heir to the throne of the Italian Courts."

Part of me wondered what the heir to a throne in Italy was doing all the way over in San Diego, but I figured we'd have time for backstory later. Hopefully over lunch.

"How's it going?" I said instead. And then, finally remembering Anastasia's instructions, I folded over at the waist. I'd never bowed to royalty before, but I was pretty sure I'd made it look good.

A snicker from the spiky-haired brunette told me otherwise.

The queen didn't acknowledge my words. Or my bow. Or me, to be honest, which was both hurtful and kind of attractive. Instead, her cold eyes remained fixed upon Anastasia.

"Last mediator?"

"A purge occurred this morning at the hands of the karkino."

"And the Rook?" If anything, Lucia's voice had grown even colder. Less crystal, more ice. I was guessing that whole Lady of Winter title had to do with her personality.

"He was the first to be slain."

"Surely not by the karkino."

"Given his own abilities, it seems unlikely. Captain Xavier and several of the Watch are at the scene now. He will have a report for us shortly."

"Excuse me?" I waved a hand in the air, like a student desperately wanting to answer whatever question the teacher had just posed. "Could someone fill me in on what's going on? I'm guessing the Rook was your usual mediator? Why wouldn't he have been killed by the crab people?"

"The Rook was not human, Mr. Smith," said Anastasia, speaking before anyone else could. Judging by the expressions on the two men's faces, they'd had a less friendly response in mind. "He would have presented a formidable challenge to their consortium."

"Got it. So who—"

A sound like a gunshot went off. I was diving for cover before I realized it had been the queen's hand striking the antique table. She rose to her feet. For the first time, I realized she too had a ring of gold around her pupils.

"Human." She let the word drop like it was a crystal glass, tossed to the floor. "Your betters are speaking. You will sit and you will be silent until we have given you permission to speak."

I felt a sudden sense of kinship with the revolutionaries who'd won our country's freedom, centuries earlier. Royalty kind of *sucked*.

I gave the queen my best insincere smile, the one I normally reserved for angry spouses and my office landlord. "No problem. I'm just saying if this *lowly human* is going to mediate between you and Lord Beer Can, it would be helpful to know what was going on. But what do I know, right? I'm only the last mediator in the city."

There was a moment of silence. Apparently, I'd impressed everyone with my logic.

Except… they didn't seem impressed. More like shocked. Even Anastasia had gone absolutely still.

I had a moment to wonder what had just happened, and then everything went to hell.

CHAPTER 6
IN WHICH HANDCUFFS ARE WAY
LESS FUN THAN EXPECTED

I wish I could say it was the first time I'd woken up in a strange place with a splitting headache, but growing up in San Diego had left me with more than a few epic drinking stories, and many of those ended in hangovers and unhappy mornings-after. The way the walls were spinning around me was depressingly familiar.

The handcuffs pinning my wrists behind my back though? Those were new.

I took a careful breath, in through my nose and out through my mouth, in what I had once read was the best way to avoid unwanted, post-drinking-binge vomiting. It didn't help. My stomach continued to toss and turn, much like the dark room I still couldn't quite see.

It took longer than it should have, but eventually my mind cleared enough for me to remember I hadn't gone drinking at all. Instead, I'd narrowly avoided death at the hands of two crab people, been hired for a job I was entirely unqualified for, met a group of depressingly attractive supposed-vampires, and then... what?

A well-lit conference room. Five people around the table, all in varied states of shock for reasons I still didn't understand. The handful of seconds that had followed felt like a stop-motion hallucination, like the one time I'd tried acid and ended up in Mike's closet, wearing socks on all of my extremities.

The two men snarling, vampire fangs fully exposed, as they rose from their chairs.

The spiky-haired brunette leaping onto the table, like Batman in eight-hundred-dollar Louboutins, and then vaulting off of it toward me.

A small fist, appearing from nowhere to land like a cruise missile across my temple.

Stars. Darkness. Some sort of dream about burritos.

If my memory could be trusted—if the whole thing hadn't been a fever dream, from crab men to painful finish—then I'd somehow managed to piss off my employers and been punched into a near-coma by a vampire teenager.

This whole mediation thing was starting to feel like a bad idea.

○○○

Both the floor and the wall behind me felt like rough stone, which meant I'd been moved while unconscious. Technically, the lack of light, glass, and beautiful people had already told me that much, but my brain had gone into fact-finding mode, and I didn't want to get in its way.

I wasn't dead, which was both an absurd thing to find myself thinking and an excellent sign. My heart was going a thousand beats a minute, so I wasn't undead either. And other than the nausea and my spinning head, I didn't feel any weaker than usual… which meant nobody had been snacking on my blood. Assuming Anastasia's breed of vampire even drank blood. At this point, all of the legends were in question.

So. Not dead. Not undead. Not a meatsicle for the vampire queen, whose epic hotness didn't even begin to make up for her attitude. And if you put all of those things together, it meant…

I stopped and sighed. I had no idea what it meant. I was in a room I couldn't see, with my hands bound, a splitting headache, and nothing but questions for the employers who had for some reason become kidnappers.

I needed answers. But I wasn't going to get them unless I could get free. With better light and my lock picking tools, I knew I'd have been out of those handcuffs in no time. I'd been watching YouTube videos and practicing in my office for almost a month, after all.

Without those tools—or a key, conveniently dropped next to me—my only shot at getting free was to dislocate a thumb and pull that hand out of its cuff. I'd seen it done before in the movies. It had looked painful, but Hollywood was known for its dramatics.

Of course, even with my hands free, I'd need to open my cell door and escape what I could only assume were the dungeons of the same heavily-guarded mansion Anastasia had brought me to. But nobody ever said being a private investigator was easy.

I was still trying to figure out how to dislocate my thumb—and which thumb I liked least—when a door cracked open in the far wall. The sudden influx of light hit me like a faint echo of the teenager's punch. By the time I'd blinked away my not-at-all-unmanly tears, someone was standing above me.

The good news was that I recognized her.

The better news was that it was Anastasia, the one vampire who'd seemed to give a crap about my safety.

The bad news was that, despite her legendary poker face, even I could tell that she was less than happy.

"Ana—" I didn't make it through her whole name before my voice gave out. I shook my head, setting off yet another wave of nausea, and tried again. "Anastasia, what is going on?"

"That is precisely what we are here to discover, Mr. Smith."

That didn't make any sense.

"What do you remember of yesterday?" she asked.

"Yesterday?"

"When I saved your life and brought you to meet my queen."

"It's Saturday already?" So much for my Friday-night plans to meet Mike for street tacos. "What the hell did that girl hit me with?"

"Her fist."

I scowled. Jet Li would never have been taken out with a single punch. Not unless the plot called for it anyway.

"Then I guess I remember everything? Crab people. Vampire queens. Some sort of mediation I never got the details on, because before I could even properly introduce myself, I was getting punched into the weekend by someone half my size." My throat was raw. I must have thrown up at some point. I could only hope I'd ruined the brunette's Louboutins. "Which brings me back to my original question: *what is going on?* This is a shitty way to treat the last mediator in San Diego!"

Apparently, my brain had decided to stop arguing about whether I was a mediator or not.

"My queen seeks answers, Mr. Smith. It would behoove you to provide them before she chooses to take a more active role in the questioning."

The way she said *questioning* gave it a definite torture-y vibe, which was both terrifying and confusing. The vampires had saved my life. They needed me as a mediator. Why was I suddenly in a cell being threatened with water boarding?

"Are you sure you're not with the government?"

"Mr. Smith—"

I held up a hand to stop her... or tried to, before I remembered both of mine were cuffed behind my back. "My head's killing me, but I guess nobody cares about that. Ask your questions. Afterwards, maybe you'll answer mine."

"Very well." For some reason, her voice didn't have the same delightful impact as the previous day. Maybe it was the whole nauseous-from-a-possible-concussion-during-my-apparent-kidnapping thing. "Who do you work for?"

"Whoever will hire me, usually." I frowned. "I thought that was House Borghesi, but either I imagined that part, or something's gone wrong to the point that you people are all suddenly eager for San Diego to slide into a hell-mouth."

"A what?"

"Never mind."

She shook her head, a sharp, angry little motion that was still somehow lovely to watch. "Were you ever in danger from the karkino or was the entire event staged for our benefit?"

"I didn't even know what a karkino was until you showed up! I thought they were cosplayers that had wandered away from Comic Con and gotten lost."

"A likely story."

"It's not a story. It's just the truth. You've known me for like an hour now. Does literally anything about me suggest I'm a good liar?"

"The best spies are those nobody would ever assume to be such."

I'd have to take her word for it. Being a spy sounded way cooler than being a mediator—or even a private investigator—but I was going to pass if it meant being imprisoned and tortured.

"I'm not a spy. Or a mediator. Some people would say I'm barely a private investigator."

"So you claim." Despite her words, Anastasia seemed thoughtful. Maybe I was actually getting through to her.

"Anastasia, could you just pause the interrogation for one minute, and tell me what's going on? How did we go from me being the mediator you all needed to… whatever this is? Was it something I said?"

"You disobeyed a command from the queen."

"Sorry about that, but she's not *my* queen." I shrugged. "Disobedience is kind of an American pastime."

"You should not have been able to do so."

"What? Why? Look… I want to help. Really, I do, but you're not making any sense."

"Very well." She straightened back up and effortlessly captured my gaze with her own. Even in the dim light, her eyes seemed to glow, the tiny golden band around the pupil catching fire. "Mr. Smith, I want you to rise to your feet, walk to the corner, and bark like a dog."

"You want me to *what?* Is this some sort of sex thing? Because if so, I want to make it clear that my *no* is more of a *not right now*." I'd done weirder things for considerably less attractive women.

She settled back, and nodded in satisfaction. "And that is why we believe you are someone's pawn."

"Because my tolerance for kinky sex is directly proportional to the hotness of the woman asking?" I shook my head. "That's not that unusual, trust me."

"I was not speaking of sex, Mr. Smith. I was speaking of the fact that you are able to resist our commands."

"And that's weird?"

"It is impossible. Humans have no defense against compulsion."

"Compulsion." I thought back to right before all hell had broken loose in the conference room. "So when Queen Angry Face told me to sit down and be quiet...?"

"It was not a suggestion."

"And I didn't obey it, so you all freaked out." Another thought occurred to me. "Hey, did you pull the same thing when you told me to get in the Escalade?"

"I did," she admitted without apology, "and you got in."

"Because more crab people were on the way! I'm not an idiot! But I'll swear on a stack of Bibles that I'm also not a spy." I paused. "Figuratively speaking. I'm not suggesting you or any other vampires pick up a Bible in some sort of fiendish plot to have you burst into flame."

"It's just a book, Mr. Smith."

"Tell that to my family's priest." I shook my head. "I don't know why vampire mojo doesn't work on me, but the only reason I'm here is because you hired me. Until you saved my life, I was clueless about all of this stuff."

"Against all odds, I think I believe you." Her voice had lost just a bit of its edge.

"Great. So can we—"

"Or at least I believe that you believe it."

My future ex-wife and the possible mother of our three adorable human-vampire children—all of whom would hopefully look like her and not me—was seriously starting to mess with my mind.

"What does that even mean?"

"The simplest explanation is that you are under some sort of enchantment. We must assume that the person responsible is an enemy."

"You mean Lord Beer Can?"

"Beel-Kasan. And perhaps, though it does not fit his reputation. Nevertheless, it strains belief that the only mediator to survive the purge would also have an enchantment which allows him to ignore compulsion."

"And?"

"And where there is one enchantment, there may be more. We dare not allow you to serve as mediator until we have examined you more thoroughly."

Something told me that whatever she was talking about would make yesterday's pat-down seem like foreplay.

She confirmed that thought moments later, as she effortlessly pulled me to my feet.

"Come along, Mr. Smith. It is time to see the Blood Witch."

CHAPTER 7

IN WHICH CARDIO IS KING

The room I had been stashed in was, as I'd guessed, a cell. One of almost twenty, all neatly spaced along a long hall on one of the mansion's sub-levels. The fact that the vampires needed their own dungeon would have been my first clue that I was in way over my head... if both the karkino and my one-punch knockout hadn't already told me as much.

I didn't have a lot of experience with prisons or dungeons, but this one seemed pleasant enough. No screams of the damned. No rats scurrying into the shadows or strange and unidentifiable fungi. It didn't smell particularly fresh, but that was mostly my fault. I'd made the mistake of taking a whiff as we exited the cell, and my current fragrance was a heady combination of vomit, fear, and body odor.

Eau de Yuck, in other words.

At the midpoint of the hall, a pair of guards manned a security checkpoint. Given their smaller size and movie-star looks, I assumed they too were vampires. They were all in black, just like the men who had spilled out of the second Escalade on the previous day. It was starting to seem less like a fashion choice and more like a uniform. I squared my shoulders and sucked in my gut—again—as they bowed us through their checkpoint and into the open elevator.

I wasn't an expert on elevators, but it did appear to be the same one we'd previously ridden. I waited until the doors had closed, taking us away from both the guards and the sub-level, before I turned to Anastasia.

"Were they bowing to you or me?"

Her silence was answer enough.

I sighed. "Figures. I think the last time anyone bowed to me was in taekwondo."

She raised one slender eyebrow and glanced in my direction. "You are combat-trained, Mr. Smith?"

"Not by your standards." I shrugged. "Or anyone's, really. But I got pretty good at tying my belt."

One corner of her mouth ticked upwards in a movement so slight I almost missed it.

"So... this Blood Witch person," I continued. "What happens if she can't remove the spell? Assuming there is one?"

"We will cross that bridge when we must, Mr. Smith."

That wasn't reassuring.

A chime sounded and the doors whisked open, depositing us on the second floor. If I'd had any doubt that we were still in the mansion, the large flight of stairs leading down to the overly impressive foyer put those doubts to rest. The floors here were polished wood—*Mahogany*, said that same voice in my brain, which had clearly given up on actual identification, and was just going to keep guessing the same wood species until it was right—and wide-planked. The hall was richly appointed, with unintelligible artwork on the walls. Once we'd moved past the entryway and the natural light its windows provided, ceiling lights and the occasional wall sconce offered their own soft illumination.

If the fourth floor had all been offices, and the basement—sub-level two, if I'd read the elevator buttons correctly—was a dungeon, this floor felt like a 5-star hotel, with suites on each side. Most of the doors were shut, but I peeked inside one room as we passed it, and was surprised to see what looked like a second fully functional kitchen.

"Do vampires actually eat?"

"We do. Like most species, the People must both eat and drink to survive."

"And the whole blood thing?"

"Provides its own necessary nourishment."

I shivered, suddenly feeling like a juice box on legs. It was time to change the subject.

"Does the whole House live here?"

"Members of the council have rooms on another floor, but otherwise, yes."

By my not-so-careful count, that meant there were almost a hundred vampires in residence. That was kind of terrifying.

"Not every suite has a resident, Mr. Smith. These facilities were built for the future of the House, not its present."

"So House Borghesi is recruiting?"

"To an extent." Despite having swapped her boots for heels, Anastasia glided along silently next to me.

"How does that work? Do people fill out applications and go through interviews? Or is it just a matter of agreeing to the change, getting drained, and then waking up as a vampire?"

Anastasia stopped in mid-stride. "We are not undead, Mr. Smith. Nor are we former humans."

"You're not?" That settled it. Bram Stoker was an idiot.

"Our two species' only relationship is a symbiotic one."

"Meaning you eat us."

"Drink, but yes." She continued down the hall, unconcerned that I might somehow slip my cuffs and attack her.

Then again, I'd seen her fight. And she'd seen me fall over. I think we both knew how any sort of attempted escape would go.

"So humans can't become vampires, even when they're snacked on. Are vampires… born then?"

"You sound surprised."

Actually, I sounded disappointed, but I didn't see any point in clarifying that. Once I'd accepted that this whole vampire thing might be real, a part of me had started entertaining the fantasy of becoming one. Especially since sun allergies weren't a thing.

John Smith, creature of the night, had a certain ring to it.

ooo

By the time we reached our destination, I had a better appreciation for the sheer size of the mansion. My non-existent Fitbit would have exploded from the sudden influx of steps taken. It was a building that cried out for moving sidewalks. Or mopeds.

At the far end of the hall was an enormous door, eight feet tall, five feet wide, and bound horizontally with strips of black iron. It was the sort of thing you usually saw in medieval castles and low-budget European horror movies. I was positive I didn't want to see what lurked behind it.

I was also positive I didn't have a choice in the matter.

Anastasia tugged the massive door open and ushered me inside.

The European horror motif continued as we entered the base floor of a circular tower. A flight of stairs started to our right and followed the curves of the wall upward to disappear somewhere high above us. The room we were standing in contained a single child-sized bed—contributing significantly to the creep factor—and several curved wooden bookcases, each custom-built to fit under the spiraling staircase. The bed frame was wooden—*Mahogany!* cheered my increasingly dysfunctional brain—and simply made, but it practically screamed antique. Even the house's main doors and intricately carved conference table seemed modern by comparison.

I was less concerned with the furniture, however, than I was with the endless flight of stairs.

"Please tell me we're not climbing those?"

"I could, but it would be a lie."

"Maybe it would be easier if you just killed me now." I'd been compliant so far, but *more* cardio was simply unacceptable. Especially considering I hadn't eaten in almost a day.

A voice came from the stairs, deep and polished. "If that is your wish, human, then so be it."

The newcomer was black, male, and way too handsome, with features almost as fine as Anastasia's, and a physique straight out of a Marvel movie. His head was shaved, his jaw was chiseled, and his black button-up shirt and straight-legged pants looked like they were allergic to wrinkles.

"I have the matter in hand, Xavier." If Anastasia was overcome by the paragon of masculinity that had appeared before us, she was doing a damn good job of masking it. Despite the lactic acid turning my legs to mush and the cold handcuffs still around my wrists, I felt the first pangs of desperate, helpless love. "You may await us above."

"Or you and I could go back to the kitchen, have some sandwiches, and talk about—"

A dark-skinned fist drove into my doughy midsection with the force of a '68 Mustang, cutting off my suggestion. I dropped like a puppet whose strings had been severed, barely aware of Xavier picking me up and tossing me over one annoyingly broad shoulder.

"Allow me to transport this chattel, Lady Dumenyova." His deep words were honey-smooth. "Our queen awaits."

I already knew how silently Anastasia could move, so the clicking of her heels as she preceded us up the stairs had to mean something. Unfortunately, after watching the first few steps pass under me, I was too dizzy and miserable to decide exactly what.

I'm not sure how many steps we ended up climbing.

I do know I lost what little bit of food was left in my stomach somewhere around step fifty.

I probably should've warned Xavier before I puked all over the back of his immaculate button-up.

Maybe next time.

ooo

By the time we'd reached the top of the tower, I was dizzy, unhappy, and too weak to find any satisfaction in the way the people awaiting us shrank back from the spectacle of my vomit-splattered attacker. Xavier dumped me onto the floor. Without hands to catch myself, I landed with a decidedly meaty thwack. After a moment's pause, the man hauled me back to my feet with one hand.

Beyond Anastasia, Xavier, and myself, there were five people at the top of the tower. I recognized four from the ill-fated conference room meeting. Like Anastasia herself, they'd all had ample time to change outfits. The men were in different-but still-expensive suits, while the queen had swapped her shimmering white power suit for an equally white dress.

I was starting to wonder if she'd made the guards wear black just to make her own outfits pop by contrast. She looked fabulous, but our one meeting had been enough to tell me that looks could be deceiving.

The last council member—the teenager who had leapt the table and sucker-punched me into oblivion—was the only person other than me in casual clothes; a long black Ramones t-shirt and dark blue jeans. She looked even more like a high school senior; disaffected, disgruntled, and more than ready to disavow all knowledge of my existence.

The final person waiting for us was clearly the owner of the little bed we'd passed downstairs. Mired in the always-awkward stage of early adolescence, she was the only person other than me who *wasn't* oppressively good looking; pale grey eyes, large ears, and a too-wide mouth that was turned down into a fearsome scowl. She wore a long yellow dress with red flowers along its ankle-length hem, and a wide red sash. Red heels completed the odd picture.

I had no idea why they'd decided to bring a little girl to this showdown, let alone why that same child lived in a tower all by herself, but if my recent experience with the supernatural was anything to go by, I wasn't going to like the answers.

CHAPTER 8

IN WHICH A SECOND MEETING GOES
AS WELL AS THE FIRST

"So... what now?" I finally dared to ask.

"Nothing good. I can tell you that much." The vampire in the Ramones shirt smirked.

"It smells," complained the little girl in the yellow dress, "and we do not like it." There was something seriously wrong with her voice. It was high and barbed and just the sound of it somehow tied my already-sore guts into a knot.

"*He*, Zorana," corrected Anastasia, her words mild. "Whatever happens, Mr. Smith deserves that much respect."

"Respect is to be earned, not given, Secundus," said the queen. "And if he is an enemy, he will die unmourned."

"Aren't you overreacting just a—"

Xavier did something to one of my handcuffed arms, and white hot pain radiated down from that shoulder. I went up on my toes trying to alleviate the pressure. His voice was a low rumble in my ear.

"Speak only when you are spoken to, monkey."

Considering he'd just spoken to me, I took that as an invitation, but when I opened my mouth, he twisted my arm even further. Instead of words, I managed only a strangled gasp.

"Your Majesty," Xavier continued, raising his voice, "I must admit surprise that we have gathered to deal with a solitary human. What significance does this man have?"

It was one of the other men—the one who didn't have a pony-tail—who answered. "He is the last remaining mediator in San Diego, Captain." The man's voice was heavily accented. Spanish, maybe... but not Mexican Spanish.

The grip on my arm didn't loosen in the slightest, but Xavier sounded surprised. "The Rook was not the only victim?"

"He was not." That was Anastasia, who had crossed to the far side of the room to stand next to her queen. "We were too late to save any but Mr. Smith."

"His paltry life is all that stands between us and war," concluded the vampire queen, her words light, as if discussing the weather, "but events last night have led us to believe his survival was no accident."

"Events?" asked Xavier.

"We should just kill the monkey and take our chances with Lord Beel-Kasan," growled the pony-tailed vampire, who I liked less with every uttered word. "Our security is stretched too thin already without inviting a potential saboteur into our ranks."

"What *events*?" Xavier's grip had tightened around my arm. If he wasn't careful, he was going to pulp the limb like an overripe banana. I was already going to have finger-shaped bruises.

"Mr. Smith appears to be immune to compulsion," answered Anastasia. "Either he is not truly human or he is under the effect of some sort of enchantment, and thus—"

"A threat." Xavier nodded across the room to the pony-tailed vampire. "I agree with Andrés."

"Each of you has a seat upon my Council," said the blonde queen, bizarrely including the little girl who didn't know pronouns, "but I alone rule. I will not discard a tool until I know with certainty that it is of no use."

I was pretty sure Ms. High-and-Mighty had just called me a tool. The allure of her beauty was fading fast.

"That is why Juliette struck Mr. Smith down last night instead of killing him."

The spiky-haired brunette—who looked a lot more like an Iggy or a Sid than a Juliette—tossed me a mock salute from across the room. I scowled back, trying to hide the fact that I was being easily restrained by Xavier's single hand.

"It is also," continued Lucia, "why I summoned you all to the Midnight Tower."

Maybe it was the fact that she'd given the place a name, or maybe I'd just gotten tired of looking at people way prettier than I was. Either way, I finally thought to look at the room we'd gathered in.

The chamber was empty of furniture or ornamentation. Gleaming floors of some sort of polished black stone gave way to curved walls of the same material and finish. In the center of the room, what looked like a birdbath rose out of the stone as if it had been grown, a spiral stem stretching three feet in height before opening like petals of a flower to form a bowl.

It should have been pretty, but everything about that birdbath seemed wrong somehow, from the way light seemed to bend around it to the fact that I couldn't see the bowl's interior even though I was only a dozen feet away. As for the lights themselves… I risked a glanced upward and froze.

There was no ceiling. There was nothing above us but stars, a thousand pinpricks of light filling the dark canvas of a night sky. As I watched, a cloud drifted past, obscuring Orion's belt. I'd lived in San Diego for my entire life, and taken more than a few trips out to the nearby desert, but I'd never seen the stars so clearly.

Even weirder, when Anastasia and I had walked past the foyer, it had clearly still been daytime.

"Why is it night?" I couldn't help but ask.

"Which part of Midnight Tower did you not understand?" Juliette rolled her eyes.

Which was no real answer at all.

"If there are no further questions—" said Lucia, her voice slicing through the chamber in a way that made it damn clear there wouldn't be any.

"I have a *lot* of questions."

The queen looked at me like I was a particularly loathsome bug that had died on the windshield of her custom white Ferrari, and continued on, as if I hadn't spoken a word.

"—then let the ritual begin."

ooo

To say it had already been a rough two days was underselling things to a spectacular extent. Assassination attempts, vomit, imprisonment, and possible brain damage had combined to make this the worst day of my life.

Second worst, I decided, after a moment of reflection. That last trip down to Tijuana had had most of the same negatives, and a few more besides.

Actually, asking Marie out in front of the entire senior class in high school had seriously sucked too.

Still, this was definitely in the top five of bad days, and outside of that TJ trip, it was by far the weirdest.

It was about to get weirder.

Xavier dragged me to the center of the room. A small click announced the removal of my handcuffs, and then the other man was forcibly extending my left hand in front of me until it was directly over the birdbath.

Up close, I could see that its bowl had been carved into the shape of a stylized sun, rays radiating out from a perfect circle. I risked a glance down, certain that something was going to leap out at me, but the birdbath was empty, its polished surface reflecting a skewed image of the stars above.

I tore my eyes from the reflected starscape to find Zorana, the little girl in the yellow dress, mincing across the room toward us. She took a position on the other side of the birdbath from me, ran one small hand around the rim of the container, and nodded imperiously.

I looked from the red ribbon in Zorana's dark hair to the still forms of Anastasia and her queen. "I'm not sure what's about to happen, but I'm guessing it won't be pretty. Are you sure this is a place for a child?"

The girl reached out and touched my arm and the breath inside of me vanished, like she'd reached into my soul and flipped the off switch. She blinked up at me, oversized grey eyes going crimson as they filled with blood.

"I am *not* a child!" Her strange voice spiked even higher, and I felt myself shaking like a leaf in the wind.

"Peace, Zorana." Anastasia's careful tone told me exactly how bad things had suddenly become. "He is a stranger to these things and did not know."

If the little girl heard, she didn't respond. Nor did she let me go. I felt my heart stutter and skip a beat. I fell to one knee, my vision starting to blur.

This time, it was the queen who spoke.

"In this House, it is my place to mete out punishment, Blood Witch, not yours. Kill him and your own fate is sealed."

Zorana spun on the queen, releasing my arm in the process. I sagged against the birdbath, mouth gaping open like a fish as I gloried in the simple act of breathing. "You need me, Lucia."

"I need you both. For now." The queen's voice hardened and a cold wind swept the chamber. "I am Queen, Zorana. You accepted my rule when you followed us into exile."

There was a long, pregnant pause—broken only by Juliette's ostentatious and fang-filled yawn—and then Zorana nodded. "So I did."

"Then work your magic, and let us see what it tells us."

As the small not-a-child vampire turned back towards me, her smile was malevolent in a way that shook me to the core.

"Come, monkey. Let us see what stories your blood will tell."

I looked from the so-called Blood Witch in front of me to my left arm, which Xavier had again extended over the bird bath, and had a depressing epiphany about what was meant to fill that empty sun-shaped bowl.

Well, shit.

CHAPTER 9
IN WHICH THERE'S NO WITCH
LIKE A BLOOD WITCH

On the other side of the birdbath, Zorana raised her skinny arms to the night sky and for the second time, her eyes filled with blood. The language she spoke sounded like nothing any human had ever uttered, with bizarre rises and falls, hisses and moans, interspersed with the occasional click.

My dad was fluent in Klingon—and way too proud of that fact—but this was something else entirely.

The pint-sized terror continued at length while looking to the moon, then spat out another dozen phrases while looking to the sun in the altar. I could feel… something… gathering about us in the tower, as if her words were altering the nature of the air itself.

Eventually, she fell silent, but despite the lack of a ceiling, her words continued to echo, and the pressure kept building. At last, Zorana let her hands drop limply to the side, and those blood-filled eyes turned to me.

She reached for my outstretched arm, and there wasn't a damn thing I could do to stop her.

This time, the scary little girl vampire did more than simply touch me. She ran her index finger in a small circle along the inside of my exposed wrist. My skin parted like it was water, and her finger moved *into* my arm, carving deeper, like she was an elementary school kid digging into her lunchtime pudding.

I'm pretty sure I screamed somewhere in there. I *know* I passed out, but when I came to, I was still at the birdbath, held upright by Xavier, and the little psycho was still digging into my arm. There was a lot less blood than Tarantino movies had taught me to expect, and the initial rush of pain was already fading, replaced by a strange lethargy and spreading numbness.

I didn't know a thing about medicine—*John Smith, celebrity doctor*, had been a fantasy that lasted only until I saw how much schooling was required—but I was pretty sure that was a bad sign.

Finally, Zorana slipped her index finger out of the mess she'd made of my wrist. She placed that same bloody finger up on the inside of my elbow, six or so inches higher than the wound itself, and tapped three times. On the first tap, blood stopped seeping from the open wound. On the second tap, I felt something gather inside my arm, tangible even through the numbness. On the third tap, blood began to flow again, but this time, it rose from the incision like it was being sucked through a straw, streaming smoothly together to form a tidy ribbon of crimson. It ignored the laws of physics, gravity, and basic human decency to flow down my arm in tight spiral loops as it moved towards my fingers. It stopped just before those fingers, leaving me wearing a striped, fingerless, blood-glove on my left hand.

In a movie, that sort of weirdness might have been kind of cool. In real life, it was gross as all hell. The fact that it was my arm and my blood made it even worse.

Zorana said another word in her alien tongue, and the ribbon of blood started moving again, charting a course down the length of my index finger. At the very tip of my nail, the stream paused again, as if held back by an unseen barrier. On cue, she spoke, and the barrier disappeared. My blood poured smoothly into the sun-shaped basin, like the smallest, nastiest waterfall I'd ever seen.

I don't know how much time passed as my blood poured into the bowl. The container was maybe a third full—and that same lethargy had been replaced with light-headed dizziness—when Zorana finally removed her hand from my arm. As if a door had slammed shut, the wound stopped bleeding. The blood that had already exited my body continued its path to the basin, leaving not a single speck of crimson behind. Moments later, the savage incision itself was gone, replaced by new skin; pink, hairless, and unlined.

I looked up from that impossibility to find the Blood Witch waving her little hands over the altar. In the basin, my blood was now moving, flowing counter-clockwise fast enough to create a whirlpool despite the absence of any drain. Even more disturbing, there were shapes in the blood, shapes that looked suspiciously like miniature faces and figures. One tiny crimson hand momentarily extended upward before vanishing again below the surface.

Why were there *people* in my blood whirlpool?

Right. Stupid question.

Zorana nodded one last time and raised her blood-filled eyes to the sky. Scrawny arms stretched upward again in silent supplication. The crimson whirlpool stilled.

The rest of us—six beautiful lunatics and one moderately overweight non-mediator—waited to hear her verdict.

ooo

After the utterly bonkers insanity of the ritual itself, the conclusion was anti-climactic. Zorana left the altar, her eyes returning to their usual grey. "No spells. No enchantment. Not even a trace to suggest the monkey has been in contact with anything but the karkino and our kind before yesterday."

"Then how did he resist Queen Lucia's command?"

"I don't know." The Blood Witch shrugged, looking disturbingly like the little girl she clearly wasn't, and darted a malevolent glance at the blonde queen. "Are you certain you weren't just… off your game?"

Lucia stiffened as if she'd been struck, but before she could blast the impertinent pipsqueak, Anastasia stepped forward.

"I verified Mr. Smith's immunity myself this morning."

"Fascinating. A monkey that does not know its place." She twirled a dark curl of hair around her still-bloody index finger. "I suggest we kill it immediately."

Both of the men in suits nodded in agreement, and I felt as much as saw Xavier do the same. Juliette, on the other hand, just shrugged her slim shoulders, clearly bored with the whole process.

Lucia turned to Anastasia. "Secundus?"

From across the room, the auburn-haired vampire's green eyes found mine. "I will not deny that Mr. Smith's apparent ability makes him a threat."

Xavier's grip on me tightened, as if he was prepared to carry out the execution then and there.

"However," Anastasia continued, "there is still the matter of our conflict with Lord Beel-Kasan. Mr. Smith is the only mediator left to us. We are not spoiled for choice in the matter."

I fought off a frown. On the one hand, she was speaking up on my behalf, and trying to save my life, yet again. On the other hand, nobody likes being chosen because they're literally the only option left.

I *wasn't* a mediator, but I still had feelings.

"A fair point. Yet I will not expose this House to further harm until we can be certain the human is not working against us."

"Wasn't that what this whole thing was about?" I asked. Xavier's hands tightened yet again, and I squirmed. "Dude, can you quit it already? I might need those arms later."

"Captain." Lucia glanced at the black vampire holding me captive, and he relented, releasing me entirely. Free of both handcuffs and the man's steel grip, I could have made a dash for it then and there... if there hadn't been *so* many stairs.

Those arctic blue eyes turned from Xavier to me. "Your species' history is rife with betrayal, human, and enchantment is rarely required."

I had absolutely no idea what the hell that meant, but I was pretty sure she was insulting all of humanity. Again.

The queen nodded as if she'd made her point, infusing the gesture with enough arrogance that it almost deserved its own zip code.

"Marcus, inspect Mr. Smith's finances. If he has not been spelled, let us make sure he has also not simply been bribed to work against us." Anastasia started to speak, but the queen held up a golden hand. "I will not admit a potential enemy into this mediation, Lady Dumenyova, let alone in a position of potential authority."

Marcus was apparently the vampire without a ponytail. He bowed smoothly, all courtly elegance. "It will be as you say, Your Majesty. I will have the results for you shortly."

Given the state of my bank account, *shortly* was actually an understatement.

"Andrés," the queen continued, "given the Rook's demise, the likelihood of open conflict has increased dramatically."

I was pretty sure she'd just insulted my mediator talents.

Which... was fair, given that I didn't have any.

"Reach out to your contacts," she continued. "We will need fodder if this should erupt into war."

"Your wish is my command." The pony-tailed vampire's bow made Marcus' look plain. Royal ass-kissing was clearly a competitive sport.

Lucia wasn't done. She looked past me to Xavier. "Have you and the Watch finished your examination of the Rook's murder scene?"

"Preliminary analysis nears completion, Your Majesty, but there is still much to do."

"Then you should focus your energies upon that task. I want your findings presented to the Council tomorrow. As the only assassination not carried out by the karkino, the Rook's murder remains our best chance to identify the true source of these attacks."

Xavier one-upped both of the other two male vampires—man vampires? No... *manpires!*—by skipping the bow entirely and dropping down to one knee, shaved head lowered. "I live to serve, Your Majesty."

"Yes." A wave of her ring-laden hand sent all three manpires headed for the stairs. Shortly later, the heavy door far beneath us boomed shut. Lucia turned to me. "If you are to be of any value to my House as mediator, Mr. Smith, you must be brought up to speed on the situation and swiftly."

"Yeah. About that." With Xavier gone, I felt a little bit of backbone seeping back into me. A very little bit. "Between the crab people and whatever the hell *this* was—" I carefully avoided looking at Zorana or the bloody birdbath. "—we never got around to discussing some of the details of this case."

"Are your ears broken, human? That is exactly what I was—"

"I don't mean the mediation itself." Maybe it was the blood loss speaking, but I got a special sort of enjoyment in seeing Lucia's face tighten as I dared interrupt her. I'd been insulted and attacked, and my blood had been co-opted for freaky science experiments, and all of it had been on her orders. I was going to help the vampires... as much as I could, anyway... but I was doing it for San Diego, *not* for some human-hating royal. And I definitely wasn't going to do it for free. "I'm talking about my fee."

"Your fee?" Queen Lucia stalked over to me, curved hips swaying like a ship at sea. "You would speak to me of remuneration when I have just given you back your life?" Her voice was sharp enough to draw blood.

Figuratively speaking.

It was Anastasia who saved me. Again. "Your Majesty, it *is* customary to pay for a mediator's services. The Concordat—"

"I attended the same classes you did, Secundus." Lucia's voice cracked like a whip, but the queen never took her eyes off of me. "So be it, Mr. Smith. Should you resolve this situation to my satisfaction, you will be granted the Rook's usual payment."

As far as I knew—which was admittedly not saying much—mediators were paid for their services whether the mediation was successful or not.

"I don't think that's how it's supposed to—" I began.

It was Lucia's turn to interrupt, invading my personal space like it was just another territory to annex. For the first time, I realized just how short she was. Without her skyscraper heels, she would have barely cleared five feet.

Which didn't matter much once she clamped a golden hand around my throat. Her fingers were hot despite the cold wind that had again filled the room. She pulled me down to her level, until my view was filled with the icy blue of her eyes.

"And should your mediation efforts fail," she continued, breath cool and sweet on my face, "rest assured that you will not live to see the war that follows."

Before I could say something almost guaranteed to get me killed, she tossed me away with a flick of her wrist. I found myself airborne, thrown half a dozen feet across the chamber. By some minor miracle, I didn't tumble down the stairs, but a second encounter with the obsidian floor told me it was just as hard as it had been the first time. I barely heard the queen's next words over the meaty thunk of my own impact.

"Juliette, he is your responsibility. See that he is fed, briefed, and for the love of the fallen gods, cleaned. I may never get this stench out of my hair."

The room was spinning around me by that point, but I heard the dismay in Juliette's voice. "Anastasia hired him. Shouldn't she—"

"I have need of both Zorana and my Secundus. More to the point, *I tire of having my commands questioned.* If I must tear this building down to its foundations to teach my subjects obedience, *I will do so.* Do you hear me?"

I looked up and saw the stars in the impossible night sky winking out, one by one, as thick clouds rolled in. The wind that already filled the tower went from cold to icy, and something that looked an awful lot like snow started to fall.

That seemed as good a time as any for me to pass out again.

CHAPTER 10

IN WHICH CLEANLINESS IS NEXT TO GODLINESS

I wish I could say it was the first time I'd woken in a strange place with no memory of—

Wait. I'd already thought that once today, hadn't I? Through sheer force of will, I cracked open an eye, but nothing about my surroundings looked familiar. Where the hell was I now?

And more to the point, what had happened to my clothes?

The last thing I remembered was being thrown across the Midnight Tower by the ridiculously strong and easily annoyed Queen Lucia, but the floor beneath me wasn't obsidian.

Or… whatever that black stone had been.

Nor was it concrete, like the cell I'd woken up in the first time. Or hardwood, like the endless hall Anastasia and I had traversed to reach the tower. It wasn't even carpet, like we'd encountered in the conference room.

This floor was as white as Lucia's wardrobe and almost as cold as her eyes.

I spent a moment marveling at the very many types of flooring I'd become intimately acquainted with over the past twenty-four hours. Then, I got back to the all-important business of figuring out where I was.

It took another herculean effort, but I was finally able to open my other eye. I looked around, squinting against the bright lights that were doing nothing for my possibly-brain-damage-induced headache.

I was in a small rectangular room, maybe five feet across and eight feet long. The floor and three of the walls were white marble tile, the sort of thing you'd find in overpriced HGTV remodels. The fourth wall was glass, opaque, and frosty blue. It didn't extend as far as the tiled wall it paralleled, leaving a three foot exit on the far end.

Someone banged on the other side of the frosted glass. "Enough sleeping on the job, mediator. Some of us are hungry."

I'd heard the voice before, but was still trying to place it when a slender bare arm reached through the gap to turn one of the many knobs I'd failed to notice on the far wall. And just like that, water was pouring from unseen nozzles in the ceiling to cascade down upon my naked body.

○○○

It was, without question, the nicest shower I'd ever seen, let alone used. That didn't make up for having woken up naked inside of it, or for nearly drowning before I realized what was going on, but it did help. A little bit anyway.

The touch of a button prompted body wash to issue forth from another recessed spigot. I'd have expected something floral or fruity, but the soap was surprisingly unscented. Even so, it smelled way better than I did. I scrubbed off multiple layers of vomit and filth, watching the steaming hot water carry a very bad day's worth of stench down the drain. Wherever my clothes had ended up, I could only hope they were being sanitized.

A second button deposited shampoo into my waiting hand, and I hummed quietly to myself as I washed my hair. There was something very comforting about the act of getting clean. True, I'd been left in the shower because my stench offended those around me, and yes, my life apparently depended upon mediating for a house of vampires who appeared to be bloodthirsty in both a literal and figurative sense… and sure, there was the little matter of pre-adolescent vampire girls performing party tricks with my blood, but… at least I was clean.

'Small victories are still victories,' as my dad often said.

Eventually, I ran out of parts to wash. I migrated back over to the other side of the shower and turned off the water. I was still pretty sure I disliked Queen Lucia almost as much as she disliked me, but she and her people had some amazing technology.

I stepped out onto the cool tiled floor, taking up the plush towel that had been left for me, and began to dry off, still humming.

"Well, aren't *you* the chipper little bird."

In the greatest feat of athleticism I'd ever managed, I caught the towel before it could hit the floor, and wrapped it around my waist, even as I spun toward the voice.

It had been twenty minutes since the woman had woken me up and then tried to drown me, and I hadn't heard a peep since, but there she was, perched on a floating double vanity, legs swinging back and forth beneath her.

Juliette.

In the cavernous bathroom's light, I saw that her eyes weren't light brown like I'd originally thought, but instead a pale shade of yellow. They were wide and delighted as she watched me struggle to hold onto my towel.

"What are you doing in here?" I tried to sound authoritative, which was surprisingly difficult when mostly naked and confronted by someone who'd already proven she could knock me on my ass with a single punch.

"Waiting, obviously." She waved a hand dismissively. "You dawdled for so long that I started to worry you were committing suicide by soap suds. Plus, I was bored. So here we are."

"Right." I waited for her to leave, but she seemed content to sit there and eyeball me, her smirk widening with every passing second. "So…" I tried instead. "I'm alive. Obviously. Can I get some privacy? And my pants?"

"I had your clothes burned." She smirked. "Besides, Lucia said I should feed and clean you. Nobody said anything about dressing you."

"I have a strict no-pants, no-mediation policy."

"That's probably for the best… although they do say laughter is the universal language." Juliette leaned back on the vanity and re-crossed her long legs. "So you've done a lot of mediations then?"

"A few," I hedged.

"How many, exactly?" Either she was the suspicious sort or I really, really needed to get better at lying.

"This will be my first." I thought about it and shook my head. "Actually, my second." Trying to play peacemaker between Susie Birkman and Jenny Douglass in second grade could count as my first. Hopefully, this one would be more successful.

"And you're the only mediator who survived." Juliette shook her head, her short, spiky hair barely moving. "I thought she was supposed to be subtle?"

"Who?"

"Nobody." Those yellow eyes focused back on me. "I hope you're a fast learner, little bird."

"I'm not a bird. Or little." I scowled, wondering just how much she'd seen before I rescued the towel. "And why are we just standing around? Didn't you say you were hungry? And aren't you supposed to be briefing me?"

Her smirk graduated to a full-blown smile. "I guess since I already *debriefed* you, it's only fair to do the opposite."

I almost dropped the towel again. Not that it mattered, since she'd apparently already seen what there was to see. If I were twenty pounds lighter and in significantly better shape, maybe that thought would have been something other than totally horrifying.

Juliette laughed at my expression, the delicate sound entirely incongruous with her appearance. In one smooth motion, she hopped off the vanity, revealing the neat stack of clothing that had been behind her all along.

"Hurry up and get dressed. Tormenting you is fun—and so very easy—but there are more important things at stake."

"Like the mediation I still know almost nothing about?"

"I was thinking lunch." She shrugged. "But the mediation works too. You have three minutes. You don't want me coming back in to get you."

"I didn't want you here in the first place," I said, but she was already out the bathroom door.

I hurried over to the waiting clothes. They weren't mine, and every item being black made me feel like a refugee from a Goth concert, but anything was better than staying naked. At least it all fit; a pair of black slacks and a black button-up shirt to go with equally black boxers and socks. I ran what appeared to be a brand new comb through my perpetually messy brown hair and glanced in the mirror. My battered and bruised reflection looked clean, but that was all that could be said for it. The fact that I was wearing the same outfit as Xavier—but looked considerably worse—didn't help.

I sighed at my reflection one last time and exited the bathroom. It was time to get some answers.

And a sandwich.

○○○

As nice as the bathroom had been, the attached bedroom put it to shame. Directly in front of me was a king-sized bed, flanked by ornate dressers dusted to within an inch of their mahogany lives. To my left was a full sitting area, complete with rug, sectional couch, recliner, and coffee table. On the other side of the bed, French doors led to either *another* bathroom or the sort of walk-in closet that my mom had been dreaming about since she was a little girl.

All it needed was a human-sized chandelier and a basketball court and it would have been the match of any of those extravagant Las Vegas luxury suites that real people could never hope to afford.

Juliette was perched on an arm of the couch, but she hopped up as I came in. "Finally! Let's go eat."

Now that I was no longer naked, I was feeling a bit better equipped to argue with the spiky-haired female vampire—womanpire? No, that was terrible. Wait… *femmepire!*—but it had been at least twenty-four hours since I'd left Comic Con to get something to eat and my stomach felt like it was turning inside out, so I dutifully followed the femmepire out into the hall. My carefully honed investigative abilities informed me that it was the same one I'd walked with

Anastasia. Juliette saying as much helped, admittedly. We went past the sweeping staircase and into the second-floor kitchen I'd spotted earlier.

The far wall was all countertops and cabinets, white on top of white, with only the patterned backsplash there to break up the effect. A stainless steel refrigerator sized for an ogre—assuming ogres were a thing—marked the end of the countertops on one side, while giant doors to what could only be a pantry did the same on the other.

The bathroom had been nice. The bedroom had been better. But the kitchen… it was almost worth every indignity I'd already suffered.

John Smith, creature of the night, would have made a few thousand midnight kitchen raids. The denizens of the pantry would have learned to fear his name.

Opposite the counters, on the other side of an island big enough to be its own sovereign nation, were chairs and tables to seat a small army, but the room was empty except for a handful of pretty men clustered around a distant table. Most were dressed in typical southern California casual—two even wore sandals, which seemed a bit much— but one had the same all-black outfit as me. Just like Xavier, he looked a lot better in it than I did.

The manpires were cleaning their table, carrying dishes to the two enormous sinks in the island. Most then slid past us and out into the hall with respectful nods to Juliette, but the man in black stopped.

"New pet, Juliette?" The manpire was clearly of Mexican descent, much like my best friend, Mike, albeit half my friend's size. He looked me up and down and his nostrils flared.

"He only wishes." Juliette smirked.

"He's rough around the edges," the other man mused, "but it's what is inside that counts, no?" The look he sent me was heavy with innuendo. "If this one doesn't treat you right, human, come find Esteban."

"Uhm… okay?"

He nodded, gave me a piercing stare right out of Zoolander, and followed the others out into the hall.

I waited for the kitchen door to close, and turned to Juliette. "Did he just… smell me?"

"Get used to it. Now that you're not a walking toxicological disaster, you smell surprisingly good."

"Seriously?" I took a whiff, but didn't smell anything. None of my girlfriends had ever commented on my scent except when it crossed the line and became an odor.

"Not your body, little bird. Your blood. AB-negative, I'm guessing?"

"Yes. And you knowing that is super creepy." I shivered. "They were all vampires, right?"

"Obviously." Juliette crossed the room and started digging through the cavernous stainless steel refrigerator.

"Thank God."

She paused and threw a look over her shoulder. "What?"

"Am I not allowed to mention the G-word here?"

"Why would I possibly care about that?" Juliette frowned, as I mentally crossed another vampire myth off the list. "I just don't know why you're thanking him."

"Oh. Well, it's a lot easier to accept everyone being prettier than me when it's a species thing. My ego can only take so much punishment."

"I'd think your ego would be used to it by now." She pulled out a beer and a Tupperware of pre-made sandwiches. "Anyway, you're fairly average looking for a human. Criminally out-of-shape even for someone in their mid-thirties, but—"

"I'm twenty-five!"

"Seriously?" She looked me up and down. "Have you ever thought of exercising?"

"I'm between active hobbies at the moment," I retorted lamely.

"Maybe you should try a crunch or two from time to time then." Juliette plucked a sandwich from the Tupperware and then took it and the beer to a nearby table. A flick of her thumb sent the bottle cap arcing across the room to rattle into a distant trash can. "If you'd like, I can have one of the chefs whip you up something with kale?"

I sighed. "Aliens would have been so much better."

CHAPTER 11

IN WHICH HAM IS NO LAUGHING MATTER

The pantry was as large as my parents' entire kitchen back home. The sheer variety of freshly baked bread available seemed like overkill—and a quick road to even flabbier thighs—but I wasn't complaining.

As tasty as Juliette's pre-made sandwich looked, I had opted to assemble my own from ingredients in the cavernous refrigerator. It was a thing of beauty; a skyscraper of honey wheat, ham, and Gouda, with a single leaf of lettuce on top to keep things healthy. It was so large that I had to carry my plate one-handed, the other hand positioned to keep that gorgeous culinary edifice from toppling over.

Juliette looked from me to the sandwich and then back again. "Overcompensating, are we?"

Given that she'd already seen me naked once, there wasn't much I could say in reply. Thankfully, that first bite went a long way to soothing my wounded ego. The bread wasn't the only thing with notes of honey; the ham had a glaze on it that was to die for.

"Anyway, we should probably—" Juliette paused, and a strange look crossed her face. She leaned across the table and took a long sniff.

I glared at her from behind the safety of my sandwich. "I get it already. I smell like a vampire buffet. Or catnip. Or human crack. Can you let me eat in peace?"

"I wasn't smelling you, idiot. I was smelling your sandwich."

"Oh." I shrugged. "Still rude."

"Where'd you get that ham?"

"The refrigerator." At the femmepire's scowl, I hurried to elaborate. "Tupperware on the top shelf."

"And was there, just maybe, a label on the container?"

"Yeah." I took another large bite and gloried in the taste. "It said *Xavier's. Do Not Touch.*"

"And…?"

"And I figured he wouldn't mind. Besides, I have you here to protect me, right?"

"Queen Lucia said to keep you alive. I'm sure Xavier would be satisfied with just taking one of your hands. It's what they did to thieves in his day."

I swallowed past the sudden lump in my throat. "I need both of my hands. For… mediation."

"I'm sure you do." She shrugged and took a long pull on her beer. "Oh well. Guess we'll see what happens."

That wasn't particularly reassuring. I took another bite, but the ham had lost its flavor. "So I guess he's older than he looks?"

"Duh. We all are."

"And Zorana? Why does she look like she should still believe in Santa?"

Juliette got a strange look on her face. "What are you talking about? Santa is real!"

"Seriously?"

"No." Her smirk fell away as quickly as it had formed. "Zorana is also older than she looks."

"Well, yeah, I kind of fig—"

"A *lot* older. She and Lucia are the two oldest members of the House. At least I think so."

And yet they looked like a ten-year-old and twenty-year-old, respectively. "Do vampires age backwards or something?"

"Like Mork?"

"Who?" I'd been thinking Benjamin Button.

She shook her head in mock-sadness. "How quickly they forget. And no. We're born as babies, just like humans. Only smarter, prettier, and stronger, of course. And we mostly age the same way as your kind at first."

"And then?"

"Puberty hits. Then comes the Thirst."

I could hear the capital T she'd given Thirst. "For blood?"

"No, I'm talking about milkshakes. They're the source of all our power."

The idea of a milkshake-powered species was actually kind of amazing, but my keenly trained powers of deduction told me she was being sarcastic.

"Anyway, there used to be a lot of debate about the optimal time to feed. For centuries, people thought the longer you held off the Thirst, the stronger you'd be as an adult. Thank the gods we stopped with that nonsense." She shrugged. "What isn't up for debate is that our first drink stops the aging process."

"And you…"

"Had my first sip on the night of my eighteenth birthday. He tasted fabulous. Bit of a disappointment in bed, but humans are gonna human."

I managed to stop myself from nodding in agreement. It had been a long time since I'd gotten any action at all, but there hadn't been any complaints afterwards. Although… it would explain why it had ended up being a one-night-stand.

"Wait. Are you saying that vampires and humans can—?"

"Screw? Bump nasties? Do the horizontal hulu?" Juliette shrugged. "Duh. We have the same parts after all."

"Oh."

"Don't get your hopes up. Moronic frat boy isn't as appealing as you think."

"Once we've hit our mid-twenties, we prefer to be called frat men."

"Of course you do." She rolled her eyes.

"So what happened with Zorana?"

Juliette glanced at the door, as if our continued utterance of the Blood Witch's name might actually summon her. "She was forced to feed before she even felt the Thirst."

"Why?"

"Another old wives' tale. If holding off the Thirst was supposed to make a normal member of the People more powerful, it had the opposite effect on Blood Witches."

"So they're born, not trained?"

"Yeah. It's like soul. Some people have it, some people don't. Anyway, she was the only one with the gift at the time, and the old king decided not to wait."

"And now she's stuck as a child forever? That sucks."

"You have no idea."

"Why did she stay with the royal family that screwed her over?"

"Different royal family." Juliette frowned. "At least I think so. I never paid much attention to ancient history. Anyway, Lucia doesn't make a fuss when the Blood Witch breaks her toys."

"Toys?"

"Pets, donors, monkeys... the usual. Zorana is as nutty as a fruitcake, but she's also strong enough to take this building apart, brick by brick. That sort of power is worth the occasional mishap. Remember that the next time you decide to mouth off to her."

"She just made my blood do gymnastics in a birdbath," I reminded her. "I'm cool with never speaking to her again."

"Huh." Juliette cocked her head, looking at me as if she'd never seen me before. "Maybe there's a brain in there after all."

ooo

Whatever else you might say about vampires—and after less than twenty-four hours, I already had a lot to say—it was hard to deny that their house came with some serious perks. First, there was the technological marvel of a shower I'd woken up in. Then there was the absurdly large kitchen Juliette and I were having lunch in, to say nothing of the sheer variety of available food. And last, but most definitely not least, was the room's *second* refrigerator, one that was stocked entirely by...

"Beer!" I threw the refrigerator door wide open, my gaze wandering across shelves stocked with every type of beer I could imagine. Cans, bottles, IPAs, lagers, pilsners, ales… "I think I'm in heaven."

"Nope. Just San Diego." Juliette polished off her own beer and set the empty bottle back on the table with a thump. "I don't think I've ever seen anyone undress beer with their eyes before."

"It's just so beautiful," I murmured.

"Where did Anastasia find you again?"

"Logan Heights. Outside my office."

"You work in *that* neighborhood? By choice? You've got bigger balls than I thought." She smirked. "That shower must have been ice-cold."

"Office space isn't cheap." I grabbed a bottle of Ballast Point's California Kölsch. "It was all I could afford. And speaking of money, when are you going to tell me about this mediation?"

"That depends on you, little bird."

"Seriously… what's with the nickname?" Given her constant verbal assault on my genitalia, I was pretty sure I knew where *little* was coming from, but the bird part made no sense at all.

"Don't blame me. You're the one who was singing in the shower while I waited outside."

I frowned. "I didn't sing… did I?"

"The Lion King."

Damn it. That did sound like me. I shook my head. "Whatever. You were saying about the case?"

"Bring me one of those," she said, nodding to the bottle in my hands, "throw in a 'pretty please, Juliette, light of my life', and I'll tell you all about it."

I liberated a second Kölsch, passed it over, and took a seat at the table. I'd only made it halfway through my sandwich so far.

Juliette waited expectantly.

"I just gave you a beer! I'm not saying please. Or any of that other stuff," I added, when she opened her mouth to interject. "Besides, Lucia told you to brief me on the case. You don't want this 'little bird' to sing a song to Queen Crazy, do you?"

"Damn, Juliette," came a new voice from the hallway. I wasn't good with accents, but I was pretty sure the newcomer was Australian. "Is your pet looking to get himself killed or something?"

Three vampires, all in the ubiquitous black that almost had to be a uniform, marched into the kitchen. The first was the femmepire who had just spoken, ash-blonde and tall. Behind her came two manpires, each built like terminators or MMA fighters. The first wouldn't have looked out of place at SDSU; tan with sandy-brown hair and a distinct 'marijuana morning' sort of vibe. The other was black— almost as dark-skinned as Xavier—with an honest-to-God mohawk dyed blood-red.

Until that moment, I'd always thought mohawks looked dumb. Now, I just wished I had one.

Juliette scoffed. "I'm offended that everyone keeps assuming he's mine. I have standards!" She waved one hand from me to the newcomers. "John Smith, meet Kayla, Steve, and Ray. John's our new mediator. And yes, he does seem to have a bit of a death wish."

The blonde femmepire nodded in my direction. "Nice to meet you, mate. You might want to ixnay on the whole disrespect thing though. Our queen and her council—"

"I'm sitting right here," pointed out Juliette.

"—sorry, *most* of her council are sticklers for formality."

"If only someone had clued me in on that fact a day ago," I muttered.

Although… *technically*, Anastasia had.

The mohawked manpire was still looking me over. For some reason, he seemed impressed. "A human mediator? That's got to be a first."

Kayla shook her head. "There was a family back in Adelaide that served as mediators for a few human generations." She winced. "Until a group of Muldjewangk took exception to something they said and wiped out the whole bloodline."

I wasn't sure what a Muldjewangk was, other than one more reason not to go to Australia… ever. Which was a pity because I was already halfway in love with Kayla's accent.

"You call yourself John Smith? Do you have... like... amnesia or something?" That came from the third manpire.

"You're thinking of *John Doe*, Ray." The mohawked manpire shook his head, his wide smile infectious. By process of elimination, he had to be Steve. "John Smith, on the other hand, is a painfully obvious alias."

"Actually," I admitted, "I come from a long line of John Smiths."

"No shit?"

"No shit. It's a family tradition or something to name the first son John. Technically, I think I'm John Smith the seventh."

"That's messed up, dude."

"Tell me about it." If I ever had a kid—and the lack of anything even approaching a girlfriend made that unlikely—I was going to name the child something respectable, like Alphonso, or Zachariah, or Lemon Chicken.

Ray still seemed confused. "Wait... why do we need a new mediator? Where's the Rook?"

Kayla smacked him on the shoulder. "We had a meeting about it this morning, Ray. The Rook's dead, remember?"

Ray shrugged. "You know I'm barely even awake before my morning feeding."

"And that's why nobody ever tells you anything, dude," teased Steve. "He turned back to me and gave an odd sort of half-bow. "Nice to meet you, John."

"Ditto." Given the circumstances, nice was a bit of a stretch, but someone who said dude twice in less than five minutes was alright in my book.

"Were any of you part of the detail that processed the murder scene?" asked Juliette.

"Kayla was, Councilwoman." Steve was already digging into the refrigerator. "Ray and I were working the House perimeter."

Kayla caught the bottle of beer Steve underhanded to her, popped the cap off with one thumb, and nodded, wrinkling her nose. "It's been decades since I've seen a bloodbath like that. Pieces literally everywhere."

The sandwich half I'd already eaten turned over in my stomach.

"These three are all part of the Watch," said Juliette, for once actually living up to her assigned role as my mentor. "The House's soldier class. Xavier is their Captain."

"Someone gave that maniac minions?"

Even Kayla's frown was delightful. "The Captain is a great man, John. Our House is lucky to have him."

"He sucker-punched me and carried me up the stairs of the Midnight Tower like I was luggage!"

"And you puked all over him, little bird. I'd say you're even."

"Is that why the janitors were up on our floor?" asked Steve.

"Yep. Our new mediator has been leaving messes everywhere he goes."

"I don't want to talk about it," I grumbled.

"Fair enough." Kayla spun a chair about and lowered herself into it. "Mind if we join you?"

"I'm not sure I could stop you if I did," I replied, trying my best not to sulk about that fact. "As far as I can tell, you could all break me in half without even trying."

"She was asking me, doofus." Juliette waved a hand at the other chairs around the table. "Make yourselves at home. I've been tasked with keeping this one alive until the mediation is set. I could use all the help I can get."

"We're in the heart of Queen Lucia's domain, surrounded by both the Watch and human security," laughed Kayla. "That shouldn't be a prob—" Her voice trailed off as I picked up my sandwich. "Is that Xavier's ham?"

"It's like I told you," said Juliette. "He's got a death wish."

CHAPTER 12

IN WHICH THE CONCORDAT COMES BACK

Of the three, only Kayla stuck around for long. Steve snagged a second beer before heading out the door with a wave, and Ray followed soon after, carrying an entire Tupperware of sandwiches, and muttering something about the munchies.

I turned to Juliette. "What's the deal with Ray?"

"The '60s were rough on him," admitted the spiky-haired femmepire. "When I came to San Diego, he was already three years into a decade-long plan to stuff his body with every psychotropic drug he could find. We're resilient, especially compared to humans, but there are limits."

So Juliette was way older than she looked too. I shook my head. I should've figured that much out from her being on the council, but she acted like a teenager. Not that I was in a position to judge. "Junkie vampires? What's next? Surfers?"

"What's wrong with surfing?" Kayla asked around a mouthful of hoagie.

"You're all supposed to be allergic to sunlight!"

"We're supposed to be a lot of things, I hear." The Aussie wiped her mouth with the back of one hand. "I take it this is your first mediation for the People?"

"It's his first time working for anyone other than humans," said Juliette. "Until yesterday, he was one of the blissfully ignorant."

The taller vampire paused with a beer halfway to her lips. "That's…" She shook her head slowly. "I don't mean any offense, Juliette, and I hope I'm not speaking out of turn, but was bringing in a total newbie a good idea, considering all that is at stake?"

"You won't get any arguments from me." Juliette shrugged her slim shoulders. "I didn't hire him; Anastasia did."

"Ah." Kayla swallowed. "Objection withdrawn."

"Hold up." I held up my hand again. "Why does it matter who hired me?"

"Kayla knows that I'm not going to just murder her for questioning my judgment."

"But Anastasia would?" That didn't fit my view of the other vampire at all. She'd been the only person in the Midnight Tower who didn't seem to want me dead.

"Lady Dumenyova—and John, you really should refer to the House elders by title—has a formidable reputation," said Kayla, neatly sidestepping the question. "There's a reason she's Her Majesty's Secundus. If she hired you, she had her reasons."

"I'm the only mediator left in San Diego," I admitted.

"Oh."

"Yeah."

Kayla cleared her throat, and tried again, voice almost willfully cheerful. "So you've had all of one day to deal with learning that humans aren't alone on this planet?"

"Yeah, although I spent a lot of that day unconscious, thanks to Juliette over here. And as far as I can tell, I'm still suffering from a femmepire-induced concussion."

"Femmepire?" asked a confused Kayla.

"Female vampire." I tried not to let on just how very proud I was of the term. "Obviously."

"And our men would be…?"

"Manpires." I wasn't quite as proud of that one.

"Unbelievable," muttered Juliette.

"Anyway," I continued, "I showed up here last night, Juliette punched me in the face for absolutely no reason, Zorana bled me so she could put on some sort of magic show, and now I've been officially hired."

"You're dealing with it surprisingly well—" Kayla stopped in mid-sentence and darted a look over to Juliette. "—or are you keeping him calm?"

"Shockingly, no. Our new mediator is a freak in a variety of desperately dull ways… including being immune to compulsion."

"I didn't think that was possible for humans."

"Tell me about it. Even the rest of the council was surprised."

"Well in that case, John, I really am impressed with how you're handling everything," Kayla told me, reaching out and patting me on one shoulder. "Bully for you."

A part of me was convinced that Anastasia was meant to be my one true love, but I couldn't help but set a little space aside in my heart for Kayla. I hadn't gotten a lot of compliments as of late.

"It probably just hasn't sunk in yet," I said humbly. "Right now, I'm trying to focus on what's in front of me."

"A sandwich full of ham that might get you killed?" suggested Juliette.

"A sandwich, a beer, and this mediation you *still* haven't told me anything about."

"Oh. Right. The mediation." Juliette yawned, exposing teeth that looked perfectly human. I spared a brief thought to wonder where the fangs she'd shown earlier had gone. Was it magic or did they just retract?

"I'll leave you to it," decided Kayla, gathering up her trash.

"Are you sure? I wasn't trying to run you off…" I told her.

"No worries. Truthfully, I was just stopping in for a snack before training." The tall femmepire stopped in the doorway. "It's open mat session if you're looking for something to do, Juliette."

"Sounds like a lot of work to me." Juliette smirked. "Have fun in the circle."

I turned and watched the ash-blonde vampire leave. Like so many of her kind, she had the sort of grace and controlled power I'd expect from a dancer or an athlete.

I turned back to find Juliette's yellow eyes narrowed.

"What?"

"Whatever's going on in your pea-sized brain," she told me, "you should let it go."

My pea-sized brain didn't know what she was talking about.

"Kayla's not interested," she expounded. "Not in you. Not ever."

"And?"

"And I could feel a crush coming on."

"You should get that checked by a doctor," I muttered. "I was just thinking she moves kind of like Anastasia."

"Of course you were." She polished off her second beer and sighed. "Finish your sandwich so we can head back."

"I thought we were going to talk about the mediation?"

"We will. But I want my tablet, and I left it behind."

I couldn't remember seeing a tablet anywhere in the enormous bedroom, but I hadn't been at the top of my game either. "I still have a third of a sandwich. Couldn't you give me the high points while I'm eating?"

"I could but I won't," she said. "Some things are best done in private."

"Then let's talk generalities," I argued. "Anastasia—excuse me, *Lady Dumenyova*—told me why mediators were necessary, but I still don't understand how this works."

"I need another beer," sighed Juliette. Instead of getting up to get one, she ran a finger through her spiky hair and shrugged. "Whatever. Would an example help?"

Not as much as charts, diagrams, and a twelve-episode Netflix series with lots of action and some gratuitous nudity, but since I wasn't being offered any of those, I nodded.

"Fine. Say the Clippers get into a dispute with a pack of chupacabras. Maybe the chupacabras wander onto tribal grounds and defecate in a sacred garbage dump or something. So then…" She paused, as I raised my hand. Her voice dropped into a growl. "What?"

"What's a Clipper? And who considers garbage dumps sacred? And how would anyone know if someone took a crap in one?"

For just a second, I had the uncomfortable feeling that Juliette was about to leap over the table and beat me unconscious. Again.

Instead, she rolled her eyes. "The Clippers are one of San Diego's goblin tribes. For whatever reason, the territorial little buggers latch on to the names of local sports franchises. They're insane about that sort of thing, although it's even worse in the UK."

"But the Clippers aren't in San Diego anymore." It was 2013, and San Diego was a two-team town. Four if you counted the Gulls and Sockers. Which I didn't.

"Don't mention that to them unless you want to be torn into tiny pieces. It's a sore subject. If you ever see a smug goblin walking around these parts, I guarantee they're a Padre or a Charger. As for the whole garbage dump thing…? Hell if I know. Goblins are weird."

"Right. So goblins and goat suckers get into it with each other. I'm with you so far."

"My hero." She swiped the half-full beer bottle from my side of the table, and took a pull. "Okay. So the goblins are pissed at the chupacabras. Two thousand years ago, they'd have just mobilized, and torn them to pieces. And that would've been the end of it… unless the chupas had struck an alliance with, say, a pack of Infected. Shapeshifters," she translated, before I could ask. "Mostly werewolves, around these parts. Anyway, if there *was* an alliance, then suddenly, the Clippers are finding themselves attacked by the Infected, which might cause them to bring in their own allies, and so on and so on until the whole city's on fire."

"But the Concordat-thingy stopped that."

"Right. So now, the goblins file a grievance. The chupacabras have three days to find a mediator to represent them, and then they, the mediator, and the goblins all meet."

"And then?"

"Mediate."

"Meaning what, exactly?"

"Aren't you supposed to already know about this part?"

"I know what a mediation is." More or less. Mostly less. "But I'm pretty sure they don't usually involve genocide."

"Whatever. As I understand it, the aggrieved party—"

"The Clippers," I clarified, mostly for myself.

"—can choose to accept the mediator or not. Assuming they do, that poor fool has up to one month to hash out an agreement that both sides can agree to. If an agreement can be forged, then great... everyone ends up happy and life goes on. But if either side ends the mediation early, they are found in breach."

"And get crushed for non-compliance," I recalled.

"Right. Those powers that created the rules in the first place would declare open season on whoever broke the rules... giving every creature on the planet hunting rights. Goblins are nasty buggers— chupacabras, less so, oddly enough—but the tribe would be erased by Tuesday, and whoever took them down would end up owning a brand new power base in San Diego."

This was starting to sound like a horrifying case of Game-of-Thrones-meets-reality.

"What if, after a month, the two sides still haven't come to an agreement?"

"Then they've all fulfilled their obligation to the Concordat and can annihilate each other."

Which was basically what Anastasia had said. It wasn't enough to just mediate... I had to be successful at it.

No pressure.

"What's to stop one group from lodging phony complaints against anyone they didn't like, waiting a month, and then wiping them out?"

"Nothing. But it gives the other group a month to recruit allies, and there are always powers happy to be hired on to see justice done. That's what Lucia has Andrés doing. There aren't a lot of groups in San Diego willing to risk their own destruction. Unfortunately, we're currently up against one of the few." She drained the dregs of my beer and tossed the bottle over one shoulder. Annoyingly, it ricocheted perfectly into the bin for glass recyclables. "Now do you get it?"

"More or less. So you guys are the accused party?"

"Bingo. The whole House is at risk and you're our one hope of salvation. Which is utterly terrifying, if you think about it." She met my sudden frown with a smirk. "Don't get all pouty on me now, little bird."

"I stopped paying attention to your insults about five minutes after meeting you," I lied.

"Then why do you look like a constipated gorilla?"

"The whole process just seems needlessly complicated."

"Tell that to the powers-that-be. Just warn me in advance; I'd like to be in another country when you do."

CHAPTER 13

IN WHICH EVEN FUTURE EX-WIVES
HAVE BAGGAGE

Without a beer, the last few bites of sandwich were difficult to get down, but I heroically persevered. Minutes later, we were walking back down the hallway to the bedroom suite I'd woken up in. Juliette's strappy heels echoed on the hardwood floors.

"I have another question."

"And I have a strong urge to murder you," replied Juliette.

I ignored the threat, secure in the knowledge that Lucia wanted me alive… and that the vampire queen was a lot scarier than my current companion.

"Anas—argh, *Lady Dumenyova*—said that you were all part of House Borghesi. Is a House just a collection of vampires?"

"A flock is a collection of vampires. A House is when that flock gets large enough, strong enough, or influential enough to become a major player in their region. In Europe, there are noble bloodlines involved. Here in America, we're a bit more casual about it."

"Except your House has a queen."

"True." She shrugged. "I ran the flock in San Diego for almost a decade, but it was Lucia's arrival that led to the formation of our House."

"And you just let her take over?" Juliette had as much trouble remembering to use people's titles as I did.

"I'm the youngest councilmember in the western world and belong to the largest and fastest-growing House in the country." Juliette rolled her eyes. "Hell yes, I let her take over! In fact, when I heard those morons in Chicago had rejected her petition, I was on the next plane out to offer an invite."

"So you brought Lucia to San Diego, she gave your flock legitimacy, and the result was a House?"

"It wasn't just the Queen that came. It was her entire council. Marcus, Andrés. Zorana…"

"And Anastasia."

"Anastasia and Xavier. They were a matched set, after all."

I didn't like the sound of that at all. "Meaning what?"

"Did your parents never give you the sex talk?"

"Oh." I frowned. "Gross."

"Tell me about it. I have no idea what he saw in her."

"What?" I stopped in the middle of the hallway. "No; I meant it's gross *for her.*"

"Hardly. Xavier has a lot to recommend him, if you get my drift." In case I didn't get her drift, she held her hands a significant distance apart from each other. Apparently, Xavier was part-horse.

"And you know this how?"

Her smile just widened.

"Ugh. So he and Anastasia…"

"Oh, they're old news now—"

"Awesome."

"—but before that, they were together for decades. Theirs was supposedly one of the great romances of the Italian court."

I'd been keeping an eye out for my suite as we walked, but every door looked exactly the same. *Mahogany*, my mind volunteered unhelpfully. Juliette finally pulled open a door and ushered me inside. Her tablet was in plain sight on the nearby table.

I had no idea how I could have missed it earlier. My PI mentor would be rolling over in his grave… if he weren't still alive and cursing.

"So what happened?" I asked, as she picked up the offending tablet and dropped into the closest chair.

"With what?"

"With Anastasia and Xavier."

"Anastasia followed Lucia into exile, and Xavier trailed along like the love-sick puppy that he was. Only to find out, *after* he'd given up everything he had for her, that the Secundus wasn't interested in continuing their relationship." With one hand, she mimed an airplane crashing and burning.

I almost felt sorry for the guy before I remembered he was a colossal dick who'd been arguing for my death.

"Why do you care anyway?" asked Juliette.

"No reason."

As usual, my poker face was the exact opposite of rock-solid.

"Seriously, little bird?" Juliette shook her head. "First Kayla, now Anastasia? I was joking about the death wish thing."

"I'm not saying—"

"Let me make this simple." She tossed the tablet back onto the table and leaned forward, smirk completely absent. "The high and mighty Anastasia Dumenyova does not care about you or Xavier or anything at all beyond what she wants."

"She saved my life," I argued.

"Because the House needs you."

"It's still more than anybody else has done."

"Oh please." Juliette rolled her eyes. "I saved your life too. Not that I want you to mope over *me* like some moon-faced virgin or anything."

I ignored the moon-faced virgin bit. Mainly because I wasn't. "When exactly did you save my life?"

"When I punched you in the face." I started to reply, but she talked right over me. "If Marcus or Andrés had reached you before me, you'd be real-dead instead of just braindead."

That was... a weird thing to think about. It had never occurred to me that being punched unconscious might be the lesser evil. "Seriously?"

"Seriously."

"Then... thanks, I guess."

"Thank me by not getting us all killed. Take whatever weird puppy dog infatuation you've stupidly developed for Anastasia and bury it. There's a reason they call her the Stone Lady."

"I thought she was Lady Dumenyova?"

"She has multiple titles. A lot of the elders do. Welcome to the world of the People."

"And what are you, the Duchess of Snark? Lady Juliette Smirks-a-lot?"

"Just Juliette. For now."

"You gave refuge to an exiled queen—" Having met Lucia, I wasn't at all surprised she'd been exiled. "—and didn't even get a title out of it?"

"Which part of youngest councilmember ever did you *not* understand?"

"I'm just saying…" I lowered myself into the chair next to her, and waved a hand dismissively. "*I'd* have gotten a title."

"I'm three seconds away from giving you something," muttered Juliette.

Which told me it was time to change the subject. As much as I was enjoying our back-and-forth—and to my surprise, I kind of was—I couldn't forget that I was there for a reason. And that reason involved saving the city I loved from catastrophe.

"Maybe we should get back to the mediation then, now that you have your tablet. Who is Lord Beer Can, and what's his problem with Lucia? Aside from her being… well… her."

"It's Lord Beel-Kasan. Not Beer Can. Get that right or it's going to be a really short mediation."

"Beel-Kasan." I sounded it out a few times and shrugged. "Got it. So is he a vampire too? A representative of another House or something?"

"Hardly. He's a local deity."

"I'm sorry?"

"More specifically, the demigod of nightmares—"

"What?!"

"—and terror." Lady Juliette Smirks-a-lot lived up to her title. "And you get to meet him face-to-face."

Well, shit.

ooo

"Gods are real? Like... *God* gods?"

Juliette sighed. "You know, I was kind of excited when this whole nervous breakdown began, but it's gotten old fast. Get a grip before I put you out of my misery."

I was not dealing well with the news about Lord Beel-Kasan, demigod of nightmares and terror. Being a lapsed Catholic might have had something to do with it. I just wasn't sure if I was now worried that the Christian God might actually exist, or if I was concerned with how the existence of other deities might impact the theological foundation of my childhood. Or maybe the real problem was that—

SMACK!

And just like that, I was lying on the carpet. Very plush carpet, naturally, but the left side of my face was burning and the headache that had disappeared somewhere in the middle of Zorana's ritual was back with a vengeance. I looked up to see Juliette standing over me.

"You *hit* me?!"

"Eureka! He speaks!"

I struggled back into the chair, rubbing my face. My head was starting to feel like a potato that had fallen off the supermarket shelf and been kicked down the aisle by hyperactive twelve-year-olds. If I'd had any rugged good looks to worry about... well... I'd have been worried.

"I think you broke my jaw."

"If I had, you wouldn't be able to speak, you idiot."

"Whatever. I hope you're happy."

"Why would I be happy? I could have slapped you ages ago, and saved myself twenty minutes of boredom!"

She did have a point, not that I was going to admit it. "Alright. So he's a god."

"Demigod."

"Demigod." I rolled my eyes. "What does that mean? What can he do? How the hell am I supposed to convince someone like that not to kill us all? And what did your House do to piss him off anyway?"

"At least you're actually thinking now." She waved a slim hand—presumably the one she'd slapped me out of my chair with—to forestall my reply. "Gods 101. Pay attention because there *will* be a test, and getting an F means we're all screwed."

Still standing, she paced back and forth in front of me. While she was far stronger than she looked, Juliette lacked the controlled grace I'd noted in Anastasia, Xavier, or even Kayla. Not that it mattered much, since she'd woman-handled me without even trying.

"As I told you the first fifteen times you asked, yes, gods are real. Lower-case g. Leave the blind worship stuff to the priests. A god is basically an immortal—meaning they don't die of old age and nobody knows how to kill them—with shit-loads of power. Most species' pantheons are at least partially represented, although there are plenty of literary characters with no real world analogue, and just as many instances where the same god shows up in multiple mythologies."

She brushed a hand through her spiky hair and shrugged. "It's a mess. There are even some gods who don't show up in any mythologies at all. I'm assuming those are the cool ones. If you have to actively seek out worship, you're either an egomaniac or *severely* overcompensating, if you know what I mean." She held her thumb and index finger an inch or so apart to illustrate.

It was becoming clear Juliette had a size fetish. I nodded anyway.

"A demigod is an immortal with *less* power. They can still do plenty, but have a smaller sphere of influence. If a god is the sun, a demigod would be... a spotlight."

"And humans would be?"

"Monkeys playing with their own poop. Obviously." She smirked. "Anyway, Lord Beel-Kasan is the demigod of nightmares and terror. One of many, though I think he might be the only one presently on this coast."

"What does that mean? Being the demigod of nightmares."

"And terror."

"And terror." I rolled my eyes again. "He gives people bad dreams?"

"That's one way to put it. Another would be that he feeds off the fear of every sentient being in California."

Given the state of our world, I was guessing the demigod was very well-fed.

"In the waking world," continued Juliette, "he appears to people as the object of their deepest fear. He's also supposed to be the ruler of some sort of hell dimension."

And here I'd thought *Lucia* was going to be the worst part of this mediation. I was so dead.

"And let me guess… he's best friends with the local horsemen of the apocalypse too."

Juliette frowned. "Not that I've heard. Did Anastasia say something?"

"Uhm… no?"

Her sigh sounded relieved. "Good."

Apparently, San Diego had horsemen of the apocalypse. Who knew?

"Anything else I should know?"

"Light behaves weirdly around him. He casts multiple shadows, and if he stays somewhere for any length of time, those shadows can stain the walls or ground they fall upon." She shrugged. "Reportedly."

"Reportedly?"

"It's not like we meet up with him for Tuesday brunch. As far as I know, we've never had any contact with him at all before now."

"Then how did the House piss him off?"

"You'll have to figure that part out. The night before last, a homeless man jumped the wall to our property, maimed two of our human security team, and wrote a warning on the wall in human excrement."

I wasn't sure what any of that had to do with Lord Beel-Kasan, but it sounded gross. And, given the sheer size of the guards, pretty unlikely.

Juliette brought the tablet in her hands to life, tapped twice, and passed it over. When I finally finished drooling over the device—light as a feather, but sturdy and sleek—I looked down to see what the ultra-bright, high definition display was showing me.

It was a photo… a glossy image of… yup, that was a wall, and yup, it did appear to have fecal matter on it. Nasty. I puzzled out the words.

People of this House
You will Return what you Stole
Or I will Send Each of You
To Gehenna where You will Make
Beautiful Candelabras

Yours in Love,
Lord Beel-Kasan

"Candelabras?"

"No idea. Word is he's at least partially insane."

"Fantastic. What does he think you stole?"

"Again, no clue. We sent a reply and received an incoherent tirade in return. We had to cite the Concordat to even get him to entertain the thought of mediation."

"So my job is to determine what he thinks you stole and figure out a solution that everyone can agree on?"

"Bingo. Maybe you're not as dumb as you look, frat man. This should be a piece of cake."

"And the fact that he's insane and will eat my fear is just a minor detail to be dealt with."

Juliette gave me a thumbs-up and the mother of all smirks. "Exactly."

"Anastasia should have just let the crab people kill me."

CHAPTER 14
IN WHICH FAMILY MATTERS

The suite the vampires had stashed me in was luxurious. It was enormous. It was furnished like a five-star hotel.

It was so boring.

I'd pestered Juliette for more details on the forthcoming mediation, only to find that we'd exhausted her knowledge on the subject. The femmepire had gone back to playing some mobile game on her tablet, and I'd been left to…

Well, there wasn't much for me to do. Which got old fast.

I'd have asked to borrow her tablet, but I'd already bobbled it once just giving it back to Juliette, and I didn't have a spare thousand dollars to replace it if I did end up dropping it.

Luckily, I owned a phone.

Unfortunately…

"Where's my phone?"

"Top drawer, on the left." Juliette didn't even look up from her tablet. Nor did she point out which of the room's seven dressers—seriously, who needed seven dressers?!—she was referring to.

I started with the one closest to the bathroom. The top drawer held stacks of identical boxers, neatly folded, next to a half-dozen pairs of black socks. On the far left was a Ziploc bag, and inside that bag were shards of plastic, glass, and electronics. Only the shredded remnants of a "Big Brother is Watching You" sticker told me the pile of scrap had once been my phone.

"What the hell happened to it?"

"How would I know?"

"You knew where it was. Clearly, you also knew it was in a bunch of pieces in a bag too."

"Yep."

"And?"

"And I have no idea how it got that way. Maybe you fell on it when I knocked your ass out?"

Or when I'd been running from the crab men. Or when Xavier had punched me. Or when I'd fainted.

I'd been spending a lot of time on the ground lately.

"I'm adding this to my fee," I decided.

"I'll let you tell Lucia that." Juliette was *still* playing on her tablet.

In the long list of terrible things that had happened to me over the past two days, my phone getting broken actually ranked pretty damn high. I'd never had an iPhone before, and if my parents hadn't opted to pitch in on the purchase, I'd have been even further behind on my rent.

Which reminded me of something even more important than a phone. "My parents!"

"Regret their decision to not use birth control?"

"What? No. What if the crab people go after my parents?" I couldn't believe this was the first time I'd thought of them. I was going to a hell reserved for terrible sons.

Juliette finally lowered her tablet, even if it was just to shoot me an eye roll. "Why would they? And how, for that matter?"

"If I'm the last mediator in San Diego—" Damn it; it was getting easier to believe that lie the more I said it. "—then I'm the final target on their hit list."

"Which is why you're here, being protected by yours truly, and not out in the world where you might trip on a curb and die."

"But they wouldn't know that. They looked for me at my office and Anastasia killed them. They'd stake out my home too."

"Assuming they could find your address, sure. But what does that have to do with your parents?"

"I live with them!"

Juliette let out a long sigh. "Of course you do." Despite her words, she was already on her feet. "I'll go talk to the Watch. Stay here."

"I'm coming with you." I met her annoyed gaze. Her almost-yellow eyes were practically glowing, but whatever mojo she was throwing my way slid right off. "They're my parents, Juliette."

"I'm starting to see why Zorana wanted to kill you," she muttered, waving me through the open door "This whole disobedience thing is a pain in the ass."

"You're wearing a Ramones tee. I'd think anti-authoritarianism would be right up your alley."

"It's more fun when I'm the one rioting."

ooo

Leaving behind my temporary bedroom for the second time that day, we headed down the hall to the elevators. A few seconds later, we were on sub-level one. Immediately opposite us was a set of glass and steel doors, through which I could see black-uniformed vampires sitting in front of workstations.

"What's this?"

"Watch HQ. This is where they monitor the feeds from all those cameras you've been seeing."

"Right... the cameras." For the first time outside of my brief and terrifying stay in the Midnight Tower, I bothered to look up. Sure enough, there was a swivel-mounted camera with a perfect view of both the elevator and the hall that stretched to our right.

It was a good thing I was a mediator now, because I was seriously starting to question my keenly honed investigative instincts.

Juliette pressed the call button to the right of those doors, and spoke into the intercom. "Juliette here. I need a protective detail put together for..." She glanced over her shoulder at me, waiting.

Oh. Right. I supplied the address to my parents' house in Chula Vista.

The voice that came back over the intercom was straight out of Texas. "Yes, ma'am. One second, please."

"Please tell me he wears a cowboy hat."

"Sometimes, that's all Case wears."

"TMI, Duchess. Way too much."

Before she could reply, the intercom crackled back to life. "There's already a flag in the system for that address, Miss Juliette. It says Lady Dumenyova addressed the issue. Do you want me to put together a fresh detail anyway?"

"Does it say how she addressed it?"

"No ma'am."

"Fine. Forget the protective detail then, I guess. Thanks, Case." Juliette turned to me and shrugged. "Sure would be nice if the great and terrible Anastasia Dumenyova could bother to tell her fellow councilmembers when she did something."

"What do you think she did?"

"I have no idea." She saw the look on my face, and something in her angular features softened. "Whatever it is, you don't need to worry about it. Anastasia's cold as hell, but she's efficient. She'll make sure your parents are safe, if only to make sure you have no distractions during the mediation."

Once again, Juliette's perception of Anastasia was wildly different from mine. I had to wonder which of us was right … the femmepire who'd spent at least a decade in the same House, or the private investigator who'd only met the auburn-haired Secundus a day ago.

It had to be me.

Right?

We turned back to the elevators. Juliette reached out to hit the button, and then paused. She cocked her head and turned to me, a slow grin widening across her face.

"As long as we're down here… want to have some fun?"

I blinked. She wasn't seriously hitting on me, was she?

"What… what did you have in mind?" I tried for suave; a mixture of confidence and mild interest.

Juliette narrowed her eyes. "Are you constipated again?"

Apparently, suave wasn't going to work today. I shook my head.

"If you say so." She shrugged. "You heard Kayla earlier. Training is in session."

"And?"

"And we should go watch. Trust me; it'll be way less boring than sitting in your room, staring at the wall."

Given my lack of a phone, it was hard to argue.

○○○

Past the Watch HQ, the hallway was far more utilitarian than the above-ground floors, disdaining natural wood paneling and art deco knickknacks for simple cement and neutral grey carpeting. There were a lot fewer doors too. Either the sub-level was unfinished, or the rooms it contained were huge. At the very end of the hall, there was another swivel-mounted camera, and a handful of doors in the left wall.

Juliette opened the first, and waved me inside.

The room was enormous, quite possibly stretching the length of the hall we'd just walked. The wall across from us was decorated with a cornucopia of weapons. I recognized everything from the two-handed swords from Braveheart to the bladed spears from The Last Samurai. To our left, multiple heavy bags dangled from the ceiling. Past them was a row of speed bags and the wooden dummies that wing chun practitioners used, and past *those* were what appeared to be tumbling mats. Directly in front of us, the floor was covered in the dried-grass mats that showed up in every Japanese martial arts movie. And to my right was an honest-to-god full-size basketball court, wooden floor and all.

The room could have comfortably held several hundred people, but there were only a couple dozen, all of them vampires. All of the individuals sparring on the mats were black-clothed Watch members, but there were a few other vampires sprinkled throughout, wearing anything from color-coordinated Lululemon to the sort of ratty, tattered clothing you'd find in a run-down boxing club or Rocky spoof. The vampires playing twenty-one on the basketball court were even sporting Air Jordans and NBA team jerseys.

Apparently, vampires liked the Lakers. It figured.

"What is this place?"

"Welcome to the House training facilities."

"Impressive." To our left, a spectacularly fit femmepire beat the holy hell out of a heavy bag. "Where's the weight room?"

"Past the gymnastics mats and through another door. Not that it sees much use."

"Why not?"

"We're not human, little bird. Strength training has limited benefit for our kind. Our physical gifts are primarily a function of power, and that power comes from will and age."

"Oh." I tried wrapping my head around that one, but it was a weird concept for someone who'd received a weight bench for his twelfth birthday. And then used that weight bench as a convenient shelf for his comic collection. Besides, if that was true, then why did some vampires have more muscle than others? The lady boxer looked like she could bench-press a car without vampire mojo. "Wait... if your power has nothing to do with training, then why have a gym at all?"

"Because there's a difference between physical gifts and trained skill." Juliette shook her head sadly, as if I was the dumbest human in the room. (I was, but given that I was the *only* human in the room, I was also the smartest. It was a heady sensation.) "Our species is strong, fast, agile, durable, and frankly gorgeous—"

"You forgot humble."

"—but we don't have any sort of ancestral knowledge to draw on. We're not chupacabras. We have to learn to fight."

"I thought that's what the Watch was for."

"They're the specialists, but we all need to be at least somewhat capable. There are worse things than the karkino out there."

As she spoke, Xavier emerged from one of the two small doors on the other side of the basketball court. He wore the standard Watch uniform, but there was no chance of him being lost in the crowd. Call it presence, call it confidence. Call it overpowering douche-baggery. Whatever it was, he was undeniably distinctive.

Next to me, Juliette was practically purring.

The Watch members formed a circle around the center mat. Even the game of twenty-one ground to a halt, as the vampires turned to watch.

"What's going on?"

"It looks like class is in session. We arrived just in time."
Juliette took a seat on the nearest mat and motioned for me to do the
same.

The object of everyone's attention strode to the weapons rack
and took down a pair of wooden swords. Taking the center of the
circle, he tossed them to two of the waiting Watch members. One was
a Samoan male with a shaved head, almost as wide as he was tall,
muscular arms straining against the confines of his sleeves. The other
was Kayla, the friendly Aussie from the upstairs kitchen, looking sleek
and deadly next to her hulking counterpart. Each caught their
respective weapons and stalked toward the weaponless Xavier. He
adopted a vaguely martial stance and waited.

For a long moment, nothing happened, and then all three
vampires exploded into motion.

Blink. *The Samoan vampire quick-steps to his left, then drives in with an
overhand strike. Kayla mirrors the action on Xavier's opposite side, though her cut
is horizontal.*

Blink. *The attacking manpire drops in a heap to the mat. His sword flies
through the air.*

Blink. *Kayla reels back from an unseen blow to her mid-section, only to
turn the fall into a roll that brings her back to her feet.*

Blink. *Xavier is on her as she rises. A loud snap echoes through the gym,
and Kayla's left arm drops limply to her side. Her weapon has somehow found its
way into Xavier's hands.*

Blink. *Kayla throws herself across the room to avoid a lightning-quick
strike from Xavier. She comes up clutching her fallen partner's sword in her right
hand.*

Blink. *The clack of wood striking wood comes so quickly that it blends
into one continuous noise. Just as quickly, Kayla is on the ground again. Xavier's
foot pins her broken arm to the mat, while his sword pushes up under her chin.*

Start to finish, the entire fight couldn't have lasted longer than
ten seconds.

A very small part of me was starting to regret stealing the man's
ham.

Xavier smoothly stepped aside, lowering his weapon. Only then did Kayla climb to her feet, handing him hers. The other vampire was being seen to, but seemed incapable of standing on his own. Xavier ignored them both and motioned to the crowd. Two new vampires stepped forward, accepted the weapons he offered, and began to circle their Captain…

"So he just beats the crap out of his subordinates?" I told myself I was whispering as a matter of courtesy, and not because I was worried Xavier would hear and cut me into tiny pieces.

"Usually. Isn't he lovely?" Juliette had a pleased, almost wistful, smile on her face as she watched the black vampire dispatch his next set of sacrificial lambs.

"If you say so." I would have gone with *sadistic*, but I was just a dumb human, after all. "Do they actually learn anything?"

"Of course. They just finished training. The circle is their chance to match skills with the Captain."

"And we're here to watch?"

Her smile reverted to its usual smirk. "What would be the fun in that? We're here to play." With that ominous statement, she hopped to her feet and led me onto the mats.

CHAPTER 15
IN WHICH CHEATERS SOMETIMES WIN

To my relief, we headed past Xavier's ritualized murder circle, where even now, the Captain was laying waste to another pair of his subordinates. Juliette found an empty space on the mats, not far from the heavy bags, and turned to face me.

"Duchess, I don't think I'm going to be able to learn self-defense between now and when I meet Lord Beel-Kasan." I took a moment to give myself a mental pat on the back for finally saying the guy's name right. It was funny how learning that he was a demigod had helped with that. "Maybe we can do this some other time?"

"Where's your sense of adventure, little bird?" At my scowl, she pouted. "I wasn't suggesting that we actually train. What would be the point? Instead, I have a proposal for you."

"A proposal?" Something told me to be very careful about what I agreed to. Maybe it was all the weapons on the far wall.

Yeah, it was definitely the weapons.

"Take your pick of training implements from the wall. If you can strike me even once in the next five minutes, I'll give you—" Her pout widened into a smile. "—a treat."

"Hard pass. I think we both know how that would turn out. I'd get one swing and then find myself waking up in *Le Dungeon Lucia*, covered in vomit. Again. Plus, I'm pretty sure I already have a concussion."

"You were pretty sure you had a broken jaw too." She rolled her eyes. "What if I promise not to hit back?"

Given my experience with Juliette so far, there had to be some sort of catch, but I couldn't find it. "What kind of treat are we talking about?"

Her smile was slow and wide and sexy as hell. "I'm sure we can figure something out."

"I want to call my parents."

"Are you—?" For some reason, the femmepire was irritated. "Fine. Whatever."

"Then we have a deal."

Despite the rapidly accumulating evidence to the contrary, I wasn't a complete idiot. Juliette didn't have the controlled grace of Anastasia or Xavier... or even Kayla and Steve, but she was still a vampire. My chances of actually hitting her were astronomically low.

At the same time... I really wanted to call my parents. As much as I trusted Anastasia—and I did—my job had taught me the value of seeking independent confirmation.

I headed over to Ye Ol' Wall o' Weapons, and deliberated over the options it offered. The claymore? There was no chance I'd be able to lift it for more than one or two very slow and awkward swings. The spear thing? I'd trip over it and injure myself. The rapier? Fencing had peaked with The Princess Bride.

Eventually, I settled for a padded stick, three or so feet in length. If all else failed, I could swing it like a bat. I dug through some of the other weapons. Hmm. *That* might work too.

Juliette eyed the stick when I returned. "A hanbo? At least you won't accidentally chop off one of your own limbs."

Was it hypocritical to be annoyed by her comment, even though I'd thought the exact same thing only moments earlier? I mentally shrugged. I'd been called worse things than hypocrite.

Her yellow eyes gleamed with anticipation. "Do you need to prepare? I don't want you to die of a strained hamstring or anything."

"Humans are tougher than you think, Juliette." I *could* have done with some stretching, given the events of the past day, but I wasn't going to suffer through more mockery. At least my outfit was loose enough that it didn't restrict my movements. I eyed Juliette's skintight jeans. They showed off her legs, but they were also going to slow her down a bit. I might even have an advantage. "I'm ready."

"Very well." She checked her watch. "Annnnnnnd begi—"

I was already swinging the hanbo. When in doubt, cheat.

Unfortunately, there are times when cheating just isn't enough. Juliette watched my stick arc towards her, waiting until the absolute last moment before she twisted to the side. My strike whistled past and bounced off the mat. She gently pushed me with one hand and I toppled over, having over-extended myself.

"Again."

To her credit, Juliette kept her word and never actually hit me, but I spent way too much of the next few minutes picking myself up off the floor. Every time I swung, she dodged, and I always somehow ended up badly off-balance, at which point, she would send me to the mat with a bump or a nudge.

I was starting to think all that time practicing my bows in taekwondo had been a waste.

I was also starting to realize that five minutes was a *long* time to be waving around a stick. By the third minute, I was gasping for breath… and I'd only lasted that long because I'd been pacing myself. My next swing was so slow and weak that Juliette actually sighed as she avoided it. I lost my grip on the hanbo altogether and watched it spin to the mats.

"This is pathetic." Juliette walked over to pick up the weapon, while I dropped to one knee, gasping and wheezing. She walked back over to me, hanbo extended. "I'll be honest, I was expect—"

I whipped out the length of weighted rope I'd tucked into my shirt sleeve and threw it at her.

Her reaction time remained inhumanly fast, and despite the short distance between us, she was somehow able to get the hanbo into position to deflect my unexpected toss. If I had thrown a baseball or a brick, I'd have been screwed. But as one end of the rope wrapped about the hanbo, the other end swung past, and smacked Juliette in the abdomen, right below Dee Dee's name on her Ramones tee.

It wasn't the kind of blow that would end a fight, let alone win one, but I didn't care. What mattered was that it had landed! And from the stunned expression on her face, Juliette knew it.

I'd have done a happy dance, if I weren't so busy sucking wind.

"Nicely done, mate!" Kayla wandered over with a smile to counter Juliette's frown. "Tricking Juliette into lowering her guard by pretending to be slow and uncoordinated was a brilliant tactic. It's not something I'd try in a real fight, but it sure worked here."

"Uhm… yeah. That was totally my plan," I muttered under my breath, trying to hide how much it pained me to straighten back up. Was there a demigod of heart attacks?

Kayla's left arm was still dangling limply by her side, but she didn't pay it any attention as she took the hanbo from Juliette in her other hand, and proceeded to whip it about in dizzying fashion. It was a nice demonstration of what could actually be done with the weapon.

When I was done picking my jaw up off the floor, I nodded to her broken arm. "Shouldn't you do something about that?"

"I'll get Steve to set it in a bit. Once I feed, it should be good as new."

"Seriously? That's handy."

"It doesn't suck," she agreed. "Still hurts when it happens, of course, but Captain X says pain is just weakness leaving the body."

"Maybe that's because he's the one dispensing the pain."

She laughed, brown eyes dancing. "Anyway, I just wanted to wander over and congratulate you on your victory. I hope you won a prize?"

"I sure did." Her reminder renewed my excitement. "I get to make a phone call."

Kayla looked confused. "Does the phone in your room not work?"

"My room has a phone?" Tablets. Cameras. Phones. I was seriously off my game.

Juliette smiled wickedly. "Bet you wish you'd taken the other treat now, little bird."

"Little bird?" Kayla snickered.

"Welcome to my life. The Duchess of Snark decided I needed a nickname."

"He sings in the shower, Kayla," explained Juliette. "I'll bring you over next time so you can hear. It's hilarious."

"Sounds like a party," said the Aussie. "I'll bring Darlene."

For a so-called mediator, I seemed to be spending a lot of my time as the vampires' entertainment.

ooo

We stayed in the gym for another hour or two, although I spent most of that watching vampires play basketball. Few of the manpires were taller than six feet in height, but every single one of them could dunk. They'd also all minored in trash talking. It was like watching an entire court of Nate Robinsons.

I'd gotten my ass kicked in my five minutes against Juliette, but I'd have fared even worse in a game of Horse or—God forbid—one on one.

The Watch slowly filtered out of the gym once Xavier's combat demonstrations had ended. The black-clad vampires were responsible for guarding the interior of the building while human security forces manned the gatehouse and walked the estate grounds. It seemed like an odd decision to involve humans at all, given how scary dangerous vampires were, but maybe it was a question of numbers. The more I saw of the enormous mansion, the more it seemed like it had been built to house four or even five times as many people as it currently did.

Recruitment had to be a bigger challenge than Juliette had made it seem. I couldn't help but think Lucia and her resting-I-hate-you-and-want-you-to-die face had something to do with that. If I were in charge of recruiting, I'd make sure the first time anyone even spoke to the femmepire queen was when they were swearing their oaths of fealty.

Not that anyone had put me in charge.

More's the pity.

Eventually, Juliette remembered I existed, and wandered back over. "Ready?"

"I was born ready."

"What is that even supposed to mean?"

"I have no idea," I admitted.

"Apparently, we've heard back from Lord Beel-Kasan."

"And?"

"And the meeting is set. Tomorrow at dusk."

"Tomorrow? What am I supposed to do until then?"

"Work very hard on not dying?" Juliette shrugged. "Don't look at me. This was not how I wanted my Saturday to go. Anyway, there's a Council meeting tomorrow also, and I've been instructed to bring you."

"Okay."

"Okay?"

It was my turn to shrug. "I assume we'll be discussing the mediation. Given what's at stake, I'm not going to complain about a strategy session."

"Huh." Juliette pulled me to my feet with only a little bit more effort than it had taken Anastasia. "Maybe you are a frat man after all."

It wasn't much of a compliment. In fact, it was still kind of an insult... but I was going to take it. *Small victories, right, Dad?*

"Stop smiling," hissed the femmepire. "You're freaking me out."

CHAPTER 16

IN WHICH YOU CAN'T GO HOME AGAIN BUT YOU CAN AT LEAST CALL

Despite the late hour, I was still full from my sandwich, so we skipped the kitchen on our way back to my suite. From the noise, it sounded like there was a party going on, but it had been a long day, and I wasn't feeling up to hanging out with the death-dealing denizens of the night.

Although it probably wasn't fair to call them denizens of the night when they were running around during the day, killing crabs, and hiring fake mediators.

Vampires were proving hard to figure out. Outside of a few notable individuals, they mostly seemed like regular people. Except they could also move like lightning, control minds, and punch holes in a brick wall. It was a weird blend of normal and supernatural. Accents, sandwiches, people shouting Kobe whenever they drained a mid-range jumper... but also ancient little girls making magic with blood.

I was putting up a brave face—as far as I was concerned, anyway—but the whole situation was still messing with my mind. And the fact that I'd soon be meeting with a clearly deranged demigod didn't help.

A demigod of nightmares and terror.

"Is everything okay over there, little bird? You're back to looking constipated."

And yes, Juliette had made herself at home in my suite again. Which didn't help. In fact, she was a microcosm of what I was struggling with. Attractive woman? No question. Someone who had twice smacked me around? Unfortunately. Fun to banter with? Hell, yes. Likely to eat me if I pissed her off?

I wasn't going to test her.

When I didn't immediately reply, Juliette took my chin in a vice-like grip and tilted my head down to look at her.

Freaky eyes in a color not found in humans? Yup. Were they amazing anyway? Duh. Her fingers against my skin were cool and soft… but if she sneezed, she'd probably pulverize my jaw.

I was a mess.

She brought her other hand up in front of me, index finger extended. "Follow the finger with your eyes."

"Damn it, Juliette, I was just thinking!"

"So *that's* the face you make? No wonder I've seen it so rarely."

"Funny." I slipped out of her grasp. "Actually, I was thinking about your species."

"That explains the drool."

I just acknowledged the point, and moved on. "Obviously, most of the myths about vampires are wrong."

"I feel like we've had this talk," she muttered.

"Right. And most of the weaknesses you're supposed to have don't exist. Sunshine, crucifixes, and the like."

"Yep. Your species' fixation on defining the People as soulless undead former humans resulted in a lot of weird ideas. Why would we be troubled by running water? Does that include showers?" She snorted, amused by the inconsistencies. "So?"

"So why aren't there more of you? You all live forever, or close enough to it from a human perspective. You're all preternaturally good looking and… *active*, sexually. Why haven't you replaced humans as the dominant life form on the planet?"

"Little bird, humans were *never* the dominant life form on the planet. As far as our numbers… how many vampire children have you seen so far?"

"Well, none, once you explained Zorana's situation. But," I added, "I assumed you wouldn't be bringing a smelly, disease-ridden human into a vampire nursery."

"The only disease you have is terminal stupidity and you're at least marginally less smelly than you were this morning. The reason you haven't seen any children is because there is only one in the entire House, and she's here because of Lucia."

"*Lucia is a mother?*" That simply did *not* fit my impression of her. Talk about the tiger mom from hell…

"No, moron. Can you even imagine?" She shook her head and actually shivered. "Summer was sent here by an allied House in Brazil to be the queen's ward."

"They're all the way in Brazil, but they chose Lucia to be her guardian?"

"It's not as weird as you think. Lucia is a Queen-in-exile. Her role as the head of this House has brought us a ton of prestige from those who don't pay homage to the Italian court. We're the second largest House in the country, remember, and likely the youngest House in the entire world. A lot of our members traveled from around the world to align themselves with her."

"Like Kayla."

"Bingo."

"Do all vampires belong to Houses? Or flocks?"

"No. There are always people who choose freedom over security. But the unaligned are few and far between… mostly because they get themselves killed."

Curiosity sated, I returned to the initial topic. "Still…. only one kid for this whole House. Is that a fertility thing?"

"I can't believe we're having this discussion."

I took that as a yes. "Don't the People have doctors?"

"We do, and they're working on the issue. But I was taught our species evolved this way for a reason."

After a moment, the answer came to me. "Blood supply?"

"Bingo. And you even figured it out without making that absurd face." She sounded almost proud.

"So, because you're dependent upon my kind for blood… wait, why do you eat normal food *and* drink blood?"

"Food fuels our bodies. Blood fuels our wills."

"So you need both to survive?"

"Obviously. Blood is the more important of the two though. A vampire who starves herself of blood will become sluggish and stupid… until the Thirst takes over and forces them to feed."

"That sounds almost like an addiction to me." *John Smith, creature of the night,* would have referred to it in his crime journal as 'Cocaine Red' or 'The Crimson.'

"Is *food* an addiction? Is it better that your kind will simply shut down when deprived of fuel, instead of being genetically wired to prolong your lives at any cost?"

"Well…"

"We've always been dependent upon your kind for food. Because of this, a lower birth rate was helpful back in the days when humans and our kind occupied only a small portion of the globe. It kept our numbers small, and prevented us from killing off too much of the herd."

I had a flash of Mike and I standing around in a field on all fours, mooing woefully.

"Now that your race has overpopulated the planet," she continued, "and *still* insists on breeding like pea-brained rabbits, food supply is less of a concern. Still, modern technology has made hiding that much more difficult. As a result, our small population remains beneficial."

"Gathering together in large mansions seems like a lousy way to stay hidden."

"Houses provide security, structure, and access to blood, little bird. All of which reduce the risk of exposure. And you'd be surprised what the rich can get away with in most countries, especially when they have the ability to erase, sway, or control human minds."

For the first time, I was the one smirking.

"Yes, yes. Except for *your* mind, which seems immune to such tricks, no doubt due to it being walnut-like in both size and density.

And before you crow too much about that fact, I'll remind you that it just means we'll have to kill you to guarantee your silence."

That took the wind right out of my sails. And cut those sails into little pieces. And set the boat on fire. As my smirk faded, hers returned. Was there some sort of universal law regarding the conservation of smirks? If so, I was seeing it in action.

"I also should point out that your family and friends—assuming you actually have any of the latter—are unlikely to share your bizarre talent. Telling them about our kind will only result in one of us mucking with their brains. It's a tedious yet trivial task."

I waved off her warning. "Nobody would believe me anyway. And I *do* have friends!" *One* friend, technically, but whatever. "But speaking of family… where the hell is this phone I've heard so much about?"

"Why are you so fixated on talking to your parents? You heard Case. Anastasia already took care of things."

"I live with them, remember? It's not unheard of for me to pull an all-nighter on a case, but they're going to worry if they don't hear from me at all."

"You've mediated for Nightwatchers then?"

"What?" I didn't know what the hell a Nightwatcher was, but it sounded cool. "No."

"Then what are you talking about?"

"What are *you* talking about?"

"I asked first."

"Fine. Most of the time, I work as a private investigator." I closed my eyes and waited for the inevitable snark.

"Cool."

"Cool?" I cracked one eye open to find Juliette actually looking impressed.

"Kicking down doors and clearing the names of falsely accused dames… I can dig it."

Apparently, Juliette had the same misconceptions about the job that I'd had. And a love for old detective movies where people still said things like *dame*. Five years into my career, I now knew the job was mostly paperwork and waiting, but I wasn't going to tell her that.

"Anyway, the phone is over there." Juliette pointed to a feature-less oblong black disc on the bedside table.

"I thought this was an ash tray." I picked it up and flipped it over to find a single button in the center, what looked like an earpiece on one end and a microphone on the other. There was no number pad or even a rotary dial, so I had to assume it pulled the number to dial out of the user's brain. Badass.

Someone on the other end picked up almost immediately, her French accent apparent. "How may I direct your call?"

Or it connected to an operator. Significantly less badass, although I remained a sucker for the accent. I rattled off the number for my family's house. There was a brief pause, and then she spoke again, sounding apologetic.

"I'm sorry, sir. This line is not cleared for external access." The fact that she called me sir almost made up for the rejection.

"Celeste, this is Juliette." Lady Smirks-a-lot apparently had no difficulties hearing both sides of the telephone conversation. "Please put this call through to the number Mr. Smith provided. I'm granting him a one-time exception, on my authority."

I shot her a victorious smile, which was met and vanquished by a casual roll of the eyes. Apparently, my choice of rewards hadn't been so stupid after all.

"As you wish, ma'am." There was an audible click over the receiver, and I heard the phone ringing.

"Hello?" answered my Dad.

CHAPTER 17

IN WHICH THE DREAD PIRATE ROBERTS MAKES AN APPEARANCE

"Hi, Dad… this is Joh—"

"Haha! Just kidding! You've reached the machine of John and Maria Smith."

Oh, you have got to be kidding me…

"We can't come to the phone right now… because we're on our way to Vegas!" In the background, I could hear my mother whooping with glee. "So, *if you feel lucky, punk*, go ahead and leave a message at the beep. But we'll be drinking margaritas pool-side, so don't expect us to get back to you!"

There was a long pause. Still no beep.

My dad's voice came back on in the background. "Yes, I set the message. Told you I could figure i-"

Beeeeeeeeeeeep.

Son of a bitch! I hung up and turned to Juliette, who had a bemused look on her face. "I'm assuming you heard that?"

"The acorn didn't fall far from the tree, did it? Does your dad understand that a message like that is an invitation to have the house robbed? Did he also post a notice on the internet, along with a map, directions, and the code to the alarm system?"

"The only thing my dad knows about the Internet is that there is supposed to be porn hidden somewhere on it, and even then, he's convinced you need a secret URL to get to it." I wasn't kidding, either.

He'd actually hinted around the subject a few times, in the hopes that I would provide him the golden ticket needed for admission. "My mom, on the other hand… Yeah, it's probably all over Facebook."

"I told you Anastasia had taken care of things."

"You think *Anastasia* sent my parents to Vegas?"

"Looks like it. What's the problem? It's out of the way and a lot more fun than a motel."

"I wasn't complaining. I just wish I'd gotten to go." I hit the phone's single button again.

"How may I direct your call?" Celeste still sounded cute.

"Hi, Celeste. It's me again. Could you call a different number please?" I provided the number for my dad's cell. With him out of the house, he might actually answer it for once.

"I'm sorry, sir. This line is not cleared for external access."

"I *just* called. Juliette gave me an exception."

"A one-time exception, sir. For the first number you provided."

"Oh, come on!" I turned to Juliette. "Seriously, Juliette. They weren't even home!"

She shrugged. "That sounds like an error in judgment on your part."

"Is there anything else I can do for you, sir?" The words were purely professional, but there was a hint of laughter in her voice.

"No, Celeste. Thank you ever so much." I disconnected with another press of the button, and dropped the useless piece of crap back onto the dresser. Who the hell designed a phone with one button, anyway? Evolution had given us multiple fingers for a reason.

Juliette was unapologetic. "We can always go back to the training hall and see if you can win another phone call."

Fat chance. I knew as well as she did that my victory had only been possible thanks to a healthy dose of luck and the fact that she had underestimated me. That sort of lightning wouldn't strike twice… and neither would I.

"Is it too late to opt for whatever that other reward was?"

"Let me think about it." She stepped back into my personal space, her hand lightly tracing patterns on my chest, and then blurred around at vampire speed until she was behind me, holding me with that arm. She stepped into me from behind, pressing her lean body against mine. She must have risen on her toes, as her fangs were suddenly at my neck, just below the ear. Her voice, liquid and sensuous, sent an electrical charge through my body. "Yes, indeed… it's far, far too late."

With a laugh that positively sang of sex and mischief, she spun away from me and headed for the door. "I will collect you tomorrow morning. Please don't leave your room tonight. If you have to, have Celeste contact me."

"Really? That's it?" Through the grace of one or more gods, my voice didn't crack, even though that had been the closest I'd come to sex in way too damn long.

"I'm sorry?"

"No bedtime story? No turndown service? What kind of a second-rate hotel is this anyway?"

"I can give you a story." Her voice was quiet, almost solemn. "Once upon a time, there was a human. Though not particularly smart, skilled or handsome, he somehow managed to find his way into the company of the best and brightest of the land. There, he was given one chance to save the kingdom. If he failed, he knew his life would be forfeit. So he took the opportunity to get as much sleep as possible, knowing that he'd need his all-too-limited skills if he were to succeed and thus survive. The End."

Those last two words sent a decidedly non-sexual shiver through me. She turned to leave, but once again, I stopped her.

"I was really hoping for a more *traditional* fairy tale, Juliette."

Still with her back to me, she snickered. "Good night, little bird. Sleep well. I'll most likely kill you in the morning."

And with that, the Dread Pirate Juliette sauntered out of the room.

ooo

After Juliette left, I showered again (still heavenly), scrubbed my face (still stubbly), and set about getting ready for bed. Then, when enough time had elapsed without any sound from the hallway, I crept to the door. This was the first time all day that I'd been left to my own devices. I wasn't going to pass up the chance to explore.

The door was a sterling example of its kind; large, heavy and made out of some sort of dark hardwood that probably wasn't mahogany, despite the voice in my head telling me so. It was also locked from the outside, a fact that I demonstrated several times in rapid succession by trying to turn the handle.

Well, shit.

Apparently, Juliette wasn't the trusting bloodsucking fiend I'd imagined her to be. Thankfully, this was an area in which my PI training might actually come in handy. I rummaged through the desk in my suite until I found several paper clips. I then bent them out of shape and began the laborious process of picking the lock.

Once again, vocational training was proving to be way more useful than a liberal arts degree.

Twenty minutes passed, and I was pretty sure the mahogany door was laughing at me. Maybe if I'd had my actual lock picking tools... Or maybe it was time to rewatch those YouTube videos. Either way, the lock seemed unpickable. Defeated, I re-evaluated my options, revised my long-term strategy, and elected to pursue Plan B.

In other words, I went to sleep.

ooo

The bed was like a cloud. The sheets were some fine, absurdly soft fabric that only pretended to be cotton. The house (or House, if you will) was cool and quiet, with none of the occasional creaks or noises you'd expect from an edifice of that size. Despite all of those facts, I found myself awake an hour later, faced with a terrible and unavoidable truth:

I was hungry.

Once again, I took my paper clips in hand. While my earlier efforts had been abysmal failures, I was now properly motivated, as only a hungry twenty-five-year-old can be.

Thirty minutes later, I was really starting to hate that door. I was on my fourth set of paper clips, the previous ones having proven defective and possibly traitorous. I was still hungry. I was also starting to think those YouTube videos had been full of shit... which raised any number of potential concerns about the rest of the course. I was going to be very disappointed if the *Top 10 KGB Tactics for Successful Interrogations* proved ineffective.

I discarded my latest and greatest set of jury-rigged lock picks and toyed with the idea of breaking one of the bedroom windows, fashioning a rope from the drapes, and climbing down to the ground floor a la Bruce Willis in Die Hard. Or setting the door on fire—with what, I wasn't sure—and making my triumphant escape during the resulting blaze.

I even briefly considered admitting defeat, and phoning Celeste to have Juliette escort me to the kitchen…. when I heard it: footsteps outside. Pushed to the depths of despair, I took the only rational course of action left to me.

"Hello!" I pounded on the door. "Is anyone there?"

The footsteps came to a halt.

"Hello?" Her voice was soft, maybe even a little bit timid.

"Hi! Could you do me a huge favor? I can't seem to open my door. I think the handle may be stuck or something. Do you mind giving it a little… wiggle?" I held my breath, waiting for a response.

"Are you John?"

Her question left me in a bit of a pickle. If I answered truthfully and word had circulated that I was supposed to stay in my room, she would abandon me to my eventual starvation. If I lied and she realized it, she might very well open the door… and kill me. A lot depended upon what the femmepire already knew. It was going to take a very careful approach to determine the depths of that knowl—

"Yeah, that's me."

Damn it. Another brilliant counter-intelligence maneuver done in by an empty stomach. Once again, I waited. The unpickable lock had left me few other options.

The door handle rattled momentarily, then turned smoothly as the lock disengaged. The door swung inward, and my savior greeted me with a shy hand wave and an even shyer smile.

She was… small. A pixie, really. Five-foot-nothing, cute as a teacup, and slender without being skinny, she had flaming red-hair, a dusting of freckles across a button nose, and warm cornflower-blue eyes. She was wearing grey sweats and a short-sleeved green t-shirt with the words *Love is Never Wrong* on it.

Unless I was wildly mistaken, she was also as human as I was.

She held up a key. "This was hanging on the outside door handle. Was someone pranking you?"

"Something like that, yeah."

"Cool. Anyway, I'm Darlene!" She gestured to her left. "I'm heading to the kitchen for a late-night snack. Want to come?"

"Darlene, I think I love you."

CHAPTER 18
IN WHICH SANDWICHES SHOULDN'T BE EUPHEMISMS

Xavier's ham was right where I had left it, and I quickly began constructing a new sandwich to put my previous sandwiches to shame. Darlene had extracted a mug from one of the cabinets, and was making herself a coffee-like drink that looked to consist primarily of milk and sugar. The coffee, it would seem, was there purely for coloring.

"I'm guessing you've got a bit of a sweet tooth?"

She smiled and raised the mug to her lips, taking a long sip with a happy sigh. Someone had clumsily painted multicolored hearts on the mug's surface, and there looked to be some sort of raised lettering on the side facing away from me. She smiled. "Kayla likes me sweet."

"Oh." I had no clue what she was talking about, so I settled for carrying my sandwich to the kitchen table. She set her mug down next to me, and scurried back over to rummage through the refrigerator herself. I took a closer look at the mug. Yup, there was writing on it in gold glitter. I turned the mug so I could read it: *Kayla's.*

Wait. Kayla had mentioned something about a Darlene, hadn't she? "So…"

She grinned at my evident confusion. "Sorry, I thought you knew. I'm Kayla's!"

"Kayla's… *what*, exactly?" Given the number of women already convinced I was a moron, I hurried to explain. "I mean… I understand what you are to her, I think. But... do vampires have a specific word or title for the relationship? Or is it just 'girlfriend'?"

Darlene shrugged. "We don't really worry about labels. It's enough that I'm hers, and she is mine." She gathered up her sandwich, a multistory behemoth of bread, vegetables and sausage, and placed it on a plate as she took a seat next to me. In the shadow of that terrible sandwich, my own snack's relative inadequacy became apparent. I knew that it was perfectly normal for men to feel size envy at some point in their lives, but I hadn't expected sandwiches to be involved. As Darlene took an impressively large bite, I noticed the two small bruises on her neck, partially hidden by her shirt.

"Wow." Obviously, I knew that the vampires in the House fed on humans. It was impossible to even pretend ignorance of the fact, given how frequently Juliette had been working it into our conversations, usually followed by a derogatory comment, threat, or invitation. But it was another thing entirely to be sitting at a kitchen table, eating sandwiches with a blood donor. She seemed very much at peace with the whole thing. "How did that happen, if you don't mind me asking?"

"Oh, the usual way. Girl grows up knowing she likes other girls. Comes out to her family a week before graduation. Gets disowned." Her cornflower blue eyes flickered with momentary bitterness and pain. "Heads west, and doesn't stop until she hits ocean. Bumps into a tall Aussie surfer chick who actually accepts her for who she is."

"And turns out to be a vampire," I guessed.

"Yeah. I guess it's not quite a Hallmark movie, huh?"

"Maybe it should be."

"And then they lived happily ever after." She took a second bite of her monster sandwich, and nodded firmly. "That's the plan, at least."

"But when and how did you find out..."

"What she is?" A dopey smile spread across Darlene's small face. "Our first time. I've never minded a little nibble, but *that* definitely took things to a whole new level. Thankfully, I was too blissed out afterward to freak much when she explained. I started spending my nights here soon after."

"That's awesome," I told her. "I'm sorry about your family though."

She shrugged, wiping mustard off her chin with a napkin. "It's their loss. It sucks but all their shit was worth it to find K."

The conversation lagged soon after, as we both got down to the serious business of eating. Food and drink were vanishing from Darlene's plate at near-record speeds, and I had absolutely no idea where she was putting it. If vampires ever wanted to come out to the public, they could make billions just by marketing the *Blood Donor Diet Plan*.

"So… what's it like? Being bitten?" I recalled Juliette's teeth at my neck with a shiver.

Darlene's blue eyes softened, gazing somewhere into the distance over my head, as she chewed her lip and considered my question. A slow blissed-out smile spread across her face.

"Orgasms like multicolored, cotton candy supernovas."

"Uhm." This had gone in an unexpected direction.

"And that's just the bite. When you mix in absolutely gratuitous amounts of sex…" she leaned back in her chair, closed her eyes, and sighed happily, "well, let's just say the last couple of hours helping her heal her broken arm were *really* enjoyable."

"That's… a lot of information." So much for Darlene being shy or timid. I struggled for something else to say.

She laughed at my obvious embarrassment, and her smile became mischievous. "I'll let you in on something else, John. As soon as I finish eating, I'm going to go right back to my Kayla," she said, blue eyes sparkling, "and I'm gonna ride that long-legged Aussie like a pony." She then proceeded to tell me exactly how.

I nearly choked on my sandwich.

ooo

It took Darlene a little under ten minutes to polish off a sandwich that could have satiated Godzilla. It took me another ten to stop blushing, something the pixie-lesbian-blood-bank found hilarious.

When she finally left to pursue the aforementioned recreational equestrian activities, I retrieved a beer from the refrigerator and slumped in my chair, holding the cold bottle against my forehead.

I wasn't a prude. I loved sex… what I could remember of it, anyway. My non-existent love life over the past too-damn-many years was a product of long, odd job hours, comparative poverty, and way too much competition from San Diego's male population, rather than any lack of interest or desire on my part. But I hadn't been prepared for the sort of girl-talk Darlene had decided to hit me with. I wasn't sure I'd ever be able to look at her or Kayla again without blushing. Even assuming I survived the next few weeks.

I popped off the bottle cap—with a bottle opener, not my thumb—and drained half the beer in one pull. It had been a long and very weird day. A few more sips and the beer was gone, leaving me slightly buzzed but no less confused. Xavier's now empty Tupperware went into the sink with the used dishes, and I trekked back to the bedroom, my bold plans for exploration forgotten.

The door to my suite remained ajar, just as I had left it, and I slipped inside, bringing the key with me to make sure nobody tried locking me in this time. I stripped off my borrowed button-up and tossed it in the vague direction of a chair, stepped out of my similarly borrowed pants, and flopped down onto the bed, determined to think of puppies, ice cream, rainbows and other entirely safe things until I fell asleep.

"Hello again, Mr. Smith." The creamy cheesecake voice sparked every nerve in my mostly naked body, and I physically twitched as the feeling swept through me.

Son of a bitch!

I clutched the sheet around me, and tried to locate her in the darkness. "Hello, Anastasia."

CHAPTER 19

IN WHICH BOUNDARIES ARE TESTED

I switched on the bedroom lamp. Sure enough, there she was, Lady Anastasia Dumenyova, Stone Lady and Secundus. It had only been a few hours since I'd seen her, but I had somehow forgotten just how beautiful she was. She was calm and composed, as if she habitually waited for people in their unlit bedrooms and saw nothing unusual in doing so again.

Finding someone like Anastasia in my bedroom would normally have been a cause for celebration, if not deep and heartfelt prayers of gratitude to the demigod of seriously lopsided relationships, but a word or two of warning would have been nice. Maybe then I wouldn't have stripped down in front of her. Or I'd have at least sucked in my gut while doing so. While the femmepire had already seen me concussed and vomiting, pudgy and mostly naked was a bad look all its own.

Anastasia waited as I gathered my thoughts. After the all-day rapid-fire banter with Juliette, and Darlene's impromptu tell-all session, I appreciated the silence. There was a stillness about the Secundus that was downright soothing; a deep lake in the woods, its surface barely rippling with the breeze.

"I didn't think I'd see you again until tomorrow's Council meeting," I finally managed. "Lucia seemed thrilled to put you to work."

"*Queen Lucia*, Mr. Smith. For your own safety."

"I'll call her Queen Lucia if you call me John."

She nodded, agreeable without ever actually agreeing. An auburn strand slipped free of its bun to trace the curve of her cheekbone. "In truth, there *were* a surprising number of things that required my attention. I finished the last of them only a short while ago, and wanted to verify that you remained intact."

"So far." I decided not to mention the ham. Or my mock battle with Juliette. "As *Queen Lucia* said, everyone has a vested interest in my surviving at least until tomorrow night."

"Yes. Nevertheless, your current minder has a long history of breaking her toys."

"I'm fine. After a day with Lady Smirks-a-lot, the only thing hurt is my ego."

"Lady Smirks-a-lot?"

I'd managed to surprise a true smile out of her. I filed that smile away in a mental folder titled 'Greatest Moments of My Life.' "Everyone else on the Council seems to have a mishmash of titles. I figured it was only proper to grant her one of her own. And since you immediately knew who I was talking about, I'd say it's appropriate."

"Titles come with age and accomplishments. At this point in her life, Juliette has neither."

Ooo. Vampire burn. "She did give you and the Queen a place to establish this House."

"I see you have been busy."

"I'm not a real mediator, but I thought knowing something about the parties involved might be useful. Juliette has helped on that front. More or less."

"Mr. Smith—"

"John." We were back to playing this game, it seemed.

"I recognize that Juliette can be charming, in her fashion, but I would warn you not to trust her. She can be... mercurial."

I shook my head. "You two really don't like each other, do you?"

"It is not that I disli—" Anastasia's voice trailed off. "What makes you say that?"

"Earlier today, *she* was warning me about *you*. Said you had a tendency to use people and then discard them."

"Of course she did. Why Lucia decided to pair the two of you together…" Anastasia's poker face was back in place, but the femmepire had to be irritated if she was referring to the queen by name instead of title. She took a seat at the foot of my bed, expression solemn.

"Mr. Smith, I will not deny that I utilize the skills of those around me. Most of our kind do so as naturally as breathing. Moreover, it is my job. However, when I choose to make use of someone, they know and agree to it, as you have done. And I am not in the habit of discarding such people afterward."

"What about Xavier?" It just sort of slipped out, as so often seemed to be the case with questions that might get me killed.

There was a long and not-at-all-comfortable silence, during which I carefully avoided eye contact by becoming fascinated with the sheet in my hands. At vampire speed, it would take Anastasia roughly a second to leap the length of the bed, eviscerate me, dispose of my remains, and head to the kitchen for midnight tea.

Instead, Anastasia laughed softly. If anything, I grew even more worried. That laugh was devoid of mirth, the closest thing to an ugly sound I'd heard from her. I looked up and found her watching me, her face cold and hard. For the first time, the title of Stone Lady made sense to me.

"Juliette *has* been busy." Her voice was equally leeched of life.

"I shouldn't have pried."

"No, you should not have. It is a personal matter and should be left in the past, where it belongs." She sighed, and it was a measure of how empty her voice had been that the tired sigh was a warm spring breeze by comparison. "But as the question has been raised, I will answer it. And if word spreads beyond this room of what I am about to tell you, I will know exactly who to hold responsible."

"I met Xavier when he was presented to the Courts, barely ten years after his first feeding. Lucia was still a princess then, in line to inherit the throne from her father. Xavier had come to Italy to pledge his sword to her service, and I was given the task of training him. In the process, we became lovers, and remained such for some time."

She looked over at me. "Did Juliette tell you that I chose prestige and power over my love for Xavier? That he willingly joined Lucia and me in exile, only to discover that he had given up everything for a *puttana* who no longer wanted him?"

"I'm not sure what a *puttana* is, but that's the general gist of it."

"Of course. The truth is more prosaic, Mr. Smith, and perhaps even less flattering. I never loved Xavier. I enjoyed my time with him, particularly in those early years, but our relationship was headed toward its inevitable ending long before my queen's coronation and subsequent exile."

"Did he know that?"

"Xavier was aware that I did not return his feelings, but believed love would come eventually. When Lucia asked me to join her, it was an easy decision... not merely because I had spent my life in service to her, but also because it offered what I was, by that time, truly looking for."

"A fresh start."

"Precisely. I ended my relationship with Xavier that night."

"So why did he follow you here?"

She smiled sadly. "He has always been a great believer in over-sized, romantic gestures. Perhaps he thought doing so would change things. If I were a different woman, perhaps it would have."

"I'm not sure love works like that," I said, from a position of limited experience.

"I must take your word for it. Regardless, in reward for his loyalty, Queen Lucia made Xavier the Captain of her Watch."

"Just like that?"

Anastasia shrugged. "He has a talent for battle. It is why she instructed me to make his acquaintance so many centuries ago."

"Oh."

"As I said, I am not the only one of the People who believes in effectively utilizing resources."

Vampire love lives weren't anywhere near as awesome as Hollywood has led me to believe. "I'm sorry again for intruding. God knows you don't need my approval, but it sounds like you handled it as well as possible. He's responsible for his decisions, not you."

Admittedly, that had sounded better in my head.

"As I said, it should be left in the past. But I appreciate your words nonetheless."

The silence that followed was surprisingly comfortable, but it couldn't last forever. Finally, I had to ask. "Anastasia, why *are* you here tonight?"

She primly rearranged her seat on the bed. If she'd been anyone else, I would have said she was stalling for time. But a mere day's acquaintance had already taught me that Anastasia Dumenyova did *not* stall for time. All she had to do was twitch an eyebrow and time would stand still of its own accord. "As I said, I wanted to verify your well-being. Additionally, I need your help."

"Aren't I already helping?" I was confused. And mostly naked, slightly pudgy, and probably smelling of onions.

"In your role as mediator, yes. However, I wish to also retain your investigative services."

I pinched the bridge of my nose. "I'm sorry. It's been a long day, and I'm struggling. Do you mind explaining what it is you're talking about? Using little words?"

"It is clear that someone seeks to prevent this mediation from occurring. Lord Beel-Kasan does not seem the sort to employ assassins, which suggests a third party is now involved. I am investigating our known enemies in San Diego, but it is also possible that the threat has come from within these walls."

"You think someone in the House might be involved?"

"Our spies elsewhere have found nothing. Either they have been fooled or suborned, or the danger originates closer to home. Either way, the current crisis may be only one more step in a campaign to destroy this House."

"Jesus." Things just kept getting more complicated. "So you want me to... what? Poke around the house? Kick over some stones and see what crawls out from under them?"

"Precisely. Look, speak, and listen. As an outsider, you may see things that I would miss. And you already have a relationship with one of the primary suspects."

I took a moment to puzzle that one out, and then made an enormous leap of logic. "Juliette?"

"Indeed."

"Why would she want to betray the House?"

"Her current position has not been the grand reward she thought it would be. There remains a divide between our European and American contingents, and I suspect she regrets surrendering her authority to become, as your countrymen say, a small fish in a larger pond."

It made a strange sort of sense, but I'd just spent the day with the other femmepire. I shook my head. "I have a lot of trouble picturing Juliette as any sort of evil mastermind. Femme fatale serial killer, sure. But mastermind? It seems kind of farfetched." The irony of defending the other femmepire by calling out her long-term strategic inadequacies was not lost on me.

"Then prove it. Find whoever is responsible so that I may stop them. Otherwise, I fear that Lord Beel-Kasan will be the least of our worries."

In a little over twenty-four hours' time, I had gone from having no cases and limited career prospects, to having two cases and a limited life expectancy.

It didn't seem like an improvement.

CHAPTER 20

IN WHICH RULES ARE BROKEN AND
HOMES PLUNDERED

The morning dawned clear and beautiful, which is the long way of saying I was still in San Diego. If the Apocalypse ever came to pass, San Diego was where we'd host the inevitable post-cataclysm barbecue.

Anastasia and I had spent some time discussing her concerns and suspicions about the possible conspiracy against the house. Her reasoning seemed solid, but there was a dire shortage of evidence, both that Juliette was responsible, and that the conspirators were part of the House at all.

On the other hand, Anastasia was quite a bit smarter than I was, and she had literal centuries of experience in this sort of thing. It was possible she was seeing connections I had missed.

In the end, my opinion didn't actually matter. When a client came to me, convinced that their spouse was cheating, my job was simply to prove or disprove their suspicions. If you took away all of the supernatural hocus-pocus, this case wasn't so different.

Also, since my mediation efforts were probably going to get me killed anyway, there wasn't any downside in taking on an equally dangerous investigation. I could only die once after all.

All of these happy morning thoughts bubbled through my brain as I kicked off the sheet and stretched, lazy as an overfed cat in the warm sunlight that streamed through my window.

"If this is your idea of a floor show, I'm disappointed. I was promised the full Monty."

I jumped off the bed. More accurately, I *tried* to jump off the bed. Unfortunately, one foot got tangled in the sheet, the other foot fell short of the floor, and the rest of me flopped onto carpet that, while luxuriously plush, was hardly designed to cushion a mostly-naked man's fall.

"Hmm. Adding in slapstick to your burlesque show? That's a bold choice. Not the *right* choice, mind you, but bold."

I tried to gather the scraps of my dignity about me, but had to settle for the sheet. "What are you doing in my bedroom, Juliette?"

"The word around the House is that you blush like a schoolgirl when it comes to sex talk. I wanted to see for myself." She bit her lower lip, canines partially extended. "Plus... I was bored. Again."

"And hungry, by the looks of it."

She shrugged off my observation with a disturbing lack of concern.

"I suppose it's too much to ask for a bit of privacy here at Vampire Central?"

"You had all night, little bird. Except you decided to sneak out of your room and *investigate* Kayla and Darlene's relationship instead."

"Is it really an investigation when someone volunteers every damn detail of their sex life?" I felt my cheeks warm even as I spoke.

"Darlene was right." Justine seemed equal parts fascinated and amused. "Like a sheltered little schoolgirl."

"Don't you all have anything better to talk about than me?"

"Better? Easily. More entertaining? Not at the moment." She smirked, but the expression faded almost as quickly as it had appeared. "Less amusing is the fact that you left your room, after we agreed you'd only do so with me as an escort."

"You mean after you locked me in my bedroom?!"

"Exactly."

"I don't take kindly to being kept a prisoner, Juliette. And in my profession, a locked door is like an engraved invitation." After a moment's thought, I stashed that winner of a line in a mental folder titled 'Things that sound badass.'

"Darlene said she had to let you out."

"Hardly. She was on her way to the kitchen, and saved me the inconvenience of opening the door myself."

"So these are… what? Art projects?" Juliette waved a handful of misshapen paper clips in the air.

I sighed. Busted. "I would have cracked it, eventually." Five years of experience as a private investigator told me she didn't believe me. Her loud snickers were what we in the business called *a clue*. "Look… could we table the mockery until after I've showered, dressed, and eaten?"

"I'm not sure that we can." Despite her words, Juliette did stop laughing. Her face was serious as she sauntered over to where I was clumsily propped up on the carpet. Yesterday's Ramones shirt had been replaced by a white, cropped Sex Pistols tee, and her jeans were tucked into knee-high, clunky-heeled, ass-kicking motorcycle boots. Juliette planted one of those boots right next to my crotch with a thump.

I may or may not have squeaked. Sources remain mixed on that particular detail. I looked down at where her boot had pinned the white sheet to the floor. The steel toe was literally touching my thigh. There was no way in hell she could have seen where the sheet ended and my body began, which meant that vampires either had some sort of psychic ability or she'd just decided to *guess*.

Certain parts of my anatomy tried to crawl their way back up and inside my body.

Juliette bent down, bringing her face closer to mine. "I asked you nicely to stay in the room. I even went so far as to say *please*, something that you can damn well believe will never happen again. I refuse to be punished because you have the sense of a turnip and decide to go romping about in a building full of individuals that can and will kill you! Do you understand me?" Using her hand, she nodded my head up and down like I was a doll and then released me.

"Now then," she continued, yellow eyes hard and angry, "what do you have to say for yourself, Mr. John Smith?"

"I was hungry?" I flinched from the blow that never came.

"And…?" Her voice took on an edge sharp enough to shave with.

"I'm sorry I left the room without calling for you."

"And…?" That edge was still there.

"Next time… I will?"

"*And…?*" Her eyes narrowed.

"Sex Pistols rule?"

"*And…?*" Out of the corner of my eye, I watched one of her hands clench into a fist.

"I have no idea what you want me to say, Juliette!"

The menace left her face as if someone had wiped it off with a towel. "Actually, I just wanted an apology. But it was fun seeing how far you'd take it." She straightened up with another snicker, dug her boot into my thigh one more time for good measure, and sauntered away.

"You do realize you could have just accidentally ended my prospects for fatherhood?"

"Little bird, there would have been nothing accidental about it. And let's not pretend that you have prospects. You're a terrible liar and I've already laughed enough for one morning."

"I didn't mean current prospects," I muttered. "Regardless, could you please not risk future Smith generations the next time you want to make a point?"

She considered the request, looking every inch the vampire elder, despite her attire. "No promises." She pulled me to my feet with one hand, while I desperately held the sheet about me. "Now, go shower. And don't dawdle this time, or I'll be forced to come get you."

"What's the hurry?" I didn't mean to sound whiny, but… I *liked* that shower. It was about the only thing in the house that hadn't threatened me with bodily harm.

"We have a business matter to discuss. And as you noticed, I'm hungry. The longer you take, the hungrier I'll be." She flashed fang.

I grabbed the sheet, and scurried into the bathroom.

Yes, I sucked in my gut while doing so.

I wish I could say it helped.

o o o

The shower was still a technological marvel, but it was difficult to enjoy it, knowing that Juliette might burst in at any point and haul my wet and naked ass away… probably into the hallway, where all the supermodel vampires would gather around and laugh as I blushed like a schoolgirl. I had just turned off the water when the bathroom door cracked open and Juliette poked her head in.

"Did I mention I was *hungry*? Stop screwing around!"

"Why don't you go grab a bite and leave me to get ready in peace?"

"Leave you alone? I don't think so. Not until I can hand your mortal ass back to Lucia, anyway."

"Then close the bathroom door! You're just slowing my mortal ass down."

"Fine." Her head disappeared from view and the bathroom door slammed shut. If I lived through the night, I was going to get deadbolts installed on both doors. And maybe the windows. I toweled myself off, ran a comb through the tangle of my hair, and started to get dressed… which is when I realized the only clothes in the bathroom with me were yesterday's boxers and my bed sheet.

"Juliette, where are my clothes?"

"Oh, I'm sorry… did you want something from me? I wouldn't want to delay you any further!"

"If you'll wait in the hall, I can get them myself. Otherwise, you're going to need to pass me some clothes so I can get dressed. I saw some Watch uniforms in the dresser yesterday."

"So now I'm your maid as well as your bodyguard?" Someone was in a bit of a snit. It might have been funny, if she wasn't minutes away from treating me like a juice box. "One second, oh exalted master…"

The bathroom door banged wide open, and Juliette marched in with an armful of clothes, completely unruffled by my nudity. I hurriedly covered my dude parts with both hands. Nose firmly lifted toward the ceiling, she tossed the clothes on the counter, spun on one heel, and stalked away. As she closed the bathroom door behind her, I heard her snicker. "Xavier would have needed *three* hands."

There's nothing quite like a drive-by emasculation before your morning coffee.

○○○

I dressed in record time. I know this because all the bedroom furniture was still intact when I exited, although the back of one chair appeared to have gained several decorative finger holes. That would have been mildly terrifying if I didn't already have weightier issues on the brain.

"Are these *my* clothes?" I had not, in fact, been supplied with another Watch uniform. Instead, I was wearing a dark grey Greendale Community College t-shirt and ripped jeans, both of which were exact matches for items I had at home, down to the spot of dried paint on the frayed cuffs of the jeans.

"How should I know?" Juliette nodded to the dresser, the top drawer of which was open and now filled with familiar clothes. "If they are, we'll add fashion to your list of transgressions—"

"Like you have room to talk." I gestured to her own shirt.

"—or is that t-shirt intended to be a warning to others that you attended community college? We used to do the same thing with scarlet A's..."

"Hilarious. I didn't go to Greendale. It's from a TV show..." Something in her lack of expression tipped me off. "But you knew that already."

"I do watch television, little bird, when I'm not stuck babysitting mediators."

"Anyway. These are *clearly* my clothes. How did they get here?"

"*Clearly*, someone went to your house to retrieve them and then *clearly* they brought them here."

"Unbelievable." So last night, a vampire had broken into my house, found my room in the basement, gone through all of my things, and returned with shoes and multiple changes of clothes, which they then deposited into the dresser... all while I was sleeping?

Clearly, vampires didn't understand personal boundaries. I dug through the drawer. "Why didn't they bring any underwear?"

"I don't see the point of the stuff, myself." I'd have chewed on that mental image for a nice, long while, but the dangerous tone was creeping back into Juliette's voice, and her canines were fully extended. For some reason, they didn't interfere with her speech. "If you have a problem with it, take it up with Lucia. Maybe she'll give more of a shit than I do."

"I'm just saying—"

"Enough!" Juliette pointed to a chair and growled. "Sit."

I sat.

"I'm going to make this brief. Afterward, I am going to take you to the kitchen, where someone else will be stuck with you, so that I can go feed, in the hope that a few pints of blood will keep me from murdering you in the next twelve hours. Understood?"

I nodded. This didn't seem to be the time to point out that she could have fed *before* waking me up.

"Good." Juliette let out a long sigh of frustration, and ran one hand through her spiky hair. "Last night, you said you were as much a detective as you are a mediator, right?"

"More of one, really. Why?"

"Because I need you to put on your detective hat for a second. I think there's something fishy going on. First, a demigod we've never even dealt with has a bone to pick with the House. Within a day, all the mediators in San Diego but you are dead. There's no way any of that is a coincidence. I think there might—"

"—be some sort of conspiracy to destroy the House."

Her yellow eyes widened. For the second time ever, I may have actually impressed her. "How did...?"

"I'm a private investigator, Juliette. It's what we do," I told her modestly. "So, I'm guessing you want me to figure out who did it?"

"I already know who's responsible. I just need you to prove it."

"And the evil mastermind would be...?" I had a sinking suspicion that I knew exactly where she was going with this.

"Anastasia, obviously."

Sometimes, it just didn't pay to get out of bed.

CHAPTER 21

IN WHICH BRUNCH HAS A BITE

It would be unkind to say that Juliette force-marched me down the hallway to the kitchen. Accurate, but unkind. Having dropped her own unique version of the conspiracy bomb and secured my promise to look into it, the vampire was no longer interested in doing anything but handing me off so that she could get her morning blood.

Since I was dying for a cup of coffee, I actually understood how she felt. A lot of people are monsters before their morning fixes... Juliette was just a bit more literal about it than most.

The kitchen was crowded. I counted nine vampires, three of whom were wearing black Watch uniforms. I was the only human present, which seemed to be an oddly persistent trend. If the People all had to feed, and there were somewhere between thirty and a million of them on the premises, shouldn't there have been a similar number of blood donors? Yet the only other member of my species that I had encountered so far was Darlene.

Juliette pulled me right into the kitchen, located an empty chair, and sat me down—hard—in that chair. She scanned the suddenly fascinated audience. "Kayla. I need you to watch him while I go feed. If he tries to get out of this chair, break his legs." She blew out of the kitchen like an angry storm cloud.

By contrast, Kayla sort of... moseyed... over to me, as the other vampires watched. She snagged a chair for herself, spun it around, and sat, leaning forward over the back of the chair to regard me seriously. "So. Darlene."

"Nice girl," I replied hesitantly.

"And mine."

"Yeah. She made that pretty clear, what with the detailed breakdown of your sex life."

Kayla didn't crack a smile. "The bond she and I have is important. Attempts to interfere with it will have consequences."

"What the hell, Kayla? I'm not going to try and steal your girl! Even if I weren't the *completely* wrong gender, I wouldn't mess around with someone else's girlfriend. I'm hard-up, not stupid."

Wait. Had I really said that last part out loud? Judging by the laughter, the answer was yes.

Damn it.

On the bright side, my pitiful admission had gotten through to Kayla. Some of the tension seeped out of her and she sat back in her chair with a nod. "It's nothing personal, John. I just want to make sure you understand."

"I know we've only known each other for a day. But give Darlene a bit of credit here. If I were the sort of person dumb enough to hit on her, I'd wind up with her knee lodged somewhere unpleasant. And then she'd go get her big, badass, vampire girlfriend—who healed from a broken arm *overnight*, by the way—to tear my freaking head off."

Finally, she was smiling. "Okay, okay. You're right." She gracefully rose to her feet, and offered me a little half-bow. "I apologize."

Three of the vampires in the kitchen stormed out, muttering something under their breaths.

Kayla's eyes flickered over in that direction, then back to me. She shrugged. "Racists."

"I guess humanity doesn't have a monopoly on them. Now that that's settled, can I get up and get some coffee? I need my caffeine."

"You heard Juliette. She's not quite the hard-ass the rest of the council is, but an order's an order. Just wait here." She poured out a mug of coffee and brought it over before making a second trip for the milk and sugar. "I wasn't sure how you liked it."

"Bitter and hot, just like my women," I mumbled, before giving away the lie by dumping in three sugars and a healthy dose of cream. "Where is Darlene anyway?"

Kayla grinned. "Sleeping it off. She had a long night."

"Lucky her." I blushed, realizing immediately how that might be misconstrued. "That she's still sleeping, I mean. I got pulled out of bed by Juliette, who was in a pissy mood because she was hungry. I guess feeding first and *then* waking me up would have worked out too perfectly for both of us."

"Yeah, that's actually my fault. Sorry." Kayla sat back down, holding her own steaming mug. "I ran into her when she was on her way to feed this morning and mentioned that you and Darlene had met. After getting the details from me, she turned around and stormed off towards your room." She grinned. "D was right, by the way; you totally blush like a choirboy."

"Choirboy?"

She nodded happily.

"Not schoolgirl?"

"Not unless you've been keeping secrets. Why?"

"Just Juliette messing with me, as usual." I waved it off. "So, it's my fault because I wanted a sandwich last night? That's fair, I guess." Once again, I'd been hoisted by my own petard... or whatever the saying was. What *was* a petard, anyway?

I was pretty sure it had something to do with boats.

"That's part of it," agreed Kayla. "In general, you might want to avoid her when she's hungry."

"I would if I could," I grumbled, "but why?"

"Your blood. AB-negative, if I'm not mistaken?"

"Uhm. Yes?"

"I thought so. It's a lovely bouquet for those who have acquired the taste."

A golden-skinned manpire at the nearest table nodded in agreement, not that either of us had asked him.

"And Juliette is one of those, I take it?"

"Absolutely. Your blood type is uncommon enough that none of the communal donors have it. So, having you around but off-limits is like being forced to guard a cupcake when all you have to eat are saltines."

I couldn't decide whether or not to be offended that I was the cupcake in this scenario. Finally, I decided I was a very manly cupcake. "Well, if Juliette starts to fang out on me, I'll just ask Lucia for a chaperone."

Kayla choked on her tea. "I'd almost pay to see that."

I leaned back in my chair, smiled, and sipped my coffee.

ooo

Flash forward ten or so hours, and I was still smiling. It had been a good day. Not how I'd expected to be spending my Sunday, but a good one nonetheless. After brunch, I'd been escorted back to my room by Juliette and Steve, the badass mohawked manpire. I'd had a very long second shower while they chatted in the bedroom.

When I emerged, Ray had joined my steadily growing bodyguard squad. I wasn't entirely sure why I would be in greater danger now than on the previous day, but I wasn't going to complain about it, especially once Juliette showed me how to operate the projector TV and game console that I somehow hadn't noticed in my room.

A Sunday playing video games? With free beer a hallway away? It was almost heaven.

I quickly learned to avoid competing against the vampires in games where reflexes mattered. After I got smoked by Steve, taunted by Juliette, and barely held my own against Ray, despite his tendency to lose interest mid-game, I demanded we switch to something I'd actually have a chance in: Trivial Pursuit.

Several games later, I realized that every person competing against me was, at minimum, two to three times my age. They were all also a whole lot more knowledgeable. Even Ray, who showed a distressingly complete knowledge of musical history.

Similarly, we only played a few games of Scene It! before I called it quits, my (self-given) reputation as a TV and film buff in tatters. As far as I could tell, Juliette had seen every movie… ever. As for Just Dance, my best and only moves were the Running Man and an odd, personalized version of the Ketchup Song dance, which I'd learned in preparation for a weekend Cabo trip, in the desperate hopes that it might make me cool.

Spoiler alert: it hadn't.

So, why was I still smiling? Two reasons, really. First, Darlene had finally woken up sometime after noon, and with Kayla on duty, had been happy to join me in a show of human solidarity. Second, we were playing the latest UFC game, and I was kicking some major ass. Ironically, given that my vampire opponents could break me into tiny little pieces even without their powers, they really, really sucked at fighting games.

"What the hell?" moaned Juliette, as my fighter dropped back into guard and I started working for a triangle. "What button do I push to bite your dick off?"

"There is no button for that," I crowed, as her on-screen avatar was choked unconscious. "It's against UFC rules."

"That's ridiculous! If you're going to be dumb enough to put me between your legs, you'd better believe I'm taking advantage of the position." She and Darlene exchanged high-fives while Steve and I shifted uncomfortably. Ray was staring out the window again, counting bunnies.

"That's the difference between sport and fighting," I was saying, when the ashtray-shaped phone on my bedside table started to vibrate.

Juliette tossed her controller down in disgust and answered. She listened to the caller for a moment more and then replied, "Understood." Placing the phone back down, she looked at me. "It's time." Steve and Ray were already up and headed for the door.

I shrugged and rolled off the bed. I took one glance in the bathroom mirror to make sure I was presentable, brushed the crumbs from my t-shirt, and followed them out the door. Darlene said goodbye, but not before giving me a hug. I hugged her back, as conservatively and platonically as humanly possible, on the off chance that Kayla was watching through one of the hallway cameras.

It pays to be careful about these things.

CHAPTER 22
IN WHICH THE COUNCIL CONVENES

Flanked by Ray and Steve, I followed Juliette through the House; down the hall, up two floors in the elevator, and back to the same conference room in which I'd had my disastrous first meeting with Lucia.

Had that really only been two days ago? I thought back to that naive and innocent version of myself, and shook my head. So young. So foolish. If I'd only known then what I knew now... well, I'd have tried to avoid getting punched unconscious, at the very least.

The other council members were already seated around the table, with Lucia in her customary chair at its head. Once again, Lucia was all in white—it seemed to be her color as much as oceanic blues and greens were Anastasia's—with golden cleavage piled up almost to her chin.

The queen nodded to Steve and he and Ray filed out of the room, closing the doors behind them. Juliette took her seat at the table by Marcus and Andrés, while I was sent to an empty chair next to Xavier.

"Now that we are all present..." Lucia's voice rang out in the suddenly quiet room. "Marcus, you may begin."

Marcus was in yet another suit, the third one I'd seen him wear in as many days. His dark eyes flickered briefly in my direction before he began to speak. If he really had come over to America at the same time as Lucia and Anastasia, the thickness of his accent indicated a stubborn resistance to assimilation.

I wanted to blame that accent for the fact that I only understood about half of his presentation, but the truth was, most of it was financial in nature, and unintelligible to someone of my delicate fiscal standing. As ordered, he'd investigated my finances and found mostly cobwebs and dust, which helped convince everyone that I hadn't been hired to work against them.

The House, on the other hand, had a lot of money, and he went into exhaustive detail enumerating the very many incomprehensible things he was doing to make that money grow. It all sounded impressive. I'd have asked him to assist with my future investments, but that would have meant breaking open my piggy bank, and I couldn't do that to Porky.

Besides, I wasn't sure Marcus had ever even seen currency smaller than a hundred.

When the manpire had finished, he took his seat, and Andrés rose instead. His briefing was a lot easier to follow, presumably because he wasn't discussing numbers so large that an act of faith was required to even believe they existed. "Per your directive, I have initiated talks with our potential allies in San Diego. Discussions are still in a preliminary stage, but I am confident that we will not be alone in our fight, should the mediator fail."

I tried not to take that personally.

"We have also extended our contract with Bayside Security. They will continue to provide us with exterior guards and drivers. However, it is my position that we should utilize the humans and other lesser species in only non-essential positions."

"I've read your security recommendations, Andrés, and I agree," Lucia replied smoothly. "Xavier, what can you tell us of the Watch's readiness?"

The dark vampire rose to his feet smoothly, his deep voice rumbling through the room. He seemed completely unruffled by the seating arrangements, making him a much better man than me. "If recruitment efforts continue at their current pace, I believe we are still a year or so away from regaining full strength, Your Majesty. On an individual basis, our warriors stack up well against any potential enemies, but numbers tell when it comes to war."

Lucia nodded. "So be it. Andrés, keep me apprised of your continued efforts. I do not like being reliant on others at a time like this, but needs must." The pony-tailed manpire sat back down, and she motioned to Xavier, who was still on his feet. "Captain, what have you discovered regarding the Rook's death?"

Juliette threw me a meaningful look at the same time as Anastasia narrowed her eyes. I gave them both a half-nod to show I'd gotten the message, and turned my attention to Xavier.

"The investigation remains in the preliminary stages. We have retrieved a small mountain of forensic evidence that we will still need to analyze." Lucia gave him a nod of acknowledgment and a wave of *get on with it*, and Xavier continued. "If Lord Beel-Kasan was involved in the Rook's death, I believe he did so through intermediaries. The Rook and his companions—we've gathered enough body parts for three individuals in total—were cut into pieces. I found traces of metal in one of the wounds, suggesting that some sort of bladed weapon was used. It sheared through flesh and bone with equal ease. There was no sign of forced entry. Whatever or whoever did this, I think it is safe to assume that it was not the karkino."

"Why's that again?" I asked.

"The karkino take a brute strength approach to locked doors, Mr. Smith," said Anastasia. "Their passage would have been apparent."

"As we've already said, they would hardly have been able to kill the Rook, regardless," murmured Lucia. "In his own way, he was formidable. Continue, Captain."

"Blood spatter suggests more than one attacker. Two of the kills were a substantial distance apart in the living room, yet appear to have occurred almost simultaneously. Unfortunately, the postmortem desecration and scattering of the bodies makes a full reconstruction of the scene difficult."

"What about security?"

"I assure you, Mr. Smith, that you are as safe here as you could possibly be," Xavier growled in disgust.

I rolled my eyes. Mentally, anyway. I'd seen what Xavier could do when angry. And he hadn't even found out about the ham yet. "I meant at the Rook's residence. What sort of security setup did he have?"

"Do we really have to listen to this mewling human speak?" Xavier's contempt was mirrored in Marcus' derisive curl of the lip. Andrés even went so far as to nod his agreement. I didn't have a lot of fans among the council manpires. Thankfully, the women were—

"He does tend to babble at the slightest provocation," noted Juliette.

Seriously?

"Most humans do," agreed Lucia. "However, our mediator has worked as an investigator in the past. His background may be of some use here."

"Very well, Your Majesty," replied Xavier, offering her a half-bow that again managed to bring attention to the way his Watch uniform shirt molded to the muscles of his chest and arms. I'm pretty sure Juliette was purring again.

Xavier turned to me, a sneer on his face, even though his voice had reverted to its usual professional tone. "How many murders have you investigated, in your vast expanse of experience, Mr. Smith?"

"None," I admitted, and waited for that sneer to grow to sufficient size. "But I've helped look into a few robberies—" And participated in the occasional illegal entry myself, not that I was going to admit that. "—so I'm familiar with a decent variety of security systems."

That wiped the superiority right off his face. Throw in a kiss from a cute young lady or two, and I could have died happy.

For the first time, Xavier had to refer to his notes. "The house had an alarm system at the exterior door and windows, installed and maintained by ALS. The system was not enabled at the time of the murders."

"Do the logs show *when* it was deactivated, and have you cross referenced that with the estimated time of death?"

More flipping through notes ensued, but the answer, when it came, was what I'd hoped for. "There does appear to be a possible correlation between the estimated time of death and when the alarm was turned off."

"You think the killers may have known the access code for the alarm, Mr. Smith?" Lucia was speaking to me as if I were something more than a bug under her incredibly expensive shoe. Honestly, it felt pretty great.

"That's a possibility, but with no sign of forced entry, I think it's more likely that the Rook turned off the alarm himself and invited them in." Out of the corner of my eye, I saw Xavier's irritation grow. Captain Amazing did not like being upstaged, especially not by me.

"Which further supports the idea that he knew his attackers." Lucia murmured, glacial blue eyes distant as she put her royal brain to work.

"Either that or they were able to convince him to let them in. I didn't know the guy… would he have been susceptible to compulsion? Or coercion? Maybe threats to a loved one?"

Marcus laughed. "The only things the Rook loved were money and himself. And he was too smart to open the door to a known threat."

"What about his companions?"

Xavier re-entered the conversation. "From the body parts, we believe they were constructs, created for the Rook's physical gratification."

"Seriously? Sex bots? Those are a thing?" My horizons had just been broadened. And my mind was officially blown.

"Magical… sex bots," he confirmed, the disgust again evident in his voice. "As such, it is unlikely they would have been granted rights to open the door."

Magical sex bots. The supernatural world had everything. "It sounds like we're back to the Rook knowing his attackers."

"Even if that were true, and it does seem like a valid hypothesis," admitted Xavier, offering me an almost-respectful nod, "our suspect pool remains substantial. As city mediator, the Rook worked with many of the creatures in and around San Diego, almost all of whom have used bladed weaponry at one time or another."

"In all likelihood, whoever killed the Rook also hired the karkino," said Lucia. "Narrow the suspect pool to those species who would benefit from our troubles."

"That would be almost every species," said Andrés. "We sit at the top of the power structure in this city. If we fall, all others rise."

"I don't suppose the Rook had cameras installed?" I asked.

"If the security system had included cameras, Mr. Smith, do you not think I would have started my briefing with stills of the attackers?" Xavier shook his head. "Despite his relative affluence, the Rook lived in a single family dwelling. One gate, but no cameras."

What about cameras that weren't part of the ALS-installed system? I knew from experience that not everyone liked the idea of in-home footage being stored on some faceless company's network. If the Rook was as squirrely as everyone seemed to think, he could have had his own camera setup indoors.

I'd have loved to say all that, to wipe the superiority off of Xavier's face, if nothing else, but something stopped me. It wasn't because Juliette and Anastasia were both in the room with us. After all, I didn't really believe either of them was responsible for the Rook's murder. Especially since they'd each hired me to solve it. And yet... if there *had* been cameras in the Rook's house, maybe it was better that I be the one who found them.

Lucia was already speaking. "Captain, keep us apprised of your efforts. Perhaps the forthcoming forensics report will help narrow our suspect pool even further."

"Of course." Xavier bowed again—seriously, was he using his other hand to pull the shirt tighter against his chest when he did so?—and took his seat.

"Which brings us to our final order of business. Mr. Smith, I understand that Juliette has briefed you on the details of tonight's mediation?"

"What few details exist." I looked around the table. "If anyone has anything to add, I'm all ears. There's not much to go on, beyond vague threats and an accusation that your House stole *something*."

"Unfortunately, attempts to communicate with Lord Beel-Kasan have been unsuccessful. He refuses to speak with anyone from my House. Even our human servants have been turned away… or worse. He only agreed to tonight's mediation because it was suggested to him by the Mer, and their impartiality is beyond question."

The Mer? More stuff I knew nothing about. "Couldn't they have served as mediators then?"

Andrés laughed unpleasantly. "Only if we wished to meet at the bottom of the Pacific."

"They are sea folk, Mr. Smith," said Anastasia.

"Never mind then." I gave the whole situation a few more seconds of thought, and then shrugged. "I guess I'll have to play it by ear. Once Lord Beel-Kasan explains what's actually going on, we can take it from there."

"In other words, we're doomed," said Juliette, in a whisper that carried through the room.

"We shall see," replied the femmepire queen. "We depart in one hour. Captain, I require two cars, and a pair of your Watch for each vehicle. Andrés, Marcus and Juliette, you will remain behind. Temporary truce or no, I will not be putting the entirety of our leadership in harm's way."

"If any of us stays, should it not be you, Your Majesty?"

"No, Marcus." Lucia's voice lost its sweet coating. All that remained was ice, and the room temperature plunged to match it. "This filthy godling has dared to insult and threaten my House. I will meet him face-to-face and I will have an apology or I will see him bleed for eternity."

Because *that* was a productive attitude to bring to a mediation.

As if she'd heard my thoughts, the queen glanced my way, arctic blue eyes still glowing. "Anastasia, I pass Mr. Smith into your care once more. When you have readied yourself, please, for the love of this House, see if you can dress him in something that *doesn't* make him look like an opium-addicted vagrant."

CHAPTER 23

IN WHICH NIGHTMARES COME
IN SHADES OF GREEN

An hour later, I'd been packed into one of two Escalades, accompanied by Anastasia, Steve, and another Watch member who introduced himself as Corey and had the cheerful sociability of a Mormon missionary.

This was my second ride in an Escalade, but despite the absence of blood and crab guts, I was actually less comfortable than I'd been the first time. Whoever had searched my parents' house had been thorough; they'd somehow found the suit I'd worn, years earlier, to my one and only job interview. The fact that it fit at all was a minor miracle. Anastasia had suggested adding a tie, but I'd finally put my foot down. My non-existent mediation skills weren't going to be helped by a lack of oxygen.

Admittedly, it was difficult to deny the vampire anything, given her own outfit. For the first time, she'd abandoned her oceanic color scheme, and was now clothed entirely in shiny black leather, from low-heeled boots to buttery-soft pants to some sort of halter top that left her strong arms and shoulders bare. Her auburn hair was up in a complicated knot that kept it out of her face without providing an opponent something to grab.

It wasn't the sort of outfit you could sneak up on someone in, but she looked dangerous, a statuesque goddess of war.

I looked like a used car salesman.

In the lead car, Lucia was wearing an identical outfit, though hers was, of course, white. The color scheme should have left Anastasia looking like the queen's shadow, but all that black leather couldn't keep the setting sun from highlighting the red in her hair or the gold in her luminescent jade eyes.

I thought about their dynamic as we waited for our small convoy to depart. How many centuries had Anastasia served Lucia as Secundus? Could Juliette be right? Was it possible that Anastasia had tired of her servitude? I didn't want to believe it. At the same time, if I were making a list of vampires with the brains and will to plot an elaborate conspiracy, she would be at the top of that list.

Ray, bless his space-cadet heart, would be at the very bottom.

Right below Juliette, if we were being honest.

The queen's Escalade finally began to move and ours followed. As the cars neared the gate, I found myself oddly panicked to be leaving the grounds. In two short days, my world had somehow become defined by the House. As bizarre a place as it was, I was suddenly reluctant to re-enter the greater world around us.

The fact that we were headed to meet with an insane demigod in the hopes of staving off supernatural Armageddon might have been part of that.

"You are quiet tonight, Mr. Smith."

"Just thinking, I guess." Anastasia and I occupied the middle seats of the lushly appointed automobile, with Corey behind us, and Steve riding shotgun next to the human driver, who had neither introduced himself nor been introduced. I promptly dubbed him Bob. Like all the other humans on the security force, Bob looked like he wrestled gorillas for fun. Which made it all the more ridiculous that he was by far the weakest person in the Escalade.

Besides me, of course.

Anastasia took my statement at face value and said nothing more. I added it to the laundry list of things I liked about her. Together, we watched the roads blur by as the sun dropped below the horizon. As we neared the 15, I shook my head. "I still can't believe the House is in Scripps Ranch."

"How so?"

"I just figured the People would have gone for something fancier and closer to the ocean. Upper-crust Del Mar or La Jolla, maybe."

"We are but one of several supernatural contingents in this city. Juliette and her flock lacked the numbers and strength to claim a territory along the coastline. When we arrived from Italy to establish the House, we decided we were better served by a more secure and remote location."

"Scripps Ranch is remote?" I was pretty sure there were tens of thousands of people living in the neighborhood.

She shrugged a well-defined shoulder. "This was many years ago. San Diego has expanded since then, and faster than we anticipated."

Our convoy took the circular on-ramp to head south on the 15. As was typical for a Sunday night, southbound traffic was light, but brake lights flickered ahead of us like fireflies. Anyone who has spent significant time in Southern California knows that traffic speeds will routinely go from eighty to twenty and then back to eighty in the span of a few blocks, without rhyme or reason for the change.

"What did Xavier mean when he said the Watch wasn't back to full strength yet?"

"Were you in San Diego for the Cedar Fire?"

"Yeah, although I was a teenager." I could tell that had thrown her for a loop. For someone who lived centuries, ten years must seem like an eye blink. For me, it was almost half my life. "Was the House caught in the fire?"

"Worse. We were its target."

I struggled to wrap my mind around that. At the time, the Cedar fire had been the largest wildfire in California history, responsible for at least a dozen deaths and the destruction of large portions of San Diego. "I thought it was started by a hunter, up near Ramona?" Ramona was a good twenty miles northeast of Scripps Ranch, which just went to show how far the fire had eventually spread.

"Indeed. But the winds that drove it southwest were the result of our enemies' intervention." Anastasia frowned in recollection. "For all the damage it did to the region, the fire was used primarily as a distraction while they assaulted the House directly."

"Who were they?" Something about the way she said it suggested something other than vampires. Witches? Satyrs? Genetically altered bunny geniuses?

"It does not matter. They no longer exist. But the damage inflicted was significant. We have been forced to recruit from around the globe to regain our strength as quickly as we have."

"I'm sorry." I frowned as a thought occurred to me. "Wait… they attacked you? Shouldn't there have been a mediation first?"

"The Rook mediated for us that year, but no agreement could be reached. Thus… war." Anastasia's jade eyes met mine. "That is what awaits us, should you fail."

ooo

We drove in silence after that. I mean… what was there to say? For all the collateral damage resulting from the Cedar Fire, I suspected it would be trumped by whatever a demigod might unleash in the heat of full-scale war.

Since the beginning of the whole mess, I'd known my death was a possibility, even a likely event, but I'd tried very hard not to think of how my failure might impact my family, Mike and everyone else I'd grown up with. Hell, Susie Birkman—my one-time elementary school nemesis, now married and the mother of twins—actually *lived* in Scripps Ranch!

"Anastasia, I'm not sure I can do this." I heard the tremor in my voice, and knew that *John Smith, creature of the night*, would never have sounded like that. But a film noir vampire legend doesn't have family to worry about, unless it's an ex-wife he still occasionally meets for booze and sex. "I'm going to get us all killed."

"It is possible," agreed Anastasia, promptly staking her claim to the title of *worst pep talk giver in recorded history*, "but I choose to believe otherwise. Despite your inexperience, you have qualities that make you the optimal person for this scenario."

"Like what?" I asked. "I'm a college dropout. The only things going for me are that my parents let me live with them, and I have some weird, one-in-a-zillion quirk that keeps the People from messing with my brain." Using vampire powers, at least. The women of the House had already demonstrated their ability to mess with that mind in other ways.

"I believe you are omitting two key strengths. The first is flexibility of mind. Two days ago, you did not know our world existed, yet you have shown an astonishing capacity to roll with the punches. Not literally, of course; Juliette had no difficulty knocking you unconscious."

From the seat in front of me, Steve coughed, stifling what sounded suspiciously like a chuckle.

"You've learned that vampires, karkino, and many other supernatural beings are real. You've been held prisoner, undergone blood rites, had your life threatened on multiple occasions, and been hired to mediate with a demigod of nightmares."

"Yeah. It's definitely been a weekend." Had I mentioned what a lousy pep talk this was?

"And how have you responded?" she continued, eyes still locked with mine. "Did you find a corner to hide in or suffer a nervous breakdown? No. You expressed disappointment that the People were not aliens, demanded payment from my queen, consumed the entirety of Xavier's baked ham—"

Apparently, Anastasia had been keeping tabs on me, even during our separation.

"—talked your way through Juliette's blood hunger *and* Kayla's jealousy, and last but not least, spoke up to offer your perspective in the middle of a meeting of elders." She gifted me with one of her rare smiles, and a warm glow spread through my chest in response. "Your ability to remain calm in the face of chaos will serve you well in the mediation to come."

"But I've been *terrified* during most of it."

"And yet here you are, alive and coherent. You are stronger than you realize, Mr. Smith."

"Oh." This was the point where Juliette would have chimed in with a suitably ego-puncturing comment. Honestly, I kind of missed the sarcasm. It was a lot easier to take than what seemed like a genuine compliment.

"Equally as important, people *like* you. Juliette went from cracking your skull to playing video games with you in the span of a weekend. Several of our Watch have shared coffee, beer, or sandwiches with you. Even Her Majesty has repeatedly elected not to discipline you for your informality."

If that was Lucia liking me, I really, really didn't want to see how she treated her enemies. "Xavier, Marcus and Andrés all hate me."

Anastasia shrugged. "Not even Alexander the Great won every battle."

"I'm pretty sure he did, actually. That was kind of what made him great."

"Is that what they teach in human schools these days? Interesting."

I decided to table *that* discussion for another time. "So, my superpower is that some people like me?"

Steve spoke up. "A lot of us think you're a trip, dude. The House has definitely been more interesting since they dragged you in." He coughed and darted a look at Anastasia. "Your pardon for the interruption, Lady Dumenyova."

"It is something he needed to hear, Mr. Duvassi."

"Huh." I was too busy thinking to pay much attention to the stilted interplay between the two. "I'd have preferred flight or laser eye beams, but I guess fake calm and non-comprehensive likeability will have to do."

"A mediator's job is to bridge the divide between warring parties, Mr. Smith. Charm is more valuable than you might think."

"I just hope it works on demigods."

"Amen to that," murmured Steve.

οοο

In the movies, negotiations between rival crime families happen someplace dark and foreboding, like the vacant lot of a crumbling, inner-city tenement building, where tension hangs in the air like cigarette smoke and rival enforcers take turns staring each other down.

With vampires and immortals added to the mix, I could see that setting becoming even more ominous… a dimly lit boiler room or an abandoned sewage facility where the rats grew to be the size of small dogs.

Instead, our two car convoy turned into the parking lot of a shopping center just west of Mission Valley mall.

"Wait… we're meeting at Gordon Biersch?" The lot was oddly empty for a Sunday night, especially on the last night of Comic Con. The restaurant itself was quiet, its windows dark. I gave Anastasia an incredulous look. *"Gordon Biersch?"*

"The Concordat dictates that the aggrieved party may choose the location," she replied absently, her eyes alert for danger. "Much of Mission Valley is deemed neutral territory, but I do not know what attachment Lord Beel-Kasan might have for this establishment in particular."

"They have great garlic fries."

"I am not entirely sure that he eats food."

"Huh. Then I've got nothing."

Bob parked our Escalade five or so spaces down from its twin, in what would normally be the valet area, and he, Steve and Corey exited to secure the location. I found the protective measures vaguely comforting, although I had no idea how effective they might be against a demigod… or a human sniper, for that matter.

Through the windshield, I watched Steve confer with Xavier. I assumed they were deciding whether it was safe for the rest of us to exit the vehicles, but they could just as easily have been lamenting the Chargers' first losing season in almost a decade.

Eventually, they reached some sort of consensus. Steve signaled to Corey, who opened the rear door for us to exit. Lucia appeared from within the confines of the first Escalade, her white leather gleaming in the electric glow of the shopping center's street lamps.

Bob and the other driver positioned themselves outside the main door to the restaurant, but the rest of us entered in two discrete groups. I guessed the idea was to minimize our casualties if someone threw a grenade. Or shot an RPG. Or sent a forest fire after us.

Being a mediator really sucked.

The interior was as dark as it had looked from the outside, with only a handful of lights to lessen the gloom. A building that could hold several hundred was now eerily empty of patrons or employees. We were greeted instead by a young Korean girl, her dark eyes enormous behind extremely thick-lensed glasses. She had long black hair, straight-cut bangs, and was wearing a Catholic school girl uniform. Not the sexed up version that Hollywood and anime sells us, but the real deal; a dark V-neck sweater and white-button-up shirt of some heavy cotton blend, a tartan skirt that extended well past her knees, and clunky, low-heeled Mary Janes. Over the entire ensemble, she wore a bright red cape, as if she were in training to become Supergirl.

"I am Jee Sun!" she said, a little bit too cheerily. "He is waiting. Follow, please!"

Xavier took point while Corey and Steve flanked the Council members. The fourth Watch member, a no-nonsense male vamp whose name I had yet to learn, served as our rear guard. I leaned over to Anastasia as we walked, taking care to speak as quietly as possible. "You see her too, right? What is she? Demon? Ghost-child? Cyborg?"

"She appears to be a member of your species. Female. Somewhere between five and ten years old."

"What is she doing here?"

"I do not know."

If Lord Beel-Kasan was in any way harming this girl, I was going to mediate my fist right into his face. And then I'd die, and the city would descend into apocalyptic chaos, and a bunch of vampires would somehow be made into candelabras… but still. Some things just couldn't be allowed.

Jee Sun led us to one of the large tables in the Gordon Biersch common room. Four chairs had been placed around the table. With an overly cheery smile, the little girl motioned for me to sit at the head, and for Lucia and Anastasia to take the two chairs that had been placed together. Our guards spread out to form a semicircle behind the femmepires, and Jee Sun went to the only unoccupied chair. For just a moment, it occurred to me that *she* might be Lord Beel-Kasan. Which would have been a little bit weird, frankly, even after the whole Zorana thing.

Instead, she took a position just behind and to the right of the chair, where she stiffened to attention like a miniature soldier. Her voice squeaked as she announced: "Lord Beel-Kasan, Scourge of the Zoroastrians, Lord of Gehenna, God of Nightmares, Terror, and Vindication."

Vindication? Nobody had mentioned that one. It sounded like Lord Beel-Kasan and I had something in common.

I was looking to Lucia and Anastasia when Lord Beel-Kasan chose to make his appearance, so the first thing I saw was the vampires' reactions. Xavier clenched his jaw and one fist. Corey took an uneasy half-step backward from the table. Steve shivered and dropped his eyes. Anastasia gave no reaction at all, and Lucia… the queen tapped her long, opalescent nails on the wooden table as if she was bored.

I wasn't sure if the queen had already mastered her greatest fear or if she was simply too pissed off to let it trouble her.

Dreading what I might see, but knowing I couldn't put it off forever, I turned back to the now-occupied chair. Seated there in all his diabolical glory, the demigod of nightmares appeared before me as…

…a seven-foot-tall spear of asparagus?

What the hell?

Someone had attached two pieces of coal for eyes and a carrot nose, as if he were a skinny green snowman rather than an impossibly large, animated vegetable. A mouth had been crudely drawn with magic marker, just below the carrot. Both coal eyes and carrot rotated slowly around the asparagus body, taking us all in, before the mouth began to move of its own accord.

"Please, call me Bill."

CHAPTER 24

IN WHICH MANY THINGS ARE BROUGHT TO THE TABLE, BUT NONE OF THEM ARE GARLIC FRIES

Eventually my upbringing kicked in. "Hi, Bill. I'm John Smith."

A protuberance appeared from the side of his body, a leafy stalk with a hand on the end of it extending towards me. Bill's skin didn't feel like human flesh or vegetable matter, but something else entirely; cool, moist, and slightly spongy. I very carefully refrained from wiping my own hand on the tablecloth afterward.

The face stayed pointed in my direction, although coal for eyes made it difficult to know exactly what he was looking at. His mouth was even weirder. Beyond the fact that it was drawn by magic marker, I mean. There were no teeth visible. There was no cavity or gaping maw. In fact, were it not for that marker outline, I wouldn't have even known there was supposed to be a mouth. And yet, he was able to speak. Weird.

"You're taking this REALLY well for a human." The hand-drawn mouth wriggled as Bill confided in me. His voice was deep, with a slight Southern twang. Maybe that was normal for vegetables? "What do I look like to you? A dead relative? Naked pygmies? A winged bloodshot eyeball?"

Corey twitched at that last one. I guess I knew what he was seeing.

"You look like asparagus, actually. Except... with a face."

"And are you TERRIFIED of asparagus?"

"Not really. I'm a breakfast burrito kind of guy, " I admitted, "but I do eat my vegetables."

"Huh." Bill pondered that for a while. "Is it possible that you're broken?"

Lucia grew impatient with our meeting of the minds and interjected. "Mr. Smith's mind appears to be shielded from our gifts as well."

Bill's mouth turned upside down into a cartoon frown. "Well, that explains—" The coal eyes rotated around the shaft of asparagus to point in Lucia's direction. "DO NOT WIGGLE YOUR FACE TO ME, QUEEN OF REFUSE AND THIEF OF MOONBEAMS!" One of the few working lights above us blew out in a shower of sparks and glass. In the deepening gloom, something unseen stirred with a rasp of scales on stone.

Jee Sun's smile never wavered.

I didn't even see Lucia move. She went from being seated one moment to standing several feet away the next. Her lovely features were twisted in rage, and I shivered as a cold wind blew through the empty restaurant. Around her, Xavier and his Watch prepared for battle.

"Stop!"

I wondered what moron had just jumped into the middle of that war zone... and then realized it was once again me. Just that quickly, I was the center of attention for both vampires and demigod. I couldn't speak for whatever beast lurked in the darkness, but even Jee Sun had turned to look in my direction.

"Can we all take a breath, sit back down, and *not* start Armageddon?"

Nobody moved.

I tried again. "Normally, the point of a mediation is to reach an agreement without the expense of a lawsuit or courtroom." I'd read that on Wikipedia, when Juliette finally granted me ten minutes of carefully chaperoned internet access. "For us, it's bigger than that. We're here to avoid a war. If you want to work with me towards that goal, that's great. Maybe we can make some progress tonight." I looked from Lucia to Bill and back. "But if you'd rather just jump straight to murdering each other, at least give me a running head start. My family, friends, and I will head for Arizona, while you all get wiped out for breaking the Concordat."

Lucia gave me a hard look, but she returned to her chair with a muttered oath. Her guards relaxed, once again tucking away the weaponry they weren't supposed to have brought with them. Anastasia was the lone vampire who'd kept her seat during Bill's outburst. She watched me from her chair, projecting an air of calm and confidence.

I turned to Bill. Again, he frowned, but the shattered light bulb slowly reformed in its socket and began to glow. Something slithered away from us and faded into the darkness.

"Thank you." I couldn't believe that had actually worked. "Obviously, tensions are high." And craziness was running amok, but that wasn't the sort of thing you said to the inmates at the asylum. "Assuming Bill agrees to me being mediator, we're going to have to set up some ground rules. Especially if we want Gordon Biersch to still be standing tomorrow." Which reminded me… "Why did you pick this place, anyway, Bill?"

"I once knew a monkey named Gordon," he replied sulkily. "He wouldn't eat the bananas."

"Right. So… rules. First, rather than having you address each other directly, let's have all communication go through me, OK? That might lessen the shouting and chance of mayhem."

I didn't get agreement from either side… but I also didn't get stabbed or boiled alive. I took that as a win.

"Second, if you *do* lose your temper, take a break and walk away until you calm down. We're not going to be able to accomplish anything at that point anyway. Cool?"

Lucia gave me a stiff nod and immediately pushed away from the table to stalk deeper into the restaurant. Which wasn't quite what I'd been hoping for. Xavier and the nameless fourth Watch member trailed behind the queen, while Steve and Corey held their positions by Anastasia.

I turned to Bill, who was back to being armless. His mouth was wobbling up and down, but I couldn't hear any words. Talking to himself, maybe? There was no way to know for sure. However, Lucia's absence did offer an opportunity of sorts.

"Bill, I get the sense that you're the sort of demigod who appreciates honesty." No reply, but his face rotated back in my direction. Well, most of it did. One eye stayed behind, presumably keeping watch for Lucia. "So I'm just going to ask: before I was 'hired' for this job, there was another mediator, known as the Rook, who turned up dead. Do you have any idea what happened to him?"

"I don't know who that even is, Johnny-boy!" he replied. Jee Sun whispered something to him and his mouth became a perfect circle. "OH! THE CORVUS! Squawky little fellow. Never cared for him." He leaned in toward me, which was a neat trick for a vegetable. "He was a WINE drinker!" He turned to Jee Sun. "Did I kill him? Please tell me I killed him!" The young schoolgirl shook her head silently, and Bill's smile faded. "I guess I don't know what happened to Mr. Squawky."

It had been worth a shot. I thanked him and looked around. Lucia was still nowhere to be found. "If you don't mind, Bill, I'd like to get started. I've already heard the People's take on the situation, but it was a little bit short on details. You believe they stole something of yours, and want it back?"

"Belief is for bumblebees, Johnny-on-the-spot." His voice was merry. "I *know* that they stole it, and I MUST HAVE IT BACK." Jee Sun did a slow pirouette behind him to music only she could hear before getting tangled in her red cape.

"OK, let's start there. What is it that was stolen from you, and how?"

He decided to answer the questions out of order. Naturally. "They snuck onto my boat like rats looking for cheese while I was away at an appointment." His smile widened until it stretched around the entirety of his body. "I look in on Barry every Thursday!"

"Barry?" I wasn't sure I wanted to know, but at least he was talking.

"Yes!" he crowed. "Squat guy, very hairy, with a fear of balloons! *Globophobia*... it's one of my favorites, you know? And so very rare!"

"Sounds like a party." There were times when you just had to accept things and move on. "So, knowing that you'd be off tormenting someone with balloons, they came onto your boat, and stole... what, exactly?"

His entire body shivered. "THEY STOLE IT!" His chair began to rock from one leg to another, and a crack in the floor appeared between us. Instead of the building's foundation, or the city dirt below that, I caught a glimpse of some sort of desert abyss. Were those *people* mounted on silver fixtures...?

The crevice vanished as quickly as it had appeared. I looked up to find Jee Sun poking Bill with one finger. His magic marker mouth frowned, but he stood up and moved away from the table. Jee Sun walked with him, one small arm wrapped around his mid-section. I was so relieved that they were heading in the opposite direction of Lucia that it didn't occur to me to wonder how Bill could be walking, given that he lacked both legs and feet.

"And then there were none." I looked down the table at Anastasia. "Still think I was the right person for the job?"

"We are still alive, Mr. Smith," she pointed out, "and they seem to be obeying your rules. All is not lost."

"Bill seems pretty convinced that the People stole whatever it is that he is missing. I know Lucia's not in the mood to even entertain the thought but... is it possible?"

"Our House is large and has many members, Mr. Smith, but we are not thieves. To do such would be a betrayal of all our House stands for." Her eyes met mine as she was speaking, and she narrowed her eyes.

Oh, right. The anti-House conspiracy. So, it was possible, but if so, whoever had done so was probably the same person who had killed the Rook and hired the karkino.

I looked to my left, and found Bill back in his chair, with Jee Sun nowhere to be seen. "Sorry about that, Johnny Dangerous. I got a little bit hot under the collar. HA HA! What was it you wanted to know?"

"The item that was stolen. Can you describe it to me?"

He was silent for a bit, and I watched nervously for cracks in the floor. Finally, two arms grew out of his body. He waved them about in the air. "It's bigger than a breadbox, roughly square in shape, and has a light grey top and a dark grey bottom." I couldn't read his expression, mainly because he didn't have actual features, but I got the impression that he was looking at me hopefully.

"Did it have any other distinguishing features?"

"Nope nope nope." He actually rotated his face back and forth about his body to simulate shaking his head. "Oh. Well, it did have some words on it."

Now we were getting somewhere. "That's great, Bill. Can you remember what those words were?"

His mouth briefly became one straight horizontal line. "Of course I can, John. I'm not a moron." He waited for me to acknowledge the point, then continued. "They said *Nintendo Entertainment System.*"

CHAPTER 25

IN WHICH ONE CONSOLE IS WORTH A CITY

"Someone stole a *video game console* from your boat?"

"That's what I've been telling you! And not someone. THEM."

"Bill, could I just *buy* you another one? Those old Nintendos sell for like $50 on eBay."

He shook his face stubbornly. "It must be that one. It must be recovered. And the THIEVES MUST BE REPAID IN BLOOD AND FIRE."

I tried again. "Is it a… magic Nintendo?"

Bill's mouth became a smile. "You are very silly, Johnny-come-lately."

"Right." I mentally scratched my head. "So, the issue here is that your Nintendo was stolen, and you want it back." Out of the corner of my eye, I saw Lucia and her escorts returning to the table. Unfortunately, I wasn't sure we'd made any real progress in her absence. "Is there any tangible evidence that it was taken by the People? Like you said, you were away at the time."

"I was, but Jee Sun was not," he replied affably. The girl in question stepped out of the shadows behind him and assumed her customary position. "Tiny Flower, tell Mr. Smith what you saw."

"They took the Nintendo box!" Jee Sun bounced up and down, waving one hand about wildly. She now held a detached controller for the console in question.

"Thank you, Jee Sun." Honestly, she creeped me out more than the immortal asparagus. "Could you, by any chance, *describe* the ones that took the box?"

She nodded, and did another pirouette in her Mary Janes. "Yes, Mr. John!"

I waited.

She smiled.

Eventually, I realized my mistake.

"Please tell us what they looked like."

She screwed up her face in concentration, causing her large glasses to inch up her nose. "They were yellow," she finally decided.

"Yellow?"

"Yes!" she agreed happily. "Yellow!" This time, she gestured towards the vampires on the other side of the table. The controller cord swung out in an arc, nearly smacking me in the face. Once again, her Supergirl cape fluttered in a non-existent breeze, and once again, I decided to ignore the phenomenon.

"Am I yellow, Jee Sun?"

She giggled, sounding more like an infant than a young girl. "No, Mr. John! You don't have a color! You're like me!"

It's a sign of how much my head was spinning that I actually looked to Bill for an explanation. "What does yellow mean?"

His mouth formed a round circle of surprise at my ignorance. "It means vampire, of course!"

"So, she sees colors instead of faces?"

"I see faces!" asserted Jun See with a pout. "Only monsters have colors." She snuggled up to the seven-foot tall asparagus demigod, sticking her lower lip out as far as it would go.

"And only vampires are yellow?" She nodded, still pouting for all she was worth. "What color is Bill?"

The outrage on her face was remarkable. She shook the controller at me threateningly. "Mr. Bill is not a monster!"

"So he doesn't have a color?"

"He's green," she admitted.

"Thanks, Jee Sun." On the reliable eye-witness scale, she fell somewhere between crack-head and narcoleptic. I turned to the vampire queen. "I assume you heard everything that's been said to this point?"

She nodded imperiously, sitting straight-backed in the restaurant chair as if it were a throne.

"Great. So what are your thoughts on the matter?" I reminded myself that my role in mediation was to facilitate discussion, rather than to try and solve the mess single-handed. Thank God. Or gods. Or demi... maybe I needed to hold off on that sort of phrasing entirely until I had a better grasp on my own belief system.

Lucia didn't even look at Bill, which was probably for the best. Despite having returned to the table, her crystal blue eyes were even colder than normal. "I think the whole thing is absurd. A lunatic demigod misplaces his archaic entertainment device and accuses my kind of thievery because a defective human child saw the color *yellow*? Come now, Mr. Smith. We are rational creatures. You know this is a farce."

I resisted the urge to duck under the table. I also resisted the urge to leap *over* that same table, tackling Anastasia to the ground and shielding her from the impending magical fallout. Which would have been a noble, but ultimately stupid gesture, considering she was way tougher than me.

Halfway through my internal debate, I realized something important: I was still alive. The restaurant remained in one piece. None of us had been forcibly mounted on candlesticks. In fact, nothing at all had happened. I looked over at Bill, and found his inhuman face regarding me.

"Did *you* hear something, Mr. Smith? *I* didn't hear anything at all." His mouth quirked upward and his charcoal eyes scooted around his body to point at Lucia, in case I needed the hint that he was actively ignoring the vampire queen. If he'd had a tongue, it would have been sticking out at her.

It was childish and it was stupid, but with the alternative being fiery oblivion, I kind of loved the big, green bastard for it. Next to him, Jee Sun had extended one hand towards Lucia, making a very non-child-like gesture. Clearly, she hadn't liked being called defective. I offered Bill a grateful smile, and turned back to the vampire.

"It's an unusual story, but it should be easy enough to verify. If you'll just let Lord Beel-Kasan into the House to look for his—"

"That *thing* is not setting foot in my domain," snarled Lucia.

I gave her a look of exasperation. Was she actively *trying* to start a war? Anastasia, my supposed ally, remained silent in her chair. No help there.

"Fantastic." I turned to Bill. "What if the People searched their House for your Nintendo? If it's there, they can find it and return it to you."

His entire body quivered in outrage. "Why would I trust the THIEVES to look for that which they already STOLE?" Jee Sun had stopped flashing Lucia the one-fingered bird, but nodded angrily in agreement, mouthing the word *yellow* as she did so.

"Call us thieves again, demigod, and you will spend eternity bleeding from all seven of your limbs!" Xavier had decided to involve himself in the discussion, because there wasn't already enough ego being thrown about.

And... seven limbs? I had no idea what the hell he was seeing when he looked at Bill.

"You!" I pointed at the angry Captain. "Shut the hell up or get out of here. You're not helping." It felt pretty damn good to yell at him, until I remembered his demonstration in the training facilities. Despite all evidence to the contrary, I really didn't want to piss him off. He took a step toward me, and I tried not to flinch.

Anastasia was (still!) silent in her chair, but Lucia halted Xavier's advance with a cold look and an irritated wave of her hand. "I speak for the honor of this House, Captain. Not you. If you cannot control yourself, I will send you outside to wait with the humans."

I shared a confused look with Jee Sun, before realizing that Lucia was talking about her drivers.

To nobody's surprise, Xavier decided to stick around. He contented himself with brooding moodily from a distance, looking like an extra from Twilight or any of a dozen television shows on the CW. If anyone deserved a trip to candelabra land...

Lucia and Bill were both watching me expectantly.

"Hmm." I muttered intelligently, having completely lost my train of thought. Let's see. Yellow. Leather. Armageddon. Middle fingers. Oh, right: searching the House. "What if we had a neutral party perform the search? Someone that you, Queen Lucia, would accept in your House, and who you, Lord Beel-Kasan, would trust to be truthful with you. There has to be at least one unaligned group in the city that you both would trust?" I had my first truly brilliant thought of the night. "What about the Mer?"

"The Mer are ocean-dwellers, Mr. Smith," Lucia reminded me. "They would drown soon after leaving sea water."

Right. Not as brilliant as I'd hoped.

"Why don't you perform the search, Mr. Smith?" Anastasia *finally* spoke, proving that she was both the smartest person in the room and still perfectly willing to use me in whichever manner she deemed fitting.

"Me?" I squeaked, but both Bill and Lucia were already nodding.

"My Secundus speaks wisely," acknowledged Lucia. "I have no objection to Mr. Smith performing a non-invasive search of my House."

"And I'm convinced that Johnny-be-good is a right proper enchilada," agreed Bill. Which I could only assume meant he was also okay with the idea.

"Okay. I'll do it. Happily." I regarded my vegetable client. "Bill, if I find your special Nintendo and return it to you, will we be able to put this whole disagreement behind us?"

"Of course," he said, his magic-marker mouth smiling widely at me. "All I want is my box and THE HEADS AND HEARTS OF THOSE RESPONSIBLE."

Well, shit.

ooo

The mediation stalled at that point, predictably. The good news was that Bill had accepted me as mediator and we had agreed on the first course of action. Oh, and nobody had died. Fear my mad skills.

The bad news was sobering.

First, even if I did somehow find the missing game console, I didn't think I'd be able to prevent a war. Bill wanted blood, but the queen was never going to agree to hand over one of her subjects to the demigod's tender mercies. So, while it was great that we had made some progress on our very first night, it felt a bit like we'd painted a smiley face on a nuclear warhead. For all our efforts, that warhead was still primed to take out the west coast.

Second, the task Anastasia had volunteered me for was basically impossible. Over the previous two days, I'd seen sections of five of the House's six floors, and the one thing they all had in common was that they were Godzilla-sized. Meanwhile, a Nintendo was roughly a foot wide, eight inches deep, and a couple of inches high.

This wasn't just a needle in a haystack. It was a needle in a football stadium... featuring a needle that could be moved at any time by the thieves.

Bill had an answer to that issue, at least. As I was preparing to go, Jee Sun came to my side and poked me in the ribs. Which seemed really unnecessary, given that I had both seen and heard her approach. That bright red cape wasn't exactly stealthy. When she finally realized that she had my attention, she handed over the Nintendo controller she'd been waving about like a weapon. "This will take you to the box, Mr. John, when you're in the yellow castle."

I looked over her head at Bill. "Wait, so it *is* a magic Nintendo?"

He and Jee Sun both giggled, the girl skipping back over to again hug her demigod.

"Cheerio cheerio, and when Johnny comes marching home again with our box, hurrah tada. I will be on our boat, unless I am not on our boat, in which case I will be SOMEWHERE ELSE. Call me?" Bill grew an arm for the sole purpose of making the telephone sign with his thumb and pinky finger.

I nodded, but he and Jee Sun disappeared, before I could get his number. It wasn't like they'd been beamed up in Star Trek, or the darkness had washed over them and swallowed them whole, or anything like that. They just... weren't there anymore.

As I followed the vampires out of the restaurant, the lights began turning off behind us, one by one. Eventually, only a single light remained. I knew without looking that it was the bulb Bill had destroyed and then resurrected. I also strongly suspected it would never go dark again.

Hell of a party trick.

○○○

The security protocols for departing were every bit as complicated as they had been upon arrival. The drivers brought the Escalades around to the front of the restaurant, where they kept their engines running. Xavier flowed out at vampire speed to open the rear passenger door of the lead car so that Lucia could enter. By contrast, the queen positively strolled to the car, arrogant and unafraid.

When she was seated within, Xavier joined her, and the unnamed vampire took a seat riding shotgun. The door closed, their car peeled out of the lot with a squeal of rubber, and it was our turn to repeat the dance. As Bob began to accelerate out of the lot, I had the urge to yell out *The package is secure! Repeat: the package is secure!* at the top of my lungs... but that was probably my tension talking. That or the fact that I'd watched a lot of terrible spy movies as a kid.

We were stopped at a red light, a block away from the overpass that would take us onto the 8, when I leaned forward between Bob and Steve. "Is anyone else hungry?"

Corey piped up from the back seat. "I could definitely eat."

I pointed down the road to our left. "There's an In-n-Out in the shopping center just past the mall. All those in favor?"

A chorus of ayes filled the Escalade. If there's one thing most Californians can agree on, it's that In-n-Out is the greatest burger chain in the history of the world. The universe, maybe. Even Bob chimed in with an agreement, bless his human heart.

Crap. Now *I* was starting to sound like a racist.

It was only when Steve looked to Anastasia that I realized she had remained silent. Unfortunately, she was also the final authority and decision maker in our car.

I turned to her. "What do you think, Anastasia? I can't speak for the rest of the guys, but I suspect my ability to find Bill's Nintendo and save the House from a costly war would be improved with a double-double. And some fries. And maybe a vanilla shake."

That won a small smile from her, which made Steve blink in surprise. "Very well. I think we could all do with some nourishment." As Bob hit the blinker and slid over into the left-hand turn lane, Anastasia held up an ultra-thin cell phone and speed-dialed a number. "Your Majesty, we are stopping to get food, and will meet you back at the House."

I watched her closely after the phone call, trying to figure out where she'd produced the phone from in the first place. She sure as hell didn't have any pockets. I'd looked. Several times. A quality private investigator always keeps his skills sharp.

Sensing my interest, Lady Dumenyova quirked an eyebrow and gave me a long, cool glance, phone still in hand.

Blushing for no reason at all, I turned away and pretended to be interested in the night sky.

Oh, neat; stars.

CHAPTER 26

IN WHICH ICE CREAM CURES THE BLUES

Grandpa Chuck died when I was five. He wasn't the first of my grandparents to go, but his death was the first that I was old enough to really experience. I don't remember crying, even at the wake, where I couldn't bring myself to believe the object in the coffin was really him, but I do remember being confused, sad, and a little bit scared. If death could happen to the kindly old man who'd always had a new magic trick for me, it could happen to anyone. For almost a week, I did cry whenever my parents left the room, convinced that I would never see them again.

Finally, my dad bundled me into the car and drove until we had reached the most magical place on earth: Baskin Robbins. He bought a banana split for us to share, and as I dug into the gooey chocolate syrup and ice cream, he talked to me about death, about life, and about how the two were part of a natural cycle and something something something.

I don't remember exactly what he said; I was five. I mostly remember how good the ice cream tasted, the way I managed to get chocolate all over my grubby little fingers, and the deep satisfaction I felt when the sundae was entirely consumed.

Then and now, I knew that there was nothing so dire that it couldn't be improved, in some fashion, by food.

And so, as Bob drove us back up the 15, I found myself looking at the current situation with fresh optimism. Yes, there were a lot of obstacles, and the slightest misstep would mean the end of San Diego as we knew it, but the immediate task was simple enough. In the morning, I'd walk the house with the Nintendo controller. If I didn't find the console, I could tell Bill as much, and he'd have to look for someone else to threaten with his vegetable wrath. Problem solved.

If I *did* find the Nintendo…

Well, we'd cross that bridge when we had to.

In the seat behind me, Corey polished off his third double-double. That boy ate like a champion, not that you'd know it by looking at him. Steve had finished two burgers of his own, plus a large chocolate shake and fries, and appeared to be blissfully entering a food coma. Even his mohawk seemed relaxed. And Anastasia…

"I can't believe you've never eaten at In-n-Out before. And you've been in San Diego for *how* long?" The elegant vampire had a paper place mat in her lap over her leather pants, and was slowly finishing her own meal. She seemed bemused by the whole experience.

"Since well before your birth, Mr. Smith." She wiped her mouth delicately with a paper napkin, and set the container aside. "That was not my usual fare, but it was enjoyable nonetheless."

"Next time, you can choose where we eat. We can go to one of your usual spots." Yes, I was *definitely* feeling optimistic. Vanilla shakes have that effect on me.

She gave me a considering look, which warmed me every bit as her rare smiles. "You'd have to wear a tie, Mr. Smith," she teased.

"For you?" I grinned the slow, easy grin of a man with a full stomach. "It's a date, Lady Dumenyova."

Behind me, Corey choked.

Served him right for eating so much.

ooo

My second time seeing the vampire house was no less an event than the first. If anything, it was even more impressive at night. Jee Sun had called it 'the yellow castle,' and the high walls surrounding the estate grounds did bring to mind those of a medieval fortress. So did the gatehouse access-point, staffed by armed human security guards who carefully verified our identities before opening the heavy iron gate.

Street lamps lined the driveway and ringed the house in golden light, making a stealthy approach virtually impossible. Those lamps also offered occasional glimpses of the additional guards who patrolled the grounds, from the orchards on our left all the way to the small pond down the hill on the right.

When we came to the building itself though, only the Midnight Tower, rising into the air like an apocryphal middle finger, looked the part of a medieval institution. It was almost ten, but a number of interior lights were still on, visible through windows on the second and third floors.

I tried, in vain, to determine which dark window was mine.

The wide driveway forked as we neared the House, one path descending to the underground garage. Bob drove all the way up the hill instead, parking in the loading zone and allowing us to disembark. Two additional human guards flanked the massive wooden doors, outfitted in the Kevlar and assault rifle combo that was all the rage with paramilitary types.

"If the mediation does go belly-up, you all seem ready to fight a war," I murmured to Anastasia.

"Xavier and Andrés are both determined that we will not suffer a repeat of 2003," she acknowledged. "None of us like relying so heavily upon an outside security firm, but there is something to be said for overwhelming force as a deterrent."

"Why hasn't the U.S. Government flagged this property as a place of interest?"

"Because we told them not to." Her lips curved in quiet amusement.

The ground floor was dimly lit and empty except for a small number of human servants. We proceeded through the foyer to the elevators. For once, I would have been okay with taking the stairs, but nobody else seemed overly concerned with working off the fast food we had just consumed.

Steve and Corey said their goodbyes and took one elevator down to one of the sub-levels while Anastasia and I entered the other. I went to push the button for my floor, only to pause and look over at Anastasia.

"Yes, Mr. Smith?"

"If I'm going to wear a tie for you, you *will* eventually have to call me John," I teased.

She smiled, but said nothing.

"Anyway, I just realized that I have no idea what floor your room is on."

Anastasia regarded me evenly, an indecipherable expression on her beautiful face. Then, with a smile that would have done the Mona Lisa proud, she leaned past me to press the buttons for both the second and third floors. Her hip brushed mine and her delicate scent, mixed in with the almost imperceptible smell of leather, swirled about us.

I'm fairly certain I forgot to breathe, and not just because I'd had onions on my burger.

Without a word, she returned to the other side of the elevator.

Either Anastasia had no idea what she was doing to me, or Juliette wasn't the only vampire that enjoyed screwing with my head. Her voice, however, was matter-of-fact. "I would not advise visiting the third floor unannounced, Mr. Smith. It is reserved as living space for the council, and the Watch on that level look poorly on uninvited guests."

I nodded my understanding, as the doors closed. "I'll need access tomorrow though. I'm going to have to search every floor when looking for Lord Beel-Kasan's uhm... lost item." With the asparagus demigod far away, the notion of a Nintendo scavenger hunt was seeming more and more ludicrous.

"I will alert them to that fact, if Her Majesty has not already done so. Even with an appointment, it is unlikely you will be allowed to wander without a chaperone."

"I'm getting kind of used to that." The doors opened on the second floor, but I stayed put. "If there *is* a thief, what's to prevent them from smuggling the Nintendo out of the house ahead of our search?"

"It's a good question." I puffed up with pride that slowly dissipated as she continued. "Which is why Queen Lucia has restricted knowledge of the impending search to those of us at the mediation.

And ordered that nobody be allowed off the grounds until tomorrow night."

"How do you know that?" Other than the brief phone call she'd made to let Lucia know about our fast food detour, Anastasia hadn't spoken with the queen since leaving the mediation.

"Because I suggested she do so, Mr. Smith, upon your agreement to search the House."

"Back in Gordon Biersch?"

"Indeed."

"Wow. You know, you'd make a pretty great private investigator yourself, Lady Dumenyova."

"It is no longer my focus, but I have many, many years of experience in matters of security."

I grinned again, not even caring as the elevator doors tried— and failed—to close for the fourth time. A full belly and a beautiful woman who smelled fantastic and hadn't threatened to kill me in more than a day? What could be better? "How many years exactly, would you say?"

"A lady never tells."

She was *definitely* flirting. At least... I thought so. I finally exited the elevator, only to turn and look back at the lovely vampire. "Are you sure I'll be safe walking all the way to my room unchaperoned?"

"Good night, Mr. Smith." Jade eyes sparkled as the elevator doors closed between us.

oOo

The second floor was still busy, even at this time of night. I passed a handful of vampires, Watch and otherwise, on my way back to my room. I even saw a few humans, presumably blood donors like Darlene. None of them seemed concerned that I was wandering about on my lonesome, and none of them seemed particularly interested in kidnapping me and killing me in an empty bedroom. I decided that Juliette had, yet again, just been screwing with me that morning.

The kitchen was packed, and there seemed to be a fantastic quantity of beer being consumed, but I was way too tired to deal with more socialization. As every good mediator knows, a tension-filled encounter with an insane demigod can suck the energy right out of you. I pushed open my door and stepped into the dark room with a sense of relief.

I'm not the world's smartest man. I'm not even the neighborhood's smartest man and my neighborhood in Chula Vista isn't exactly crawling with Ivy Leaguers. Some people were put on this earth to solve complicated formulas and create things that make the world better, one brightly colored gadget at a time, but I am not one of those people. I'm not even one of the people that can afford to buy their gadgets. In the ongoing cycle of world improvement, I'm largely a spectator and I'm okay with that. It's kind of the unofficial philosophy of beach culture; when confronted with an unpleasant truth about yourself, shrug, drink a beer (or smoke a bowl), and move on with your life.

But I'm not a complete moron either. I occasionally learn from my mistakes, and I'm even pretty good at recognizing the patterns that I see around me. That last part was the reason I'd thought I could be successful as a private investigator, and the only reason my parents had co-signed the office lease.

So when I closed my bedroom door, I didn't just strip down and hop into bed as I'd done the previous night. Instead, I reached over and turned on the lights. I placed my suit coat on a hanger in the walk-in closet, where it looked forlorn and lonely all by itself. Then I turned to the femmepire sitting in one of the tableside chairs and nodded a greeting. "Hello, Juliette. How long have you been waiting?"

"Since Lucia and Xavier returned." Her tone was light, but her yellow eyes were hard. "No one will tell me what happened in your mediation with Lord Beel-Kasan."

Ah. That explained it. And her current snit.

"So you decided to seek out the one person you thought you could intimidate into talking?" I took a seat in the chair next to hers, rolling my eyes. "I can't tell you how loved that makes me feel."

"Little bird, intimidation only needs to come into play if you…" She stopped and looked at me, nostrils flaring. "What have you been *doing* with her?"

"With who?"

She narrowed her eyes, unamused. Vampire senses were scary good. I was starting to think all those comments about my smell hadn't just been hyperbole.

"Anastasia? Nothing."

"Then why do you smell of her? Like she rubbed herself all over you?"

"Maybe because we shared a car *and* an elevator? How can you smell anything over the burgers and grease anyway?" Juliette's yellow eyes were glowing, which was pretty cool, but also something I was starting to recognize as a Bad Sign. "Seriously, Duchess… what is your problem?"

She was out of the chair in a blur, looming over me. "What is my problem?" she hissed. "First, I'm excluded from the mediation with Lord Beel-Kasan, then I'm informed the details of that meeting are confidential, despite my being a member of the freaking COUNCIL! And then you waltz in here a half hour late, reeking of the vampire who I *told you* was a traitor!"

"So," I asked archly, "you're *not* just jealous?"

And just like that, I was airborne.

Only the thickness of the carpet and my half-remembered adolescent lessons on how to fall saved me from serious injury. Mostly the carpet. Not being naked this time helped too. Even so, the wind was knocked out of me. I rolled onto my back, looking frantically for Juliette.

The good news was that, after physically throwing me across the room, the Duchess of Snark had returned to her chair, which put me a solid eight feet beyond her immediate reach. The bad news was that she could cross that distance in an instant, and her eyes were *still* glowing. I needed to get a handle on the situation before she killed me. I wracked my brain for something safe and diplomatic to say.

"You are such an obnoxious, pain-in-the-ass, vampire punk!"

That really, really wasn't it.

"The world doesn't revolve around you, Juliette. If you'd stopped to check, you'd have seen that Lucia didn't inform Marcus or Andrés of the details of the mediation either, and they're on the council, older than you *and* Lucia's pals from Europe."

She scowled but said nothing.

"Also, I'm getting *really damn tired* of being tossed around by you people whenever something doesn't go your way. Learn some freaking impulse control, damn it!"

It was, in retrospect, a textbook example of the pot calling the kettle black.

Juliette's mouth twitched, like she was struggling not to smile. We looked at each other across the room for a long moment, the silence broken only by the low hum of the ceiling fan. Then, as if on cue, we both began to laugh.

"Did you," she snickered, "of all people, just lecture me on self-control?" Her snicker turned into a full-scale cackle as she saw my expression.

"I knew it was dumb the moment I said it," I admitted, struggling to contain my own laughter. "But seriously... can we just talk for a moment, like halfway-civilized beings?"

"Civilized..." Juliette looked down at her Sex Pistols tee and then over at me, and broke down again. The femmepire actually snorted when she laughed, which was enough to set me off. If the bedroom hadn't been soundproofed, we'd have drawn a crowd.

By the time our laughter started to peter out, my stomach was hurting and I was once again finding it hard to breathe. Juliette waved a hand. "Alright, alright... we'll talk."

"And you're not going to beat me up anymore?" I was still sucking wind like I'd just run a mile. Or even a quarter-mile.

"It depends." She flashed her trademark smirk. "Are you going to tell me what happened at the mediation?"

"And disobey Her Majesty Queen Lucia's express instructions to the contrary, despite my deep and abiding love for authority figures?" I gave a mock gasp of horror, then grinned. "Of course."

CHAPTER 27

IN WHICH PROPOSITIONS ARE REJECTED AND PLANS ARE MADE

It took a while to bring Juliette up to speed, and I had to dig the Nintendo controller out of my jacket pocket before she accepted that I wasn't just making everything up. Afterward, I took a quick break to brush my teeth. Goodbye, onion breath! When I came back out into the bedroom, she was idly toying with the controller.

"I remember when I had one of these," she confided. "Great little system for its day, but I'm not sure I understand why a demigod would be so desperate to get one back."

"Apparently, it's a magic Nintendo."

She gave me a dismissive look. "Magic doesn't work that way, little bird. Still," she mused, "there has to be some reason for him to value it so highly. The old Nintendos are getting a little bit long in the tooth these days."

"You would know," I agreed, and then winced when I heard what I'd said. "Sorry... what I meant to say is that I never owned one, myself."

"No?" She smirked. "Were you *naughty* that year? Couldn't convince Santa to leave one for you under the tree?"

"I hadn't even been born yet. My first console was the PlayStation."

"But..." It was kind of fun watching the emotions play across Juliette's normally fierce features.

"I'm only twenty-five, Juliette. The Nintendo came out almost three years before I was born." The fact that I knew that off the top of my head said a lot about the state of my social life.

Juliette ran a hand through her short hair as she mulled it over. I was amused to see the spikes pop right back up as soon as her hand had moved on. Either she was using some serious product or vampires had hair-related superpowers nobody had told me about.

"I can't believe it's already been that long," she muttered. "I remember the first time I played Super Mario Bros. like it was yesterday." She turned a yellow-eyed look of horror in my direction. "You're a baby!"

"Juliette, my parents might be considered babies by your standards."

That got her attention. "Exactly how old do you think I am?"

Even without my conversation with Anastasia in the elevator, I knew a loaded question when I heard one. "I don't really know..."

"Take a guess."

"Juliette, seriously..."

"*Guess.*"

"Hell, I don't know... maybe a hundred?" I braced for the inevitable blow.

Instead, a genuine smile broke out on her face. "Really? One-hundred-years old?"

I moved slowly, sensing some sort of trap. "Maybe?"

Juliette tossed the controller up and snatched it out of the air without even looking. She was beaming. "I'm only seventy-nine, Mr. Mediator, but thank you for the compliment!"

My over-guessing her age by twenty-something years being a *good* thing threw me for a loop. Then I remembered that age equated to power for vampires. Being older was actually a positive.

It was a weird concept, given my species' attitude towards our own elderly. Twenty-one had been the last birthday I'd looked forward to at all, and anything after forty was reportedly a terrifying downward spiral of hair loss, senility, and incontinence.

If the Christian God actually existed, and I did choose to start worshipping Him again, He and I were going to have some strong words about the shitty hand He'd dealt mankind.

"You're welcome. Anyway, I can't imagine your blood donors are much older than I am, are they?"

She shrugged, continuing to fiddle with the controller. "I have no idea. Until your hair goes grey or starts to fall out, most humans look the same age to me. You know, somewhere between twenty and fifty."

"You've never asked them?"

"They're blood donors, little bird, not tea party socialites. Do you hold discussions with *your* food?"

"Well, no. But my food is dead and cooked, and not a living, breathing intelligent species. I don't think it's the same thing."

"I'm not convinced," she replied thoughtfully, "that humans *are* an intelligent species. While all three of my donors are lovely blood bags in their own way, they're strictly temporary."

"I'm afraid to ask, but... temporary?" Why did I always end up playing the straight man in Juliette's comedy routines?

"I lost Claude and Diana in 2003. Since then, I've just foraged from the House larder."

I had a sudden image of a large room with humans stacked atop each other like firewood.

"However, I *am* looking for a more permanent donor solution. How about it, little bird? Feel like doing something useful with the rest of your miserable, short life?" Juliette gave me a suggestive look that somehow blended pure contempt, sexual invitation, and homicidal menace. She casually extended both canines and ran her tongue down the length of one of them.

"If that's your sales pitch, I know why you're stuck with temporary donors. You're not going to attract the cream of the crop by flashing fang."

"You'd prefer another kind of flashing, I assume?" Before I could respond, she shook her head. "Wait, what am I thinking? Someone like you would prefer..." Placing her hands in her lap, she looked at me with her eyes wide. "Help me Obi-John Smith. You're my only hope!"

I swallowed.

"That would do it." And then some. Star Wars may have been released way, way before my time, but my dad had insured I'd grown up loving the franchise as much as he did. "But I'm a little bit busy with the whole mediation thing, not to mention the possible conspiracy to destabilize the House."

"Another time then. I'd love to hear exactly how you plan to proceed with your investigation. The Stone Lady is many things, but she's not so stupid as to just give in to your feeble charm and confess."

"Yeah. About that. If there's a conspiracy—and I'm still not convinced there is—I don't think Anastasia is behind it."

"Are you *serious*? Oh, for the love of—" She jumped out of her chair and began pacing angrily, her boots leaving deep impressions in the plush carpet. "I leave you alone for just a few hours and she warps your peanut-sized brain. It was the leather, wasn't it? Put a woman in leather and suddenly boys are falling over themselves to proclaim her innocence."

"Of course not." Even as I said it, I realized it was true. Anastasia had the brains, the motive, and the resources to have orchestrated the whole thing, but I just didn't buy it. It was little more than gut instinct, but that was the sort of thing we investigators got used to listening to.

"Yeah, right. She buys you a burger and you immediately lose all perspective. What reason could you possibly have to think she was innocent?"

"For starters, she hired me to look into the conspiracy last night, a good ten hours before you did. And she thought *you* were the most likely suspect."

"What? That *bitch*!" Juliette seethed. Then her voice got quiet and dangerous. "And you took the case?"

"Well, yeah. But," I assured her, "I told her that you couldn't have been responsible."

"Of course I'm n—" Another pregnant pause. "How were you so sure?"

Oops. Something told me that citing her lack of patience, subtlety and strategic mindset wouldn't go over well. "It just didn't seem your style," I said instead. "Besides, I couldn't see what your motive would be."

"And what did the great Lady Anastasia Dumenyova have to say to that?"

"Well, she said there's a divide between the American and European vampires and that you might not be as happy in the House as you'd anticipated."

"Huh." Juliette's voice lost its edge as she considered the idea. "Well, she's not wrong about that…"

"So you *are* a suspect?"

I didn't even see the hand that lightly smacked me on the back of the head.

"Of course not, idiot. My future is linked with this House. If it falls, I'd be unaligned, and as I've already told you, that's not a safe way to live in the new millennium."

"Aren't there other Houses in the U.S.? Chicago and New York?" I vaguely remembered Anastasia mentioning both.

Juliette looked away, pensive. "I grew up in the New York House. There may have been a few… incidents." She noticed the smile I was trying to hide, and snapped, "Why the hell do you think I started a flock in San Diego, of all places? I wasn't spoiled for choice!"

"Half the country wants to live here," I pointed out. "I assumed you'd come for the beaches."

"New York has beaches too. And the water is a hell of a lot warmer." She shrugged. "The surf is nice here though and you can't beat the weather."

"Okay, so you're not going to do something that would wreck your only House. And I don't think Anastasia has any desire to do so either. So that rules you both out. What now?"

"You're the detective, little bird. I'm just the irresistible badass who hired you to figure this all out for me."

I gave it some thought. My cases usually involved married people having affairs in seedy motels. Unraveling a grand conspiracy was well outside my wheelhouse. "At this point, the only indication of a conspiracy is that someone pissed off Bill and a bunch of mediators are dead. Unless something else happens, that's all we have to go on. The first step then is to look into the incidents. We could try to track down the karkino and see if they'll tell us who hired them—"

Juliette's swift head shake told me that wasn't going to work.

"—or we can take a closer look at the one murder that the karkino weren't involved in."

"We need to get a look at the Rook's house," Juliette agreed, "and without anyone else knowing. Including Anastasia." I started to object, but she cut me off. "The fact that she hired you may mean she's innocent. But I *know* I am innocent, and I know *you* are innocent, and that's as far as I'm willing to take things for now. Got it?"

"She could get us access to the murder scene."

"I can do that on my own, thank you very much."

"Fine. See if you can figure out a pretext for getting me out of the House tomorrow night, and we'll go together. In the meantime, I'll search for the game console. Who knows? Maybe we'll have this all wrapped up by Tuesday."

"Do you really believe that?"

"No," I sighed. "That would be way too easy."

CHAPTER 28

IN WHICH NOBODY LIKES A SCAVENGER HUNT

Monday was cold and grey. Cold for San Diego, anyway; it was somewhere in the mid-60s, which just didn't happen very often in July. The cloudy sky was also a downer. I had never understood how people in Seattle could handle the gloom. It seemed like the sort of thing that might drive a person to drink.

Kind of like being responsible for an entire city, really.

"Knock, knock!" Kayla's smiling face peeked around the partially open door, one hand covering her eyes. "Are you up, John? Not still starkers, are you?"

"I'm up." I waved to her from my seat by the window. Up, showered, and fully clothed. I'd had a surprisingly restful night of sleep. Thank you, In-n-Out!

Kayla let herself in. "Sorry to intrude, mate."

"On Saturday, I woke up in a cell with a marching band in my head. Yesterday, a hungry Juliette was creeping on me while I slept. Polite knocking on my door is a massive upgrade." I gave her a smile, and then gestured to her Watch uniform. "I see you're on duty. What can I do for you?"

"Actually, you *are* my duty," she proclaimed with a grin. She snapped to attention, and offered a crisp salute. "Lance Corporal Kayla Walker, reporting for duty, sir!"

"Nice salute. I bet that impresses the hell out of Darlene," I mused.

"You'd best believe it. Especially when she's playing General."

"Where *is* your pint-sized commander-in-chief?"

"It's Monday," Kayla pointed out. "She's got classes today and tomorrow."

"Classes?"

"At UCSD," she clarified. "Bachelor's degrees don't earn themselves, you know?"

Neither did associate degrees, as I had learned during my brief and unsuccessful tenure at community college. "Wait, D got to leave the House?"

"Uhm... yeah?" Kayla wandered over to peer out the window over my shoulder. "Most of our blood donors do have their own lives, you know. Why?"

"I just thought Lucia had put the House on lock-down."

"How did you hear about that?" Kayla eyed me curiously. "Oh, I forgot... you've been rubbing elbows with the Council, poor fool. Darlene left for her dorm around the same time you went to the mediation, long before they shut the gates. She stacks her classes on Mondays and Tuesdays, and won't be back until tomorrow night." She shrugged. "She was one of the lucky ones though. We'll all be glad when we're allowed to leave."

"Tell me about it. I've been a prisoner here since Friday," I reminded her.

"Oh, you're not a prisoner!" exclaimed Kayla. "You're more like... an honored guest."

"Who isn't allowed to leave?"

"That does seem a bit prisoner-ish." Her ash-blonde hair was pulled back into a ponytail, and it swished around her as she shook her head. "I'm sure it's just temporary, right?"

"Honestly? I wish I knew." Now that Bill had accepted me as a mediator, it would be against the Concordat to kill me, right? Did that apply to contracts that predated my current role? "So, when you said I'm your duty... what did you mean?"

"I'm your escort. The Captain said you would need one again?"
She eyed me curiously. "Anyway, think of me as your—"

"Babysitter?"

"Bodyguard."

"Fair enough." I marshaled my thoughts. "Okay, first things
first, Corporal—"

"Lance Corporal," she corrected, somewhat cheekily.

"I bet *Darlene* doesn't let you interrupt her."

"Oh, she does. But then she punishes me thoroughly in the
manner I've grown accustomed to." Kayla's brown eyes darted over to
delightedly note my glowing cheeks.

"*Anyway.* I think our first order of business, *Lance Corporal*
Walker, is to get some coffee. Troops don't fight well when still half
asleep. Hip hip cheerio, and all that." I scooped up the Nintendo
controller from the dresser and marched past her to the door.

"And then are you going to tell me what we'll be doing today?"
She fell in beside me like a seasoned soldier. For all I knew, she had
been one, back when I was in diapers.

"Absolutely. But first, I need you to answer one question."

"Oh really? D didn't fully satisfy your curiosity?" That was an
evil, evil grin spreading across her face. So much for Kayla being the
'nice' vampire.

"Argh! Take pity on my non-virgin ears, woman!" I tried again
to scrub the memories of *that* conversation from my brain. "That's not
it at all."

"Too bad. So what's your question?"

"Do you believe in magic?"

"Since it exists… sure. I guess?" She seemed a bit confused. It
was nice to have someone else in that position for a change. After all
the teasing she and her girlfriend had given me, I was ready for
payback.

"Excellent. Then you can hold onto this, while I drink my
coffee." I handed her the controller.

"It's… an old video game controller," she noted, her confusion
only growing.

"Yeah. Or a locating device. I'm not really sure, to be honest. Hopefully, it will lead us to its matching video game console, which is either a thirty-year-old archaic piece of junk or a magical artifact of unimaginable power. I guess it doesn't really matter which, since it's *also* a ticking time bomb. Metaphorically speaking."

I entered the kitchen, nodded to the few vampires who weren't intent on ignoring me, and made a beeline for the coffee. Kayla stomped into the room after me, still clutching the controller.

"John…what the bloody hell are you talking about?"

"Uh uh uh," I wagged my finger at her, before taking a long sip of piping hot coffee. I could feel my brain cells waking up one at a time, like flowers unfolding in the sun. "A good soldier is seen but rarely heard, Lance Corporal."

With a muttered curse, she went to pour herself a cup of coffee. Someone snickered audibly. I was making friends.

ooo

"So, how does it work?"

We were down on sub-level two, the deepest, darkest floor of the House. I had memories I would always treasure of this place, like the time I'd woken up in handcuffs and the time I… no, that was pretty much it. Ah, nostalgia. Kayla was regarding the Nintendo controller curiously, as if waiting for it to glow.

"I haven't a clue, actually. Bill is not a great believer in explanations. Or being coherent." I took the controller back, and examined it carefully. Unlike modern controllers, there wasn't a lot to it; a directional pad and four buttons; A, B, Select, and Start.

"Bill?"

"Sorry… Lord Beel-Kasan. Apparently, seven-foot-tall vegetables prefer informal nicknames," I replied absently. Did I swing the controller by the cord? Would it vibrate when I neared its console? These old controllers didn't support force feedback, did they?

Kayla was looking at me oddly. "I'm not sure your time here has been good for you, John. You were a lot less weird yesterday."

"To be fair, my world was a lot less weird yesterday too." I gave the controller an experimental swing, to no effect. At a loss, I just gave in and started pushing buttons. When I hit the Start button, the controller jumped in my hand. "Did you just see that?"

"Yeah. Does that mean it's working?"

"Either that or I've primed it to detonate, and there's an asparagus somewhere laughing through his magic marker mouth at us." I waited. The controller didn't move after that initial twitch, but it felt… attentive in my hand. "Well, we're still alive, so I guess we should start with the search, and see if anything causes it to perk up."

There were a truly depressing number of cells on sub-level two, but the lingering stench made it obvious which had been mine. Given a vampire's superior sense of smell, it was astonishing that Ana had even come inside.

We walked the entirety of the level, but the controller remained still. I wasn't surprised; it had seemed like an unlikely place for a thief to stash the Nintendo. Assuming that they had stashed it in the House at all. "One floor down, five more to go… unless there are any secret levels nobody has told me about?"

"Nope!" replied Kayla, "Although… we probably want to check the garage too, don't you think? And maybe the grounds?"

I groaned. "This is going to take freaking forever."

"It does seem that way. But think of all the fun we'll have!"

I gave the cheerful vampire a cross look. "And you say I'm weird…"

oooo

We did search the garage, which only reinforced my innate envy of rich people. Why the hell did they get to have so many lovely toys?

Oh, right. Money.

To make it worse, the People had a lot of nice cars, and they all looked brand new, even the ones that were older than I was. They ran the gamut from sports cars to luxury automobiles, and every one of them was probably worth more than my parents' house. Unfortunately, the controller didn't react to any of them. I circled the 1968 Shelby GT500KR three full times, just to be sure.

I also tried not to drool, unsuccessfully.

"Which one of these is yours, Kayla?" I could easily see her in something sleek but muscular. Maybe a convertible?

"Oh, D is driving our car," she shrugged. "We have a cute little Wrangler with a surf rack on top. Anything fancier seems like too much trouble to me."

I looked around us at the multiple rows of gleaming automobiles. "Yeah, fancy would totally suck."

For the first time in days, it occurred to me to wonder what had happened to my gently-used Corolla. After three days on the street in Logan Heights, I suspected it was now missing its tires and hubcaps. Some artistic up-and-comer had probably also given it a paint job that was a long way from kid-friendly.

If I survived this mediation—and the investigation—I was going to make Lucia pay to get it fixed.

ooo

Sub-level one would have been a quick search, except for two things.

First, nobody wanted to let me into the glass-and-steel-enclosed security room. They had no issues with Kayla, but I was apparently a 'grade-seven security risk', and might cause incalculable damage if allowed into their nifty little computer closet. To be honest, I didn't hate the designation. It would fit right in with my growing set of titles:

John Smith

Creature of the Night

Mediator to the Gods

Grade-Seven Security Risk

As phenomenal as it would look on my business cards (once I had business cards), it was a problem in this particular instance. I was the only one Bill trusted to perform the search, therefore I had to be the one searching every single room.

Finally, we appealed to a higher authority. Xavier showed up so quickly that I suspected he'd been lurking in the shadows just out of sight. Or training in the gym, I guess. He nodded gravely as we explained the situation, and turned to the Watch member blocking the door.

"It's okay, Ricardo. Allow Mr. Smith to do a quick walk-through, and he will be out of your hair immediately afterward." He gave me a respectful nod. "If he touches anything, cut off one of his ears."

Son of a bitch.

Inside the room, there was a lot of fancy equipment, including video feeds of the outside grounds and many of the public areas of the House. I'd have protested the invasion of privacy, if the NSA and the U.S. government hadn't already thoroughly conditioned me to being spied upon. There were four Watch members present, not counting Kayla, and they all eyed me as I wandered about, no doubt anxious to be the first to take my ear.

Thankfully, the controller didn't react, and the room was small enough that the entire search took only a minute or so. Then, as Xavier had told Ricardo would be the case, we moved on. Once we were out of sight, I double-checked that both of my ears were still attached.

You never know, right?

We encountered the second problem when we were almost done walking the football-field-sized gymnasium. The doors in the near wall, just past the basketball court, turned out to be locker rooms. I was in and out of the men's room—which smelled of feet and sweat, just like human locker rooms do—in no time at all. The ladies' room, however, presented more of an issue.

With a sigh, Kayla had me wait outside as she went in to see if anyone was currently changing, showering, or doing whatever amazing things happened in female-only places. It took a while, and I could only assume that she was busy hiding the evidence of the pillow fights that Cinemax had taught me occurred so frequently behind closed doors.

Eventually, the blonde Aussie made her way back out to me, followed by the über-fit vampire I'd seen punching the hell out of a heavy bag on Saturday. Her chin-length, curly brown hair was still wet, and she gave me a look of ill-disguised annoyance as she headed for the exit. I turned and watched her leave.

"Is something wrong?" Kayla asked.

"Wasn't she down here on Saturday?"

"Brenna practically lives down here, but even normal people go to the gym more than once a week, John." She didn't quite look at the small gut I'd forgotten to suck in, but I could hear the tease in her voice. "Most of us, anyway."

"God save me from vampire comedians." The women's locker room was... depressingly functional, and not very different from what I was used to as a guy. Another illusion callously destroyed forever. It did, at least, smell better. I walked up and down a few rows of benches, and peeked into both the numerous stalls and the shower room, but the controller stubbornly stayed still. Only that persistent sensation of watchfulness told me it was even on. "So, is this what your life is like? Patrol, train, sleep, and... well... stuff with Darlene?"

"You mean the hours and hours of sweaty, passionate sex?"

"You know what I meant." We exited the gym and began the long walk back to the elevators.

"I just wanted to be sure," she replied with a grin, "but no. Being in the Watch is just a job, like any other. I have my free time to spend as I wish. D and I go surfing regularly, and we've been busy working our way through hiking trails here in San Diego." Her grin widened. "Beyond that, I like concerts, barbecues, long walks on the beach, and spicy little Irish-American cuties. What about you, John?"

"I'm fine with cuties of any ethnicity or nationality, to be honest. They're rarely fine with me though." That earned me a riotous laugh from Kayla.

"That's not what I was asking. What is your life like? Being a private eye *and* a mediator must be interesting."

"I'm new to mediation... and I'm not a very successful private eye," I admitted. "I'm sure the big agencies get better cases, but I tend to deal with unhappy housewives who are convinced their husbands are cheating on them... or vice versa. I spend a lot of my time sitting outside office buildings and homes so I can tail the person to a potential late night rendezvous, and get the proof my clients are looking for."

"That sounds... dreary." We reached the elevators and waited for one to arrive. "Anything non-sleazy?"

"Missing people. One time, I was hired to find someone's birth father."

"There you go! That must have been gratifying!"

"It would have been if the father had still been alive," I agreed.

"I guess detective work isn't as glamorous as they make it seem on the telly. You must have been thrilled when Lady Dumenyova hired you to mediate instead."

That was definitely one way of looking at it.

CHAPTER 29

IN WHICH A HOUSE JUST KEEPS GETTING BIGGER

I'd only ever passed through the first floor a few times, but it had seemed fairly innocuous. However, fiction had taught me to suspect the unexpected, and that made it the ideal place for someone to have hidden the Nintendo.

Which just went to show the difference between fiction and reality.

Next to the foyer was the People's version of a dining room. To me, it looked more like a medieval banquet hall, complete with twin chandeliers and two long tables for the common folk. A third table, perpendicular to the others, sat at the head of the room on a slightly raised platform. All that was missing was a throne. And people. As usual, the room was empty.

"Do you guys *ever* use this room?" I ran a finger along one table's surface as we paced the interior. No dust, which was a pretty impressive feat in a room that size. I only had one bookcase in my basement room back home, and the dust on its shelves still had multiple layers.

"Not often," admitted Kayla. "Everyone's hours are different, so large get-togethers are rare. There's another, more reasonably sized, dining room on the second floor, but we mostly just use the kitchen. And the Council members have their own dining areas on their floor." She waved at our surroundings. "This is for formal occasions. Visiting dignitaries that wouldn't be comfortable eating out. That sort of thing."

"Did the Rook ever eat here?"

She shook her head. "He never came to the House at all. Queen Lucia only ever met with him at the corporate office."

We wandered back into the foyer. On the other side were rooms for the House's permanent on-site staff and the unclaimed blood donors who lived on the premises. Juliette's so-called larder. I immediately dubbed the place The Hall o' Humans, but Kayla seemed reluctant to adopt the phrasing. Genius is often misunderstood and unappreciated.

I'm not sure what I was expecting from the blood donors' living quarters. Maybe a single room with shackles along the walls, a concave floor, and grooves to channel the blood to the center. You know, like in the first Blade movie. Instead, what I found was remarkably similar to the second floor. There was a sizable kitchen and a dozen or so bedrooms.

That kitchen was occupied by the House's human chef, the culinary genius responsible for most of the food I'd been consuming over the past few days. We had a harder time convincing *him* to let us search the kitchen than we'd had with the security center on sub-level one. Cooks. Give someone a mixing spoon and the next thing you know, they're speaking French and insulting your parentage. At least that's what I assume he was doing. Despite my crush on Marie, I'd never been able to master the language.

According to my mom, I had yet to master English.

Kayla soothed the chef's ruffled feathers rather than physically bulldozing him out of our path. It seemed like a waste of superpowers, but I appreciated her restraint. This was the man who had created Xavier's honeyed ham. Snooty or not, he might be the next best thing to a national treasure.

Under his baleful eye, we made a hurried circuit, but the controller didn't even twitch.

The dorm rooms were a bust too. The few humans present all seemed rather average, if unreasonably cheerful. Not a goth among them. Hell, two of the men were wearing pastels, which, next to Zorana, was the scariest thing I'd seen so far. They didn't have any problem with our brief room inspections, and there was very little to see. Despite my fervent hopes, we didn't stumble across any in-progress feedings or lurid vampire orgies.

I was starting to develop a case of the Mondays.

We retreated, yet again, to the foyer. Three floors finished, three to go, (plus a tower). I started to head for the elevators, but Kayla stopped me.

"Uhm, mate? Why don't we just take the stairs?" She nodded to the grand staircase right next to us. "Cardio is king, you know?"

○○○

On the second floor, we searched the small dining room and the kitchen I'd already spent so much time in, finding a handful of curious vampires in each. After that, we wandered the length of the long hall like door-to-door salespeople, knocking courteously at each bedroom suite. Many of those rooms were occupied, sometimes by the resident vampire, sometimes by their blood donor (or donors... one particular bedroom had enough people in it to field a basketball team), and sometimes by both. More often than not, a barely clad, sweaty individual would eventually let us inside. Here was all the kinky sex I'd been expecting to find in The Hall o' Humans.

Kayla wasn't the only vampire who batted for the other team; a large number of the vampires we encountered had same-sex donors. And the House itself was overwhelmingly male.

Anne Rice had been closer to the truth than anyone could have suspected.

I worked only a few miles from Hillcrest, San Diego's predominantly gay neighborhood—great food, great culture, ruthlessly expensive real estate—and I wasn't at all concerned with other people's sexuality, regardless of species. But I was quickly discovering that the number of male/male pairings in the House drastically increased the chances of accidental penis exposure during our search.

Accidental. Penis. Exposure.

There was a phrase I'd never expected to think, let alone experience.

After the fourth or fifth such eyeball-scorching encounter, I was starting to question how accidental it could really be. I might never order sausage on my pizza again. And hot dogs at a Padres game? Eternally out of the question.

As I tried to scrub the images from my short-term memory, Kayla knocked on our latest door. We had made significant progress, helped by the fact that at least half of the suites on the second floor lacked residents entirely. We'd still searched those rooms, of course, but it didn't take much time to walk through empty suites. It also drastically reduced the chances of further... exposure. We only had three rooms left before the Midnight Tower. So far, the scavenger hunt had been a colossal waste of time and energy.

The door opened to reveal a vampire straight out of a surf movie; long blonde hair, faded t-shirt, broad shoulders, and vacant expression. He eyed us sourly. "What?"

Kayla went into her standard spiel. By that point, I was tuning it out, so only occasional words slipped through, chief among them "queen" and "search." As always, Lucia's title worked its magic. Surfer-boy grudgingly stepped aside.

Many of the bedrooms we'd seen had been exquisitely decorated... the sort of style that my mom would kill to afford. This suite was a lot closer to my basement bedroom. I'm sure there was some sort of underlying motif or theme, but it was pretty hard to tell what that might be, given the clothing and books strewn haphazardly about.

It was kind of gross, actually. I resolved to do a better job cleaning up after myself in the future, in the event that I actually ever made it home.

I was picking my way around one particularly impressive tower of books—which somehow remained stable despite the fact that several wadded up socks were sandwiched between the fourth and fifth layers in the pile—when something caught my attention.

No, not the controller; that continued to sit in my hand like the lump of grey plastic it was.

This was way better.

On a grey day in July, the Monday after Comic Con, I had stumbled onto one of the most impressive comic collections ever. If we'd been outside, the heavens would have opened up, the clouds would have peeled away, and a golden shaft of light would have given the glass case the glorious halo it deserved. As it was, my imagination had to supply those effects, accompanied by a few bars of the Battle Hymn of the Republic. *My eyes have seen the glory*, indeed.

"Holy crap, is that an Action Comics number one—" was all I got out before I found myself smashed against the far wall.

"Nobody gave you leave to speak, filthy monkey," hissed the not-particularly-clean-himself vampire, whose breath smelled like stale Cheetos and what I really hoped wasn't blood. (Because, if so; yuck. It was like snuggling with a smoker.) "And you definitely won't be touching anything of mine."

It would have been a great time for me to fire back with a classic John Smith one-liner but I was busy trying not to scream as Mr. Surf Psycho began slowly crushing my wrist in his vise-like grip. These are the little details the movies never seem to mention. It was my right hand too, damn it all. Much more of that and I'd never be able to drive stick again.

Almost as quickly as it started, the pain stopped. I fell back onto the carpet (and a wadded-up shirt that had clearly already been worn), and watched as Kayla kicked the legs out from under the surfer vamp. She followed him to the floor in a blur of motion, one knee in his back, and twisted his arm at what had to be an incredibly unpleasant angle.

"Miles, which part of 'the queen's business' did you not understand? At this point, John Smith is worth more to our House than you are."

"Miles?" I asked disbelievingly. "His name is *Miles?*"

"Not helping, John." Kayla stayed focused on the vampire wriggling under her like a worm on a hook. "Now then, Mr. Smith is not going to touch any of your precious possessions, and you in turn are not going to give me an excuse to do some serious damage. Agreed?"

Miles' voice was tight and strained. "Agreed, damn it! Let me go!"

I finished my walk-through of the room at triple my usual speed, keeping a careful distance from the vampire's comic collection.

After successfully facing down vampire royalty and vegetable
demigods, it was a sad commentary on my life that I'd just almost been
killed over a comic book.

Miles stayed in the center of the room as we left, but the glare
he gave me promised some sort of messy revenge. As if I could ever be
afraid of someone named *Miles*. Was Kayla still between us? Oh, she
was? Excellent. I tossed him a mocking hang-loose *shaka* sign over
Kayla's shoulder, along with my best approximation of one of Juliette's
trademark smirks. As soon as we crossed into the hallway, the door
slammed shut behind us.

"I'm suddenly glad I have a bodyguard," I told Kayla. "Thank
you." I rotated my right wrist. Nothing seemed broken. This would go
down in my diary as another overwhelming victory.

"When you told me we'd be searching the entire House, I
wasn't sure what to expect," she acknowledged. "Nobody likes having
their privacy intruded upon. Thankfully, most people have chosen to
be amused by your somewhat puritan sensibilities instead. They seem
to be making a game of flaunting themselves. I guess Miles was the
exception."

Puritan sensibilities? Flaunting themselves? "Wait. You mean all
those dudes were naked *on purpose*? Because of me?"

"Well, they certainly weren't starkers for *my* benefit, John."

I freaking hated vampires.

CHAPTER 30

IN WHICH THE THIRD FLOOR IS THE CHARM

I was unreasonably excited about visiting the third floor. First, it was the only floor I hadn't seen. Second, it contained the bedrooms for the entire Council, and I was expecting some seriously over-the-top décor. I was already laying odds that Lucia's room would be white marble, roman columns, and buff dudes in togas.

On our way up, Kayla gave me a look. "Remember, John. You need to be on your best behavior. The Council is a lot more hardline than the rest of us."

"Juliette's pretty casual."

"She's an exception, being both the youngest and American. But still," she shivered, "these are the heavy-hitters of our species. I'm the Captain's second-in-command, and I wouldn't want to face anyone on this floor if they were truly angry."

"You're the Watch's number two? But Xavier..."

"Wiped the floor with me?" She nodded. "He's got a century or two on me. And combat is his Talent."

The way she said it, talent had a capital T. "What does that mean?"

"I forget sometimes that you don't know this stuff. It already feels like you've been here forever." She grinned. "As we age, our kind develops additional abilities beyond the usual strength and speed. Andrés is a Firebringer. There's an elder in Madagascar who's a

Stormcaller. And Xavier's a Battlelord. He's the standard against which we in the Watch are measured and found wanting."

"You really like him, don't you?" It seemed hard to believe, but the reverence in her voice was clear.

She nodded. "I owe Queen Lucia my fealty and loyalty, but Xavier is my Captain. He would die for us and we for him."

"Wow." Her simple statement put things in perspective a bit. If Xavier engendered that sort of loyalty in someone like Kayla, he couldn't be all bad. Maybe I shouldn't go out of my way to be a dick to him. "What about the others?"

"I'm not sure about Marcus or Anastasia, actually," she admitted as we boarded the elevator, "but you should be able to figure out at least one of Queen Lucia's Talents."

"Hotness?"

That got a laugh out of her. "Never change, John. But no. Quite the opposite."

Hmm. I pictured Lucia angry, which was surprisingly easy. Her eyes hard and glowing, her words hurled like daggers of ice... Oh. "Cold?"

"Right you are, Mr. Smith!"

"I thought the whole Lady of Winter thing was just another title."

"It most definitely is not. Remember what I said about best behavior. I'd hate to tell D that she has to find a new midnight sandwich buddy because her last one was turned into an icicle."

"Point taken," I muttered.

Our elevator opened onto a small lobby. Two Watch members guarded the sole door in the far wall. I greeted the one on the right. "Hey Ray, what's up?"

Ray blinked and looked at me for a long moment. Earth to Ray. Finally, something clicked, and he smiled. "Hey, John. Just hanging out and, you know, guarding."

Kayla gave him a slightly exasperated look. "On the Queen's orders, John is to be given access to the Council suites while I accompany him."

The vampire next to Ray nodded. "Yeah, she and the Captain told us." He gave me an indecipherable look, and opened the door for us. "Try not to piss anyone off, human."

"No promises."

ooo

As nice as the rest of the House was—and it was really, really nice—the third floor put it to shame. The hall was half again as wide, and though it was every bit as long as the halls below, only eight doors opened onto it. Nine, if you wanted to count the one between the security checkpoint and the hall itself. Hardwood floors gleamed and some trick of engineering gave the appearance of skylights in the ceiling, even though I knew there was another level above us.

The first door on our right was already open. We stepped through into a foyer, and were immediately greeted by an oversized, slightly faded poster advertising The Clash's "Give 'Em Enough Rope" tour.

I turned to Kayla. "Pretty obvious whose room this is."

"Juliette is one of a kind, isn't she?"

Past the foyer, the space opened up into an enormous suite. The primary bedroom was heavily decorated with punk rock memorabilia, and the bed, a double-sized king with blood-red sheets, had a Fender Telecaster casually laid atop it. The floor was still hardwood, without a single rug or carpet in sight, and cleaner than I would have expected. An ornate wooden desk held two wide screen monitors and a MacBook Pro. Much of the wall facing the bed was covered with an eighty-four inch LCD television.

I couldn't for the life of me understand why Juliette would have wasted her time playing games in my room when she had this monster waiting for her only one floor away. "So this is how the better half lives," I muttered to myself.

"Too right!" Kayla agreed, looking about in amazement. "I guess rank does have its privileges!"

"You've never been up here?"

"Not past the guard post." She shrugged. "The elders like their privacy."

The suite had two other bedrooms where I assumed the vampire's blood donors would normally live. In their absence, Juliette had converted one room to a heavily sound-proofed music room, and the other to a walk-in closet… if the word *closet* could be applied to a thousand square feet of space. There was a small dining area that looked to be used regularly, and a fully functional kitchen that had an unwashed bowl in one of its two sinks.

I checked the contents; Fruit Loops. It figured. I was more of a Frosted Flakes sort of guy, but I'd always had sophisticated tastes.

The real prize was the bathroom. It had all the amenities of my own guest suite, including the space-age telepathic techno-shower, but was twice the size. There was even what I took to be some sort of foot bath or urinal but which Kayla said was a bidet. I was sure Marie could have explained what it was for but I didn't have a clue.

Past the bidet was an honest-to-god, over-sized Jacuzzi that could easily seat four. The jets were turned off, but the water steamed at an even one-hundred degrees. Overhead, the steam was sucked away into partially concealed vents, leaving the rest of the bathroom dry and comfortable.

"If I'd known the job came with a private Jacuzzi, I might have actually considered being Juliette's blood donor."

"Has she asked you?" Kayla seemed surprised.

"Let's just say she's dropped some pretty obvious hints."

"I'm not one to tell someone how to live their life," said Kayla carefully, "but you might want to think long and hard about agreeing to that sort of contract with anyone in the House. Especially if you want to go back to your normal life when this is over."

"That's an odd thing for you to say, considering Darlene."

"D is different. We have an actual relationship. She's my love, and my friend, and my partner. Being *just* a blood donor isn't like that."

I thought back to Juliette's comments on 'blood bags.' Maybe Kayla had a point. "I have no plans to become anyone's donor," I admitted. "I'm just trying to survive this mediation, so I can go back to my old life, albeit a little bit richer."

"Speaking of, has the gizmo reacted at all?"

I looked down at the controller in my hand. I'd completely forgotten about it in my rush to take in Juliette's living situation. "No, Juliette's suite seems to be clean. Awesome but clean."

"Then let's get going, shall we?" Kayla asked, a bit of tension leaking into her voice. I gave her a questioning look, and she grimaced. "The more time we spend on this floor, the likelier it is that you'll somehow get yourself killed."

"That's kind of insulting. But probably true."

ooo

The suite across from Juliette's belonged to none other than Xavier himself. He met us at the door, giving Kayla a nod and me the cold shoulder. As I wandered about, controller held before me as if it was a holy talisman and not part of a dusty old video game console, he questioned Kayla on our progress. Because abject failure always appreciates an audience.

His suite shared a floor plan with Juliette's, but that was the extent of the similarities. In contrast to her cluttered shrine to the punk rock gods, Xavier's rooms were spartan, and though I hated to admit it, elegant. The style looked Japanese; low tables with cushions instead of chairs. Screens of paper and wood broke the enormous space down into smaller areas without making it feel cramped.

The bed was an oversized king, but it rose only a few feet off of the ground on a wooden frame. In place of a television, the facing wall had an ink brush painting of some sort of mountain-top landscape. A long table below was bare except for a stand that held a wakizashi and a katana, both sheathed, their blades pointed upwards and their hilts to the left. My expansive knowledge of martial arts movies told me that those details all had some sort of significance.

I nodded to the painting. "That's beautiful, dude."

His eyes widened slightly in surprise. "Thank you, Mr. Smith. I believe I have improved in the years since I painted this, but it reminds me of simpler times."

He was the painter? That just figured. I hated to admit it, but I kind of wanted to be Xavier. Except cooler. And human. And with Steve's mohawk. "So you fight like a ninja and paint like a master artist.

If you can dance, I may just have to hate you." I smiled to show I was joking.

Mostly joking.

"He dances like a dream, John," Kayla added helpfully, as she joined us in the bedroom. "There are a lot of similarities between dance and combat."

Xavier's eyes flickered over to her and then back to me. He offered a self-satisfied smile.

"Of course he does," I muttered, moving past them both into the bathroom, where I waved the controller around like an idiot.

"How exactly does that device work?" Xavier asked. I could practically hear the smugness in his smile.

"No clue. I'm just the dumb monkey tasked with carrying it around."

"At least there we are in agreement, Mr. Smith."

o o o

Our search of Xavier's suite left me in a foul mood. It wasn't anything he said. As Kayla gently pointed out, Juliette said worse on a regular basis, and I didn't seem to care. Maybe it was just a guy thing—stupid, in other words—but some vampires were a constant reminder of my own thoroughly mundane nature. It wasn't rational, but these weren't rational times; by the time we'd left Xavier behind, I was pretty damn irritated.

Then we moved on to the next suite, and I forgot all about my inadequacies.

CHAPTER 31

IN WHICH SUMMER HAS HER SAY

The door to the suite was wide open. We knocked anyway, and over a fair bit of giggling, heard someone call us in. I glanced at Kayla, but she just shrugged and waved me on.

It was like walking into a meadow, if that meadow had been crafted by Walt Disney on a Star Trek holodeck. The walls were painted with bright trees, shrubbery, and ankle high grass, making it appear as if the vegetation was growing directly out of the hardwood flooring. Above the greenery, the walls and ceiling were sky blue, with subtle hints of golden sunlight. Small cartoon animals peeked out at us from around the room.

"This is different."

Kayla had a wide smile on her face. "I'm pretty sure I know whose room it is. Summer, dear, are you okay with having visitors?"

I felt like I'd heard the name before, but couldn't place it. Regardless, the person who came to greet us wasn't her.

"Juliette? What are you doing here? We just came from searching your suite."

"If you touched anything, I will know it, and I will break you, little bird," she warned me with a disturbingly gleeful smile. "It's my day to watch Princess Pea."

"That's not my name!" The voice, coming from around the corner, was that of a small girl. My guts didn't clench at the sound, so I knew it couldn't be Zorana.

We followed Juliette deeper into the suite.

The paint scheme continued here, giving the room an airy and open feel. In lieu of a kitchen or dining area, a large portion of the space had been transformed into a child's playroom. Toys were everywhere. Off to one side, small, exquisitely crafted chairs ringed a matching table. Two of those chairs were occupied with stuffed animals; a worn grey rabbit and a tiny golden retriever. The third chair was empty, but the fourth held the little girl we'd just heard.

She was adorable. Maybe five years old, with a halo of fine dark hair floating about her head in wisps and curls. Her features were doll-like and perfect. Guileless blue eyes blinked up at us over a small mouth that was all the more noticeable because of the lower lip extended in a pout.

"John Smith, I present to you Summer, known to some of us as Princess Pea, presently the ward of Queen Lucia. Summer, this is John Smith, a human."

"That's not my name!" she protested again. On the wall behind her, a big-eyed fox peered from behind a tree stump. I blinked. Had that fox been there a second ago?

I crouched down to speak to her at eye-level. "Princess Pea isn't your name?" She shook her head vigorously, dark curls whipping about. "How about Summer? Is that your name?"

She thought about it for a long moment. "Sometimes," she admitted, pulling the grey rabbit out of its chair to hug it tightly, "but not today!"

"What would you like your name to be today then?"

I could tell the question stumped her. She clutched the rabbit closer, chewing on one of its ears in thought. Finally, a great big smile blossomed on her face. "Tea Leaf!"

"That's not even a real name, Summer," Juliette began, but the little girl and I both ignored her.

"It's a pleasure to meet you, Tea Leaf," I said solemnly, "my name is John."

I held out a hand to shake, but she blew right by it to give me an enormous hug and a sloppy little-girl kiss on the cheek. Over her shoulder, I glanced at the wall. The fox was nowhere to be seen.

"I like him!" she announced, turning to Kayla. "Is he yours? Can I have him?"

Kayla coughed to cover up a laugh. "John isn't anyone's, dear."

"Oh goodie!" Tea Leaf's blue eyes swung back over to me like heat seeking missiles, packed with cuteness instead of explosives, but no less deadly for that fact. "My first donor!"

"Uhm." How had this gone so quickly awry? "Tea Leaf…" Her bottom lip immediately started to quiver, forcing me to reconsider what I was going to say. "You're not feeding yet, are you?"

Her unhappiness vanished in an instant, and she giggled. "Of course not, silly! I'm five!" To my right, a flock of bright blue painted cartoon birds took flight from a two-dimensional tree branch. She skipped over to her own chair and pointed to the empty one nearest me. "Let's play dolls!"

In a shocking turn of events, it was Juliette who swooped in to save me. "Actually, John and Kayla are on a mission for Queen Lucia. They won't have time to play with us today."

"Oh poo!" pouted the adorable little hell-spawn.

Juliette folded herself into the empty chair and turned to look at the stuffed golden retriever to her right. "So then, Mr. Arf, would you care for a spot of tea?"

"Juliette!" protested Tea Leaf with another giggle. "Mr. Arf doesn't drink tea! But Sir Floppy and I would like some very much!" She carefully tucked the stuffed rabbit back into his chair.

Kayla and I took the opportunity to make a strategic withdrawal from the scene, completing our search of the suite in considerate silence. As we walked, the foliage that had been painted on the walls rustled, as if in a breeze.

ooo

"Tea Leaf is from a House in Brazil, right?" I asked, once Kayla and I had retreated to the hallway.

"Yes. Sent to live with us when she was just a newborn." Kayla grinned. "I'm afraid we've spoiled her shamelessly, but children are a treasure." She raised an eyebrow at me. "And you… didn't we *just* talk about you not agreeing to blood donor contracts?"

"I didn't agree to anything!" I protested feebly. "Besides, she's five. By the time she's ready for her first feeding, I'll be..." I did the math in my head. Sometimes, I impress even myself. "Thirty-eight or so." I paused. "Holy crap; I'll be ancient! Anyway, she'll have forgotten about me by then, and found a donor closer to her own age."

"You'd better hope so, John." Kayla didn't sound optimistic, but shrugged and smiled. "She's a cutie though, isn't she?"

"Adorable." I pointed to the next suite, whose door was firmly closed. "Who's next?"

"I think that's Andrés," she supplied. "With the exception of Summer, the suites should be ordered by rank. After Juliette and Xavier, Andrés is the youngest on the Council."

I nodded, as if I'd already known that. And frankly, I probably should have. With Anastasia as Secundus, which I'd figured out roughly translated to 'second-in-command', it would have to have been either Andrés or Marcus. "So then," I pointed to the four rooms further down the hall. "Marcus, then Anastasia, then Lucia, and...?"

"Actually, Marcus, then Anastasia, then Zorana, with Lucia's room being at the end."

"I didn't realize Zorana lived up here." My mind briefly went blank at the thought of having to search the Blood Witch's rooms. After meeting Tea Leaf, I was that much more aware of how *wrong* Zorana's condition was.

Plus, she was able to make my blood do gymnastics. That was the sort of thing that could worry a man.

"She doesn't, really. As a Council member she gets a room, but she spends most of her time in the Midnight Tower. Thus the bed. I think she enjoys looking at the stars."

"She wasn't there when we searched it," I reminded her.

"True. Well, as long as you don't do something dumb like calling her a child, you should be fine." The evil version of her usual grin made another appearance.

Clearly, word had spread. Thanks again, Juliette.

I was trying to think of an appropriately sarcastic response when the controller started to glow. "Oh crap!"

All traces of amusement vanished from Kayla's face. "In there?" She nodded to Andrés' room.

"Maybe?" I took a step back from the door, and the nimbus of green light around the controller faded. A step forward, and it started to glow again. Back, fade. Forward, glow. It was a pretty cool effect, really. Almost like a night light being plugged in to a socket. "Yeah, it looks like it. What now?" I hadn't expected to find the Nintendo at all, and I definitely hadn't expected someone on the Council to be the thief.

Never trust a man with a ponytail.

Kayla thought quickly. "Captain?" Her voice echoed down the hallway, and Xavier's dark form flowed through his doorway in a blur, sword in hand.

I knew he'd seen the glowing controller and realized what it meant. He stopped next to us, eyes cold and locked on the door in front of us. "Queen Lucia is in her chambers, Kayla. Tell her she is needed."

Kayla looked toward me for a moment, and I could see the worry on her face. "But Mr. Smith…"

Xavier dropped a hand to the hilt of his sheathed katana, and his voice hardened. "He will be safe."

Kayla saluted, fist to chest, the first time I had seen her do so. Then she turned and raced further down the hallway.

"I owe you an apology, Mr. Smith," Xavier said quietly. "You have found a thief I did not believe existed."

"What should we do?" My voice was hushed as well. Given vampire hearing, the only reason Andrés hadn't heard us yet was the sound-proofing in each suite. With the door closed, he might still be unaware of our presence.

"We wait. We need the Queen as witness. She is also the best suited to counter any attack Andrés might bring against us."

Right. Ice vs. fire. For once, I felt on top of the situation. It helped that I didn't have to do anything more complicated than holding the controller.

Down the hall, Lucia appeared, followed closely by Kayla. The queen did not seem to hurry, but covered the hundred or so yards in only a few seconds. She looked at the controller in my hand, looked at the door, and gave one sharp nod. "Open it, Captain."

Xavier tried the handle, to no avail. With a shrug and a tightly controlled intake of breath, he struck the heavy wooden door with the heel of one hand.

The door blew inward with a boom to crash into the far wall. I was vaguely aware of Juliette appearing behind us, quietly closing the door to Tea Leaf's room. Down the hall, Marcus appeared in his own room's doorway, wielding what looked an awful lot like a trident. Of Zorana and Anastasia, there was no sign.

Xavier swept into the room in a black-suited blur, followed closely by the furious Lucia. I started to join them, but a hand on my shoulder stopped me in my tracks. Literally; it was like being welded to the floor.

"Hold until they give the all-clear." Kayla's words were clipped and economical.

"Do you need to be in there?"

"No." I couldn't see her, but I sensed her shaking her head behind me. "Those two together can handle anything short of an army. We need to make sure you don't become collateral damage."

"She's right, little bird," Juliette agreed. "Until the mediation ends, your life actually matters."

Xavier appeared in the doorway, sword still sheathed. "There is no sign of Andrés. Mr. Smith, bring the talisman with you."

As large as the suites were, it took less than a minute to find the stolen console. When I entered the room, the controller's glow brightened and began to vibrate, tugging me in a particular direction. It led me to a black wooden chest at the foot of the bed. Inside, next to some knickknacks that were just ugly enough to be incredibly valuable, was the two-toned grey console. I lifted it out of the box, and the controller in my other hand seemed to purr.

Having retrieved the Nintendo, I realized for the first time that the suite hadn't been entirely empty. Two human women, similar enough in appearance to be sisters, knelt on the hardwood floors, their eyes clouded and staring blindly into the distance.

I shivered suddenly as a thin layer of frost crept past me and over the hardwood floors. Lucia turned to Xavier, and the temperature continued to plummet.

"I want him *found*, Captain. Alive, if possible. In pieces, if you must." He saluted and left the room, and her gaze fell upon the two human women. "And someone get me Zorana. I would know what Andrés' blood donors have seen."

CHAPTER 32

IN WHICH THE MANHUNT FOR A MANPIRE BEGINS

Andrés was gone. Nobody had seen him since Sunday night, and none of the cameras had footage of his departure, but the bat had somehow flown the coop. Or whatever it was bats lived in. Caves? I wasn't a zoologist.

His donors weren't any help either. They remained in a semi-catatonic state, and not even Zorana could deduce anything from their blood. Lucia had called an emergency meeting, and now the entire council, minus the traitorous Spaniard, was trying to figure out who to blame.

"We locked down the House last night. How is it that Andrés was able to leave without anyone being aware of it?" The Lady of Winter was less than pleased. I was glad to not be her target, for once.

"Our security is designed to keep intruders out, not to keep someone in," Xavier explained.

"Now they tell me," I muttered under my breath.

Everyone ignored me.

"Additionally," continued Xavier, "as a Council member, Andrés is well acquainted with our protocols. Outside of the individuals in this room, who would have had the power to stop him from leaving?"

"Yes, Captain!" Lucia practically spat the words out. "You've already said as much. Are you going to repeat yourself all night?"

"Only if you keep asking the same questions," I muttered again.

This time, nobody ignored me. Across the table, Juliette pinched the bridge of her nose, as if she had a headache. Anastasia's face was carefully blank, but I could practically feel the disappointment.

Lucia looked down the table, her voice low and dangerous. "Did you have something to share, Mr. Smith?"

It was like being called out for talking in class, except she was far prettier than any of my high school teachers and could do a lot worse to me than detention.

"Yeah, I do." The words surprised even me. "In college, I took a journalism course. The key questions every news article is supposed to answer are who, what, when, where, why, and how."

"Not that I'm questioning the quality of education you might have received at whatever crap college admitted you…" Juliette began, before stopping herself and waving a hand dismissively. "Actually, I *do* question it. Regardless, what does this have to do with anything?"

"Well, it seems like we need to ask some of those same questions here."

"Were we not just now questioning *how* he might have escaped, human?" Marcus looked at me like I was the sort of thing he'd pay someone to scrape off his shoe. I was pretty sure he'd learned that look from Lucia.

"Yeah, but it wasn't getting us anywhere. A better question would be 'How did he know to leave?'" There was silence as my words sunk in. I turned to the queen. "You didn't tell Andrés or Marcus that I would be searching the House, did you?"

"She did not," growled Marcus, "and the lack of faith in her own council sits poorly with me."

"You'd have more of a point, Marcus," put in Anastasia coolly, "had the culprit not turned out to be one of our own."

"So if Lucia didn't tell either of you, how did Andrés know to make his escape? An even bigger question," I continued, "is why? Why steal the Nintendo at all? And why leave it behind in his room, when he clearly had a way of sneaking out through the security perimeter?"

"These are all questions we will ask him, Mr. Smith." Lucia scowled. "But they do not get us any closer to finding him."

"Fair enough," I agreed, "but what about *who*?"

"Why are we listening to this blood bag?" asked Marcus angrily. "We already know the who, you inbred monkey!"

"Actually—" I began, but Anastasia was way ahead of me.

"Andrés had an accomplice." She shared looks with Lucia. "Lord Beel-Kasan's witness saw more than one vampire on the boat."

"Exactly." I sent her a smile of gratitude. And appreciation. And undying love. "And Xavier said the Rook was killed by multiple assailants. So, if we want to find Andrés, we should identify his partner-in-crime."

Lucia nodded sharply. "Captain, assemble the House in the banquet hall. We will see who else is unaccounted for."

"And if nobody is missing?" asked Xavier.

"Then we will know the accomplice remains in the building, and I will put every member of this House to the question until I find them."

"As you wish." Xavier gave a short bow, and left the room.

The blonde turned her arctic eyes back in my direction. "And what will you do, Mr. Smith?"

I hadn't thought that far ahead. Luckily, my own next move seemed pretty obvious. I nodded to the Nintendo and controller on the table in front of me. "I'm going to return *this* to Bill before it disappears again. Who knows? Maybe he'll be satisfied having his console back, and the rest of this can become an internal matter for the House."

Lucia considered for a moment. "Very well. I'll arrange for a driver to transport you. But you will need an escort."

"Your Majesty, I—" Anastasia began.

"No, Anastasia. I need you with me. Juliette, you will accompany Mr. Smith to his rendezvous with Lord Beel-Kasan. Have Xavier lend you one of his Watch for protection."

"Sure thing," said Juliette. We'd come a long way. Just two days ago, she'd practically had a conniption at the thought of being stuck with me. "It's a small price to pay to get out of the house early."

"So be it." The femmepire queen rose to her feet. "And when you return, you will submit to Zorana for questioning, Juliette."

"Is that really necess—"

"This is *my* House!" Lucia's voice cracked like a whip. "You will listen, and you will obey!"

Juliette actually flinched in the face of the queen's wrath. When she spoke, her words were stiff and formal. "Of course, Your Majesty."

I gathered up the Nintendo and followed Juliette to the elevators. She gave me a look of annoyance. "If you say anything, I will hurt you."

I raised my hands in a warding gesture, Nintendo and all, and nodded my understanding. "Totally fair. It's just…"

Juliette turned to face me, yellow eyes glinting in the light. "Yes?"

"I'm just saying… that was one hell of a flinch." I grinned.

For a moment, I thought she'd follow through on her threat. Then she shook her head, trying to fight off an answering smile. "You are *such* an asshole."

ooo

Thankfully, I wasn't invited to the all-vampire assembly. Being the only human in the middle of a roomful of upset vampires could have had life-ending ramifications, and I tried to avoid those, the last few days notwithstanding. I ended up waiting in my designated bedroom for a little less than an hour before Juliette returned.

"Let's go, little bird."

"Go where?"

"To return the Nintendo, moron. Where did Lord Beel-Kasan say he would meet us?"

"Uhm."

Her eyes narrowed. "Yes?"

"I don't have his phone number. And you revoked my telephone privileges." Yes, I was still bitter about that.

"Do I have to do everything around here?" Juliette grabbed the phone from my nightstand and stabbed its single button with what seemed like unnecessary force. "Celeste? This is Juliette. Do you have the phone number for Lord Beel-Kasan's houseboat? Excellent. Yes, please put me through."

She tossed me the phone, which I actually managed to catch, thanks to my elite fifth grade intramural baseball skills.

As the telephone started to ring on the other end, I looked at Juliette. "Is Celeste *always* on duty?"

She gave me a look of mingled pity and exasperation. "Obviously not. Celeste is one of several operators for the House. Even the People need sleep, you know."

"I do now." Someone finally picked up on the other end. "Hello? Bill?"

"Seven!" yelled Jee Sun merrily, at a decibel level usually reached only by foghorns and football arenas.

ooo

After being deafened by Jee Sun's enthusiastic but nonsensical greeting, I had her hand the telephone over to Bill. I could hear her skipping through the houseboat, phone-in-hand. Was it a cell phone? If so, where did Bill store it when he went out? Vegetables didn't have pockets, did they? Half the time, the demigod didn't even have arms!

"Johnny Appleseed!" Bill's drawl came through loud and clear. "Wiggle your face at me, AMIGO!"

It had only been one day. How had I already forgotten how weird he was? "Good news; I managed to find your Nintendo."

"Aces!" I could hear Jee Sun's voice in the background, but the words themselves were unintelligible. "Tiny Flower wishes to know if the box has any ouchies. IT DOES NOT HAVE OUCHIES, DOES IT?"

"No, Bill," I assured him, "it doesn't look to be damaged at all." Before he could further derail the conversation, I continued. "So, I was hoping I could meet with you to return it?"

"Absolutely, Johnny One-Note!" He paused. "How about Gehenna? You bring the sandwiches, and I'll bring the beer! NO ANCHOVIES FOR ME!"

Juliette shook her head vigorously in my direction, as if I needed her help to figure out that going to a hell dimension was a bad idea. I'd seen the fricking candelabras. "Actually, could we meet here on Earth instead? Preferably in San Diego?"

"You're a crazy one, Johnny Sunshine!" I had to laugh at that, and he joined in merrily, although I suspect we were laughing about different things. "But okay! Hmmmmmmm." He thought about it for several seconds, humming the theme song to Cheers the entire time. "What about The Bitter End?"

This time, Juliette nodded, a wide smile on her face. Least subtle charades partner ever.

"You mean the bar, right, and not some sort of literal ending?" It seemed worth clarifying. One misunderstanding with the insane vegetable demigod and whoosh! There went San Diego. Or at least San Diego's least-favorite, barely-employed private investigator. "Because I'm pretty sure it was renamed a few years ago. Now it's The Drunken Seagull or something like that."

"Absolutely!" he crowed. "The bar under the bar by the bar! There will be beer! And music! THINGS WITH LEGS WILL MOVE THOSE LEGS!" Another pause. "No, Tiny Flower, you cannot go again. You are TOO YOUNG. Next year, maybe." Then, back to me. "Let us meet when Mickey's small hand points at the seven!"

Sadly, I didn't have any trouble translating that into real time. "That sounds great." I looked over at Juliette, who remained visibly excited for some reason. Which reminded me... "Is it okay if I'm accompanied by a couple of the People, Bill? They're a little over-protective at the moment."

"You won't bring the cold one, will you? WE DO NOT LIKE HER FACE."

As many problems as I had with Lucia, her face wasn't one of them. Nevertheless, I assured him that Lucia had other things to do.

"Then it's okey dokey with me, Johnny Rotten. I will be waiting for you at The Bitter End."

I still didn't love that phrasing. I handed Juliette the phone. "What are you so happy about, Duchess?"

"I love The Bitter End! Finally, something good comes out of the tedium of babysitting your worthless ass."

I ignored the insult to my ass. Truth be told, it *had* seen better days. "Are we talking about the same bar? I've only been once, and it was nice, but kind of sedate." And way too expensive for someone like me. "And like I told Bill, they changed the name a while ago."

"That's the human bar. The *real* bar retains its original name, and is located below the other." Juliette gave me an arch look. "Stick with me, little bird, and I'll show you the world."

"That's what scares me," I muttered.

"One of many things, no doubt. We're meeting at seven? That should give us just enough time."

"For what?" It was a few minutes after five. On a Monday evening, even with rush hour traffic, it shouldn't take more than an hour to get downtown.

"For me to get ready and for you to transform into someone I won't be embarrassed to be seen with."

CHAPTER 33
IN WHICH A DEMIGOD, A VAMPIRE, AND A FRAT MAN WALK INTO A BAR

Juliette and Anastasia had very different ideas on what constituted appropriate attire. The one thing they agreed on was that I was very much lacking in that department.

A little bit before six, Juliette whisked back into my bedroom, wearing a black mini-dress that was probably illegal in parts of the Midwest. It clung to her slim curves and stopped mid-thigh, exposing a lethal amount of leg. A diamond pendant dangled between her breasts on a platinum chain. She'd even used some sort of black magic, alchemy, and/or makeup to make her eyes appear twice their usual size. Given their distinctive color, the effect was profound.

"Try not to drool on the carpet, frat man," she said smugly. And then, with a frown, "That's not what you're wearing, is it?"

I'd showered and dressed in my usual standby; worn jeans and a t-shirt. My hair was combed, my face was shaved of its eleven o'clock shadow, and I was manfully not complaining about having to go commando yet again because nobody had grabbed boxers from my house. In short, I was as presentable as I could be without three months of weight training, a stylist, cosmetic surgery, and appropriately dim lighting. "We're going to a bar, Juliette, not walking the red carpet."

"If you wear that, we're not going anywhere." She stalked over to me. "Does that t-shirt have *holes* in it?"

"You're losing your punk rock street cred by the minute." I glanced down at what appeared to be yet another pair of Louboutin heels. "If you didn't lose it entirely the moment you put those on."

Juliette drew back, momentarily offended, then slid back in front of me with a smirk. She thumped her chest. "Punk is in here. There's no reason I can't also enjoy the occasional pretty. You, on the other hand, appear to be representing the 'dirty hippie' demographic. And that will simply not do."

And so, for the second time in two days, a femmepire dug through the dresser to examine the clothes that had been retrieved from my house.

"This. And this." Juliette tossed me a pair of less-worn jeans and a blue button-up. "The blue will help minimize your blotchy complexion."

My complexion and I were both equally insulted.

"And these," she continued, pulling out the dress shoes I'd worn to the mediation and another pair of black socks. "If you ever wear white socks and sneakers again for a night on the town, I will drown you in a puddle."

Finally, she looked at my unruly hair and shrugged. "I'm not a miracle worker. Maybe you'll free a djinn someday. Or go bald. At least now you're borderline acceptable."

ooo

Bob was waiting for us out front in one of the Escalades. And riding shotgun was our designated Watch member.

"Hey, Ray."

The spacey manpire blinked in my direction, and threw up a halfhearted, absent-minded wave. Of all the Watch members available, Xavier had picked Astronaut Ray to go with us? Maybe he was a lot deadlier than he looked.

Or maybe Xavier didn't care overly much if I died.

Juliette joined me in the Escalade, having added a slightly cropped black leather jacket to her outfit. She saw me notice and smirked. "I decided to make allowances for your leather fetish." She brushed the back of her hand against my cheek, sending a charge of electricity to my extremities. "We'll see how Lady Dumenyova likes you carrying *my* scent."

"I wish you two would leave me out of whatever this competition is that you've got going on."

"I don't believe that for even a second, little bird."

"Are you going to tell me what happened at the assembly? Was anyone other than Andrés missing?"

"Briefly." She waved off my confused look. "Mouth shut, ears open, Mr. Smith. It's the only way you're ever going to learn anything." Her red lips quirked. "When we first assembled, one other person was missing: Brenna. You don't know her, but—"

"Dark, curly hair, spends most of her time in the gym? Yeah, she and I go way back. Pen pals and workout buddies. She used to hate me back in high school."

"That last bit I could believe... if she'd ever attended high school." Juliette rolled her eyes. "Anyway, she showed up late. Seems she'd been out walking the grounds when the call to assembly came."

"So we still don't know who Andrés' accomplice is?"

"Nope. Lucia gave the House the five-cent recap, and said she'd be merciful if the individual came forward and turned themselves in. But whoever it is didn't seem to buy what she was selling."

"I can't say I blame them." Lucia was many things, but merciful wasn't a word that came to mind.

"I guess not. But it means the House is stuck on lock-down for another day, so that Zorana can perform her mass interrogations."

"What if Zorana herself is responsible?" I asked, using my keen insight and well trained detective instincts.

"The Blood Witch doesn't leave the House, little bird. Ever. And teaming up with Andrés? Please. She does not play well with others."

Now *that* I could believe.

"So Zorana is innocent, and Lucia's innocent, and I'm innocent," I mused, "but the rest of you are... People of interest."

Somewhere in the magical fun-land of my imagination, there was a rim-shot and canned studio laughter.

ooo

The Bitter End was only a few miles from my shabby office, but the two neighborhoods couldn't have been more different. The Gaslamp Quarter had been rescued from the depths of urban decay somewhere around the time I was born, and was now one of the nicer areas in the city, full of bars, clubs, and restaurants, with Petco Park, Seaport Village, and the convention center all in walking distance. Even on a Monday, there were a fair number of people milling about—mostly tourists—but we found a parking spot by the bar on F Street.

I pointed to the black and gold awnings across the street and the yellow sign which featured a stylized black bird. "Tipsy Crow! I knew there was a drunk bird involved somehow."

"For the last time, nobody cares what the human bar is called." Juliette strutted out into the street—literally stopping traffic—and Ray and I scurried along behind her. Well, I scurried. Ray sort of… ambled. When an annoyed driver in a red Mini Cooper beeped her horn, he turned and waved with a smile.

I don't think she smiled back. And I'm pretty sure the gesture she gave him wasn't a wave.

Juliette ignored the main entrance of the bar entirely, and instead headed to a staircase that led below street-level.

"I think this just goes down to the dance floor—" My words cut off when, at the base of the stairs, the femmepire vanished into the opposite wall. I looked around in confusion until Juliette reappeared, an exasperated look on her face.

"Are you coming or what?"

"*Into* the wall?" I carefully passed one hand through what should have been solid concrete. There was a slight flickering of light as I did so. "This is an illusion?"

"No. It's a portal, accessible only by the supernatural community."

"How does that help me? Last time I checked, I was human."

"As if I could ever forget. After I enter, the portal should remain active long enough for you to follow. Don't worry; it hasn't accidentally eaten any humans for at least a month." She smirked. "But you might want to hurry, just in case."

I jerked my hand out of the portal-wall. All five of my fingers appeared to still be intact. Wait... had that scar always been there? Oh. Yes, it had. Whew.

Juliette rolled her eyes for the thousandth time and disappeared into the portal. This time, I followed on her heels.

Against all expectations, walking through a supernatural portal in the middle of San Diego was a kind of disappointing experience. There was a minor glow, like someone was fiddling with the world's dimmer switch, but that was it. No feeling of transportation. No nausea as my body was re-assembled from spare atomic parts. No wailing of damned souls as I took a side route through hell. I simply stepped into the wall, and emerged somewhere else.

As for that 'somewhere else', we were at the top of yet another flight of stairs, but these were a far cry from what we'd walked down in San Diego. The ceiling, walls, and steps were all rough black stone, like unpolished obsidian. Striations of metallic gold glinted in the flickering light of the torches that lined our steps. The torches looked like the sort you'd find at Hawaiian luaus or Disneyland, but their pure white flames didn't give off any heat or smoke.

Ray bumped into me from behind, interrupting my inspection. Juliette was already nearing the bottom of the stairs. I'd never seen someone in heels take stairs so quickly. Then again, she'd been wearing heels just like those when she hurdled a table to bludgeon me unconscious.

It's possible I was still a little bitter about that.

At the base of the steps, two larger torches flanked an imposing, iron-bound door. Standing in front of that door was a slab of grey beef with legs. Bloodshot eyes peered out from a face that would have been most remarkable for its twice-broken snout if it weren't for the two tusks jutting upward and outward from the lower jaw.

Other than those tusks, the grey skin, and the fact that he was larger than an NFL lineman, he seemed fairly normal. His coarse grey hair was cropped short, and he sported a neatly trimmed goatee. He was also dressed much nicer than me, in slacks, a gold button-up shirt (tucked-in, no less), and a blazer that looked like it had come straight from the dry-cleaner. No tie, but that was probably because ties weren't made to fit thirty-five inch necks.

Maybe the femmepires were right. If I was being out-dressed by orcs, I really did need to step up my game.

By the time Ray and I reached them, Juliette had already said her piece, and the bouncer was stepping aside to allow us entry. My head barely reached his chest, and the sound of his breathing was reminiscent of the noise an inner tube makes when being inflated. Which made sense, I guess, given that his lungs were roughly the same size as one. As I squeezed past, he bared his teeth in the world's least friendly smile. I ducked my head and hurried in, followed by what was either his low chuckle or a minor earthquake.

On the human side of the portal, the Tipsy Crow had three floors, partly because horizontal space was at a premium downtown, and partly because it allowed the owners to orient each floor to serve a different need or class of clientele. The top floor housed the VIP section, which I'd somehow never gotten to experience, the ground floor featured the main bar, and the basement was reserved for dancing.

On this side of the portal, space was clearly less of a concern. A long bar stretched thirty or more feet along the wall to our right. Behind it, shelves carried hundreds of bottles, everything from scotch to something called *Menschlichemwein*. The men and women working the bar were a very long way from human. The nearest sported a third arm, scaled and green, sprouting from a bare and otherwise attractive abdomen. That arm was vigorously shaking a cocktail while her two standard-issue arms poured a second drink.

I bet she made a killing on tips.

The sitting area was filled with a number of round tables and wooden chairs. Private booths lined the left wall, and a dance floor was barely visible past the tables. Some sort of jazz emanated from that same direction, but I couldn't locate the band. In fact, my vision was oddly distorted, like I was looking through a slightly dirty window pane.

I blinked my eyes a few times, but the effect stubbornly remained. There's never a bottle of Visine when you need one.

In place of tiki torches, glowing balls of colored light floated about the bar's interior. For the most part, they accumulated in the rafters above us, but here and there, a lone globe drifted down towards the floor. One particular globe, shining a pretty blue, hovered directly above me. At this distance, I could see that it lacked any sort of visible shell or container. It was as if the glowing light had simply coalesced of its own accord into a rough sphere. How had the owners managed that trick? I reached up to give it a tap, only to have Juliette grab my wrist in a steely grip.

"Don't bother the Mistborn, little bird. The last thing we need is for you to start an interspecies war. You can look, but don't touch." She saw how my eyes were avidly darting around the room, taking in the exotic sights and sounds. "Actually, try not to look either. You'll just end up pissing someone off… and this is a new dress."

"Wait," I hissed, "the floating light bulbs are *people?*"

The blue globe slowly floated away from us. Hopefully, I hadn't hurt its feelings. I had a sudden vision of my house being swarmed by balls of colored light. It would be like Christmas in July.

"They're sentient, yes. Most beings here are," I think Juliette was beginning to reassess the wisdom of bringing me here. She brought us to an empty table and glanced around the room. "Do you see Lord Beel-Kasan anywhere? Remember; I have no idea what he'll look like."

I shook my head and placed the Nintendo and its controller on the table. "You'll know him when you see him, but I don't think he's here yet. I'm having a hard time seeing anything though."

"Oh, right. I'd forgotten the effect this place had on humans." Juliette shrugged. "Don't worry about it. Your body will acclimate and you won't even notice it anymore. Either that, or you'll implode."

I was still digesting that when a waitress arrived at our table. Or a waiter… it was hard to tell, given that the creature was entirely hairless, with two iridescent eyes and lightly scaled skin in a fire-engine red.

"Nice to see you again, Juliette. What can I get for you folks tonight?" I wasn't sure how that long and forked tongue was able to contort to shape sounds I understood, but the voice was undeniably female. She nodded in my direction. "While you're welcome to bring your own drinks, there will be a nominal corkage fee."

Juliette shook her head. "Actually, Mercedes, I'm letting this one age a bit first." Three guesses who they were talking about. "I'll take a glass of AB-negative, if you have any that's fresh. And a Pickled Mary."

I *seriously* hoped that was just the name of a drink. I'd attended high school with a girl named Mary, and despite her many, many faults, she hadn't deserved to be pickled.

The waitress looked over to me.

"Rum and coke, please."

"What rum would you like?"

That one stumped me. The bars Mike and I frequented never asked. I wasn't even convinced they always used actual rum. "Uhm… a good one?"

Juliette looked like she wanted to cry.

"Of course, sir." Mercedes' strange face quirked in what may have been a smile.

"I'll take a Guinness." Just like that, my opinion of Ray kicked up a notch. Anyone that drank Guinness was okay in my book.

Our waitress headed towards the bar with our drink orders, and I turned to find Juliette eyeing me with a disgusted expression.

"What?" I checked to make sure my fly was still zipped.

"'A good one?' Really? Could you try even a little bit to not embarrass me in public?" She shook her head sadly. "A good one…"

I did my best to ignore her. She'd been right about one thing, at least; my vision was slowly clearing. As the room came into view, I saw that only a few of the nearby tables were occupied. Most of the people around us could at least pass as human.

And then there was the blob of goo that occupied three chairs around a circular table. Or… were there three globs of goo that just happened to form a single mass under that table? It was difficult to be sure.

Orc bouncers and snot elementals?
Bill would fit right in.

CHAPTER 34
IN WHICH ONE GOOD DEMIGOD
DESERVES ANOTHER

As if my thoughts had summoned him, the seven-foot-tall asparagus appeared in the entryway. That part of the room darkened as nearby Mistborn made a beeline for other locales. Past Bill's spindly body, I could see the bouncer, looking several shades whiter than usual.

"John-o-Rama!" Bill cried out in joy, growing an arm to shake my hand as he ambled over, still lacking anything that could serve as legs. "IN THE BAR BY THE BAR UNDER THE BAR!" His charcoal eyes spun in place, and the magic marker mouth widened into a grin. At some point since I'd last seen him, something had taken a bite out of his carrot nose. The end of it now dangled by a thread.

"How's it going, Bill?"

"It goes places we did not expect, and other places too," he replied cheerfully, "and then the mouths wiggle and we are here. Is this the box?"

"Recovered as promised." I passed him the Nintendo and its controller. He grew a second arm to hold them.

"Cheerio, good chap!" Two additional arms appeared, clapped once in evident excitement, and then disappeared back into the green stalk of his body. "All that we need now are the HEARTS AND HEADS OF THOSE WHO TOOK IT!"

The snot elementals at the nearby table separated into three equally sized globs, and began to ooze their way toward the door. I guess that answered my earlier question.

"About that…" His face didn't move at all, but I could feel his focus intensify. It was a very creepy feeling. "We've identified one of the thieves, but he fled the House before we could capture him. The People are hunting for him now, and hope to find him and his accomplice shortly. I hope that's okay?"

"Of course it is, Johnny Bones! I'm a reasonable sort of guy."

"Anyway," I continued, after an awkward pause, "I thought you'd prefer getting that back as soon as possible."

"Yes! Tiny Flower was very upset by its disappearance, and we CANNOT HAVE THAT EVER NEVER EVER." His magic marker mouth grew jagged, like a jack o' lantern's maw. Our table was now almost completely dark, and a mass of Mistborn appeared to be hiding behind the bar.

"Lord Beel-Kasan." A cloaked and cowled figure approached from the direction of the dance floor, seemingly unruffled by Bill's current state of mind.

Bill's face rotated around his body to regard the newcomer. "Lord Kala, my amigo! It is very dark in here!"

Next to me, Juliette, who had remained uncharacteristically silent the entire time, looked as if she wanted to crawl under the table. Ray didn't seem too worried though.

Which might have comforted me if it had been anyone other than Ray.

"It is dark because you're scaring the Mistborn again," Kala explained, reaching out with a skeletal hand to pat the asparagus on his back. "Perhaps, we could move your party to a private room instead?"

"Will there be beer?" Bill asked hopefully.

"I will make certain of it."

"THEN LET US GO AND DRINK THE BEER!" Even as Bill shambled after Kala, his face rotated around to look back at our table. "Bring your friends, Johnny boy, and we will wiggle our faces while libations soothe old wounds. And," he added reproachfully, "maybe then you can make proper introductions."

"Absolutely, Bill," I told his back. Ray went on ahead, but I took Juliette aside for a moment. "Are you okay, Duchess? You're being very un-you at the moment."

"He seriously looks like an asparagus to you?" She shuddered. "Lucky damn human. And Lord Kala—"

"Yeah, who is that dude anyway?"

"Keep it down, moron," she hissed. "He's the owner of this place. And a demigod, just like Lord Beel-Kasan."

"Seriously?" How many demigods could one city hold? "What's he a demigod of? Creepy fashion choices?"

"Time." She nudged me with one hip, and we started across the bar after Ray. "And death, I think."

Of course he was. "Where is the demigod of puppies and rainbows when you need him?"

"Orlando, last I heard."

I honestly couldn't tell if she was joking.

"Anyway, Lord Kala's domain is limited to this one dimension, but within it, he is not someone to screw with."

"What a marvelous idea it was to meet here then."

"Stuff it, little bird." Juliette's acerbic attitude was making a comeback. "Great booze, hot guys, and dancing. This place is normally awesome."

Hot guys? I could only hope she wasn't talking about the bouncer. If she was, we had vastly different ideas about male beauty.

"I've been coming here for longer than you've been alive, and this is the first time Lord Kala has ever made an appearance." She scowled at me. "I don't know how, but this is your fault. You're some sort of a magnet for horrible things. If we fired you into space, I bet the world would suddenly become a paradise."

"Sure, but think how bored you'd be without me."

"I'm willing to risk it!"

Still trailing Ray and the two demigods, we made our way across the empty dance floor. On the far side, the source of the jazz music I'd been hearing was revealed to be a rotund purple elephant in a tuxedo. His mouth was open, and from that yawning orifice came the sounds of at least four distinct instruments.

I didn't even pause to stare. It was far from the strangest thing I'd seen that night. I did feel kind of bad that nobody was dancing though. It couldn't be easy to sing jazz. When we finished our business, I'd tell Juliette to tip him.

On our left, the booths had given way to private rooms. Kala took us to the last of those rooms and opened the door with a bony arm, inviting us to enter. I risked a peek into his shadowed cowl as I walked past. A skull with candle flames for eyes grinned back at me.

Yeah. He seemed like a death god alright.

Inside, more traditional lighting illuminated a long table and ten or more chairs. Kala offered a half-bow. "I will instruct Mercedes to bring your drinks here. What do you wish to partake in, Lord Beel-Kasan?"

"Kala, if we're going to keep wearing sombreros, you really should call me Bill," replied the vegetable demigod. "Could I have a bottle or two of Waldhaus Gold?" He smacked his lips together, all the more disturbing because he didn't actually have lips.

Juliette shuddered.

"Consider it done." The hooded skeleton bowed again and left, gently closing the door behind him.

Bill's face rotated to me. And waited in silence.

Oh, right.

"Lord Beel-Kasan, allow me to introduce you to Lady Juliette, youngest member of House Borghesi's Council. And this is Ray, a representative of the queen's Watch." I turned to the two vampires. "Ray, Juliette… this is Lord Beel-Kasan, Bill to his friends, and the owner of the Nintendo we recovered today."

Bill grew a hand and waved, his magic marker mouth wavering briefly before it settled on a smile. He turned to Juliette. "Your eyes are yellow like the PAC MAN WHO EATS GHOSTS! I like you!" Then, to Ray: "And you have an extra face on your head! Ha!" His voice quieted ominously. "I will reserve judgment until your face wiggles."

Bill's own face rotated towards me. "But actually, Jack-be-nimble—"

That was a new one.

"—the box is not mine. It belongs to Tiny Flower, and she will be very happy to have it back."

The door opened to admit our crimson-skinned waitress, Mercedes, carrying a tray full of drinks. As she passed out glasses, I decided this was as good a time as any to indulge my curiosity.

I leaned over to Bill, who mirrored my pose in a way that still shouldn't have been possible for an asparagus. "Do you mind if I ask you a question, Bill?"

"Go right ahead, tomodachi! I have nothing but time." He suddenly squirmed about in his chair. "Mickey's not pointing at the nine yet, is it?"

I eyed the clock on the wall. It was about half past seven. "No, we still have a while to go before then."

"Excellent," he enthused, "I have to see a guy about a thing at that time." He leaned closer again, speaking in a whisper louder than most people's shouts. "He is afraid of BUTTONS!" He giggled again, before the mouth abruptly stilled. "What did you want to know?"

I hesitated, trying to phrase the question in a way that wouldn't result in San Diego's destruction. "What's the story with Jee Sun?" The magic marker mouth drew down into a frown, and I hurried to elaborate. "How did you two meet? Is she human? You know, that sort of thing."

"Tiny Flower is as human as you are, Jackie-O." Bill's voice was unexpectedly solemn. "She was broken by the thing that called himself a father, and I came into her nightmare, and took her away and gave her a cape and NOTHING WILL HARM HER!"

A crack appeared in the center of the heavy wooden table, spider-webbing outward like a map of fault lines. I grabbed my glass before it could spill. Priorities, right?

Thankfully, the cracks stopped before the table fell apart entirely. Bill's half-eaten carrot nose spun in place and his mouth slowly stretched back into a smile. "And now we are happy and we play with the box on the boat, and she calls me Mr. Bill and I call her Tiny Flower and other names of that sort."

Poor Jee Sun. It was oddly fitting, that a demigod of nightmares had saved a human child from her own waking horror. "And her dad?"

The charcoal eyes regarded me solemnly, the magic marker mouth a flat line. "He burns, John Smith. He burns."

CHAPTER 35

IN WHICH GOOD DRINKS MAKE GOOD NEIGHBORS

"…and then the moth says," I paused, trying to hold in my giggles, "well, your light was on!"

I waved my arms wildly, nearly knocking over the assortment of glasses that had collected in front of me. Bill, on his fourth or thirtieth beer, laughed uproariously, his shadows cavorting wildly along the wall behind him. Juliette was dancing around the room, her own glass in hand, and Ray… well, Ray was passed out face-down on the table, after only two beers.

What a lightweight.

"This has been a good night, Jack and the Beanstalk, even if I did miss my appointment with the button man," burbled Bill, whose partially eaten carrot was now pointing in the opposite direction from the rest of his face. "You and Lady Pac Man and silly face head are CRAZY!"

"I'll drink to that," agreed Lady Pa… err, Juliette, tossing back the remainder of her cocktail.

"And soon, you will find the thieves and there will be bloodshed and everyone will be happy except for the thieves whose blood is shed!"

"You know what's funny?" I choked out, trying to keep my latest rum and coke from going up my nose as I snorted. "Nothing about the theft makes even the tiniest bit of sense!"

Tiniest. I found myself growing momentarily maudlin. A long time ago, I'd had a pet mouse named Tiny. He'd been cute, like a pink-eyed snowflake in my hand. *Oh, Tiny. Why did you have to go away?*

I blinked away tears and bravely continued. "I mean, why would someone steal the box, and then keep it in their own room, where anyone with a magic controller could find it?"

Juliette flounced back over. It had taken her four cocktails to get over her fear of Bill. By the tenth, they were old friends. "Tweet tweet goes the little birdie! Remember," she drawled, poking me in the chest with one finger, "nobody on the council would expect to have their privacy invaded like that!" She looked over at Bill. "*I'm* on the council, y'know! Youngest in the West. It's verrrrrrrrry impressive!"

"Still, it doesn't make sense!" I maintained, with a stubbornness born of two rum and cokes, a screwdriver, and half of Ray's second Guinness. And possibly other drinks I couldn't remember. I looked at Bill and Juliette, wide-eyed. "I think Andy was framed!"

"So the THIEF IS NOT THE THIEF?" Bill seemed confused. "Then who is the THIEF THAT MADE THE NON THIEF LOOK LIKE THE THIEF?" He lifted another glass of dark beer near his magic marker mouth, and the alcohol disappeared, as if by magic.

"I haven't figured that part out yet. But I think all of this," I waved my arms, sending an empty bottle to the floor, "was just a setup!"

"NO!" Bill hooted in shock. "Why would Lord Kala DO THAT?"

I collapsed back into giggles.

"Not the bar, Bill!" I waved my arms about again. "I mean the other stuff. Rook dead. Mediators murdered. Nintendo gone. Vampire snob framed." I leaned in close and whispered loudly. "We think it's a conspria... a conps... a plot!"

"We do?" asked Juliette, a confused look on her lovely face. A moment later, her expression cleared and she giggled. "I'd totally forgotten about that!"

"Anyway," I continued, shushing Juliette, "Ana thinks so too, and she's like *way* smart."

"Not *that* smart," mumbled the femmepire.

"But the wiggling of faces makes my head all twisty," complained Bill. "Why would someone do this?"

"We haven't figured that part out yet either. What we need…" I began, lifting a glass to my lips only to discover that it was empty. I fumbled about for one that still had its contents, and tried again. "What we need… is a plan!"

"YES!" crowed Bill, his magic marker mouth wobbling in excitement.

"Awesome!" agreed Juliette. They both looked at me expectantly, and then the femmepire snorted with laughter. "You don't have a plan!"

"My plan was for us to make a plan. I leave the details up to you."

"Well, my plan is that we follow your plan and come up with a plan!" She stuck her tongue out at me. Brat.

"And my plan is that the plan must involve beer and yellow ribbons!" chimed in Bill.

Stymied, we looked about us for further inspiration. As if caught in a gravitational pull, all eyes—yellow, charcoal or otherwise—fell upon Ray at the same time.

And so it was that Ray found himself being woken up by a human, a demigod, and a House elder. He handled it with his usual style and grace.

"Whu…?"

"Silly face head, we need you to make a plan to undo the plot by the thief who is a thief but not the thief you thought was a thief!" Despite not having a real mouth, Bill's breath smelled strongly of hops.

"Whu…?" Ray managed again, feebly. His gaze skated over me, flinched away from Bill, and landed on Juliette. Or, more precisely, on Juliette's cleavage, which was, as I'd noted more than a few times, looking very nice that night.

The femmepire slid one slender finger under his chin, and lifted his eyes to her face.

Busted!

"We think there's a plot against the House," she explained, "and we four are going to solve it! Like the Justice League!"

Oh.

My.

God.

Juliette read comics! Not the right comics, clearly, if she was making Justice League references, but still…

"Or the Avengers!" I corrected her.

We glared daggers at each other, as only fans of superhero groups from competing comic publishers can do.

"Or the Wonder Twins!"

We both looked at Bill for a long moment, then shrugged. Sure, why not?

"But isn't Andrés the thief?" Ray was still confused.

I shook my head, which set the room spinning. "We think he was framed, dude! Someone wants us at war with Bill!"

"But we're not at war with him. Right?" He was starting to harsh my buzz something fierce. Juliette rode in to the rescue.

"The *point* is that we're going to find out who is really behind it all. And then," she muttered to herself, "we'll see who is *way smart*."

"But we need-a-plan-need-a-plan-need-a-plan!" sang Bill, his face rotating several times around his body.

"And that's where you come in, Ray." I smiled at the bewildered vampire, glad that we were back on track.

He gave it some thought. "Maybe we could start by going to bed, and figuring it out tomorrow?"

"YES! That is a GREAT plan!" Our resident demigod was officially on board.

"But I wanted to dance," whined Juliette, doing a pirouette that nearly decapitated Ray. "Actually, I may be a little bit drunk."

I didn't reply, because as soon as Ray had mentioned bed, my eyes had started to droop. Sleep sounded good. Really good. I might not even shower first.

And just like that, the first joint meeting of the Justice League, Avengers, and Wonder Twins came to a loud but successful ending. Our cause was just, our faith was strong, and most importantly, we had a plan.

ooo

Our exit from The Bitter End was a great deal noisier than our entrance, but none of the other guests chose to make an issue of it. Bill was the only one of us walking in a straight line, and he and Juliette were singing a song that had been popular before my parents were born.

I staggered through the bar, trying to avoid the tables and chairs in my path. Somehow, the room was affecting my eyesight even worse than when we'd arrived… only instead of a general haze, the whole place was spinning.

Eventually, we made it through the portal, and up the stairs to F Street, where the night air was cool on our faces. Juliette had settled our tab, but we'd forgotten to tip the jazz elephant. Next time.

Bill took his leave of us, Nintendo in hand, and began walking in the general direction of the harbor. Several tourists took one look at him and hurriedly crossed the street. One of them, braver than the rest, took a picture with his phone. Moments later, the phone erupted in a fountain of sparks. Pieces of expensive plastic fell to the curb.

Bob and the Escalade were still parked just across the street. He opened the rear door, and Juliette and I climbed inside. Eventually, I managed to fasten my seat belt. Safety first, San Diego! In the other chair, Juliette stretched with a yawn and snuggled into her leather jacket. It was adorable, like watching a baby tiger go to sleep. Bob climbed back in, and fished out his keys.

"Hey, where's Ray?"

Where had the vampire gone? I double-checked the front seat, but he still wasn't there. Blearily, I spotted him across the street. For some reason, he was watching our car intently. The wave he gave me was a twin to the one he'd offered the driver of the Mini Cooper a few hours earlier.

Bob didn't hear my question… or notice Ray's absence. Instead, he turned the key in the ignition. The Escalade's engine roared to life, the air conditioning kicked on with a purr, and the world around me erupted in fire and light as our SUV exploded.

CHAPTER 36
IN WHICH HEAVEN IS CLOSED FOR REMODELING

"John, sweetie? Are you almost ready?"

"Just a second, Mom!" I checked myself out in the mirror. I was as presentable as a rented tuxedo could make me, my hair darker than normal thanks to all the product I'd put in it. The corsage was still pristine in its plastic container on my bedroom dresser.

[Corsage? Why do I have a corsage?]

I ignored the stray thought, straightened my bow tie, and readjusted my cummerbund one final time. At least I didn't have a gut, unlike some of my classmates. I'd spent the last four years of high school trying to put on muscle, but it seemed my destiny was to remain a beanpole forever.

The basement door cracked open, and I could hear someone on the stairs. "Your date's here, son. Better come on up, or I might just go to prom in your stead. Plus, you know your mom is going to want pictures before you lovebirds head out for the night."

[Date? Lovebirds?]

Again, a random thought struggled to make itself known in my mind. Weren't Mike and I going to the prom as heterosexual life partners?

I snickered. That sounded like something we'd have done, if I hadn't already had a date. I grabbed the corsage in one hand, and took the stairs two at a time.

As expected, Mom had her camera ready. The flash blinded me as I left the stairwell. I blinked spots out of my eyes and posed for a couple more solo shots, before heading into the living room, where my dad was no doubt entertaining... whoever it was I was going to prom with. Why couldn't I remember?

All the stress of choosing a university was clearly taking its toll on my brain.

I rounded the corner, and there was Ana, wearing a lovely silk dress in deep green, her long auburn hair curled and styled to fall about her face. She smiled and rose to her feet as I presented her the corsage we'd selected to match her dress. Even after all this time, it was hard to believe that the most beautiful girl in school had chosen me as her boyfriend. What had I done to get so lucky?

"You didn't become a private detective, for one," pointed out my dad... but when I looked over, he was busily engaged in conversation with my mother. Sensing my gaze, he offered a big smile and a not-so-subtle thumbs-up while nodding in Ana's direction.

"I need pictures of the lovely couple!" My mom had taken control of the situation, as usual. "Ana, dear, would your parents like copies?"

[She doesn't have parents.]

Another weird thought. Of course Ana had parents! Hadn't I spent the first month of our relationship terrified that her father would find out I'd kissed his daughter? And if Ana's mother was any indication, my girlfriend was going to be lovely for a long time.

[A very, very long time.]

We posed for photos until my dad intervened on our behalf.

"Maria, you can't keep them here all night." He looked past my mom to us. "You kids, go and have a wonderful time. We won't wait up! Be safe!"

And just like that, Ana and I were headed out the door. I had a moment of panic when I realized I didn't have my car keys with me... which was ridiculous, in retrospect. After all, I'd rented a limo for the occasion!

It was parked out front, and the lady chauffeur hurried to open the door so Ana and I could enter. She doffed her cap and made a funny little bow. "Ma'am. Sir." Yellow eyes twinkled with good cheer, and I couldn't help but smile back at her. This was going to be the greatest night of my life.

Ana slipped into the limo and I followed. The driver closed our door, walked around the car, and took her own seat behind the wheel. And then... nothing. She sat there motionless.

"I think we're ready to go," I suggested.

She met my eyes in the rear view mirror, her smile gone. "Aren't you forgetting something, John?"

[Forgetting something?]

"Oh, of course. Our other passenger!" Ana scooted over to the window to make space and a dazzling blonde in a white slip dress took a seat next to me.

"Hi there, Lucia! Glad you could make it!"

"I wouldn't miss it for the world, John." Her pale blue eyes were ice cold.

With everyone finally present, the limo pulled away from my parent's house. I was saying something to Ana when Lucia clamped a hand down on my thigh. For a cheerleader, she had a hell of a grip. Almost painful, even.

I turned to tell her to knock it off only to find that the limo's windows were melting, dripping down the car doors like condensation.

"I think something might be wrong."

The chauffeur didn't reply. Lucia's fingers continued to dig into my flesh.

"John..." Ana tugged at my left shirt cuff.

"I'm telling you, this is very wrong!" I reached for the chauffeur's shoulder but it crumbled under my hand. Her cap fell into the passenger seat, exposing a grinning skull staring blindly over the dashboard.

"John...!" Ana was persistent.

"What?!?" Didn't she realize a skeleton chauffeur could never get us to prom? I turned to look at my girlfriend, but she'd been replaced by a gray-skinned man with tusks jutting out from his lower jaw. He growled.

"I really think you need to wake up."

And so I did. And immediately wished I hadn't.

ooo

Heat.

That was my first sensation.

No, wait. There was a lot of pain too.

Heat and pain and pain and heat.

Also, someone was groaning like they'd been in a car accident.

Oh, wait. That was me.

I cracked open one dry and dusty eye, and squeezed it shut again immediately to block out the blinding light. I tried again, opening that eye a tiny sliver at a time. After a while, I was able to make out shapes and colors within the brightness. Taking a leap of faith, I opened the other eye.

I was lying flat on my back. Thunderclouds gathered above me in a starless sky that was somehow still overly bright. I squinted up. Why were the clouds varying shades of red and orange? As I watched, magenta lightning lanced down from one thunderhead, followed almost immediately by a dull roar. The air was thick and charged with electricity.

San Diego can always use the rain, I thought, before my body decided to remind me of the sheer pain it was experiencing. My left arm was pinned to the ground, but my right arm was free and mobile. Gingerly, I patted my chest and abdomen. Everything seemed to be in one piece. Using that same arm, I tried to roll over onto my side. Liquid fire immediately erupted in my right leg, the leg that Lucia had been…

I shook my head as the thought slipped away. The dream was already fading.

I took the coward's way out and decided to focus on my other issues first. Whatever was wrong with my leg could wait until I had a clear head and two functional arms. I looked down and found my left arm held tight in Juliette's unmoving grasp. The spiky haired femmepire was lying in a heap next to me, unconscious or…

No, I told myself, *she's definitely just unconscious. She has to be.*

I peeled away her fingers until I was able to pull my wrist free. With both arms available, I was finally able to leverage myself into a seated position. That was the good news. The bad news was it let me take inventory of the damage.

My one nice pair of jeans were a complete loss. From the right thigh down, my jeans were shredded and soaked in blood. I scraped wet scraps of denim from my skin and winced at the sight. The entire leg was a mess of lacerations, but the wide gash across my inside thigh was one of the grossest things I had ever seen. Above that cut, someone had tightened my belt into an emergency tourniquet. It was likely the only thing that had saved me from bleeding to death.

The world went grey for a moment, and I choked back vomit. What the hell had happened? We'd met Bill at The Bitter End. There'd been a lot of alcohol, and then... the memories came in a flood. Ray. Our car. An explosion. Pain.

Why wasn't I dead?

And where the hell were we?

The Duchess of Snark was in even worse shape than me. Both of her formerly fabulous legs were torn and bloody, and the right one was scorched all the way up to mid-calf. One arm was bent at an awkward angle. Most worrying of all was the fist-wide shard of metal piercing her abdomen. I could just see the far end of it poking through her back, dangerously close to the spine.

Still, she was a vampire, right? This sort of thing was probably just a minor setback, like stubbing a toe, or cutting yourself shaving. Except her skin was so devoid of color as to be almost translucent. Juliette was usually pale, but now she looked downright sickly. Her skin was cold to the touch, and when I felt for a pulse, it was slow and weak.

Gripping her face in my hands, heedless of the tracks my bloody fingers were leaving on her pale skin, I thumbed back an eyelid. Her eyes had rolled back in her head. Breath tickled the hair on my arms, but it was weak.

I didn't know what to do.

"Juliette?" Nothing. I laid her head back down, hoping that slight movement wouldn't cause any more damage to her spine. Juliette remained motionless in the dirt, her tattered leather jacket in scraps next to her.

Wait… dirt?

I looked around us. We were seated in red dirt, dry and warm to the touch, a far cry from the cracked asphalt of San Diego's streets. How had Juliette gotten us out of the car and to… wherever we were? New Mexico? Arizona? Tatooine? Just how long had I been unconscious?

A slight noise turned my attention back to Juliette. Her cracked and torn lips were now slightly open. As I watched, her tongue slid out and made a slow foray around the corner of her mouth. It took me a moment to realize that she'd licked up the small traces of my blood that had trickled down her cheek.

It was pretty disgusting, but it also gave me an idea.

I tried to find more blood to feed her with, but it was drying on my skin as quickly as it oozed to the surface. Beneath me, the parched earth greedily swallowed every drop that spilled down onto it. Undoing the tourniquet would change that fast… but it would also probably kill me.

My eyes fell on the bloody scraps that had once been a pair of expensive, almost-fashionable jeans. The denim, at least, was still wet. I took hold of one of the larger scraps and tore at it with both hands. Somehow, I managed to not pass out with the effort. An agonizing length of time later, I held a piece of blood-drenched cloth in my hands.

I turned back to Juliette. Holding the scrap above her face, I squeezed the blood from it and into her mouth. A truly pitiful amount of liquid emerged. The femmepire's tongue made another slow circle to gather up the blood, and she swallowed once.

I nearly wept at the thought of tearing another piece of denim free, but there didn't seem to be any other option. Then the choice was taken away from me. Juliette reached up and caught my hand in her iron grip. Eyes still closed, she yanked my arm to her mouth with inhuman strength and bit down savagely.

Either Darlene had a different idea of pleasure than I did, or something had gotten badly garbled in the message, because being bitten *hurt*. A lot. And not just because my whole body spasmed, sending new waves of pain through my shredded leg. I could feel the points of Juliette's teeth digging into my skin, accompanied by the gruesome sounds of skin being torn, and the nauseating sensation of a tongue lapping at broken flesh.

As she drank more and more, my vision started to flutter. I felt exhaustion sweeping through me, drowning out the pain. I tugged at my hand, trying to pull free, but it was like trying to lift a house. With my consciousness slipping away, there was only one thing for me to do.

Juliette's head snapped back, fangs torn free from my arm and shiny with blood. Her yellow eyes opened wide, full of an animalistic fury that only marginally lessened as she became aware of her surroundings. She rubbed one hand against her cheek.

"Did you just punch me?"

'This isn't a full service bar, lady'. Or 'No shoes, no service.' That's what I should have said. That's the sort of thing *John Smith, creature of the night*, would have said while tossing back a shot of rye whiskey and cracking the knuckles of his uninjured hand.

Being merely human, I had to settle for a helpless shrug.

And then I fainted.

Again.

ooo

Consciousness returned in fits and starts. Eventually, my eyes decided to open and actually stay that way. Above me, unnaturally colored clouds were still gathering, but the throbbing in my left arm was now competing with the burning pain of my right leg for attention.

It was progress. Just not in the right direction.

I looked to my left. No sign of Juliette. It was a lot harder to get back upright with only one arm. The faint smell of burnt flesh reached my nose a moment before I felt a hand on my back, gently helping me sit up. Juliette sat down to my right.

She looked better. The shrapnel was gone from her mid-section and the wound had sealed. In her right hand, she held the remnants of her designer leather jacket. Her left arm swung freely, and the worst of the burns were rapidly fading from her legs. There was even a little bit of color in her cheeks.

"Damn. My blood kicks ass."

"It has its moments," she agreed lightly, patting my shoulder. "John, I'm sorry…"

"Don't worry about it." I'd have waved it off but wasn't sure I could stay upright without the support of that arm. I gave her a look. "I'm not going to become a brainless zombie now or anything, am I?"

She snorted. "Zombie? No. Brainless? That ship sailed a long time ago. Seriously, though. I owe you one, little bird."

"I think we're even," I replied, with a nod at my leg. "Both for the tourniquet and the follow-up bandage." A scrap of blue cotton, torn from my button-up shirt, had been wrapped tightly over the cut, and the bleeding had apparently slowed sufficiently for the tourniquet to be removed. It was weird that such a large a cut had managed to clot though. A quick inspection showed that the wound on my wrist had similarly stopped bleeding. "Besides, if it weren't for you, we'd both be in little pieces all over F Street. I'd say any debt is more than repaid. How did you get us out of the car?"

"I was half-asleep when the bomb went off," Juliette said with a frown, holding up her leather jacket, "or I'd have made sure my favorite jacket hadn't been destroyed."

"Then how did we get here?" I frowned. "And where the hell are we?"

"Got it in one." Her voice remained uncharacteristically quiet. If it were anyone but Juliette, I'd have thought her scared.

"You're going to have to run that by me again, Duchess. Where are we?"

Instead of replying, she pointed over my shoulder.

I turned to look, and my blood ran cold. "Is that…?"

"Yeah. We're in serious trouble."

In the distance, across a mile or more of red, cracked earth, was a field of what looked like scarecrows. But even from this distance, I could see the figures were writhing in pain as flames leapt skyward from their heads and outstretched arms. And the frames they'd been tied to weren't made of wood but silver, like candelabras.

Holy shit. We were in Gehenna.

CHAPTER 37

IN WHICH HELL IS BEING STUCK WITH
THE WRONG PERSON

"Where are we going?" I asked for at least the tenth time. Knowing we were in Gehenna somehow made the heat even more noticeable. Sweat trickled down my body, stinging whenever it ran across one of my cuts or scrapes.

"The answer's not going to change just because you keep asking it." Juliette's voice was tired, and more than a little bit irritated. "We need to find a way out. Given that neither of us has any idea *how* we ended up in Bill's hell dimension, our best bet is to make it to somewhere he might actually notice us. Like—"

"—the field of human candelabras," I finished. As she said, it wasn't the first time we'd had this discussion. "I just think we'd have been better off staying back where we landed. It's the first place Bill would look for us."

"You're assuming he even knows we are here."

"He's the only person who could have brought us here in the first place…"

"Then where is he?! He's not here, and I'm not going to just sit around baking to a crisp waiting for him to remember us!" She took a deep, calming breath, and started moving again. "Besides, he was as drunk as we were last night, and didn't have the luxury of a car bomb and near-death experience to sober him up. He might not remember anything at all."

I sighed. We'd been through this debate multiple times, and I still hadn't found a winning argument. Maybe that should have told me something. "We've been traveling for an hour and the candelabras don't seem to be any closer."

"What are you complaining about? You're not even walking!"

It was true. Something about Gehenna was causing my body to heal way faster than normal, but I wasn't up to walking just yet, let alone hiking across the nightmarish desert landscape. Instead, I nestled like a six-foot-tall infant in Juliette's arms. And the only complaint she'd uttered to this point was...

"Have I mentioned how badly you reek? It's like carrying an armload of garbage."

"Some of it's blood. I'd think you'd enjoy the scent."

"Once it's cold, it loses its appeal, little bird. And the dirt, sweat, smoke and vomit don't help." She adjusted her grip, and kept walking, her nose thrust upwards. "Also, could you try not to breathe in my direction? Or at all? I'm getting sick of the smell of stale beer."

Take away the red sands, the weird clouds, and the people mounted on candelabras, and it felt like we were back at the House.

○○○

We walked in silence for a time. I did my best not to breathe into her face, which is harder than it sounds when cradled in someone's arms. I'd have killed for a mint, if there were any mints to be had. Or people to kill, for that matter. The candelabra victims were the only other beings we'd seen and they, quite frankly, would probably appreciate the release.

I eyed their silhouettes in the distance. Juliette's bare-footed pace was steady, and we'd covered an awful lot of ground over the past few hours. So why did the candelabra field still seem so far away?

An even better question came to mind. If the field was tens or even hundreds of miles in the distance, how were we able to see it so clearly?

It was a bit early to be making judgments, but I decided then and there that hell dimensions kind of sucked.

Now that the shock of being in Gehenna was wearing off, boredom was setting in. Yes, we were in another dimension, and that was alternately horrible and cool, depending on your frame of mind. But beyond the weirdly colored clouds, near-constant electrical storms, and field of human candelabras, there wasn't much to differentiate it from Arizona or New Mexico.

I craned my neck to get a better look around us. Actually, Arizona and New Mexico were more interesting. At least they had mountains, rock formations, and road-side tourist shops.

Gehenna just had dirt.

I looked up at Juliette. "I'm telling you, Ray was watching from across the street when the car blew up. He even waved. There's no way he wasn't in on this."

"Talk to the ground and save me from your gods-awful breath." Juliette was going to give me a complex if this kept up. It didn't help that her own breath was somehow cool and fresh. I'd been punched in the face enough times to know my blood wasn't a breath freshener, so how had she managed that? Vampirism's main purpose seemed to be making me feel inadequate.

"I'm serious, Juliette."

"So am I. And I've known Ray a long time. A very long time. I don't buy it."

"I know what I saw," I insisted stubbornly, "and he didn't come to the car with us. What other explanation could there be?"

"Maybe he was just that drunk? Maybe he stopped at the restroom on the way out of the bar? Maybe he actually was in the car with us and burned up with Bob? There are a lot of possibilities to cover before I'll accept that Ray Jennings is a traitor."

"You believed Andrés was one, on the basis of nothing but a Nintendo."

"Andrés came over with Lucia. I trust him about as far as I can throw him. Ray was part of my flock before all that. He had more than enough chances to betray me, but has always been someone I could rely on."

"Are we talking about the same manpire? Space Cadet Ray?"

"He's not always like that."

"That sounds like wishful thinking to me."

"Wishful thinking is me leaving you to fend for yourself in Bill's rock garden of delight." She bounced me effortlessly in her arms and gave me a meaningful look.

"Fine," I conceded, "we can table the Ray debate for now." But I was going to inform Anastasia as soon as we'd made it out of Gehenna. She'd believe me.

I hoped.

We traveled another mile in silence, and I was reassured to see that the candelabra field was, in fact, just a bit closer than it had been. The heavens continued to shake and storm, but we had yet to see rain.

Juliette adjusted her grip again, and I folded my legs to try to avoid kicking her as she walked. "So you're sticking with your theory from last night? That Andrés was framed?"

"Just because we were drunk doesn't mean we were wrong." Except about the worthiness of our plan. We'd been very, very wrong on that front. "Andrés didn't strike me as someone stupid enough to stash a stolen video game console in his own room. And what was his motive? Why would he want to start a war between the House and Bill?"

"Why would anyone at the House want to?" she shot back.

"I have no idea." My honesty was rewarded with a snort of disdain from the femmepire, which I manfully ignored. "I've only known you all for like three days. I don't understand your motivations, and I can't begin to guess why any of you do what you do, let alone figure out why you'd do something you might not have done."

Juliette puzzled through that last sentence for a while. To be honest, it wasn't one of my best. "Well, you'd better think of something before we get out of here. Assuming we ever do. Lucia's going to want answers."

"At this point, I don't give a damn what Lucia wants." Maybe it was the oppressive heat, or the nagging pain of my injuries, but pleasing the blonde queen was currently very low on my list of priorities. And then, as if the irritation had burned away the last bit of alcohol/pain-induced haze, a thought struck me. "Besides, none of that really matters. I don't worry about motivation in my usual cases. Why should I start now? All that matters is the evidence."

"Of which we have precisely none, save for the Nintendo which we found in the room of the manpire—" her mouth twisted as she spoke the word. "—who you maintain was framed."

"True. But my point stands. If we can't figure out the motivation, we should focus on opportunity. Who and how instead of why."

"If you start talking about your journalism class again, I'm going to bite you just to put you out of my misery."

"I'm serious. We have four incidents that we think were part of a larger plot, right?" I ticked them off on my fingers. It was really handy being carried everywhere. "One: the Nintendo gets stolen. We don't know why someone wanted a war with Bill, and we don't care... yet. Two: the Rook gets murdered and a hit is put out on other mediators. We think the goal there was to prevent a successful mediation between the House and Bill. Three: the Nintendo gets planted in Andrés' room so that I can find it in my search. And four: our car blows up, presumably in an effort to kill one or both of us."

"And?"

"Who was in a position to do all of those things? The theft..."

"Any of the People could have done it! It's not like stealing something from a boat is particularly difficult, especially if Bill wasn't there." She gave me an irritated glare. "Congratulations, you've narrowed the subject list down to every individual in the House. Assuming that it wasn't someone *outside* of the House."

"I think that's a reasonable assumption at this point. I don't see an outsider sneaking past the Watch to plant it on the premises, do you?"

"So it could have been one or more of forty-three People, fifty-plus donors, and at least ten maids and cooks. Great job, detective."

"This is why I was able to hit you with the rope thing in the gym," I muttered. "Sometimes, I think you're intentionally obtuse."

Juliette dropped me into the dirt. The fact that I didn't scream said huge things about how quickly I was healing.

"That rope thing is called a *kusari fundo*, you moron." She angrily strode off towards the field, leaving me behind. "And you can walk on your own from now on."

I shakily climbed to my feet. Everything hurt, but again, I felt far healthier than I should have. My injured leg even held up under my weight, which was definitely something that wouldn't have been possible even two hours earlier. I started limping after Juliette. Even fully healed, I wouldn't have had a prayer of catching up to her... so when I did, I knew she'd purposefully slowed down.

"Apology accepted, Duchess." A manic light appeared in the depths of her yellow eyes. "Errr... I mean, I'm sorry about that."

The light didn't exactly fade, but she nodded.

"Anyway, you're right. Anyone in the House could have been responsible for the theft itself. Thanks to Jee Sun, we know at least two of them were." I breathed heavily, ignoring the slight burning in my leg. This had been easier with a personal servant to carry me. "But that's just the theft. How many of the People could have killed the Rook and his magical sex bots?"

"You can't even say magical sex bots without smiling, can you?"

"I can't. It's just too ridiculous. Let me guess... they were invented in Japan?"

"As I understand it, they are summoned, not built. But yes, the spells originated in Japan. As for the Rook," she continued, her tone thoughtful, "I'm not sure. Certainly, the House servants and donors couldn't have killed him. But as for the People... I guess it depends on how many attackers there were."

"Let's say no more than three," I decided. "Remember, the evidence suggests he let them in, and I doubt he would have done so for a small army of vampires."

"That changes things a bit." Juliette thought hard, unconsciously picking up her pace in the process. When the femmepire turned back to speak, I was a good ten steps behind her, limping as fast as I could. With a long-suffering sigh, she swept me back into her arms, as easily as I would pick up a bag of lightly packed groceries. "One word about me sweeping you off your feet, and you're going right back in the dirt."

I blinked up at her, the very picture of infantile innocence.

"Anyway, I think three of the stronger Watch members could have taken the Rook. If a Council member was involved, it was probably doable with only a single accomplice. Which means Andrés is still a suspect."

"Sure. It's entirely possible he's just an idiot. If so, this whole thing will have been wrapped up by the time we get back. But let's proceed on the assumption that he's not." I tried not to be lulled into sleep as I rocked in her arms. For any other man, being carried through the desert might be the tiniest bit emasculating, but for me… oh hell, it was plenty emasculating. But it was still better than walking. "Out of our smaller suspect pool, who has ever had dealings with the Rook?"

"Andrés," came the quick reply. "And Lucia. And Anastasia. And pretty much everyone on the Council or the Watch. Remember, he was the city mediator for a long time before you came along."

"That doesn't help much. Next incident then. Who has access to Andrés' room?"

"Again, pretty much everyone on the Council or the Watch," Juliette retorted. "This isn't getting us anywhere!"

"Actually," I pointed out, "Kayla said she'd never been past the guard post on the third floor. It sounded like that was the case for everyone on the Watch."

"Huh." Juliette thought about it a while longer, and shrugged. I rode up and down in her arms like I was on a carnival ride. "That's true. I never really thought about it, but they do stay out by the elevator."

"So that just leaves the Council."

"I guess. Any of whom could have done it. It's not like we spend a lot of time in our rooms. Other than Summer and Lucia, anyway."

"Still, we've narrowed things down from a hundred people to…" I did the counting in my head instead of using my fingers. Mrs. Bernstein, my third grade math teacher, would have been proud. "…eight of you?"

"Seven. I didn't do it. I think we can cross Summer off the list too."

"And you already said Lucia and Zorana were innocent. So that takes us to four?"

"A number that includes Andrés," she reminded me, "and the ever-perfect Lady Dumenyova."

"True. I think we can cross off Marcus too. He didn't know the results of my meeting with Bill, so he couldn't have anticipated the search that would locate the console."

"Andrés didn't know either, but he disappeared from the House."

"Without the Nintendo. That still doesn't make sense. But yeah, if he somehow found out, I guess Marcus could have also. So we have four suspects."

Three, really. There was no way I believed Anastasia had done it. And if it wasn't Andrés or Marcus...

It didn't take a detective to see who was left, but I didn't say anything. I wanted to see if Juliette would reach the same conclusion "Which brings us to the attempt on our lives. I know you don't want to think that Ray—"

"I told you we were done with that topic! He is not a traitor!"

I knew what I'd seen, but there was no reason to belabor the point, and risk having to walk under my own power again. "Let's look at it a different way, then. Who knew that we were going to meet with Bill last night?"

"Everyone that attended the Council meeting after Andrés' disappearance," she said slowly, "which does suggest Andrés himself wouldn't have known."

"Right. And who knew what car was taking us and had access to that car to plant a bomb?" I watched comprehension come to her, followed quickly by wide-eyed shock.

"It would almost have to have been..."

"Yeah," I nodded, "I think it was Xavier."

CHAPTER 38

IN WHICH CANDLELIGHT IS FAR FROM ROMANTIC

"It's thin," said Juliette, "and based entirely on conjecture and shaky logic."

"But it makes sense, right?"

"Other than the open question of his motive… yeah. But there's no way you can accuse Xavier without evidence. And that's something we don't have."

"If there was only someplace we could go to find that evidence," I mused smugly. "Some crime scene that Xavier has been carefully managing to this point, probably to keep the truth hidden."

"You want to go search the Rook's house?"

"Why not? It was part of our original plan anyway. This would be the perfect time to do it. Assuming we figure a way out of here."

By now, we'd covered at least ten miles. The good news was that we were finally coming up on the candelabra field. The bad news was… well, we were coming up on the candelabra field.

There were more than a hundred people present, mounted in three long rows, the ground covered in what I hoped was just wax. Each candelabra was at least twenty feet tall. At the top, unclothed figures—most of them men, given the dangling dude-parts—were bound to silver frames by thick, barbed wire around their ankles, torsos and outstretched arms. Wax had been poured over their heads and hands. It was that wax that burned, while the figures writhed in agony. The end result was a horrific blend between candelabra and crucifix.

If I'd had anything left in my stomach, I'd have vomited. Probably all over Juliette, which would have been the last the world heard or saw of John Smith. Thankfully, my stomach was empty, leaving me free to simply stare up in horror and disgust.

Thinking about Jee Sun's father helped. There was at least one person who deserved to be here.

"Any ideas?" I asked.

"We could call him, I guess?"

I looked at Juliette, outraged. "You have your phone?!?!" Why had we just walked all the way across Gehenna?

"Look at me, you moron." In her tattered leather jacket, and even more tattered dress, she looked like a post-apocalyptic barbarian queen. "Does it look like I'm carrying a phone on me? Besides, it's not like we'd get service in another dimension."

"Then what did you mean?"

"I meant call out to him. When he got pissed off at Gordon Biersch, you said he opened a portal right to here. Maybe he'll be able to hear us."

It was the best idea we could come up with, but after ten minutes of yelling his name, the immortal asparagus was nowhere to be found.

"So much for that." Juliette shrugged. "Your turn to think of something."

"I have an idea, but I don't think you're going to like it."

"What else is new? Your one good idea was to go to The Bitter End, and even that ended in someone blowing up the car and murdering my wardrobe."

"And Bob."

"Who's Bob?"

"It's the name I gave the driver."

"Oh." I waited for Juliette to make some sort of joke, but she just nodded. "And Bob. So what's your idea?"

"Well, the only thing I can think of that would get Bill's attention would be to mess with those." I gestured up at the human candelabras. "Maybe you could push one over?"

"I notice that you're not volunteering to commit this suicidal act."

"Only one of us is Wonder Woman." Given the size of the candelabras, it would take superhuman strength. Mine barely even qualified as human strength.

"Figures." She sent a smirk that was so refreshingly Juliette I wanted to cheer. "At least you're finally citing a character from a real comics publisher."

"I meant She-Hulk! Or Titania! Or..." I desperately tried to think of other super-strong Marvel women, but the damage had been done.

"I knew you were a DC fan boy, little bird." The femmepire walked over to the nearest candelabra, planted her feet, and started to push.

I'd seen the Watch spar in the House's gym. I'd been knocked unconscious by Juliette, manhandled by Xavier, and nearly killed by a strung-out surfer vamp named Miles. But it wasn't until I watched Juliette push over a twenty-foot-high, thousand-pound candelabra that I realized just how strong vampires really were. Her bare feet dug into the red earth, and the base of the candelabra started to warp under her grip. Then something gave way in the foundation. The ground beneath us rippled, and the silver crucifix toppled, crashing to the wax-coated earth.

Despite the fact that the man chained to it was now hanging parallel to the ground, his flames continued to burn.

We looked around, but nothing had changed.

"Another one, I guess?"

Juliette scowled and stalked over to the next candelabra in line. She squared her shoulders, set her feet, and took hold of the base... when the reaction we'd been trying to provoke finally happened.

Magenta lightning speared the earth around us, close enough that the hair stood up on my arms and legs. Crimson clouds shuddered and retreated, leaving behind an expanse of clear yellow sky. Then that sky cracked open and darkness poured into the world. We watched, wide-eyed, as the waterfall of darkness resolved itself into a figure that towered over the candelabra field. Its features were impossible to make out, but it had bonfires for eyes, and its mouth was a gaping maw of magma. An arm as dark as night and twice the length of a city bus reached down to right the fallen candelabra. The world shuddered as the entity spoke in a voice that screeched and strained like grinding metal.

"WHO DARES TO—" The hellfire eyes fell upon us. "Johnny Appleseed?"

"Bill?" I struggled to my feet.

Within moments, the figure shrank down to his usual height. He still shared a silhouette with the asparagus I'd come to know, but everything else about his appearance was different. "Be careful, amigo! Someone is PUSHING OVER MY CANDELABRAS!"

"That was us." I nodded over at Juliette.

"Oh." Bill seemed nonplussed. "Wiggle your face at me then, bro! What it is you were thinking when you thought to do so? Also," he added, tilting his head as he looked at both of us, "what are your faces doing here? IT CAN BE DANGEROUS! I think there might be snakes," he added in a whisper that could probably be heard throughout the entire dimension.

"Actually… we think *you* brought us here," I explained.

"HAHA! You and Lady PAC MAN are so SILLY!" He paused, and asked in a small, confused voice. "Why did I bring you here? Were you naughty?"

"No!" I hurried to nip *that* in the bud. "Do you remember meeting us for drinks at The Bitter End?"

"Of course I do, John," he replied in an injured tone. "That was just a couple of Mickey rotations ago."

A couple of… "We've been here more than a day?!?" I stomped down on my growing hysteria. Now was not the time to freak out. "After we said goodbye, the car Juliette and I got into… uhm… exploded."

The shadow version of Bill just looked at me for a long moment, saying nothing. Then his eyes opened wide, and the temperature around us rose by at least a few degrees.

"YES!!! THE CAR THAT WAS AND THEN WAS NOT SOON AFTER YOU AND LADY PAC MAN JOINED WITH IT."

He danced around in jubilation, while above us, people burned. "So I moved you here and then," he began to giggle, "I FORGOT!"

"It could happen to anyone, Bill." A thought occurred to me. "Did you manage to save Bob too?"

"Who is THE BOB?"

"The human driver of our car."

"Was he... at the FRONT?" At my nod, he shook his head. "I was too late to GET HIM! I was almost too late to save you as well!" It was impossible to read any emotion, given that he had no features here in Gehenna. I find myself missing the magic marker mouth.

"Still, you saved our lives," I reassured him. "Thank you."

"Good fences make good neighbors, amigo, and good neighbors don't let friends burn up in fiery explosions unless they have been asked to do so by those same friends."

I guess that made sense in Bill's head.

"So," he continued, "do you want to vamoose our way out of here? Tiny Flower and I are having milkshakes!"

At our relieved nods, he smiled a lava-filled grin, and began to grow again. One enormous paw of darkness swallowed Juliette in the blink of an eye, and then I was similarly engulfed. I found myself unable to breathe. Starbursts of nameless colors appeared in my brain. And then, as I was starting to do with annoying frequency, I passed out.

CHAPTER 39

IN WHICH MILKSHAKES, LIKE REVENGE, ARE BEST SERVED COLD

In the past week, I'd been beaten and strangled. I'd been blown up by a car bomb and had my blood drained by a painfully sarcastic femmepire. I'd even been thrust from one dimension into another through a whirling shadow vortex in the sky. But nothing compared to the agony I was currently experiencing.

"Ow!" I put a hand to my head, and groaned. The other three occupants of the boat's main cabin turned to look at me with varying levels of concern.

"Brain freeze," I explained, and watched that concern disappear. No one understood my pain. Cautiously, I took another, much slower, sip of my vanilla milkshake. Better. And yum.

Jee Sun sat on the very edge of one of the cabin's couches, swinging her feet and focusing every ounce of attention on getting the last drops of her strawberry shake. The little girl was wearing her omnipresent Supergirl cape over a pair of powder blue, footed pajamas. Her black hair was braided into three tails, and the light reflected off her thick glasses.

Now that we were back on Earth, Bill was in the asparagus shape I'd grown accustomed to. I couldn't decide if what I'd seen in Gehenna was his real form or not. If it was, did his appearance here in the real world mean I really *was* secretly terrified of asparagus? I wrote

myself a mental post-it note to ask Juliette what she'd seen when Bill
came to fetch us.

Speaking of the femmepire, she was wrapped in a fluffy white
robe, sipping a shake of her own. Chocolate, which she'd calmly
explained was the superior flavor. The robe had been a donation from
Jee Sun's wardrobe, and I decided not to mention that it was both far
too large for the little girl and had the Marriott logo stitched on the left
side in maroon thread. When Bill had led us down into the main
stateroom of the forty-foot-long powerboat he and Jee Sun called
home, I'd spotted slippers, dishware, and towels bearing the same
brand.

As we were currently moored at a slip just outside the Marriott
Marquis, it wasn't too difficult to deduce where they'd acquired the
merchandise. I *was* a detective, after all.

My return to consciousness had roughly coincided with our
return to Earth. I'd found myself on the upper deck of a shiny white
coastal cruiser. Uneducated plebeian that I was, I thought of it as a *boat*,
but Juliette referred to it as a yacht, and Jee Sun, who'd been sitting out
in the sun waiting for us, called it a pickle. Kids. Pickle or not, it was
much nicer than I had expected. The stateroom and two bedrooms
were all larger than my office.

Growing up in San Diego, I'd spent plenty of time out on the
ocean. Most of it had involved me getting seasick. There'd been one
fishing trip with a girlfriend and her dad where I'd spent the entire
afternoon hanging over the side of the boat. Her dad hadn't been
impressed. Come to think of it, she hadn't been either. Our
relationship had fizzled out within the month.

Thankfully, sea sickness wasn't going to be a problem on a boat
this large, particularly given the marina's location in the harbor and the
fact that we were bracketed by even larger vessels.

At least it shouldn't have been.

Sadly, nobody had though to tell my stomach that.

As Jee Sun slurped noisily through her straw, my stomach
decided that the combination of the gently rocking boat and a rich
vanilla shake was *not* one it approved of. It followed that declaration

with an all-too-familiar rumble. I rushed up the companionway, lunged for the guard rail on the main deck, and retched over the side.

Maybe I should move my failing detective agency somewhere farther inland. Like South Dakota. Or the moon.

"Sea sick?" Juliette's voice was close enough to suggest that she'd followed me to the main deck, but far enough away to communicate her unwillingness to otherwise get involved. "In the harbor?! Unbelievable, even for you."

"So, he IS BROKEN after all?" Apparently, Bill had joined us on deck. Because illness appreciates an audience. At least Jee Sun was still down—

"That's gross, Mr. John!"

Lovely. I wiped my mouth and looked about for a Marriott-branded towel. "Sorry, everyone. I think I might need to stay up here for the time being. Fresh air and all that." I swallowed and winced at the taste in my mouth. "Also, does anyone have a mint?"

ooo

One mint, two cups of mouthwash, and twenty minutes later, I was doing okay. And by okay, I mean I'd finished sharing my milkshake with the San Diego harbor. As the sickness finally passed, I found myself capable of thinking of something other than my own misery.

"So, Bill… wiggle your face at me. What's been going on since Monday?" Juliette and I had confirmed that it was, in fact, Wednesday afternoon, which meant we'd lost the majority of two days in Gehenna. Either we'd been unconscious a lot longer than we knew, or time moved differently in the hell dimension.

"Well, partner, first your car EXPLODED and then I walked home after stopping for a MILANO MOCHA and some cookies for Tiny Flower. And we watched WINNIE THE POOH ON THE TELEVISION!"

"Piglet's Big Movie!" Jee Sun added with a giggle. "Because he is small, like me!"

"And I am big, like Christopher Robin, and wise, LIKE THE POOH!" Bill crowed, his magic marker mouth stretched into a triumphant smile. "And then we went to sleep but Tiny Flower was cold, so I made her warm milk, and then she was not cold, and we slept in and then we had breakfast and played on the box!" His charcoal eyes rotated back to look at me, and his words were measured. "We have not found any ouchies on it so far."

"That's good," I admitted. "But I meant the situation with the People. Any new developments there?"

"Haha! Amigo, your face doesn't know what it is wiggling when it wiggles!" His mouth narrowed into a perfect circle, smaller than the circle he used to indicate surprise, and his voice dropped to what, for Bill, was a low whisper. "There are people everywhere, Johnny boy! Hundreds, at least! How would I know what the situation is with all of them?"

"Well, yeah, but—"

His eyes spun to opposite sides of his asparagus stalk, each pointing at a different one of the boats flanking his. "Do you want me to tell you what is going on with these ones, Johnny-be-good? Because Mrs. Etelstein and the head crewman have been sneaki—"

"Actually, that's OK," I assured him, my five years as a private investigator enough to know that story was headed places a girl of Jee Sun's age shouldn't know about. "I meant People, not… people."

He still didn't get it.

"You know, vampires." I made the universal sign for vampire, pointing my fingers down from my upper lip to mimic fangs.

"Yellow!" shouted Jee Sun, contorting her face into a pout immediately after. She launched herself at Bill and hugged him tightly around his lower stalk.

"Ohhhhh," Bill chortled, "vampires!" He came over to join me at the railing. "Did you know, amigo, that there is a vampire ON THIS VERY BOAT?"

Either my brain freeze had returned or I was starting to get a headache. "Of course, Bill. That's Lady Pac Man. She's our friend, remember? Since she was with me in Gehenna, we need to know whether anything new has happened with House Borghesi in our absence."

"Negative, kemosabe! It's been as quiet as a mouse in a house!" He turned to Jee Sun. "Can we get a mouse, Tiny Flower? And build him a house?"

Jee Sun pondered the thought for a moment. There were times I questioned which of the two was the adult and which was the child. "I think so, Mr. Bill, but this time, you should—"

"GET DOWN!" cried Juliette, blurring into motion.

Bill staggered. An enormous hole appeared in his chest, right where his heart would be, and pieces of him sprayed across the deck. Jee Sun screamed as another hole appeared in the asparagus demigod, just as the sound of the first shot finally reached our ears.

Bill's eyes turned to regard me, and his mouth formed a giant O of surprise. His voice was hushed and devoid of its usual maniacal intonations, almost inaudible beneath the echoes of that second shot. "Johnny Dangerous, I think the vampire situation may be escalating."

And then he melted away, leaving behind a puddle of viscous goo, two pieces of charcoal and a half-eaten carrot on the deck.

ooo

I stood there in shock, looking at what was left of the demigod, when I suddenly found myself face-first on the deck. I started to panic, before I realized I wasn't in any pain. Getting shot hurts, right?

"Which part of 'get down' did you not understand, little bird?" Juliette growled, pulling me across the deck and away from the guardrail. "Do you *want* to die?"

"I'm a private detective, Juliette! I'm not used to worrying about snipers!" Baseball bats through rear windshields, courtesy of irate husbands? Sure. But snipers? Hell no.

We'd reached the companionway and were solidly under the cover of the upper deck, when another sound reached us.

A child was screaming.

"Jee Sun!"

"I've got her." Juliette blurred over to where the Korean girl was bawling her eyes out by the puddle that had been Lord Beel-Kasan. Another blur brought the two of them back to me, Jee Sun kicking and waving her arms in an attempt to get free. Juliette set her down, and the little girl threw herself into my lap, hugging me and crying at the same time. I shared a look with Juliette. What the hell had just happened and what were we going to do now?

The Duchess read the question in my eyes and shook her head. First, the crab hitmen. Then the car bomb. And now, Bill had been shot by what had seemed like a bazooka but was probably a high caliber rifle. Things were escalating, and one of our only allies had just been assassinated.

"Why is Tiny Flower crying, amigo?"

"Because she just watched you get—" I turned to find the demigod standing by the guardrail, his mouth drawn in an 'S' of uncertainty and distress. As I watched, the pieces of charcoal and half-eaten carrot attached themselves to the base of his stalk, and like an elevator, ascended until they'd retaken their place above his mouth.

"Mr. Bill!" Just like that, Jee Sun abandoned my lap and launched herself at her demigod friend. Two arms extended from his stalk and caught her in mid-air, returning the hug. "You're okay!"

"Of course I am, Tiny Flower!" He patted her braided hair soothingly. "I went to wiggle my face at the people who thought it would be a good idea to SHOOT THE GUNS AT THE BOAT WHERE THE FLOWER WAS SITTING!" His face spun to regard me, and his mouth quivered. "Did the milkshakes survive?"

"We'd already finished them," I reminded him. "Do you and Jee Sun want to come over here, under cover?" It was all well and good if Bill could survive being shot with an elephant gun, but I was pretty sure that the same wasn't true for Jee Sun, and the two of them were standing right out in the open.

"That's a big ten-four, good buddy," he replied, carrying Jee Sun over with him. "But Smokey has left the building."

"The shooter's gone?"

"That's what I said." His eyes slid down to the child in his arms, and he whispered loudly to her, "Mr. John is broken."

Jee Sun giggled.

"Now, Jee Sun, you must go below and find the movie you wish to watch tonight!" He paused and thought to himself. "Maybe the one with the video games and the little girl WHO IS A PRINCESS?"

We watched Jee Sun tear down the stairs at a pace that might kindly be described as brave, or unkindly described as borderline suicidal. When the vegetable demigod turned back to us, his mouth had assumed its jack o' lantern shape. I was uncomfortably reminded of the magma-filled maw he had shown in Gehenna. "And I will go to the House that believes it is OKAY TO SHOOT AT BOATS WITH TINY FLOWERS ON THEM, and I will BURN IT DOWN AND PLANT A NEW FIELD OF CANDELABRAS. Maybe next to the snakes."

"Bill, wait!" I reached out a hand to stop him, only to think better of it at the last moment, leaving me with my hand extended awkwardly as if I was saluting him in Nazi Germany. Not a great image. Thankfully, he stopped as soon as I spoke, and his face rotated around his stalk to look at me. "You can't leave Jee Sun like this. Who's going to watch over her?"

Bill was quiet for a long moment. "I was thinking that would be you, John."

"You know I'd be happy to help," I assured him, "but wouldn't she rather have you with her? Plus," I added, my mind racing just fast enough to stay ahead of my mouth, "you attacking the House may be exactly what they want."

"Then they are FOOLISH, John-o, and will regret their plan's success." Face still pointed at us, he resumed his leg-less march in the opposite direction.

This time, I did grab him, trying to ignore the moist squishy texture of his asparagus body. He stiffened, and the magic marker mouth drew downward into a severe frown.

"Please, Bill. Hold on a second." I put every ounce of reasonableness I had into my tone. "I'm trying to prevent a war, remember?"

"Bang-up job so far, little bird," quipped Juliette.

"Not helping!"

"Lady Pac Man has a point, Johnny-boy," rumbled Bill. "You found the box, but this has moved past the face-wiggling stage."

"Give me one day," I pleaded. "At The Bitter End we talked about a conspiracy, remember? I think that the car bomb and the sniper are part of that plot. And the whole point of it is to start a war!"

Bill's mouth wiggled uncertainly. "I do not know if I REMEMBER THIS, amigo." He thought for another long, tension-filled moment. "Was there… a plan?"

Oh, thank god. Or gods, even. "Yes, Bill," I assured him, "we had a plan to go home and think of a plan."

"That is a GOOD PLAN!" The top half of Bill's stalk dipped in what I decided was a nod.

"Yeah," I agreed, "and while Juliette and I were in Gehenna, we thought of the next step."

"Does it involve fire?" the demigod asked, a mixture of sadness and terrible yearning audible beneath his southern twang.

"No." Once again, I snipped *that* in the bud as quickly as possible. "We need to do some investigation so that we can expose whoever is behind the conspiracy here."

"Hip hip cheerio!" Bill's good mood was instantly restored. "Let us go investigate, amigo!"

I thought seriously about having him come along. A demigod—even one like Bill—would be a pretty handy thing to have around in a fight.

But when it came to sneaky investigations… not so much.

"I think you need to stay and watch over Jee Sun, my friend. Her safety is the most important thing."

The asparagus nodded again, and his magic marker mouth reformed into a smile. "OKAY THEN! But if you find out anything, give me a ring, compadre!"

"Absolutely, Bill!" Neither Juliette nor I had our phones anymore, nor did we have his number, but those were trifling issues. What mattered was that the House, and San Diego in general, had been granted a temporary reprieve.

Juliette removed her robe and we crossed over to the pier before the demigod could change his mind.

CHAPTER 40

IN WHICH AN INVESTIGATOR
FINALLY INVESTIGATES

There may have been a time when firing large-caliber weapons in downtown San Diego was considered perfectly acceptable. But this was post-9/11, in the era of the Patriot Act, NSA wiretaps, and highly trained, killer-robot CIA death drones. As we were leaving the marina, a police car had already pulled up outside the entrance. Uniformed officers were speaking with a pedestrian, the latter individual waving the cell phone he'd called 911 on.

"Should we warn Bill?"

"This isn't television, little bird. So what if people heard two loud bangs? Without a shooter, a victim, or even a crime scene, it'll just be another random gunshot report."

A lifetime of CSI and Law & Order viewing told me otherwise, but I decided to accept Juliette's confident reply. Behind us, Bill's boat blended in with the hundreds of other vessels in the marina. There was an outside chance that Jee Sun's scream had drawn attention, but it seemed unlikely that anyone would connect it with gunshots that had clearly come from somewhere outside the marina.

Plus, the little girl made a lot of noise on a regular basis. The neighbors were probably used to it.

That still meant Juliette and I needed to find a way past the police. We'd cleaned up in Bill's boat, but between the dried blood and our tattered scraps of clothes, we looked like horror movie extras. And that was what officers of the law might consider *suspicious.*

Before I could mention my concerns to Juliette, the spiky-haired femmepire waltzed right past the investigating policemen and the small crowd of tourists that had gathered to join in on the excitement. Nobody even looked in our direction.

It wasn't until I saw the golden gleam in her yellow eyes that I understood she'd used compulsion to mask our presence. Vampire mojo was powerful stuff. No wonder humanity still had no idea their kind existed.

We crossed through the back lot between the Marriott Marquis and the Manchester Grand Hyatt and proceeded down and across Harbor Drive. Petco Park was dark and quiet, with Comic Con long over and the Padres away playing a doubleheader against the Rockies. Playing... and probably losing. The less said about being a professional sports fan in San Diego, the better. If our weather wasn't so nice, we'd have basically been Cleveland.

"You weren't much help back on the boat, Duchess. Why am I the one who always has to talk down the angry demigod?"

"Hey... I helped!"

"Your little joke almost started the war we're trying to prevent!"

"It's not my fault," she protested in an injured tone. "I have... a condition."

"Tourette's?"

"Make-fun-of-John-itus." She stuck her tongue out, yellow eyes bright in the late afternoon sun.

Sure she did. I shrugged. At least we were still alive. The sun was starting to set, painting the western sky in beautiful hues. Nobody was running away screaming. And most importantly of all, nobody could see that, thanks to the car bomb, I was effectively wearing denim capris. The horror.

"Can you keep *this*," I gestured around us to indicate whatever hoodoo she was utilizing to keep people from noticing our appearance, "going while we walk to the Rook's house?"

"Oh, hell no." She sounded horrified by the notion.

"Then we should probably… what are you doing?"

Juliette brushed off the question. Leaving me behind, she turned and entered the sandwich shop on K Street. I watched her approach one of the customers in line, a thirty-something guy in designer jeans and a collared shirt. She sidled right up to him and wrapped an arm around his waist, a gesture which he immediately reciprocated, as if they were a long-time couple. When she whispered something in his ear, he laughed and gave her something. She patted him on the butt and came back out, keys dangling from one finger.

"Why walk when we can drive?"

○○○

"I can't believe you just stole some dude's car."

"You were there. That makes you an accomplice." She smirked. "Besides, he gave me the keys, so it doesn't count as a theft. I'll just make someone drop the car back off when we're done."

"And if he has to go anywhere in the meantime?" I kind of felt bad for the dude, designer menswear or not. At the end of the day, we humans had to stick together.

"I'm sure his girlfriend will be pissed when he doesn't make their rendezvous, but that's not really our problem now is it? Maybe he'll spend the night with his wife instead."

"How did…" I thought about it for a long moment, my horror growing. "Can the People read minds?!"

"Even if we could, my little partner-in-crime, I wouldn't go poking around in yours without a hazmat suit." She shrugged, changing lanes at high speed and with little regard for traffic laws or human life. "He was wearing a ring, but was—" She cut herself off, mid-speech, and shot me a sly look. "On second thought, I'm not going to explain. A good magician never reveals her tricks."

Before I could reply, the Duchess of Snark dropped the pedal to the metal. We rocketed forward at speeds my Corolla had never even dreamed of.

I stopped talking, and started praying. I was too damn young to die.

ooo

Somehow, we made it to North Park without even scratching the paint job of our stolen Acura. Clearly, the local demigod of reckless drivers had heard my prayers. I'd pour out a forty whenever I got the chance... it seemed like the sort of offering he or she would appreciate.

The Rook's place was a narrow, multi-story house with a small front yard, secure behind a tall brick wall and black iron gate. With the sun having now fully set, the house sat like a slim shadow between the two brightly lit residences on either side.

Or maybe I was projecting. I knew what had happened inside.

"If this is the sort of place the Rook could afford, I can't wait to get my paycheck." I'd briefly thought about renting office space in North Park, or even in Hillcrest, which was just to the west, but the properties had been way out of my price range. "Why did we park a block away, anyway?"

"When you stake out a house or a hotel, do you park directly in front of it?"

"No, but... you don't think someone will still be there, do you? Between Andrés' disappearance, and our death by car bombing, I can't imagine the House is focusing on the Rook's murder anymore."

"You're probably right. But whoever shot at Bill on the boat may know we're alive. And Xavier is a control freak. If he is behind this, I can't see him leaving anything to chance. He'll want to know if someone comes snooping."

We watched the house for a few minutes. In my shredded clothing, I was starting to get cold, but I kept that to myself. Between the fainting and the vomiting, I was getting tired of all the jokes. I changed position slightly, using Juliette as a wind break.

"I don't see anyone. Do you?"

"It would defeat the purpose of posting a guard if you could just see—" Juliette gave me a side-long glance. "You're cold, aren't you?"

"You try crouching in the shadows while wearing capri jeans and what's left of a shirt!"

"Thanks, but no thanks. I actually have a fashion sense."

I eyed the tattered remains of her own outfit and raised one eyebrow.

Juliette's face colored, and she scowled. "I really do hate you." She stalked across the street toward the Rook's house. It looked like we were done being sneaky.

The gate was closed and locked, and I still didn't have my lock picks. Getting in would take time we didn't have, especially if someone was watching the house. I turned to tell Juliette we should look for a back entrance and just managed to catch a flash of pale skin as she leapt and pulled herself up and over the eight-foot brick wall. If I'd been capable of even a single pull-up, I might have tried to follow her. Instead, it looked like I was going to have to find my own way in.

A sharp hiss got my attention. The Duchess was lying flat atop the wall, belly-down, with one arm extended toward me. "Jump and catch my arm, moron. I'll pull you over."

I kept forgetting that she had super strength. I reached up and clasped her hand. Before I knew it, we were over the wall, and standing in the tiny grass courtyard.

The house's front door was similarly locked. I peeked through the narrow sidelights that flanked the door. There was no sign of movement.

Before I could suggest we look for paper clips that I could use to pick the lock, Juliette drove her fist through the plate glass pane. It was quieter than I would have expected, maybe because the sidelight was so small, but we were *definitely* done being sneaky. She reached in and unlocked the door from the inside with a triumphant smirk.

"How did you know the alarm would still be turned off?" The quick flash of concern on her face sent me racing to find the alarm panel just inside the door. To my relief, it really *was* off. I shot Juliette a look of exasperation, but she just shrugged.

"What do you want from me, little bird? It's not like I do this for a living." She closed the door behind her. "What now?"

I shrugged. My brilliant idea was seeming a little bit less brilliant in practice. "Look for cameras, I guess. Do you remember where the Rook was killed?"

"The living room." She gave me an arch look. "Some of us actually listened to Xavier's briefing."

"Oh, please. You were too busy checking out his pecs," I retorted.

"His shoulders, actually, but I'm an excellent multitasker." She sighed. "It will seriously suck if he's the evil mastermind behind all of this."

"No more booty calls?"

"Those ended a long time ago, little bird. But a girl still likes to have pretty things to look at."

I followed her into the living room which looked... well, totally normal. There was nothing to say that a murder (or three, if you counted the sex bots... and I did) had occurred less than a week earlier. This was my first, and hopefully last, murder scene, but I'd expected homicide to leave more of a mark.

Instead, it was just a room, richly decorated and completely innocuous. The bodies had been removed, of course, and the lack of blood stains suggested the walls had been repainted. Even some of the furniture had been replaced or at least re-upholstered. The next owner would never know the home's bloody history.

From what I could tell, the Rook had been a bit of a tool, but he still deserved more than to have his death erased like it had never even happened. We were brothers in mediation, after all.

On the other hand, if I ever had to make a triple-homicide disappear, I'd damn well be calling in the House's cleaning crew. Moral quandaries aside, their work was impeccable.

I wandered around the room. The Rook had expensive tastes, but it was all a bit gaudy, even for me, from black and white nude photographs to the giant sculpture of a woman's legs over in one corner. Just the legs, mind you, but they were easily seven feet tall, with less than a yard of overhead clearance. Next to the sculpture, a spiral staircase led up to the second floor, and I found myself wondering if the torso that went with the legs would be found up above.

It was just that sort of house.

To our right, a hallway led to what I assumed was a powder room and floor-level bedroom. For the time being, I ignored both the hall and the staircase. The killings had happened in the living room, so that was where we needed to look for cameras.

The problem was that hidden cameras came in any number of shapes and sizes. They weren't particularly useful for my kind of stakeout, where I still made do with my dad's camera, but I'd read about spy cams that could be hidden in anything from clock radios to Bic lighters. Amazon even had a whole shopping category for hidden cameras, which was kind of amazing.

I started with the framed pictures. Plenty of interesting views of the female anatomy, but no cameras. The wall clock hanging over the entryway seemed another likely candidate, but a quick search didn't turn up anything. The same held true for the giant legs sculpture, not that I'd really expected it to be anything but a monument to bad taste.

A series of heavy bookshelves flanked the hallway entrance, stocked from floor to ceiling with literature. Many of the books looked like they'd never been read. None were hiding cameras. Nor was the giant fern whose fronds were rapidly going brown.

Several feet in front of the bookshelves, a couch faced the opposite wall and the flashy big screen television that had been mounted there. Below it was a sideboard. The Duchess had already searched that area but come up empty.

"This sucks," she complained, putting the last few DVDs back into the cabinet. I didn't even giggle at the vampire pun. Much. Frankly, I agreed with her. Technology seemed to be outpacing mankind's ability to detect it, let alone protect against it.

I searched for the kitchen (which turned out to be upstairs, and no, the other half of the sculpture wasn't up there), and grabbed a pair of scissors from one of the drawers. Then it was back to the ground floor, where I had the joyous task of removing the covers from the living room's three light switches, two air vents, and six electrical outlets. Four of those outlets only had partial views of the living room, and one of the air vents was closed, but I checked them all anyway. You never know, right?

Again, no luck. Juliette's scowl was growing with every fruitless minute, and she'd flopped down onto the couch to watch me work. If this all turned out to be a waste of time, I could only imagine the level of sarcasm I'd be subjected to on the drive to the House. Assuming we survived the sheer terror of Juliette driving on the 163 and the 15.

I looked to the heavens to offer another prayer to the demigod of reckless drivers… and that was when I saw it.

"Juliette, could you grab a chair, please?"

She rose to her feet and casually picked up one of the overstuffed La-Z-Boys that flanked the couch.

"I meant something I can stand on."

She scowled and disappeared into the first-floor bedroom, eventually returning with a large wooden chair.

It would have to do. I carried it over to the center of the room, trying not to grunt as I did so. I really, really needed to start working out. Passing the scissors to Juliette, I climbed onto the chair, and took a closer look at the smoke detector.

It was a fairly standard model; circular with several vents, a button in the center and a light that would presumably flash while its air-raid siren scared the hell out of everyone in a two block radius. But next to that light was another, much smaller hole. Yes! I took back the scissors and unscrewed the cover. There was a small camera behind it, along with a wireless broadcaster and what looked like the parts to an actual working smoke detector.

I pointed it out to Juliette with a smug smile, and waited for the accolades to come pouring in.

CHAPTER 41

IN WHICH THE ACCOLADES DO NOT COME POURING IN

"That's it?" Her yellow eyes narrowed as she looked closer. "Wait... it's wireless? Couldn't we have used a scanner to find the WiFi network?"

"We didn't know it was WiFi until we found it. And between the two of us, we don't even have a phone... where are we going to get a scanner?" I shot her a dirty look. "Now, if we'd stopped by my office, like I suggested..."

"I told you: it's too dangerous. For all we know, Xavier or the karkino have your office and house staked out."

"My parents—"

"...should still be in Vegas, remember?"

Right. The week-long vacation package Anastasia had hooked them up with. I was still jealous. Once all of this was over, I might have enough money left over after back rent and utilities to afford a Vegas trip of my own. Assuming Mike was free. And that I survived the next few days.

"Well, whatever. Now, we just need to find the router, and the computer that's being used to store this stuff." Hopefully, the Rook hadn't heard of the cloud. I had no idea how we'd get the video if it was stored somewhere on Amazon or Microsoft's servers.

Something else occurred to me. "Why does the house still have electricity anyway? The Rook's dead. And for that matter, why isn't this a crime scene for the SDPD? Are you brainwashing the entire police department?"

"I assume the electricity is paid through the end of the month." Juliette shrugged dismissively, as if she'd never paid a bill in her life. Which was entirely possible. "As for the police, it's unlikely anybody even notified them. It's not like the Rook had friends who'd get concerned just because he disappeared for a week."

"That's kind of sad." I glanced over at the sculpture. "Understandable, but sad."

"Anyway, standard procedure is to clean up the house, once the scene has been processed." She nodded to the room, which had looked a lot nicer before we started searching it. "As you can see, that's been done. In a few weeks, an accidental fire will end up burning the whole place down to its foundation. The authorities will be left with a very cold missing persons case."

The fact that the People even had standard procedures for something like this was frightening.

In the bedroom suite, I started my search with the armoire. Nothing there, except clothing. I moved to the closet. Same deal. A really nice, hip-length leather jacket was on a hanger, along with a half-dozen suits. The floor was covered with pairs of dress shoes. Apparently, the Rook had fancied himself something of a fashion hound. Or fashion-bird. Or whatever.

I started to close the closet door, but Juliette stopped me, frowning. "Do you hear that?" She crouched down and leaned in past me, her shoulder bumping my leg. Extending her fingers, she tapped the far wall. A hollow thump sounded.

"A hidden compartment? Nice find. See if you can find the release lever or—" I swallowed the rest of the sentence as the femmepire made a fist and punched through the wall. "Or you could just do that."

Glass windows, false walls, mouthy humans... Juliette really liked punching things.

She peeled back the facade, exposing a computer that was barely larger than the wireless router it sat next to. The sound she'd heard was the system's internal fan. Even with the fake wall removed, it was just a murmur.

Atop the computer was a seven-inch LCD. The hidden alcove was only slightly larger than the electronics it contained. "The Rook wasn't... exceptionally tiny, was he?"

Juliette rolled her eyes and ignored my question.

The keyboard, at least, was reasonably sized, once unfolded. I plugged it into the computer, turned on the monitor, and did my best not to embarrass myself using the built-in trackpad. Thankfully, the UI was straight-forward. As far as I could tell, the computer's sole purpose had been to store video recordings. I skipped the file folders for "UBR", "KIT", and "DBR", proceeding instead to "DLR", which my masterful code cracking skills told me stood for downstairs living room.

No wonder the women of San Diego were so hot to date me.

I drilled down through sub-folders until I found the file for the previous Friday and double-clicked that file to launch the video. Judging by the varied file sizes for each day, the cameras were triggered by motion sensors. Even so, we had a multi-hour video to review.

The good news was that the video quality was stellar, and the picture was in full color. The bad news was that there was no audio, and footage of the living room got very dull, very quickly.

"Bored now." Reaching past me, Juliette dragged the progress bar about twenty-five percent of the way to the right.

After a brief pause, the video resumed, looking down onto a scene of carnage that had once been a person and two magical sex bots. Given the quantity of blood involved, I was surprised the cleaning crew hadn't had to sandblast the hardwood floors. They'd definitely replaced the couch and rug. All the new furniture seemed like a waste, if they were going to burn the building down anyway, but I was far from an expert in criminal behavior.

Anastasia stepped into the video, wearing the clothes I'd first seen her in. She stepped carefully around the blood, and crouched to take a closer look. The room's halogen lamps picked out the red tones in her auburn hair. It had only been two days since I'd seen the Stone Lady, but I'd honestly forgotten how beautiful she was, as if mere memories couldn't do her justice. Even surrounded by the blood and ugliness, she shined like an angel of—

Juliette dragged the progress bar back to the left with a huff of displeasure. "Indulge in your creepy stalking later, little bird."

I let the comment slide, because, by sheer chance, she'd found the exact right time on the video.

The Rook seemed like a reasonably normal, human-looking guy, albeit with greasy looking black hair that had been slicked back from a pale forehead. We watched as he got up from the couch in a movement that seemed almost boneless, leaving behind two barely clad, extremely nubile women. *These* were the magical sex bots? After the footage we'd just seen of Anastasia, they seemed like soft core stereotypes; inflated breasts, long legs, and sun-bleached blonde hair.

I peered at the one on the left. She was holding something in her hand and stroking it. Was that…? Yes, it was definitely a tail.

That was new.

The Rook re-entered the frame with at least one guest behind him but out of the picture. The mediator seemed perfectly at ease, gesturing to one of his sex bots with a smile. He was almost to the couch when that guest, still unseen, made his move.

From that point on, everything was at vampire speed. The only things the camera captured were a black-clad blur and the room's lamps reflecting off something metallic as the Rook was literally carved to pieces.

A second blur, slower, but still beyond the camera's capabilities, leapt toward the couch, and made quick work of the hapless sex bots. If they'd come with any sort of self-defense programming, it hadn't done them a bit of good. Body parts were still tumbling to the ground when the two attackers blurred back out of the frame.

Start to finish, the whole massacre took no more than fifteen seconds, and we hadn't gotten anything that would amount to actual evidence, beyond proof that there were two attackers, moving at vampire speed.

"Well, shit. Maybe one of the Watch techies can slow it down some?" I turned to my companion. "I'm sorry, Juliette. I really thought this was going to turn out—"

"Shhh." She motioned to the monitor. I turned, trying to see what she was gesturing at. The living room floor was covered with scraps of what had once been bodies, and there was no sign of the attackers. Wait. Was that...?

"Holy crap." I watched the legless torso of the Rook pull itself across the rug with its single remaining arm. Most of the man's head was missing, and it was impossible that he could still be alive, but apparently nobody had told him that. "Tough bastard."

"For all the good it did him." We watched in silence as the former mediator crawled away from the rest of his body. And then we got the break we had been hoping for.

One of the attackers strode back into view, disdaining vampire speed now that resistance had been crushed. He walked over to the squirming torso and pinned it to the ground with one booted foot. The naked, bloody blade in his hand flashed again, bisecting the torso. Even then, the arm was still trying to drag the remaining section away. The attacker used his blade to brush aside the gore, and I saw something black and bulbous protruding from the top chunk of the Rook's much diminished body. It pulsed gently.

The fact that the camera caught that detail at all was a testament to the quality of its lens, but I was too disgusted to be properly appreciative. We watched as the attacker carefully stabbed down into the pulsing organ. That finally did the trick. The arm twitched one and went still.

The Rook's killer swept his blade out in a smooth motion, sending blood arcing across the room. As he turned to leave, one of the room's halogen lights perfectly illuminated the masculine features of the prettiest man I'd ever seen.

And then Xavier left the building.

ooo

"Shit." Juliette's heartfelt expletive from behind me said it all.

I nodded, even as I looked through the alcove for a flash drive or something to copy the video to. It didn't take long to conclude that we were out of luck in that regard. With a shrug, I shut the computer down and unplugged it. That old quote about Mohamed and the mountain seemed appropriate, and I was pretty sure the computer was the mountain in this scenario. I picked it up easily in one hand.

It was only when I finished backing out of the closet to join Juliette that I realized her cursing hadn't been in response to the video at all. The Duchess was on her knees and facing me, hands pinned behind her head. And behind her, with an ugly-looking assault rifle leveled at her back...

"Hello, Ray." The sleepy-eyed vampire spared me a glance, but his focus remained on the femmepire in front of him. Apparently, Xavier had had someone watching the house after all. And Ray really was Xavier's accomplice, just like I'd tried to tell Juliette back in Gehenna. I met her furious yellow eyes and gave her a silent look of 'I told you so.' She gave a short nod of acknowledgment.

Being right didn't make me feel any better.

"Hi, John," Ray replied amiably. He nodded at the computer in my hand. "I'm guessing that has information that implicates the Captain? Something we missed?"

"If I say no, will you give Rambo back his favorite machine gun and let us go?"

"I'm afraid I can't do that." He shook his head, looking genuinely regretful. "You're supposed to be dead already. How did you survive the car bomb, anyway?"

"Didn't you hear? I'm an international man of mystery." If I had to die, I was going to get in as many cool one-liners as possible.

From her kneeling position, Juliette rolled her eyes.

"It doesn't really matter." Ray shrugged. "Getting blown up after a fun night out would have been better than being shot in a pervert's home, but dead's dead, after all." His eyes were strangely sad. "Why don't you take a seat next to Juliette, John?"

"Why should I? You just said you were going to kill us, regardless of what I do. I'm not sure what leverage you have left."

"Get down on the carpet, or I fill Juliette full of holes."

"Which you also said you were going to do anyway." Juliette was staring daggers at me, but I was starting to feel like I had the situation under control. An evil genius, Ray was not.

He scowled. "Do it and I'll finish you both quickly. Keep yanking my chain, and your death will take hours."

That was a surprisingly good threat, actually. I really didn't want to be dead, but I didn't want to be tortured for hours either. I'd have paid good money for a third option. I looked at Juliette, who was now making some sort of face at me. She was evidently every bit as scared as I was.

"Sure, Ray." I assured the just-smart-enough manpire. "Whatever you say."

I faked like I was going to my knees and then threw the computer at him.

As distractions go, it served its purpose... probably because the person in question tended to be easily distracted. He batted the computer aside with his gun, which gave Juliette the time and space to make her move. One moment, she was on her knees, the next she was standing, wrestling with Ray for the machine gun. The computer ricocheted onto the king-sized bed and I ran to recover it, thanking both the god of miniature computers and the goddess of soft foam mattresses for their shared benevolence.

Computer secured, I tried to figure out how to help Juliette. The first step was to identify which of them was the femmepire, but that was surprisingly difficult. Two vampires fighting at top speed and in close quarters looked an awful lot like a Looney Tunes melee; a wild blur where only the occasional arm or leg was recognizable.

With no strategy presenting itself, I fell back on Plan B and crept past them toward the door, computer in hand. If Ray won, I was going to run like hell. Juliette would understand.

A loud crack stopped me in my tracks. I turned to find Ray sagging to the ground, one side of his torso caved in where a knee had struck home. Juliette stood behind him, her grip on the manpire's head the only thing holding him upright. Another crack sounded as she violently spun his head a full three-hundred-and-sixty degrees. Ray's corpse slumped to the floor in a heap.

"What the hell happened to you, Ray?" A furious, slightly battered Juliette wiped blood from her face and glared down at the body of the friend she'd just killed. She turned suspiciously shiny yellow eyes on me. "And you! What took you so long?"

"To do what?!" I waved the computer at her as a reminder that I had totally saved our lives. Or at least given her the opportunity to save our lives. Yeah, that was a little bit more accurate.

"To distract Ray, like I was telling you to do!"

Huh. That put all the faces she'd been making into perspective. I decided not to share my wildly incorrect interpretation of our silent conversation. "Well, I—"

"Forget it." As quickly as it had come, her anger faded. She looked down at Ray's body again. "He's the last person I'd have expected to turn traitor." She spat blood to the side. "And he should have known better. He could never take me, even in the old days."

"I'm sorry it came to this, Juliette."

She shrugged, pretending like she hadn't just been blinking back tears. "One down, one more to g—"

Music blared loudly, interrupting her. Reggae music. Juliette pulled a cell phone from Ray's front pocket, and Bob Marley's voice filled the bedroom.

"Speak of the devil." On the bright, enormous screen, the caller was identified merely as 'Captain.' We stared at the phone in silence for almost a full chorus before I snatched it out of her hand and swiped across the screen to answer it.

"Did you identify the disturbance?" Even across the digital divide, I recognized Xavier's voice. "Mr. Jennings?"

Without stopping to think, I replied. "Afraid not, asshole. But if you start running now, you might just manage to escape the pile of shit we're about to drop on you."

"Mr. Smith. And somehow still alive." His voice tightened. "Is Juliette with you as well?"

"Actually," I decided, ignoring his question. "I think you're screwed, no matter how far you run. And I can't wait to watch you burn."

I hit the end call button, and gave Juliette the phone.

"You are weirdly hot right now," said the spiky-haired femmepire. "Letting him know you survived probably wasn't a smart thing to do though."

"Smart? No. But satisfying? Hell, yes." Flush with adrenaline and triumph, I went back to the Rook's closet and took the dead man's leather jacket. There was no point in letting it burn, after all. Somehow, it actually fit.

Juliette shook her head again in amazement. "Weirdly hot."

CHAPTER 42

IN WHICH PHONE TAG ALWAYS ENDS
WITH SOMEONE BEING IT

"Borghesi residence, this is Akiko. How may I direct your call?"

I took a moment to glory in the smooth maple syrup of the new operator's voice. "Could you transfer me to Lady Dumenyova's line, Akiko?"

"Of course, sir. Please hold."

I couldn't help smiling as the hold music came on. I was never going to get tired of being called sir by the House operators.

In the driver's seat, Juliette's irritation was obvious in the set of her shoulders and the clenching of her jaw. "This is stupid. Why the hell are you calling Anastasia? We've been doing fine without her."

Apparently, getting drunk, being blown up, sucked into a hell dimension, and almost dying to the most spacey of manpires qualified as 'fine' to Juliette.

"I agreed not to call her from Bill's boat, since we didn't have any proof yet, but now we have the evidence and Xavier is on the run. Anastasia can mobilize the House to hunt him down. And she'll be the one breaking the news to Lucia instead of us. I've already spent too much time around a pissed off Lucia as it is—"

I broke off as the music ended, and Akiko came back on. "I'm sorry, sir, but Lady Dumenyova is unavailable right now. Would you like to leave your name and number?"

"Actually, this is John Smith, Akiko. The mediator. Could you try her cell instead? Please? It's important that I reach her as soon as possible."

Akiko's voice lost none of its smooth courtesy, but there was a note of surprise added to the mix. "Mr. Smith? Aren't you supposed to be dead?"

"I got better," I replied, scratching one more phrase off my badass bucket list. "Juliette is here with me as well."

"Some people will be very happy to hear that." I could hear the smile in her voice. "Hold on while I connect you to Lady Dumenyova's cell."

The elevator music made its triumphant return with a series of muted piano chords and otherwise unintelligible instrumentals.

"Look at it this way, Duchess. We did all the important stuff. We returned the Nintendo, we appeased Bill, we found evidence implicating Xavier, *and* we killed one of the House traitors. I mean you," I amended, as her yellow eyes narrowed, "you killed one of the House traitors. We're going to come out of this looking like heroes. Trumpets, medals and adoring crowds. It's okay to have Anastasia help with the cleanup."

I could feel the moment when Juliette's mood turned. She looked at me as a crooked smile spread across her face. "The Stone Lady acting as my gofer? I could get used to that."

I waved her to silence as Akiko finished transferring me to Anastasia's cell. After a single ring, it picked up.

"Hello, you have reached Anastasia Dumenyova, but I am currently unavailable. Please leave your name and number so that I may get back to you soon. Thank you."

So much for that idea. I scowled and waited for the beep.

"Anastasia, this is John. John Smith. I'm with Juliette. We're both alive... obviously... and we have evidence that proves Xavier is the person behind the House's current troubles. He knows we know, and I'm pretty sure he's running for his life, but I think I can end this whole mediation if the House brings Xavier to justice. Anyway, I'm not sure where you are at the moment, but call us back as soon as possible."

"I guess she's busy doing her own thing, little bird. As usual. What now? Dinner? There's a nice little Indian place over in Hillcrest."

"Bombay? I know. My parents take me there for my birthday every year."

Juliette gave me a look that was half scorn and half pity. "You really don't have *any* friends, do you?"

"Yeah, yeah, laugh it up." I punched in the number for the House again.

"Borghesi residence, this is Akiko. How may I direct your call?"

"Hey Akiko. This is John again," I said with a smile. "We ended up leaving a message for Lady Dumenyova. Could you transfer me to Kayla's room?"

"You know, Mr. Smith, our residents do have numbers that you can call directly," Akiko teased. Yeah, I liked her.

"I know," I fibbed, "but trying to remember all those numbers would strain my fragile human brain." Great. Now, even I was making fun of my species.

It was worth it when Akiko rewarded me with a low chuckle. "We can't have that now, can we? Please hold while I transfer you to Kayla's line."

If my life ever became a movie, I'm pretty sure the soundtrack would consist entirely of elevator music. I tapped my toe slightly to the muffled beat.

"First, Anastasia. Now, Kayla? You really *are* doing everything you can to avoid talking to Lucia, aren't you?"

"You know it. Plus, as the Watch's second-in-command, Kayla is the logical choice to lea—" Again, the ringing on the other end of the line silenced me. It was surprisingly difficult to hold a conversation while being transferred from number to number.

"Hello?" The distinctly American accent suggested that this was not, in fact, Kayla. I took a wild guess as to the recipient's identity.

"Darlene?" If she was back in the House, the lockdown had already ended. Which was weird. How had Ray and Xavier slipped through Zorana's questioning?

"This is she. Who's this?" Her voice sounded a bit foggy, as if I'd woken her up.

"Hey Darlene, this is John." For the second time, I got to explain that I was not, in fact, dead. The undeniable happiness in D's voice kept it from being a chore. I'd only known the pint-sized pixie for a few days, but I definitely considered her a friend. "I'll give you the whole story when I get back, but in the meantime, I really need to chat with Kayla."

"She'll be as happy to hear from you as I was, John, but K's not here right now. She's at Captain X's assembly."

That one stopped me cold. I looked at Juliette, whose eyes had gone wide with concern. "Uhm, just to clarify, do you mean an assembly about Xavier, or an assembly that he called?"

"X-man called it," she confirmed. "I'm not sure what the big news is, but all of the Watch is attending."

"Oh shit," I breathed. That did not sound like the actions of someone on the run. Next to me, Juliette had already turned the key in the ignition. For once, I didn't mind that she was using her vampire hearing to eavesdrop.

"John? Is everything okay?"

"Xavier is a traitor, D. He and Ray were behind the attempts on my life, as well as the murder of the Rook, and the theft of that stupid Nintendo." There were a series of loud honks, as Juliette pulled out into traffic. Without even a retaliatory middle finger, the spiky-haired femmepire gunned the stolen Acura's engine, and we were quickly doing seventy on a residential road.

There was a moment of stunned silence on the other end of the line. "Oh no! Kayla!"

"Darlene!" I had to shout her name a few times before I broke through to her. "D, I don't know what is going on, but you could be in danger. I want you to lock your door and barricade yourself in your room. Can you do that?"

"But Kayla—"

"Is a badass who can take care of herself," I pointed out. "But it would crush her if something happened to you." I waited for her shaky acknowledgment, then continued. "I'm going to call Lucia. Whatever happens, stay put and stay safe."

I ended the call and grabbed the 'oh shit' handle above my passenger-side window as Juliette took the roundabout to the 805 without even easing off of the gas. We skidded from the right lane all the way into the left, but somehow kept from spinning out. Once that particular moment of death defying derring-do was over, I dialed the number for the House one more time.

"Borghesi residence, this is Aki—"

"Akiko, this is John again," I cut her off.

"You know, Mr. Smith, if you keep calling me, my boyfriends are going to get jealous," she teased.

"I'll uh, keep that in mind, Akiko, but I need to talk to Lucia. Right now." Another thought occurred to me. "I'm not sure where you and the other operators work out of, but you might want to barricade yourselves in. I think something horrible is about to go down, unless Lucia can stop it."

"Horrible… how?" Akiko's smooth voice was marred a little bit by the mingled notes of concern and suspicion.

"I don't know. A bomb or an invasion or something. All I know is that Xavier's at the center of it."

"Barricade, hell. I'm going to go kick some ass," muttered Akiko. "Thanks for the warning, John. I'm transferring you to Lucia now."

This time, the elevator music only played for a few seconds. During that brief time, we crossed the 8 at a speed somewhere between one hundred miles per hour and Mach three. As soon as the phone started to ring, it was answered.

"HELLO!" The voice was full-volume, child-like, and nothing at all like that of the ice queen's.

"Tea Leaf?" Her responding giggle told me I'd guessed correctly. Not that there were many children in the House to choose from. "Is Queen Lucia there?"

I had a sinking feeling. Were we already too late?

There was a series of unidentifiable noises on the other end, followed by Tea Leaf loudly proclaiming her displeasure as someone took the phone from her.

"Who is this?" Lucia's voice was surprisingly soft, colored by the affection she felt for her tiny charge. Suddenly, I had no problem seeing Lucia in the role of a mother. Weird.

"Lucia, this is John Smith."

"But—"

"Yes, I know. Dead, etc. There's no time. You're in danger."

"Explain." Her voice was back to its usual pissed-off shaved ice timbre.

"Xavier is a traitor." That's all I got to say before the sound of gunfire broke out over the phone. Immediately after, the line went dead.

CHAPTER 43

IN WHICH PEOPLE DIE

With no traffic, it can still easily take thirty minutes to get to Scripps Ranch from North Park. During rush hour, that same trip will be more than an hour.

We made it in fifteen. We didn't just break the speed limit, we kicked its ass and dropped it out of an airplane. We drove on shoulders, we cut across lanes, we ran red lights… after the first half-dozen near accidents, I stopped looking. It was just going to give me a heart attack. Instead, I punched redial on my phone, on the off-chance that anyone might answer.

Nobody did.

When we reached the House, however, human guards were manning the gate as if nothing had happened. Juliette slowed the stolen Acura to a halt and impatiently waved at the security guard.

"Good evening, ma'am." The guard's hands were empty, his assault rifle on a strap over one shoulder. His tone was courteous, but professional.

"Hi," Juliette responded, mystified, "you can buzz me in any time now."

"I'm sorry, ma'am." He sounded sincerely apologetic. "These grounds are private property. No trespassing is permitted."

"I know that," Juliette protested, "I live here."

He gave an 'aw shucks' laugh. "Well, I *am* new to the job, ma'am, so I'm afraid I don't recognize the residents on sight." He gave us both a brisk once-over. "Do you have any identification with you? I'm sure we can clear this all up in no time."

Juliette bit back a curse. When she spoke, her eyes were glowing with a golden light, and her voice had a sugary sweetness that should have sent the man running for the hills. "Look at me, meat. You will let us in now. You will forget that you saw us, and when you get home tonight, you will drink a bottle of laxative as punishment for your interference."

I was happier than ever that vampire mojo didn't work on me.

We waited for the guard to buzz us in. Instead, he spoke, the friendliness in his voice forgotten. "I can't see why I'd do that, ma'am. It seems to me like you're just asking for trouble."

While Juliette was busy gaping at the human who'd just ignored her compulsion, I caught movement out of the corner of my eye. The passenger side mirror showed a second guard coming around the rear of our Acura, his gun held at the ready. "Juliette…" I warned.

The words were barely out of my mouth when the guard on her side brought up his gun. At the same time, Juliette swung her door open at full strength. I'm pretty sure the steel hinges groaned, but it was difficult to hear over the sickening crack of a man's bones being broken by the impact. The guard flew into the wall of his security shed, and crumpled in a heap, his neck cranked at a thoroughly unnatural angle.

Even as he was flying through the air, Juliette was out of her seat. She pivoted and leaped over the car. In my side mirror, I saw the guard who'd been flanking us go down under a flurry of femmepire. Juliette tossed the man's limp body to the side, walked back around the Acura, and reached inside the shed. Moments later, the gate started to slide aside. She took her seat back behind the wheel, and powered us through the widening gap.

"What just happened?" I squeaked out, as we careened up the two-lane drive onto the estate. "How did he resist your voodoo?"

"It's hard to override someone else's compulsion." She spit the words out like a curse. "Xavier is using our own security force against us. Even so, they're cannon fodder. He couldn't take the House with just humans. What is he doing?"

"Maybe Ray wasn't his only accomplice." I'd been thinking about it since my aborted phone call to Lucia. How had someone gotten past the guards on the third floor? "He wouldn't have stuck around if he didn't have additional allies in the House."

"Shit." Apparently, that was *not* something Juliette had considered. She looked over at me, yellow eyes wide, as the full implication sunk in. "The House may have already fallen."

We screeched to a halt at the base of the stairs exterior stairs. The enormous wooden doors were wide open and there were no guards in sight.

Juliette cocked her head in response to a noise I couldn't hear, and a slight smile appeared on her face. "That was gunfire. The battle's not over yet." She stepped out of the car. "John, get out of here. Take the Acura and go someplace safe. When the People war, humans are just casualties waiting to happen." She dropped the keys in my lap and turned away. Before I could say anything, she was gone, bounding up the stairs in her tattered dress and bare feet.

Juliette was right. Either of the gate guards could have killed me as easily as breathing, but she'd handled them like children. And Xavier was on another level entirely. The traitorous asshole was a freaking Battlelord, for God's sake.

Whatever the hell that meant, I knew it wasn't good for us.

But thinking of Kayla inevitably made me think of Darlene— human like me and half my size—stuck in her bedroom on the second floor.

Shit.

I tucked the mini-computer with its now superfluous evidence into the glove box, and unbuckled my seat belt. And then, like a red-shirted crew member on Star Trek or the boneheaded best friend who dies in every horror movie, I left the car and ran straight toward danger.

ooo

I made it almost two feet into the House before coming across the first body; that of a security guard whose Kevlar vest had failed to protect him from whatever had punched a hole straight through his chest. To my right, the door to the human quarters was hanging from one hinge. A glance down that hall showed many more bodies, few of them armed or armored. The French cook sprawled in the doorway to the kitchen, a cleaver on the floor near his outstretched hand.

After that, I tried not to look too closely.

I left the human quarters and went across to the banquet hall. It held the largest collection of bodies yet, all of them vampire, and many clothed in black. I remembered Darlene's words about Xavier meeting with the Watch. This was clearly the place where it had happened.

But what about Kayla? Steeling myself, I stepped inside.

At first, the enormous room was just a chaotic scene of savaged bodies and blood. As I moved between overturned tables, I started to piece together the puzzle. In contrast to the human quarters, very few of the dead here had fallen to gunfire. Instead, bodies were broken and torn, cut down by bladed weaponry or shredded by tooth and claw. One particular pair of corpses said it all; two vampires, both in the black uniform of the Watch, one dead from the second's fist through his chest. That second vampire's throat had been torn away, even as she struck the killing blow.

Watch killing Watch. This was bad.

Several vampires had been killed in their seats. The initial victims of the surprise assault? I mentally labeled them as the good guys, for all the good that label did. Others had died back-to-back, having gained sufficient warning to at least attempt a defense. Corey, my In-n-Out eating manpire buddy, had been forcibly separated from his head. Blue eyes stared accusingly at me from across the room. A thick knot of four or five bodies was surrounded by a slightly larger pool of attackers. And in that knot, I saw a spread of long, ash-blonde hair.

Kayla.

I ran to the pile. Leeched of blood and life, the vampire corpses were surprisingly light. I grimly shifted them off of the femmepire. The Aussie was a broken shell, bone protruding from a shattered left arm, and at least three large gaping wounds visible in her torso. Something had taken a bite out of her right shoulder; the marks left there far too large to be human, or even canine.

"Kayla, I'm sorry." If only we'd been faster somehow. Or I hadn't answered Xavier's call.

Pale lashes fluttered, and the woman I'd assumed to be dead looked up through brown eyes darkened by pain. Her mouth worked a few times before any sound emerged.

"Xavier."

"I know," I assured her. "We're still fighting."

Her eyes, already drifting shut, suddenly widened. "Darlene…!" Impossibly, she tried to struggle to her feet.

"Is barricaded inside your room. If anyone survives this, she will, but we need to help you first." I extended my arm over her mouth, and braced myself for the pain. "Feed."

"Can't." She shook her head stubbornly. "Wouldn't be able to stop." She took a deep breath. I could hear the air wheezing in and out of her one working lung. "Get me to Darlene."

"Kayla, I—"

She grabbed my extended wrist, and pulled me closer. "Get. Me. To. Darlene."

ooo

The only thing worse than navigating a massacre was helping a badly wounded femmepire do the same. I don't know how we made it up the stairs, or why Kayla didn't pass out from the pain. The sucking sounds from her chest intensified as we traveled, and she leaned more and more heavily on me with each step.

Compared to the first floor, the second was relatively undisturbed. There were bodies, but it wasn't the charnel house that the banquet hall had been. Part of that was because a good portion of its inhabitants had been elsewhere when the fighting started, but I suspected a greater part was that the fight was focused on the third floor. If Lucia died, the House was pretty much doomed.

I could only hope Juliette was up there and still kicking.

Many of the rooms we passed were empty. Some, like my own suite, showed no signs of forced entry at all, while others had clearly been targeted by the attackers. Kayla and Darlene's room was ten or fifteen suites past mine down the hall, and I was relieved to see the door was shut. I leaned Kayla against the wall, and banged on the wooden portal.

"Darlene, it's John. I've got Kayla with me, but she needs—"

Help. She needs help. That's what I was going to say, before someone grabbed me by the arm and hurled me down the hallway.

I landed with a thud and a moan, bruised by the landing, but lucky to have not struck anything mid-flight. Back down the hallway, Kayla had fallen onto her side. Above her loomed a strung-out surfer vampire. Miles' ultra-white teeth flashed as he smiled evilly in my direction.

"Hey, monkey. Remember me?"

ooo

Miles let loose with a savage kick that actually lifted Kayla up off the floor, the sound of his foot connecting flesh audible from almost thirty feet away. I desperately looked about for something or someone who could stop him. Unfortunately, I'd left my asshole-killing laser gun in my other pair of pants and the suites near me were empty. And further down the hall was nothing but...

I squinted to bring the massive iron-bound door at the end of the hall into focus. Why was the door barred? As I watched, the door itself seemed to shiver. Either I'd finally gotten that concussion I'd been dreading all week, or—The door shivered again, as if something had struck it heavily from the other side. As Miles went to kick Kayla a second time, I pushed myself to my feet and ran for the Midnight Tower.

It was like trying to outrun an avalanche. I'd taken maybe six steps when Miles caught me. He didn't even slow but simply ran with me in one hand, turning me about to slam my back against the very door I'd been running for.

"Where were you going? I haven't even begun to play." He ragdolled me against the door, rattling my teeth and brain in the process.

"I should have known you'd be part of the coup," I spat, trying in vain to get some form of leverage while being held a foot off the ground.

"Is that what's going on?" He raised an eyebrow. "Huh. Can't say I'm sorry to hear it. Things have been getting stale anyway." His blue eyes darkened as the pupils widened, and his fangs began to extend. "Too bad you won't live to see what comes next."

Suspended in mid-air by someone vastly stronger than I was, with my shoulders pinned against the door, I didn't have a lot of options. It was time to break one of the most sacred of dude-laws...

I kicked Miles in the nuts.

It wasn't the testicle crunching blow I'd been hoping for, but Miles groaned and dropped me as he grabbed at his groin. When he straightened up, he was in full manpire fury. I was still standing at the door, which seemed to confuse him. His angry eyes focused on the iron bar I now held in my hands.

"You think that's going to save you, fool?" he asked in a mocking tone. "I'm going to take it away from you and shove it up—"

"This?" I tossed the bar aside. My arms were tired from having even held it that long. "I wasn't grabbing a weapon, dude. I was just opening the door."

His brow furrowed in confusion at my words. Then the door blew open and the Blood Witch was tearing his arms off.

CHAPTER 44
IN WHICH THINGS COME TO A HEAD

Good old Miles never stood a chance. Zorana, dressed in a navy pinstriped dress, straddled what was left of the manpire, and held one hand in the air above his corpse. A thin stream of blood rose from Miles' mouth and nose to coiled around her hand like a liquid snake.

"Human." Her child's voice was barbed, her words thick with fury. In other words, she was Zorana. "What is this I hear about a coup?"

I explained as quickly as I could, and Zorana made for the elevators in a swish of long skirts and slipper-clad feet. With Miles dead, Darlene had brought Kayla into their room and was preparing some sort of funnel with which to feed the Aussie her blood. Her wide eyes met mine as Zorana and I marched past, and then she closed the door and set to work trying to keep her lover alive.

At the elevator, Zorana stabbed the button to call it to our floor. It didn't light. She stabbed it again. Still nothing.

"I don't think it's working." I didn't want to attract the angry Blood Witch's attention, but time was not on our side.

The tiny vampire shot me a look of annoyance. "Lucia must have hit the panic switch in her room. The third floor won't be accessible." As reasonable as both her tone and words were, they still made my intestines twitch.

Maybe it was just a Blood Witch thing.

"Where would Xavier go? She has to be his primary target."
Look at us, just a guy and a Blood Witch, talking almost like regular
people.

"Be silent, meat!" She turned back down the hall, the coil of
animated blood trailing behind her like a pet. I followed her into the
first open suite to the left.

I hadn't known this suite's resident either, although I vaguely
remembered her face from the kitchen lunch crowd. She and her blood
donors were well and truly dead, the femmepire's hand outstretched to
the window as if still trying to escape. Zorana brushed the corpse aside,
picked up a blood-spattered chair, and threw it through the bedroom's
main window. Tossing me over one shoulder in a fireman's carry where
both my head and feet almost touched the ground, the Blood Witch
climbed out the window.

If the portal to The Bitter End had been a thoroughly mundane
experience, being carried by an ancient vampire in the body of an
adolescent girl as she scaled the exterior wall of a multi-level mansion
was anything but. Like a little spider monkey, Zorana moved up the
wall as if she were walking on a level surface. And she only banged my
head against the stone a few dozen times on the way.

We climbed right past the third floor. Thick sheets of steel had
come down over the windows, preventing access. Apparently, the
entire level was one big panic room. Assuming Lucia had survived the
initial assault, she was probably safe for now.

When we reached the fourth floor, Zorana kicked out with one
slipper-clad foot and shattered the nearest conference room's window.
She swung inside and deposited me on the carpeted floor. Right onto
the shards of broken glass. Through a minor miracle, I avoided real
damage, but my exposed skin gained a few new cuts and scrapes, and
my tattered clothes acquired a coating of glass. In the recessed lighting,
those fragments shined like sequins.

If I died, at least my corpse would be fabulous.

Our entry didn't go unnoticed. The door burst open, and
several black-clad vampires piled in, accompanied by one of the few
still-living human guards. The barrel of the human's assault rifle swung

up, tracking my chest, and the vampires launched themselves forward in a blur of steel and fury.

As quick as they were, Zorana was faster. She spoke three words in that alien tongue from my blood ritual. Miles' blood uncoiled and struck like the serpent it resembled. Neither body armor nor vampire physiology seemed to offer any resistance; I watched the enemy wither before my eyes. Zorana minced over to their bodies and repeated the gesture she'd made over Miles' corpse. The coil of floating blood quintupled in size. Her small doll's mouth curved in the closest thing to a smile I'd seen yet from her. "Death will have her day, Mr. Smith."

Something enormous and shadowed leapt from the door, bowling her little child's body over like it was a toy. The two of them went right out the window, tumbling to the estate grounds below.

ooo

Once again ignoring every lesson I'd learned from horror movies, I risked a glimpse over the window's edge. Miraculously, nothing reached up and pulled me to my death. In fact, there was no sign of Zorana or… whatever that thing had been.

I reversed direction, and peeked out into the fourth floor hallway. From the far end of the hall, near where I'd first met the council, I could hear loud banging. I crept closer. Ninja stealth. That was my mantra.

As I walked past a conference room, a slender arm dragged me inside. "Little bird, what the hell are you doing here? And why are you making so much noise?"

Including Juliette, there were a handful of vampires clustered around me, their faces grim, not a one of them entirely free of injury. I gave a nod to Steve, the only other one in the group I recognized.

Juliette had a long cut across her face and blood—not hers, I hoped—spattered across her still mostly exposed chest, but she otherwise seemed okay. Somewhere, she'd found a sword. She even looked like she knew how to use it.

"I couldn't just leave," I explained quietly. "I found Kayla and got her to Darlene."

"K's alive?" Steve looked relieved.

"So far. And I freed Zorana from the Midnight Tower."

It sounded a lot more heroic in the retelling. Clearly, this was how the legend of John Smith would get started.

"Zorana? Thank the gods," said a manpire I didn't know, who, I swear to God, had an actual mullet. Someone needed to take that dude aside and explain to him that certain things just weren't acceptable in Southern California. "Where is she?"

"She went out the window under something big and growly."

"The Infected," muttered Juliette with a curse. "At least it's out of the picture for the time being. We may have a chance."

"Are you crazy, Juliette? I don't know if you noticed, but we're outnumbered. And this is the Captain we're talking about," said mullet-boy. "We don't have a chance."

"Where is everyone else?" I asked Steve in a low voice. Even with all the bodies I'd seen, there were a lot of vampires unaccounted for.

"Down in the sub-levels, we think," the mohawked vampire replied. "We were headed there to pitch in when Juliette redirected us here."

"Were the elevators still running then?"

"No; we took the back stairs." He frowned. "Like you, I assume."

I flashed back to my nightmarish ascent up the exterior wall and shook my head, shuddering. The debate was still in full swing behind us.

Finally, Juliette overrode her companions' objections.

"I'll handle Xavier." The spiky-haired vampire's voice was hard, devoid of her usual sarcasm. "You all focus on the other traitors." She looked about her at the noncommittal manpires. "If this House falls, what do we have? Not a flock in the country will take us. I've spent years on the outside. I'm not going to let some arrogant asshole put me back on the streets."

Without another word, she spun and headed for the door, the blade in her hands shining like a steel toothpick.

Nobody else moved.

"Free In-n-Out to anyone who survives," I announced over my shoulder as Steve and I followed the femmepire down the hall. I'm not sure if it was the offer of food or the ignominy of a human being braver than vampires, but the last three manpires fell in line behind us.

Steve handed me a heavy handgun. "I noticed you don't have a weapon, John. This isn't going to stop one of us for long, but it's better than nothing."

"Cool." I felt kind of like Rambo. "Is there a safety or something?"

He showed me where it was. Judging by his expression, he was already regretting having armed me.

ooo

The noise grew the closer we came. It sounded like a half-dozen angry house flippers, each doing their own version of demolition day. In the largest conference room, the vampires had moved the antique table aside, peeled back the carpet and were trying to bang a hole in the floor. Worse, they were actually making progress.

Xavier stood by, speaking quietly to one of his Watch members, as several others swung their hammers repeatedly at the section of exposed floor. The Captain looked like he'd just stepped out of a recruitment poster. In one hand, he held a bared katana, one of the two weapons I'd seen in his suite. It was also the blade he'd used to cut the Rook into tiny pieces. Now, as then, blood trickled down the blade's edge to drip onto the carpet.

We were quiet. Vampire quiet, even. Like mice sneaking up on a watchful cat. But somehow, Xavier knew we were there. His eyes whipped up to the doorway and he barked a warning as we charged inside. And then there was chaos and blood.

As promised, Juliette leapt to engage the Captain, sword in hand. Steve, Mullet-boy and the others rushed the vampires in the center of the room. Which left one unaccounted for... the vampire Xavier had been talking to. He turned to the door and, with a sinking feeling, I recognized his face.

"Ricardo." I lifted my gun to menace the vampire who'd denied me access to the security room during the hunt for the Nintendo. Why did I always get the assholes?

The manpire blurred by me, and my left arm was suddenly burning. I looked down to see a narrow cut, just below the shoulder. It was superficial, but bleeding freely. The handsome vampire snickered. "Did you *really* bring a gun to a knife fight, human?"

So I shot him.

I tried to, anyway. The gun bucked in my hands and the vampire blurred to the side, dodging the bullet with ease. All I got for my trouble were a pair of sore wrists.

This was a lot easier in video games.

"Is that all you've got?" he taunted.

I turned to face him again, the hall door to my left. "Not even close."

I shot again.

And missed again. He was barely even trying. I pivoted to the left again to track him, for all the good it was doing me.

Another shot.

Another miss. Out of the corner of my eye, I watched Steve take down one of the sledgehammer wielding vampires with a nifty slide-roll-stab combo. Steve was a bit of a badass. I wondered how much of it was because of the mohawk.

A line of fire stroked across my chest, as Ricardo struck at a speed I had absolutely no hope of matching. Before I was even aware of his assault, he'd returned to his defensive position, an arrogant smile on his face. "I can keep this up all day, human."

He proved the point, dodging another shot with ease. Again, I turned slightly left to follow him. He was now almost flush with the wall. "And you can't have many bullets left—"

I squeezed off a shot, and then immediately rotated back to the right and fired again. In a blur, Ricardo dodged the first bullet, carrying himself directly into the path of the second.

In the grand history of pitched gunfights, there have almost certainly been more impressive shots than one made at ten feet by an untalented amateur… but I seriously doubt any of them were even half as satisfying.

"How did…" The strength vanished from Ricardo's legs in an instant. He slumped to the ground, still alive, but very confused.

"You let him back you into a corner," came Xavier's baritone reply, as the manpire himself entered my field of view. "Your options for evasion were limited, and he guessed correctly which way you would go."

"Captain…" mumbled Ricardo. "I can't feel my legs."

"The shot must have clipped your spine," mused Xavier. "You'd heal from it eventually but neither the Court nor I have any use for stupidity." His blade flashed and Ricardo's head rolled to the side.

The sounds of combat around us had ceased. Steve was backed into a corner by two vampires. Mullet-boy was face down, and struggling to stand. Our other two allies had joined the bodies littering the room. But where was Juliette?

In retrospect, looking away from Xavier wasn't the brightest of ideas. Before I could turn my gun back on him, he had grabbed me from behind, spinning me to face the far side of the room.

Juliette was on the ground in a heap.

"She's still alive," he whispered into my ear, casually squeezing a nerve cluster until my hand spasmed and dropped the gun. "For now, anyway. For her, much will depend on the decisions she makes when you are dead."

"Why are you doing this, Xavier?"

The traitorous Captain pushed me away, his blade coming up and tracking my motion as if to prove he could skewer me at any time. "Is this the part where, out of respect for a formidable foe, I explain my motivations, the full details of my plans, and in doing so, give you the opportunity to make one last attempt to stop me?"

"Uhm… yes?" Apparently, we'd seen the same movies.

"The problem, Mr. Smith," he shook his head sadly, "is that you were never all that formidable. And while you've caused me no shortage of difficulty, it would be a stretch to consider you a foe. An irritant, perhaps. I consider this a mercy killing." The sword came up, and his smile widened.

The conference room window blew inward, and two shapes entered the room in a cloud of glass and wood. Marcus landed easily on his feet, bat-like wings melting back into his body. The other figure came out of a controlled roll, auburn hair whipping about her head like a swarm of bees. Her beautiful face was expressionless, but gold glittered in Anastasia's jade green eyes. Unarmed, she advanced on Xavier.

The handsome vampire dismissed me entirely, turning to face his one-time paramour. "I'd hoped you'd be stuck down in Mexico while this all played out, my love." He shook his head sadly. "You would have had plausible deniability for Lucia's death. Not a shred of scandal to tarnish your sterling reputation."

"And then what, Xavier?" Her words were cool. "What would you do once the bodies were all buried?"

"I would go home. Back to Rome. King Tomasso will lift our banishment once this house is broken and his sister dead." He lowered his sword and held his free hand out to her. "Come with me, Anastasia. We can return to our life together, to the way things were before this whole miserable exile."

I'd hated the guy even before he started massacring my friends, but listening to him now, I could almost feel...

Nope. Still hated him.

For the first time, a sliver of anger made it into Anastasia's voice. "We were finished a long time ago, Xavier. If you think that murdering our own House members would somehow change that—"

"For you of all people to speak of murder..." He shook his head. "I regret these deaths, and will honor the courage of all who fell today when I return to Rome, but this House was always doomed. Some level of collateral damage was unavoidable." His voice hardened. "Lucia stole you from me. Until she's gone, nothing will ever be right again."

"Then this all has been for nothing. I was never yours to lose, and you will not reach her alive."

I watched the light go out of Xavier's eyes. After a long moment, he shrugged, his deep voice heavy. "So be it. If I must choose between this worthless half-life and a future in Rome alone, I choose Rome."

His blade darted toward the femmepire in a blur. Anastasia barely moved, but the blade somehow missed her. Still unarmed, she stepped inside the manpire's reach, and struck him twice, knocking him back.

They were the first hits I'd ever seen Xavier take. He growled angrily, and moved back in, sword darting like a serpent to strike at the auburn haired vampire. Using the length of his weapon to keep Anastasia at bay, he drove her across the room. Her motions were slight and controlled, perfectly chosen to avoid his strikes, but the disadvantage of being weaponless seemed too great to overcome. She was only prolonging the inevitable.

Finally, it happened.

Stepping backward, Anastasia stumbled on carpet that had been peeled away for the traitors' hole. Before she could recover, Xavier's sword slipped in impossibly fast.

There was no way for her to dodge his blade.

Instead, she caught it.

One slim hand halted the downward flash of the sword entirely. The blade should have sheared straight through the fingers and palm of that hand, should have kept cutting down into the arm and torso of the female in its path. Instead, it was like the force of the blow had dissipated entirely. I looked at that hand, and saw her usual pale skin was now grey and rough, like unfinished granite.

The title Stone Lady suddenly took on entirely new significance.

With a twist of her wrist, she pulled both the blade and the vampire holding it closer. Her other hand blurred and drove through Xavier's chest several times, like a jackhammer bursting through tissue paper.

Xavier let go of the sword and fell to his knees. He looked up at Anastasia, face empty of anything but pain, and said something to her, too quietly for me to hear.

Two hands, one stone, one bloody, came forward to cup the manpire's cheeks. Anastasia's large jade eyes were sad.

"I know."

And then those hands tightened, and she tore Xavier's head from his body.

CHAPTER 45

IN WHICH SOME THINGS AREN'T FOR SALE

With Xavier dead, his revolution fell apart. Marcus and Steve made short work of the last two enemy vampires in our room, and then the bat-winged Councilman and mohawked guard headed into the sub-levels to help crush the remaining pockets of opposition. Anastasia set up triage for the wounded vampires, including Juliette and Mullet-boy, and when I left, blood was already being ferried in to aid with the healing. With so many donors dead, I had no idea where it was coming from.

For my part, I retreated to the second floor, where I grabbed three beers from the kitchen. A very tired and white-faced Darlene and a now-conscious and slightly healed Kayla bandaged my own wounds and we sat together in silence, Darlene cuddled under Kayla's no-longer-broken arm. I was too tired to even register that I was within the confines of their fabled den of iniquity. The chair was comfortable, the beer was cold, and the two women made an awfully cute couple. That was all that mattered.

An hour later, Anastasia tapped on the door and let me know that my presence was required. Kayla and Darlene were asleep before I even reached the door.

I followed the beautiful Secundus to the elevators, which were again operational. Neither of us spoke during our journey to the third floor, but Anastasia squeezed my shoulder before we exited. I felt the warmth of that hand on my shoulder, long after it was gone.

The third floor hadn't escaped damage entirely, testament to the assault that had ended my phone call with Lucia. Frost coated the hallway, and two different former Watch members were now ice sculptures, flash-frozen in mid-motion. A third such statue had been struck by something heavy, leaving behind only two upright legs and what would be a truly revolting mess when the ice finally thawed.

Tea Leaf was skating down the hallway in bare feet, giggling delightedly as she slipped and slid past the statuary. That cost her quite a few points on the adorableness scale. But what the hell... at least *someone* was having fun.

It came as no surprise that Lucia's suite was the biggest in the entire building. Marcus was already present, supporting a woozy but healing Juliette. Next to them stood Zorana, small hands clutching a monstrous head almost as large as she was. If I squinted, it looked vaguely wolfish. Vaguely. Apparently, Hollywood had gotten werewolves wrong too. The Blood Witch was in no hurry to put the head down, heedless of the black blood dripping onto her slippers.

I nodded to each of them as I entered, offering Juliette a smile that she shakily returned. The femmepire's yellow eyes darted to my wrist and throat before she forced her gaze away. Whatever she'd been fed, she was clearly still hungry.

Lucia had been facing out the window when we entered, clad in a simple white dress. She held something in her arms, but it wasn't until she turned around that I recognized Xavier's sword. Her golden hands rhythmically squeezed its hilt. And oh yes, she was furious. One look in the queen's glacial blue eyes told me that, if the fact that I could see my own breath hadn't been sufficient warning.

"Thank you for coming, Mr. Smith." She nodded to me without ever looking in my direction, her gaze instead directed at her Secundus. "Andrés?"

Anastasia shook her head.

"Then it seems we are all here. Lady Dumenyova, I would very much like to hear your reconstruction of this debacle."

"Yes, Your Majesty." Anastasia picked her words carefully. I guess spending centuries as someone's closest companion teaches you how to handle their moods. "Several of the survivors admit to coming to our House under false pretenses, at the behest of certain families in Italy."

"Certain families?" Something about the way Lucia asked the question told me she already knew the answer.

"Your brother and his allies." Lucia gave a short nod of acknowledgment, and Anastasia continued. "I believe they sought to take advantage of the losses we suffered ten years ago. Xavier made certain that our new recruits would include a large number of their agents."

"Is it possible Xavier was behind the attacks back then too?" I dared to ask.

Nobody seemed inclined to kill me for the breach of etiquette. Anastasia tilted her head to consider the idea. "I think it is more likely that the war left our House vulnerable enough for the Court to take notice. Whether Xavier was already plotting at that point may never be known. Regardless, he did take cues from that war. He saw how the distraction of the fire had left us more vulnerable to assault, and devised a distraction of his own."

"The theft of Lord Beel-Kasan's property," concluded Lucia. A thin film of frost was starting to form over the sword in her hands.

"Yes. It appears to have been his intention to set our House at odds with the immortal. Xavier slew the Rook and hired the karkino to deprive us of a mediation, and kept the stolen item on these premises to insure that the demigod would attack. But Mr. Smith's survival complicated matters. When you and Lord Beel-Kasan agreed to have Mr. Smith search the House, Xavier planted the item in Andrés' room."

"Why?" This was from Marcus, but it was the question on everyone's lips.

"I don't know. It is possible that he was simply buying time at that point." She spared a glance in my direction. "None of us anticipated the success Mr. Smith would have with Lord Beel-Kasan. I believe Xavier was trying to turn that setback into an advantage."

"And Andrés?" Lucia skipped right over any acknowledgment of my mad mediation skills. Which was fair, since I hadn't had a clue what I was doing. In the end, I'd just been lucky that Bill had taken a liking to me.

"Marcus and I left this morning to pursue a tip regarding Andrés' whereabouts. It is now apparent that Xavier leaked that information in an attempt to lure us from the House. With Zorana imprisoned in the Midnight Tower and Juliette presumed dead, you were isolated." Anastasia frowned. "We found Andrés' body in the slums of Tijuana. A fire had devoured a city block there in the early hours of Monday morning. We don't know how Andrés was lured down into Mexico, but we believe that Xavier himself was the killer."

"How?"

"The Spaniard never concerned himself overly much with physical confrontation. This time, it cost him."

Lucia nodded gravely. "To our sorrow. But we have gotten off topic, and ahead of ourselves. Please, proceed with your original timeline."

Anastasia took a moment to reorganize her thoughts. "When Mr. Smith proved competent, Xavier saw his hopes for a war with Lord Beel-Kasan slipping away. I believe that is why he set the bomb. At worst, he would have rid himself of the last mediator in San Diego. At best, we would have taken it as an attack by the immortal and started the war we'd been trying to avoid."

"Which we might have," Marcus put in, "had you not spoken against such action, Lady Dumenyova."

"Perhaps," acknowledged Anastasia. She nodded to Juliette. "Unbeknownst to Xavier, Lady Middleton and Mr. Smith survived the attempt on their lives."

I saw Juliette perk up, her face flushing with pleasure at the title. Outside of the nicknames I had given her in jest, this was the first time I'd heard her referred to by anything other than her given name. It looked like she'd gained some status in the eyes of her fellow Council members.

Good. She was a pain in the ass, and entirely too hungry for my blood, but we'd faced death like a dozen times together, and that made her a friend.

"She and Mr. Smith returned to the scene of the Rook's murder, where they uncovered evidence of Xavier's complicity in the plot against our House. They also overcame another attempt on their lives, but Xavier had become aware of their survival. Concluding that the war with Lord Beel-Kasan could not be achieved in the time he had left, he settled for a direct assault on the House. With the entirety of the Human security force at his disposal, a large number of our own soldiers on his side, and the majority of the Council dead or absent, his chances of victory were high."

Anastasia paused for a moment, smiling coolly. "What he hadn't counted on was Mr. Smith calling the House to give warning. Akiko and Celeste were able to marshal resistance on the lower levels, and you, Your Majesty, were able to kill your own attackers and secure the third floor. And the message left on my phone convinced Marcus to fly us back here at all possible speed." She spread her slender hands aside in a 'how do you like them apples' sort of gesture. "And thus, your House survives."

Silence fell, thick and hard, each of us imagining what could have been, or perhaps thinking of those who *hadn't* survived. Somewhere in vampire afterlife, I hoped Corey was drinking a Guinness and chowing down on double doubles.

Lucia finally broke the stillness to turn on Zorana. The Blood Witch met the queen's gaze without blinking, looking terrifying as hell even in her pin-striped dress. The wolf-monster head in her hands probably helped.

"Zorana, you completed your questioning of the House a full day ago. How is it that we had a House full of traitors, and yet none of them, not even Xavier, was discovered?"

"I never questioned Xavier. When Lady Middleton and Mr. Smith were killed—" she looked over at us and amended her words, "—thought to be killed, he told me you'd decided other matters took precedence. It seemed a reasonable enough decision. As for the other traitors... it's quite simple." Her little doll's mouth twitched into a scowl. "They were thralls."

"*What?!?*" The shock on Lucia's face was unmistakable, mirrored by similar expressions on Marcus, Juliette and even Anastasia.

"What's a thrall?" Apparently, I was the only person in the room who didn't know.

"Compulsion is temporary, little bird," said Juliette. "A thrall is when it's made permanent. The only problem is—"

"The People cannot be enthralled." Lucia seemed certain.

"Incorrect," said Zorana. "There have been cases where members of the People gained the Talent to compel our own kind. It's a rare gift, but I've seen it with my own eyes. The last such instance was a hundred or so years before your time."

Which answered the question of who the oldest vampire in the room was.

"It appears Captain Xavier had been holding out on us. At some point in the recent past, he came into a second Talent."

"Son of a bitch!" That was from Juliette. I nodded in agreement. It'd have been nice if someone had told me that was even possible. Then again, it was only thanks to Kayla that I even knew what Talents were.

Marcus, however, did not seem convinced. "So he held all of the attackers—as well as an entire company of human security guards—in thrall? I find that exceedingly difficult to believe."

"Your lack of imagination is why you will forever remain a glorified accountant, Marcus." Zorana's voice dripped with adolescent scorn. She looked to Lucia. "Enthralling humans takes little effort. Enthralling our own kind takes significantly more… unless those thralls are willing. In this case, most must have been, and the remainder must have been weak of will. Upon our House's fall, I assume the Captain was meant to dissolve those bonds, granting the individuals in question their freedom."

At the 'weak of will' comment, Juliette and I shared a glance. Perhaps Ray hadn't been a traitor after all. Not willingly, at least.

"And thralldom of the People cannot be discovered through blood magic?" This time, Marcus sounded honestly concerned, rather than skeptical.

"It can, had I been testing for it. Which I was not. As far as the questioning itself… such a bond muddies the water, making truth and lie more difficult to distinguish."

Zorana sounded angry at the admission, and I feared for anyone that might get in her path over the next few days.

Looking at the enormous head still held in her hands, I revised that thought; anyone or *anything*.

"I will think upon how to prevent this sort of colossal security breakdown in the future," said Lucia, her voice flat, "but it seems the matter is settled, for now. Members of my council, thank you for your efforts today. Our House is in desperate need of the resilience you have displayed." She turned her cold blue eyes on me for the first time since I'd entered the room. "Which brings us to you, Mr. Smith."

ooo

At any other time, a line like that might have stuck me as ominous, but I was exhausted, and fear required way too much energy. Plus, Anastasia had just spent ten minutes meticulously recounting the myriad ways in which I had (often inadvertently) saved House Borghesi. My gut feeling was that I was about to be richly rewarded for those actions. Maybe I'd become the first honorary Council member in human history?

Which just goes to prove that you can't trust your gut where vampires are involved.

It started off pleasantly. Lucia ensnared my gaze with her own as she crossed the room in a swish of white silk, her skyscraper-high heels silent on the hardwood floors. That wasn't how heels or hardwood floors were supposed to work, but I was starting to get used to the weirdness.

She nodded to Anastasia, and the other femmepire pressed something into my grasp. I rubbed it between my fingers. Paper. An envelope. Aha! Without even looking down, I knew what it contained. Cash just has a certain smell to it. Like warm apple pie, expensive cigars, and fairy-tale endings. That heady aroma wafted up, and I nearly swooned.

"For services rendered, Mr. Smith, per our agreement. As well as a sizable bonus for your assistance in this other matter." Lucia's full lips curved into a smile that was as sultry as it was unnerving. Since when did I merit smiles from her?

"You might want to hold onto this. Technically, my job's not done until I speak with Bill and verify his satisfaction with the outcome." I tried handing the envelope back to Anastasia, but couldn't seem to convince my fingers to let it go.

Lucia's smile widened. "Lord Beel-Kasan has his property back, and those responsible have been exterminated. I consider the matter closed, and suspect he will agree." She closed my hand firmly around the envelope, her skin as hot as if she'd spent the day soaking up the sun. Her eyes actually twinkled as she continued. "Besides, I am no longer concerned with staying in Bill's—" She spoke the nickname like it pained her to say. "—good graces. The demigod should be concerned with staying in mine."

That statement broke through my cash-induced haze, leaving me puzzled. Her House had just barely survived a coup, and in the process, lost roughly half its population, a council member and their head of security. As far as I could see, Bill had nothing at all to fear from them. "I don't understand."

"Really, we have you to thank for it." She gave my hand a final, firm squeeze, and then spun away to pace in front of me. "I'll admit it was a problem that concerned me, from the moment Lord Beel-Kasan's minion first left his message. How do you confront an opponent who is immortal?"

"And?" There was an empty void in the pit of my stomach and it was growing swiftly. On some subconscious level, I did not like where this was going.

"And the answer, it turns out, is very simple. You target those he cares about." Her smile hardened, and the angry light flared in her glacial blue eyes. "If Lord Beel-Kasan *ever* crosses my House again, the child dies." Her gaze pinned me to the floor. "You will make certain that he is aware of this, won't you, Mr. Smith?"

I stood there, stunned by both the callousness of the threat, and how little she understood Bill.

The queen took my silence as agreement, and gave a small, triumphant nod. "To other matters then. I will admit that I allowed your appearance, demeanor, and species to negatively influence my opinion of you, but in the end, you have proven to be an effective employee. And that is why I have chosen to keep your services on retainer."

Her warm smile returned, but its impact was significantly blunted by the anger rising in my chest. "You think I would want to work for you again—"

"At a rate more commensurate with your abilities, of course." She named a figure that would have given me heart palpitations ten minutes earlier. "And you will be—"

It was my turn to cut her off. "You're holding a little girl's life hostage against an insane demigod's behavior. That's the sort of shit even pond scum would think twice about, yet you're actually proud?!" I was so mad I couldn't stand still. *This* was what we'd all spent the last few days nearly dying to protect? I took a step toward the door, then spun back around to point at the nonplussed queen. "You have no idea what that little girl has been through. If you touch a hair on her head, Bill will burn this whole gingerbread house to the ground—" I lowered my voice to a hiss. "—and I'll bring the goddamn marshmallows."

It wasn't the best of parting lines, but they couldn't all be winners. As far as I was concerned, it was good enough.

It was also, in retrospect, not the most diplomatic way to decline a job offer. That much became clear when Lucia pinned me against the door. I barely avoided becoming intimate with the doorknob. One hand wrapped around my throat and squeezed, as the queen glared up at me with near-homicidal rage, all vestiges of nobility forgotten. "I strongly suggest you reconsider."

"If you're going to kill me, kill me." I forced the words out in a croak. "But I will never work for you again."

The angry queen cocked her head, and those lush lips spread in a smile more terrifying than anything Zorana had managed. "We will see about that."

A cold wind came out of nowhere to encircle us, immediately sapping the warmth from my skin. My vision narrowed until all I could see were her starkly beautiful eyes. Unable to look away or even blink, I found myself falling through the golden rings that circled her pupils.

And then Lucia bit me.

It was every bit as painful as Juliette's bite in Gehenna. Maybe even more so, as these fangs were at my neck instead of my wrist. Beyond the pain, there was a sound echoing in my brain, the tinkling of glass, like a hammer smashing through glass windows. For the first time in my life, I could feel another being inside my head.

"Your Majesty, what have you done?!"

I couldn't tell if it was Juliette or Anastasia asking the question, but I was gratified by the anguish in their voice, in that fraction of a second when I still had the ability to feel anything at all. Then I sank into black waters, chased by the echoes of Lucia's reply.

"I have made him my thrall."

EPILOGUE
IN WHICH THRALLDOM AND 5 BUCKS
WILL GET YOU A SMALL ICED COFFEE

The waves crashed upon the La Jolla shore, their size a harbinger of the rare summer storm poised to strike San Diego in the next few hours. Here and there, a surfer was taking advantage of the unexpected conditions, although the majority of them were up in Oceanside or down south at Black's Beach. With the sun hidden behind multiple layers of thick grey clouds, I had the beach at Torrey Pines almost to myself. A few hikers trudged up the long hill into the state reserve, and a pot-bellied, gray-haired old woman was walking along the tide's high water mark, digging through seaweed on the beach. I leaned back on my hands, grateful for the towel and change of clothes I'd picked up at my house, and watched the storm clouds sweep in from the west.

The crunch of sand told me I had a visitor, but I kept my eyes on the horizon. The sweet scent of roses filled my nose as the Lady Anastasia Dumenyova carefully took a seat beside me on the towel. Her fragrance should have clashed with the salty air, or the electrical charge of the oncoming storm, but somehow the resulting mélange worked. Go figure.

We sat together in silence. The old beachcomber—who was a mere fraction of the age of the creature beside me—had trundled out of view before I finally spoke. "I wondered who would find me."

"I tried your office first." She joined the conversation almost eagerly. "And I believe Kayla checked your house. Your parents, you should know, will be returning from Vegas tomorrow."

"Yeah. I've talked with them. How did you know to find me here?"

As always, Anastasia was elegantly attired. Today, she wore wide-legged black pants, a pale green silk top and a waist-length jacket. She was altogether too beautiful for words. Even if I had watched her decapitate a man with her bare hands. Even if the queen she served had...

A fresh wind came in off the ocean, and I shivered, and wrapped my new leather jacket around me. It was, by far, the nicest article of clothing I'd ever owned and it wasn't like the Rook had needed it anymore.

She shrugged strong shoulders. "Opinions were split on whether you would end up at a beach or a bar. This is the third location I checked. Juliette—" She shook her head. "Your pardon. *Lady Middleton* would have been out walking the streets, if she were not currently struggling to take on Andrés' former duties."

"Couldn't Lucia—" I growled the name. "—have just told you where I was?" I knew the answer to that, without even asking. From the moment I'd woken up in my House suite, newly enthralled, I had been aware of the queen's position, relative to my own. Distance helped, a little bit, but even here, I could close my eyes, spin around, and instinctively point in the direction of the femmepire queen.

"Queen Lucia is discovering anew that actions have their consequences." Her jade eyes were cool and hard. "Not even Summer is speaking to her, unless so commanded."

I didn't say anything, but my mind was conjuring up images of an entire vampire House giving their leader the silent treatment. It didn't entirely suck.

"A monarch rules at the sufferance of her people," continued Anastasia. "That was the lesson of the Mad King, deposed by Lucia's own father, yet it is something that she has struggled to accept throughout her long life. Perhaps this exhibition of our collective displeasure will finally drive that lesson home." Her rich, chocolate-cheesecake voice was soft and quiet. "For what it matters, I am truly sorry, John. If I had not come for you that day…"

"Then the karkino would have killed me and a lot of other people I love would be dead."

"Even so. If I had known what she was doing…"

"So there's no way to undo this? Didn't Zorana say the bond could be dissolved?" I turned back to the ocean. The clouds had crept closer, and were now menacing the shoreline.

"Between People, yes. Even between People and humans, if Zorana is to be believed, but there are degrees of thralldom, dependent upon the power expended."

"And Lucia expended a lot of power on me." I still remembered the feeling of her voice crashing through my mind, and the way my defenses, natural or otherwise, had been swept aside.

"Yes," she said simply. "Whatever it is that makes you… you, forced her to invest a significant amount of power in the act." She shook her head, the wind toying with strands of auburn hair. "I could not have done it. Nor, I think, could Marcus. I do not believe Lucia could remove the bond now, even if she desired to do so."

"Fantastic." We lapsed back into silence. The last surfer came in off the water, combing long hair out of his face, and striking a nonchalant, wetsuited pose the moment he saw Anastasia. Jerk. He held the pose for a moment or two before giving up. If I'd been less depressed, I might have given him the finger.

Once he was gone, I spoke again. "I'm not going back, Ana. Not to the House. Not to being a mediator. You are the most amazing, complicated, spectacular woman I've ever met, but your world is going to get me killed."

Anastasia took one of my hands in hers, which might have been a lot more pleasant if Lucia hadn't done the same thing right before she enthralled me. Recognizing that, she let my hand drop, and lamely patted my shoulder instead.

"We are better for knowing you, Mr. Smith, but I understand your desire to leave this life behind. However…" She wrapped her coat more tightly around herself, as if she were cold. "I do not think Lucia will let you go free."

"It's not up to her." A thought struck me. "And if she thinks she can threaten my parents to earn my cooperation…"

"No!" Anastasia shook her head fiercely. "Your family has nothing to fear from us. On this, you have my oath in blood and bone."

That was actually a huge relief. Even my dad would eventually get sick of Las Vegas.

"Then Lucia doesn't have the leverage to make me do anything."

Anastasia curled long, slender legs up under herself, and brushed hair back out of her face a second time. If she were human, I'd have said she was either embarrassed or nervous. Since she was Anastasia, she probably just wanted to get the hair out of her face.

"She doesn't need leverage, John. When a bond is created, the vampire gains a modicum of control over their thrall. They know where they are, they are able to take nourishment from them even without blood, and—" Her voice faltered for a moment, but she soldiered on. "—they can direct their thrall's actions with no more than a simple thought." She smiled sadly. "I'm surprised that Lucia has not called you home yet. Perhaps she already regrets her actions."

"Nah, that's definitely not it."

"Pardon?"

I turned back to the femmepire, and tapped the side of my temple. "She's been demanding my return, almost from the moment I left the House."

"Truly?" Anastasia's luminescent jade eyes widened. "And you do not feel compelled to attend her?"

"Not particularly." I gave her a quick smile. "It's kind of annoying, like having someone drunk dial you at all hours of the day, but that's it. Mostly, I just," I pantomimed pushing a heavy object with my hands, "push her to the back of my brain and ignore her."

Anastasia looked at me in stunned silence for a long moment. Then she leaned back, shook her head, and laughed.

ooo

The rain was coming down in droves by the time I made it to my office, but the Corolla managed to navigate the rapidly flooding streets. I'd been amazed and gratified to find my car still in possession of its wheels, despite having been left curb-side in Logan Heights for an entire week. It almost made up for the combination of expletives and penises that had been painted across the exterior.

I opened the building's front door with my key, and extracted a pile of mail from the overflowing box. I didn't have any active cases, but the mediation had left me with enough cash to ride out a slow month or two. I even had a small surplus that I was thinking about using to buy some form of online advertising. The old yellow pages ad had clearly run its course.

Or I could splurge on that trip to Vegas. It was a thought.

When I went to unlock my office, the cheap plywood door swung inward at a touch. I brandished my keys in front of me like a weapon and stepped inside. With my free hand, I flipped on the lights.

The intruder was… cute. A bright shock of pink hair topped a round, freckled face that was dominated by liquid brown eyes. She spun gracefully to regard me, long and colorful skirts spinning with the motion, her diaphanous wings beating the air like a hummingbird's.

Wait… wings?

"Mr. John Smith?" Her voice was every bit as cute as the rest of her. Admittedly, at least some of that cuteness was because she was, from the bottom of her crystalline heels to the top of her outstretched wings, maybe ten inches tall.

"My name is Kristin, Mr. Smith. My congregation and I wish to hire you to mediate a dispute on our behalf." She made a mini-curtsy while hovering in mid-air. "You come very well recommended."

Well, shit.

AUTHOR'S NOTE

Investigation, Mediation, Vindication was the first book I ever wrote. In 2013, many months into a multi-month severance package from my day job, I sat down at the computer and began to write. I didn't know what the plot was. I didn't have a cast list. I just knew that it was set in San Diego, that the main character's name was John Smith, and that there would be vampires of some sort.

Two months later, I was done with the first draft and had a *slightly* better grasp on the plot, characters, and themes. The book needed some serious editing, but I instead started on a sequel. And then another one. And finally, a fourth, at which point, I realized this little series was going to be seven books long, and I should probably think about getting them into shape for release at some point.

That realization happened five years ago. In the interim, I released *See These Bones*, the first book of my post-apocalyptic superhero series, and two novelettes set in the same world, but John and his adventures have continued to lurk in the back of my mind, waiting for their moment. After a truly ludicrous number of revisions, I'm thrilled that *Investigation, Mediation, Vindication* is finally seeing the light of day.

While used fictitiously, many of the locations in this series do exist, or at least did so in 2013. The Chargers were San Diego's football team back then, instead of Los Angeles' second and far-less-popular franchise. That particular Gordon Biersch location is now closed, but for a long time, it sat right by the Mission Valley mall, and the garlic fries were as tasty as advertised. The Tipsy Crow is a very nice bar in the Gaslamp Quarter that was once known as The Bitter End. I can't speak to whether it houses a portal to another dimension, where snot elementals and a demigod of time and death reside... but would anyone truly be surprised?

Look for *Blood is Thicker Than Lots of Stuff* to be released in spring 2021. Thank you for reading!

ABOUT THE AUTHOR

Chris began life as a gleam in someone's eye, but birth and childhood were quick to follow. He's been fortunate enough to live in Spain, Germany, and all over the United States of America, and is busy planning a tour of the distilleries of Scotland.

A graduate of the Johns Hopkins University's Writing Seminars program, he put that degree to ill use for twenty years as a software engineer, but has finally circled back around to the idea of writing for a living.

Chris currently lives in Nevada with his angelic wife and ever-expanding whisky collection and occasionally ventures outside to peer upwards, mutter to himself about 'day stars', and then scurry back into the house.

Chris frequently shares new content on his author website at https://christullbane.com.

Made in the USA
San Bernardino, CA
23 May 2020

72204653R00202